Praise for

the queen *of* water

A *SCHOOL LIBRARY JOURNAL* BEST BOOK OF THE YEAR

★ "[A] compelling collaboration between Resau and Farinango. . . . The authors' candid narrative richly depicts Virginia's passage from a childhood filled with demoralization to a young woman who sees her life through new eyes."
—*Publishers Weekly*, Starred

★ "Riveting. . . . By turns heartbreaking, infuriating and ultimately inspiring."
—*Kirkus Reviews*, Starred

★ "A moving, lyrical novel that will particularly resonate with teens caught between cultures."
—*Booklist*, Starred

★ "A poignant coming-of-age novel that will expose readers to the exploitation of girls around the world whose families grow up in poverty."
—*SLJ*, Starred

"The details of Virginia's experiences are absorbing, and readers will share both the terror and triumph through the recounting of events."
—*The Bulletin*

"Virginia's voice will compel readers, who will find 'truths' here, no matter how true the story is."
—*The Horn Book Magazine*

"A richly described coming-of-age story set in a culture both foreign and familiar."
—*VOYA*

Also by Laura Resau

laura resau

and maría virginia farinango

the queen *of* water

EMBER

Text copyright © 2011 by Laura Resau and María Virginia Farinango
Cover photograph of María Virginia Farinango copyright © 2011 by Ken Burgess

The Library of Congress has cataloged the hardcover edition of this work as follows:
Resau, Laura.
The Queen of Water / by Laura Resau and María Virginia Farinango. — 1st ed.
p. cm.
Summary: Living in a village in Ecuador, a Quechua Indian girl is sent to work as an indentured servant for an upper class "mestizo" family.
ISBN 978-0-385-73897-2 (hc) — ISBN 978-0-385-90761-3 (lib. bdg.) — ISBN 978-0-375-89680-4 (ebook)
1. Quechua Indians—Ecuador—Fiction. [1. Quechua Indians—Fiction. 2. Indians of South America—Ecuador—Fiction. 3. Indentured servants—Fiction. 4. Social classes—Fiction. 5. Ecuador—Fiction.] I. Title.
PZ7.R2978Qu 2011
[Fic]—dc22
2010010512

ISBN 978-0-375-85963-2 (tr. pbk.)

RL: 5.5

Printed in the United States of America

10 9

First Ember Edition 2012

For my son, Yanni; my husband, Tino; and all the indigenous girls who were mistreated and humiliated as servants to mestizos

With love,
María Virginia Farinango

Acknowledgments

WRITING THIS BOOK was a six-year journey, and a great many people have contributed along the way. Together, we offer these people our deep gratitude. We received excellent manuscript feedback from Old Town Writers' Group, Paul and Holly Ashby, Jimena Peña, Martha Petty, Laura Pritchett, Chris Resau, and Michelle Sparks. We feel incredibly fortunate to have our editor, Stephanie Lane Elliott, and agent, Erin Murphy—both of whom are a rare mix of smart, sweet, and sincere. As always, it's been a complete joy to work with the enthusiastic and talented people at Delacorte Press. We thank the Barbara Deming Memorial Fund's Money for Women, the Puffin Foundation, and Arts Alive of Fort Collins, Colorado, for their generous grants. *Matter Journal* boosted our confidence in the early stages of our project by publishing "Magic Shoes," an adaptation of which appears as a scene in this book.

Many friends have been important sources of encouragement and practical help: Kay Salens, MaryLou Smith, Elcy

Vargas, José Quiñones, Alecssandra Rea and her family, Ken Burgess, and the ESL teachers at Front Range Community College. We'd like to thank all our other friends and family members who have supported us in realizing our dreams over the years, especially our husbands, Tino and Ian, and our sons, Yanni and Bran.

In particular, María Virginia would like to give special thanks to el Señor Jesús and her friend, Laura, who has become like a sister to her.

Laura would like to thank María Virginia for her friendship, her sisterly warmth, and the huge honor of cowriting her story.

¡Querer es poder!

the queen of water

PART 1

AS A LITTLE GIRL, I did not know I was a descendant of the Inca, the most powerful ancient civilization of South America. I did not know that when the Spanish conquistadors came, crazed for gold, they conquered us, and over the centuries, two kinds of people emerged in Ecuador.

The mestizos.

And the indígenas.

I did not know how they came to be them, or how we came to be us. For me, the distinction seemed as old and fixed as the mountains.

The mestizos thought they were as white and precious and delicate as fresh bread. They spoke Spanish and had fancy last names like Palacios and Cevallos. They were the doctors and dentists and teachers and bankers and landowners. They kept out of the sun so they wouldn't grow dark like Indians. Even if their skin was as brown as mine, they claimed they had no Indian blood and proudly held up their names and clothes to prove it.

And then there were us, the indígenas, with skin as rough and ruddy as freshly dug potatoes, cheeks chapped raw by the sun and wind. The mestizos called us longos, stupid Indians, dirty Indians, poor Indians. We had awkward, backward names like Farinango, which our grandparents signed with an X on contracts they couldn't read. In this way, our grandparents sold their land and then, forever after, paid the mestizos half their harvest to rent what was once theirs.

As a little girl, I hated those mestizos.

Yet I wanted, desperately, to be one.

When I was about seven, I left my world. I disappeared into theirs, and did not find my way back until many years later. But I am getting ahead of myself. I will begin at the beginning, on my last day in my village, Yana Urku. When I woke up that morning, I thought it would be a day like any other.

chapter 1

BEFORE DAWN, I wake up to the sound of creatures scurrying inside the wall near my head. Mice and rats and dogs have burrowed these tunnels through the dried clay, searching for food scraps. I'm always searching for food scraps too. Right now my belly's already rumbling, and it's hours till breakfast.

The house is dark as a cave except for bits of blue light coming through the holes in the earthen walls. My gaze fixes on a new trail of golden honey oozing from a crack, just within arm's reach. Bees live in there, black bees that sting terribly, but make the best honey in the world. I poke my hand in the crack and scoop out the sticky sweetness and lick it from my finger. It's gritty but good.

Our guinea pigs are hungry now too, squeaking and dancing around in their corner, waiting for alfalfa. I can see every corner of our house from my sleeping place on the floor. Mamita and Papito are snoring under their wool blanket on a bed frame made of scrap wood. My brother and sister are curled up next to me—Hermelinda on the end and Manuelito wedged in the middle—and the fleas and bedbugs and lice are crawling wherever they please. My spot against the wall is cozy, the perfect place for licking honey in secret.

Soon Mamita will awaken, standing up and stretching in her white blouse that hangs midway down her thighs. Then, yawning, she'll wrap a long dark *anaco* around her waist, golden beads around her neck, and red beads around her wrists. Then she'll open the door and a rectangle of misty morning light will shine into our house's musty darkness. Then she'll light the cooking fire and we'll all slurp steamy potato soup around the fire pit.

If she catches me with honey dripping from my fingers, her face will twist into a frown. When people tell her, "Your little Virginia is *vivísima!*" Mamita snorts, "Humph, she's clever for stealing food, that's about all."

It's true, I do use my wits to fill my belly with fresh cheese or warm rolls. Or to get something I really want, like a pet goat or a pair of shoes. But there's more. I have dreams. Dreams bigger than the mountaintops that poke at the clouds. In the pasture, I always climb my favorite tree and shout to the sheep, "I'm traveling far from here!" and my tree turns into a truck and I ride off to a place where I can eat rice and meat and watermelon every day.

In the half-light of dawn, I plunge my hand deeper into the darkness inside the wall, searching for honey, dreaming, as always, of golden treasures.

After breakfast, I'm in the valley pasturing sheep under a sky the dull gray of cow intestines, when Hermelinda appears on the hill. I squint up at her. The mountains loom behind her, peaks lost in heavy clouds. She waves her little arms at me, the wind whipping her hair in all directions. "Virginia!" she cries in her squeaky toddler voice. "There are *mishus* at the house. Mamita says to come right away!"

Mishus are what we call the *mestizos*. It's a mean word, in the same way that their names for us—*longos*, or dirty Indians— are mean. With my golden goat, Cheetah, at my side, I climb toward home, urging the straggling sheep along with my stick. Feeling suddenly sick, I call out, "Hermelinda, which *mishus?*"

"Alfonso and his wife and two others."

I stop in my tracks. Alfonso owns the land my family farms. Lately, he and his wife, Mariana, have made a point of talking to me whenever they visit the fields, asking me questions, eyeing me up and down, then murmuring to each other as they walk off. Alfonso is the one who took my cousins Zoyla and Gregoria away from their parents two years ago. Zoyla and Gregoria and I used to play market together while we pastured the animals. And then, one day, when they were near my age now—about seven—they left with the *mishus*.

We never heard from them again.

I head up the path, pushing against the crazy wind, kicking at rocks and smacking trees with my stick as I walk. Past the corn and potato fields, my house comes into view, looking small and weak against the mountains towering behind it. I can make out the forms of the *mishus* sitting on the dirt patio with my parents. My muscles are tensing, the way they do when I see dogs in the distance and I'm not quite sure if they're nice or mean.

I'm grateful Cheetah is at my side. Even though she's only a goat, she loves me more than anything in the world. And

5

she'll do anything to protect me. Once, when a vicious dog tried to attack, Cheetah hurled herself in front of me and rose to her hind feet. "Maah maaah!" she bellowed in its face, slashing the air with her front hooves. The dog had never seen such a brazen goat, and it backed away, bewildered. It's good to have someone love you so fiercely. Even if that someone is a goat.

I rest my hand on her honey brown head and rub her ears, walking slowly, my heart thumping. As I lead the sheep into their pens, I watch the patch of weeds in front of our house where Alfonso sits beside his wife with her ridiculous, huge bun, along with a thin *mestizo* man. A fat *mestiza* woman with short hair and a polka-dot dress sits a little off to the side. I take a deep breath, then head toward them, brandishing my stick like a machete. The closer I walk, the hotter my face gets, as though my blood has caught fire.

Mamita is watching the *mishus* politely as Papito chats with them, his face unusually friendly. As I come closer, Mamita looks up at me and frowns. Her glare orders me to stop swinging my stick and behave.

But I look straight ahead, ignoring them all, and, still swinging my stick, stomp straight into the house. Cheetah sets herself just outside the door, ever loyal.

After a moment, Mamita rushes inside, furious. "What's wrong with you? Why didn't you greet our guests? What will they think of you?"

Scowling, I throw my stick on the floor. "I'm not going with those *mishus*."

She doesn't hit me. Instead, with a frown, she spits on her finger and rubs at the reddish brown spots—dried blood from flea bites I scratch too much—that speckle the sleeves of my dirty white blouse.

"You're a mess," she mutters, readjusting the faded purple *faja* around my waist and then, in frustration, unwrapping the entire wide ribbon. Once the *faja* is no longer holding up my *anaco*, it falls to the ground, the thick, dark cotton pooling at my bare feet. I stand shivering in my blouse as Mamita shakes the loose dust and dried mud from my *anaco*. Then, commanding, "Hold still!" she rewraps the skirt tightly around my legs and hips and waist. With one hand holding up my *anaco*, she uses the other to wind the *faja* over my rib cage, so tightly I can barely breathe.

"Ahhh!" I scream.

"Don't be a crybaby," she says, tucking in the end of the *faja*, then standing back to survey her work. She shakes her head, frowning. "Your *anaco* is too short," she says, as though it's my fault I've grown. It's true, the tattered hem hangs only to midcalf, exposing my scratched-up ankles. But my other two *anacos* are even shorter, and she knows it.

"I'm not going with those *mishus*," I say again, folding my arms over my chest.

In a tight voice, she snaps, "They're Alfonso's son and daughter-in-law. They need someone to take care of their baby. Alfonso told them about you."

Gulping down my fear, I jut out my chin and harden my eyes. "I won't go."

Mamita presses her lips together. "They'll pay a thousand sucres a month."

A thousand sucres? An unthinkable sum. I consider the

dazzling clothes and shoes and heaps of delicious white rice that so much money could buy.

Mamita watches me thinking. Her voice turns silky. "I bet they have a television."

"Really?" I've only seen TV once before, but my older sister, Matilde, watches it all the time. She's twelve years old and works as a maid for *mestizos* in Quito, about two hours away. They're nice *mestizos*, she tells us on her visits home once a month. Of course, I would be happy if she came only once a *year*. Whenever Matilde visits, Mamita gives her the biggest potato from the soup and goes on and on about how beautiful and plump and fair-skinned she is.

Mamita smiles. "And they live toward the coast. There's a lot of fruit there, mangoes and pineapples and bananas." She knows I can't resist fruit. "And watermelon."

I draw in a breath. "Maybe." Maybe if I go away and come back once a month, Mamita will tell me how beautiful and plump and fair-skinned I am, too.

She pats my head and tucks my wild hair behind my ears. I follow her outside, then stand beside Cheetah, keeping one hand on the fur of her neck. "Good afternoon," I mumble to the *mishus*.

Alfonso's son looks at me carefully. His skin and hair and lips are all as pale as dried-out cornstalks. "You're pretty," he says, grinning. His teeth are the same bland color as the rest of him. "How old are you? Six? Seven?"

I shrug. I don't know exactly how old I am, or when my birthday is. My parents don't bother keeping track of these things.

He leans closer. "Do you speak Spanish?"

I don't answer, even though I've learned a good bit of Spanish from playing with some *mestizo* children in the cow pasture. That's how I learned about Tarzan and Cheetah, playing jungle with them.

"She understands more than she speaks," my father says. "And she'll learn fast."

The *mishu* glances at his wife, raising his eyebrows in a question. She nods and taps her toe impatiently, which makes the flesh of her calves jiggle.

The man turns to his father. "She'll do. We'll take her."

We'll take her? Is that it? I blink, searching my parents' faces. They're nodding, satisfied.

I want to hear more about the thousand sucres and the fruit and the TV, but no one says another word to me. The men talk a little more about the harvest, while the two *mishu* women swat at flies and battle against the wind to smooth their hair. The younger woman is looking restlessly into the distance, as though she just wants to get this over with and leave.

Suddenly, I understand that I have no say in this. Not a shred of power. The decision has been made. Even though I'm an expert at making deals to get what I want—my goat, warm rolls, purple lollipops—this is somehow different. This is happening whether I like it or not.

Panic latches onto my throat. Why have my parents agreed so quickly? They know these *mishus* are thieves and liars. Don't they understand that I might disappear like Zoyla and Gregoria?

I bite my lip. Maybe they *want* me to disappear. I whine and cry too much, and I always want to do everything myself and always my way. Just last week, Mamita threw up her arms in anger and snapped, *Virginia, I'd be happy if one day you left and never came back.* The words stayed in my head like rocks, too heavy to move out. That must be it. She wants me to leave forever.

Shaking, I press my face into Cheetah's fur, breathing in her sweet-sour goat smell, wrapping my arms tightly around her.

Mamita hisses in Quichua, "Get your face out of that filthy animal's fur. Or else we'll eat it for lunch."

I lift my head, but turn away from Mamita, keeping one hand on Cheetah, my fingers playing with her velvety ears.

Finally, my parents stand up and shake hands and agree that the next day I'll go to Alfonso's hacienda, and from there, I'll leave with his son and daughter-in-law for the half-day truck ride to their town. Tomorrow I'll be gone.

They walk down the dusty path, the woman tripping every few steps in her pointy high-heeled shoes. Without a word to me, Mamita goes inside to heat up soup for lunch, and Papito heads for the potato fields. The *mishus* grow smaller and smaller, and finally, on the next hill over, disappear into the big white house.

chapter 2

ALL AFTERNOON, the *mishus'* truck bounces over rocks, around potholes, jerking us this way and that along mountain roads. Whenever another truck passes, I have to wind up the window fast so that the baby won't breathe in the clouds of dust. On the way, the lady shouts at me over the wind. I understand some of the words in Spanish, and the rest I can more or less fill in. "Listen, *longuita,* you must call me Doctorita, because I'm a dentist, and a teacher, too."

"Yes, señora," I say, absorbed in watching her chin jiggle as she talks.

"Yes, *Doctorita,*" she corrects me. Her mouth opens wide and her chin jiggles extra hard.

"Yes, Doctorita," I say.

"And you're to call my husband Niño Carlitos."

Niño is like *Amo,* or *Patroncito*—what *indígenas* call their *mestizo* bosses. "Señor Carlitos," I whisper to myself defiantly.

"Say it," she insists. "Niño Carlitos."

"Niño Carlitos," I mumble, wondering how soon I can get away from these people.

As we wind along the narrow mountain roads, I try to remember everything I can about what happened to my cousins Zoyla and Gregoria. I remember overhearing my aunt and uncle talking about it one day when liquor had made their faces red and damp and their tongues loose. "We asked those lying *mishus* what they did with our daughters," my aunt said.

My uncle spat a glob of yellow phlegm by his feet. "And that *misha copetona*, Mariana, said our girls don't care about their poor families and their filthy homes anymore." *Misha copetona* means something like "mestiza lady with the ridiculous bun." "She says they're perfectly happy in their new lives."

They each took another swig of liquor, and then my uncle kicked a stone and my aunt wiped her eyes and folded her hands in her lap.

As much as everyone grumbled about Alfonso and Mariana, no one ever stood up to them. "Why don't you yell at them?" I asked Papito one day, thinking he had no trouble yelling at me and my brother and sisters and Mamita. His face stayed stony. "Because that's where our money comes from." Then he took a swig of *puro* and looked away.

I wonder what Zoyla's and Gregoria's lives are like now. A lump grows inside my throat and a creepy feeling spreads through my belly. I look out the window at the fields whizzing past and try to push the girls from my mind.

It's dark by the time we arrive in these *mishus'* town, which the Doctorita calls Kunu Yaku. I climb out of the truck, my dread mixed with curiosity. We go up a flight of rickety wooden stairs to the second floor; when I stumble, Niño Carlitos puts his hand at my back to make sure I don't fall.

Inside, red velvet fills their apartment, spilling over two fat sofas and two big armchairs, the kind that look like they would be fun to jump on. It's a red that makes me think of juicy berries one moment, and blood the next.

High up are two long windows, too far above my head to look through. Cross-stitched roses in plastic frames hang from the walls, and crocheted doilies are draped over every surface. A fern sits in the corner, and more plants dangle from the ceiling, a forest creeping into the house.

The apartment is one room, with a giant wooden wardrobe dividing the living room from the bedroom. I peek behind it, and my mouth drops open in pure delight. I'm face to face with a bed like a birthday cake topped with a fluffy icing-pink blanket with a white llama design, and two poufy pillows, all facing a glorious TV. I imagine myself sprawled on the pink blanket watching TV and eating watermelon.

The Doctorita breaks my reverie with a sharp *"Longuita."* She taps her foot on a grubby piece of sheepskin next to the sofa. "You'll sleep here, on the rug." Then she points to a cardboard box with a folded-up blanket inside. The blanket is orange and turquoise, crocheted in a zigzag pattern. "Here you'll put your clothes."

That night, beneath my cheek, the gray sheepskin rug

turns into Cheetah's fur. I nuzzle my nose into her softness and when my tears come it doesn't matter because Cheetah licks them off.

This is not the first time Mamita has given me away. But the first time was different. A couple of years ago, she gave me to an *indígena* woman named Marta. Only Marta wasn't a poor field-worker like the rest of us. No, she was one of the rich *indígenas*, one who owned a two-story house and a TV and a truck. She was exactly the kind of business lady I've always dreamed of becoming, one who wears finely embroidered, shiny white blouses tucked into soft black *anacos* hemmed with silvery trim, and thick, gold-beaded necklaces. One who travels confidently to far-off lands, selling clothes and crafts to foreigners and tourists. When Mamita heard that Marta wanted a little girl as a *compañera*—a travel companion—she offered me.

On the day Mamita brought me to Marta's house, Marta fed us juicy meat and asked, "You like television, Virginia?"

"I don't know," I said eagerly. "I've never seen one."

Smiling, Marta led me upstairs, to a big box that held moving pictures of flashing lights and colors. A skinny rabbit, tall and gray, stood upright like a person, using his paws as hands to hold a carrot. He waved it around and talked and munched and let it dangle from his mouth like a cigarette. He had unbelievably huge feet and long ears, which were pink on the insides. And two front teeth that jutted out and made me laugh. He put his hands on his hips and stuck out his bottom, which sent me into a fit of giggles.

In dazed wonder, I stood in front of the box, holding my

face close to the rabbit's, running my fingers over the slippery glass, vaguely hearing Mamita's far-off voice saying my name.

"Virginia," Mamita shouted in my ear.

"Yes?" I said, keeping my gaze fixed on the TV.

"Look at me."

I turned my head. Her frown was deeper than usual.

"I'm leaving now," she said.

I nodded, eager to get back to watching the rabbit.

Mamita looked at me long and hard. I wanted her to hurry and leave. It occurred to me that she might be sad, but I didn't think about it too much because the flashing colors were calling to me.

"Goodbye, Virginia," she said. "Behave with these people. Obey them. They will treat you well. You'll be fine."

"Goodbye, Mamita."

She left, and I watched TV until dark, and then, when my eyelids were starting to droop, Marta showed me my bed. It had a thick, soft mattress. Lying on it felt exactly how floating on a falling leaf would feel.

Early the next morning, I woke up and skipped downstairs to have breakfast. I was in the middle of sipping sugary coffee and chewing delicious bread, as fluffy as the pillow I'd slept on, when someone knocked on the door. *Boom boom boom.* Loud, frantic knocking. *Boom boom boom.*

Mamita rushed in, breathless and red-faced and sweating, her chest heaving. Her eyes were wild and panicked, and when she spotted me, she ran over and snatched my hand.

"I'm sorry," Mamita said to Marta. Her voice cracked. "I can't give her to you."

"Why?" Marta asked.

Mamita's face looked heavy, her shoulders weighed down. "I would rather my daughter live in my home, as poor as it is." Her voice was unusually soft. "Let's go, Virginia."

Slowly, I gathered my little sack of clothes and said goodbye and thank you, wishing I'd finished the bread and the coffee, because it would be nothing but potato soup at home. I took one last look up the stairs where the TV was still sleeping, and then followed Mamita outside into the bright morning light. I squinted up at her. "Mamita, why didn't you let me stay there?"

She looked straight ahead, her face set firmly in its usual frown. "You're my daughter. How could you think I'd send you away?"

Without talking, we rode back home to Yana Urku.

Judging by the rug I'm sleeping on, I have a feeling these *mishus* won't treat me as well as Marta did. Marta might have had more money than my family, but she was still one of us. An *indígena*. She would never have called me a *longa*.

If Mamita changed her mind about leaving me with someone as kind as Marta, then of course she'll change her mind about these *mishus*. In the morning, my mother will come for me, pounding on the door, her face full of wild, confused love, and she'll say, "I've come to get my daughter. How could I give away my daughter?"

I tell myself this, over and over, until dawn comes, and a patch of weak morning sunlight seeps through the high-up windows. The lady and the man start yawning, talking, shifting in bed. I jump up, smooth my hair into a ponytail and wrap it in a ribbon. I wind my *anaco* and *faja* around my waist, making sure my blouse is tucked in neatly. I want to be ready when Mamita comes.

The Doctorita starts clanking around in the kitchen, blending together bananas and sugar and milk in a mixer that shrieks like the wind. Somehow, the baby, Jaimito, is sleeping through the racket.

"Pay attention, Virgina," she says, "because soon you'll be doing the cooking." She shows me how much water to add for her husband's rice. "One, two," she says. One jiggle, two jiggles.

She sits down at the table across from Niño Carlitos. They eat from white china plates rimmed with little red flowers. Carved vines weave up the handles of their silverware. She points out a gray metal plate and cup and a dented spoon. "Those are what you use. You are not to eat off our dishes."

The Doctorita downs a glass of banana milk, then pours another. "Make sure we have everything we need and then you may sit down. And if you see our glasses are low with juice, hop up and ask if we want more."

When I see her glass empty, I hop up, playing the part for now, until Mamita comes. "More, Doctorita?"

"Yes."

"And eggs and rice, too?" I ask in broken Spanish.

"No," she says.

For the first time Niño Carlitos pipes up. "La Negra's watching her figure," he says, and reaches over to pat the mounds of flesh spilling from her waistband.

La Negra. The Black Woman. But she isn't black. Her skin is the same cinnamon-tea color as mine, a shade darker than most *mestizos'* skin.

The Doctorita frowns. Then she drinks two more glasses of

17

sugary banana milk and eats three sweet rolls, her chin jiggling as she chews. "See how she's watching her figure?" Niño Carlitos says, winking at me.

She shoots him a sharp look and glances at my half-eaten food. "Hurry up. Carlos and I have to be at work soon and I have a lot to show you first."

I stuff the rest of the bread in my mouth and gulp down the banana milk shake, which tastes sour and hits my stomach gurgling. *Where is Mamita?*

"Let's go." The Doctorita snatches my dishes, piling them on top of the others. "I'll show you where to wash the dishes." She waddles down the stairs and onto a cement patio enclosed on all sides by other apartments. In front of a concrete sink, she stops and sets down the dishes. "One. Two. Three," she says, showing me how much soap powder to add and how many cupfuls of water to use for rinsing. "Three times, you hear, *longa*? And don't talk to anyone while you're out here."

I wash the dishes quickly, because I don't want to miss it when Mamita comes banging on the door. Back inside, the Doctorita shows me how to make the bed, how many times to fold back the sheet. "One. Two. Three. Now, pay attention, *longa*."

And then come her rules, slow at first like drops of rain at the start of a storm, then more and more, pelting my skin until I want to dive under a bush for cover.

1) You may not sit on our bed.
2) You may not touch the television except to clean it.
3) Or the stereo.
4) You may not sit on the red chairs.
5) Or the sofa.

18

I stare at the Doctorita's face jiggling with rule after rule, not paying too much attention because soon Mamita will come and I will be far away from this place. But for rule eleven, my ears prick up anyway.

11) You may not open this drawer.

She taps her fingers on a small drawer in the wardrobe.

"Yes, Doctorita," I say, curious about what's inside.

And then she leads me to Jaimito, who is sleeping peacefully in his crib as she spews out more rules that I mostly ignore.

17) You must not let my son touch anything dirty.

22) You must change his diapers the moment they're wet.

On and on she rambles in a voice as shrill as the electric blender.

Meanwhile, Niño Carlitos stands over the kitchen trash can, moving a little machine over his face as tiny pieces of hair fall onto the banana peels. I watch in interest and horror. My father and uncles don't have hair on their faces. Maybe these *mestizos* have to secretly cut off their hairs with little machines to keep from turning into hairy monsters.

I glance at the door, willing it to start shaking from the pounding of Mamita's desperate fists. No pounding, only the buzz of Niño Carlitos's little machine, and the click of the Doctorita's heels on the tile as she rushes around, and the swish of the faucets she turns on and off, and her voice, laying out rule after rule like stones in a wall for my life here.

Mamita, where are you?

chapter 3

ONCE THEY LEAVE, the house is silent except for the tick-tick-tick of a clock and Jaimito's soft, sleepy breathing. I sit on the sofa and listen to the clock cutting up moments so that time stretches out forever. I watch the door, waiting for Mamita's knocking. When that doesn't happen, I make a few tentative bounces on the sofa.

Then I bounce harder and higher until I get giggly and breathless, my heart beating like crazy for already disobeying one of the zillion rules. I wander around the apartment, brushing my hands over the *mestizo* things—shelves of books, framed photos of the baby and Niño Carlitos and the Doctorita when she looked thinner and her hair was long and glossy.

I stop in front of the TV screen, which reflects my face like a black mirror. With a shivery thrill, I press a button, and the TV comes to life. Then I turn a big knob to change the channels. Little dots of color and light move around, news and talk shows, but no cartoons. I turn the TV off, then bounce on the bed, so high my fingers touch the ceiling, and it feels, for a moment, like I am flying.

Agile as a goat, I leap onto the tile floor, beside the wardrobe, smack in front of the forbidden drawer. My fingers graze the smooth wood and cool brass handle, then clutch it and pull.

Locked. Too bad.

Well, that covers rules one, two, four, five, and a good effort at rule eleven. Rule three next. *You may not touch the stereo*. It takes me a few minutes to figure out how to turn it on, but soon lively *cumbia* music fills the room, music that makes you want to dance around.

So that's what I do until Jaimito wakes up smiling and chattering in baby talk. "Bababa. Gagaga." He's a cute little boy, maybe a year old, with a chubby pink face and a halo of wispy soft hair the color of corn silk. I take off his wet diaper and drop it in a white painted basket with the other dirty diapers. "Hello, handsome. Want your diaper changed?"

"Bababa," he says, laughing. "Gagaga."

"Oh, really?" I pull a clean one from the neat stack, but I can't remember how the Doctorita folded the diaper and pinned it on him. I try a few different ways, but none seems right. Meanwhile, Jaimito is squirming around like a crazy puppy.

Quickly, I tie the cloth around his waist the way we do in Yana Urku, the way I've done with Hermelinda and Manuelito. I wrap it around him like a skirt that skims his ankles and then secure it at the waist with a piece of string. He seems happy crawling around in it, the fabric dragging behind him. As he crawls, his diaper cleans the floor, picking up bits of dust and hair and pulling it along like a little mop.

All morning, we build forts with the sofa cushions and play Tarzan and Cheetah. Jaimito crawls around the floor like a real savage and pees in little puddles that I wipe up with a towel from the kitchen. Hmmm. This diaper style probably works best when the babies are crawling outside and their pee just soaks into the dirt. After a while, we're tired out, and he's sitting in the middle of the floor sucking on banana skins with banana smeared all over his face, like a messy gorilla. I arrange the cushions back on the sofa even though the Doctorita hasn't included *No cushion forts* as one of the rules.

I finish just as a key scrapes in the lock. The door swings open and the Doctorita stands motionless, staring open-mouthed at Jaimito.

He crawls toward her in his long white diaper skirt. "Gagaga!"

Her nose wrinkles. I sniff the air, wondering if she's angry that the house smells like pee. But her face twists up into a laugh. "Ha! My son's a little *longuito*!" She laughs so hard tears come to her eyes. "A *longuito* baby!"

I cringe. Once Mamita comes, I'll tell the Doctorita one of *my* rules. Rule one: Never use the word *longuito*. Or *longuita* or *longa* or *longo*. *Ever*.

Later, after the Doctorita shows me how to fold the baby's diaper *mestizo* style, Niño Carlitos comes home. Over a lunch of fried steak and cucumber-tomato salad she tells him the story, and again her face screws up and her laughter rises like a hyena's into those piercing words: "Dressed like a *longuito*! A *longuito* baby!"

Niño Carlitos doesn't find it as funny as she does. Instead, he gives me a sympathetic look, and says, "Things feel very different here, don't they?"

I nod.

"Well, I think you're doing a fine job, *hija*."

My eyes dance a little in response, and I feel a twinge of sadness that most likely, after Mamita comes for me, I won't ever see this nice man again. This man who calls me *daughter*.

It's midafternoon now and I squint into the bright sunshine of the cement patio, washing dishes, finishing the last plate. One, two, three rinses. The water has turned my fingers wrinkled and pink.

The Doctorita comes outside with a big basket of dirty diapers. "Wash these," she huffs, and then disappears up the stairs.

I remember the Doctorita and Niño Carlitos telling my parents that all I'd have to do was take care of the baby. I don't remember anything about washing dishes and clothes. I plug up the basin with a rag, sprinkle in detergent, dump in the smelly diapers, and start scrubbing. But no matter how much I scrub, the caca stains won't come out. I scrub and scrub, but the diapers refuse to turn pure white. So I rinse them and start hanging them up, their spots of yellow glaring in the sunshine like decorations for a party.

The Doctorita teeters down the stairs on her pointy heels, the fabric of her skirt clinging to rolls of flesh. "What's taking so long?" She spots the diapers hanging to dry. "What's this?" she shrieks. "They're still dirty! Jaimito will get sick if he wears these." She tears them off the line and hurls them back into the basket. "*¡Longa sucia!* Dirty Indian!" Bits of saliva spray off her words. Her fists pound my head.

I shut my eyes tight, and my arms fly up to shield my face. Pain sears through me, and I think, *Stop, stop, stop*, but she punches and slaps until my head is a ball of aching, screaming fire. Just when my legs feel like they're about to collapse, she steps back.

"Next time I come out," she says, "these had better be white. Or else you'll scrub them with your teeth and eat the caca right off them."

She leaves. I fill the sink with soapy water again. My head throbs. The world shifts in and out of focus. My shaking hands move of their own accord, scrubbing the diapers, adding more and more soap. The bubbles grow and multiply, thin, trembling balls of rainbows. My thoughts disappear except for these fragile bubbles and the four words that play over and over in my head. *Mamita, come get me. Mamita, come get me. Mamita, come get me.* Something inside me repeats this like a mantra, like a drumbeat along with my heart and pulse and throbbing head.

Hours later, with my raw hands still submerged in the harsh bubbles, it finally hits me like a punch in the stomach: *My mother is not coming to get me.*

chapter 4

"I WANT TO GO HOME," I tell Niño Carlitos at dinner that night, biting my tongue to keep in the tears so that he won't think I'm a crybaby. My accent is so thick I hope he understands the words.

"Oh, *m'hija*," he says with a kind, bland smile. "I know things seem strange now, but trust me, soon you'll get used to our life."

I offer Jaimito another spoonful of mashed potatoes, eyeing their plates heaped with rice and meat and rolls, this fancy food I've spent my life craving. I don't want any of it. There are too many tears stuck in my throat to think about eating.

But I refuse to let myself cry. I refuse to show them weakness. Instead, I'll be clever, make a plan. I'll stay quiet and obedient until my visit home in a month. Once I'm home, I'll refuse to leave. When the Doctorita tries to grab me, Cheetah will lift her fierce hooves in warning, maahing and maahing, and if the Doctorita comes any closer, my beautiful goat will bash in her head.

* * *

Over the next few weeks, I discover that Niño Carlitos, unlike the Doctorita, never hurts me. While the Doctorita shouts and smacks my face or whacks my head whenever I make a mistake, Niño Carlitos never beats me, never yells, never calls me a *longa*. He calls me only *m'hija*, my daughter. "Oh, *m'hija*," he says at every meal. "This is *rrriquísimo*, really delicious!"

One night, they're sitting at the table, sipping the soup I cooked for dinner, while I feed Jaimito, who's in his high chair. He's refusing to eat, only interested in throwing handfuls of rice off the edge of his tray. I'm hoping the Doctorita won't notice. Somehow, his messes are always my fault.

Niño Carlitos leans toward the Doctorita and whispers, "Could you tell la Virginia not to use so much salt next time?"

The Doctorita slams down her fork. "Carlos, I'm sick of it. You always criticize me, but never that *longa*. Only, *m'hija* this, *m'hija* that. Oh, how delicious, *m'hija*. And I'm always the bad guy. Why is this *longa* my burden?" Her chin jiggles wildly, her face turning red as a bloody steak.

I try to focus on feeding Jaimito, slipping a few spoonfuls of lentils into his mouth, which he promptly spits into his hand and rubs all over his face.

Once the Doctorita stops yelling, Niño Carlitos gives me a secret look, as if to say, *You and I are normal, Virginia. My wife is an evil hyena.* Then he says, "Negra, you need to teach Virginia how to do things. You can't expect her to know everything. She's a little girl."

I wipe the green lentils from Jaimito's pudgy face and flick a piece of rice from the tip of his nose. It lands on the Doctorita's lap. I suck in a breath, but luckily she hasn't noticed.

She wrinkles up her face and narrows her eyes. "Ay, this fool *longa* can't learn anything." Her fist pounds the table. "You're the man of the house, Carlos. Why don't you ever discipline her?"

"I would never hurt la Virginia," Niño Carlitos says evenly. "I would never hit anyone."

I sneak another spoonful of lentils into Jaimito's mouth and press my lips together to keep from smiling. The Doctorita throws down her napkin and storms away.

Niño Carlitos offers me a flat smile. "Really, I think this meal is *rrriquísimo*, very good, Virginia."

I can hold it in no longer; I let my own smile escape. Seeing me smile, Jaimito smiles too, banging his tiny fists into his food, sending bits of rice happily sailing.

More weeks pass, without a mention of my visit home. I think of running away, but I'm not allowed outside. The Doctorita locks the door when she leaves me with Jaimito. The only pieces of the sky I see are flecks through the small, high windows, and a patch above the courtyard where I wash clothes, surrounded by walls. It feels like forever since I've seen the whole big sky, or run down a hill, or climbed a tree.

Niño Carlitos and the Doctorita say nothing about paying me my monthly salary of a thousand sucres. Sometimes I walk into the room where the Doctorita is lying on the sofa, grading papers, and Niño Carlitos is reclined in his chair, reading his textbook, scribbling on a notepad. With Jaimito on my hip, playing with my hair, I stare at them, waiting for them to say, *Oh, we almost forgot. It's been a month and we need to pay you. Here are your thousand sucres. And yes, we need to take you to*

27

visit your family. But mostly they ignore me. Once in a while, the Doctorita will look up and say, "What are you staring at, *longa?*" Or Niño Carlitos will say, "What's wrong, *m'hija?*"

And I try to form the words, *Where is my money? When will you take me home?* Then the tears start welling up and I bury my face into Jaimito's hair and go into the kitchen so that they won't see me cry.

At nights, on the sheepskin Cheetah rug under the turquoise and orange blanket, I think of how to run away. But I wouldn't know where exactly to run, only toward the mountain Imbabura, whose peak I've glimpsed through the high-up windows.

So I wait. Surely Niño Carlitos will have to visit his parents again sometime soon. And when they go, I'll go with them, even if I have to sneak onto the back of the truck and hide under a blanket.

In the meantime, I have to gain their trust so that they suspect nothing. One day they will leave the door unlocked by accident. One day they will have to take me outside the house. And then, I will escape.

About two months after my arrival, I'm playing blocks with Jaimito on the floor—building towers that he knocks over, squealing with delight—when the Doctorita says, "Let's go, *longa.*"

For a moment, I'm speechless. "Where?"

"The store." She grabs her purse and Jaimito's stroller, and ticks off more rules. "Don't talk to anyone. Just greet them and then shut your mouth." We walk down the bright cobblestoned street, past other apartments and children playing soccer, and stores selling ripe fruit and raw meat and shiny cookware and colorful cans of food. Over the roofs, I can see the tips of mountains way in the distance. I recognize the far-off shapes of the mist-shrouded Imbabura, the man mountain, and Cotacachi, his wife, who is covered in diamond frost that he has given her as a gift.

But that is all that seems familiar. On the street, the colors dazzle and confuse me after so much time inside. And even though the Doctorita is the one who has imprisoned me, I feel grateful that she has decided to take me out. *Thank you thank you thank you*, I tell the world that is so much bigger and brighter than the doily-filled apartment.

I peek down the cobbled side streets. They stretch for a couple of blocks in either direction, then turn into dirt roads, then into wavy fields that rise into mountains. There are patchworks of orchards and crops, all shades of green, spotted with cows and farmhouses. The town is bigger than my home of Yana Urku, but much smaller than Otavalo, where Mamita sometimes took me to the Saturday market. From time to time a donkey or horse or truck passes us, but most people are on foot. In Otavalo, there are *indígenas* everywhere, and in the market there is booth after booth of gold beads and dark *anacos* and shiny white blouses. But here, I'm the only one dressed in an *anaco* and puffy blouse. No one looks like me.

Almost everyone who passes us stares at me with curiosity, then makes smiley baby faces at Jaimito, then greets the Doctorita with respect, "*Buenos días*, Doctorita." It must be true, what she's told me—that she is an important person in town. She says that people from nearby communities come to her for dental work, since she is the best dentist for kilometers. "La

29

Negra's the *only* dentist for kilometers," Niño Carlitos jokes, but you can tell that secretly he's proud of her. She snorts and says that it's out of the kindness of her heart that she lives in this backwater town and helps these country people and that one day she'll reap her just reward.

I glance at her now, walking beside me, as I push the stroller, struggling to keep up. Her face is calm at the moment, her chin lifted high, her breasts and chin and belly jiggling as her feet hit the hard ground. I search her baggy eyes for bits of the kindness she claims she has. I can't find a shred of it. Only echoes of her fists flying at me and her thin lips lined with old lipstick spitting out "filthy *longa*." Nearly every day, she finds some reason to lash out at me—punching my head for burning toast, hitting me with a mop for using dish soap to clean the floor, smacking a wooden spoon against my face for adding too much water to the rice. No, if there's any kindness in her, she keeps it well hidden from me.

I follow her into a corner store, helping her lift Jaimito's stroller up the two steps. It's dark and shadowy inside, with cool blue-green walls. Pineapples and papayas and strawberries overflow from wooden crates. The air is thick with the odor of overripe fruit. It's thrilling to be in the midst of these new smells and sights, and a little scary without the apartment walls around me. It's been so long since I've been in the wide world.

The owner, an older lady, greets the Doctorita and coos over Jaimito, who's babbling in his baby language. The lady's lips are like two shriveled worms, pale and dried-up and barely moving as she talks. "Oh, Doctorita, how good that you have this girl. What a pretty little thing she is. How long will she stay with you?"

The Doctorita picks out bananas, one bunch ripe and one bunch still green. "Oh, she's going to live with us for good."

I stare at her. *What?* I wonder if I've misunderstood.

The lady weighs the bananas on a rusted scale, nodding. "Oh, that's the nice thing about these *longuitas*, isn't it? They can stay with you forever."

"Yes, forever."

Forever? My head grows hot and my throat dry and suddenly the voices sound far away and blackness starts at the edges of my eyes and moves inward, swallowing everything, until there is only a pinpoint of light, as though I'm looking down a long, dark tunnel. *Forever?*

I stagger outside into the sunshine, blinking and blinking in the harsh light.

Soon the Doctorita comes outside, struggling to bring Jaimito's stroller down the steps by herself. Annoyed, she shoves the bag of bananas in my arms. "Come, Virginia," she says, as though I'm her pet, as though she owns me now. Forever. But unlike a pet, I have to work all day. And people pay money for a pet, yet for me she paid nothing . . . at least, as far as I know.

I gaze into the distance at Imbabura, the mountain that towers over the potato fields and sheep pastures of my home. With a sudden, deep ache, I understand that the Doctorita has no intention of taking me there. From here, the giant peak looks terribly far away, something small and feeble and half hidden by clouds.

And then I understand something else. I may be a fast runner, but really, I'm just a little girl who could never run all the way back to Yana Urku.

* * *

31

Most nights, my thoughts slip back to my village, to Mamita and my brother and sisters and uncles and aunts and cousins and the animals and the way the grass felt on my cheek during naps and the smell of kitchen smoke and how big the sky stretched above me and how I could climb trees and play market and run around in the pasture all day long.

Other nights, as I remember Yana Urku, I run my fingers over my calves, over the long stripes of scars Papito gave me. After he drank lots of *puro*, he would turn into a fiery monster and beat me and Mamita and Manuelito and Hermelinda. But worse than his whip and fists were Mamita's words. I can't stop remembering her words. *I'd be happy if one day you left and never came back.* Her words cut into me sharper and deeper than any whip. I wonder if words can make scars on your heart. And if they will ever fade.

Whatever path my thoughts take—to the good memories or the bad—at least Cheetah my goat-rug is always here to lick away my tears.

chapter 5

THE DOCTORITA IS STANDING in her bathrobe by the door, sniffling and coughing, a wadded-up tissue in her fist. Her nose is red, her eyes watery, and she's looking at me as though I've already done something wrong. "I'm sending you alone on an errand," she says in a stuffed-up voice. "I'm too sick to go out." She blows her nose with the falling-apart tissue. "Don't even think about running away. Your parents will just sell you to another family. A family who doesn't treat you as well as we do. Your parents don't want you anymore. You hear me?"

"Yes, Doctorita." I try to contain my excitement, to not fidget or bounce too much. In the past few months, I've gone on errands with the Doctorita and walks with the family, but never been outside alone.

"Run there, ask for milk, pay for it, and run right back. Don't talk to anyone."

"Yes, Doctorita."

"Five minutes. You'd better be back in five minutes. I'm watching the clock." She narrows her puffy eyes into a warning.

"Yes, Doctorita."

She hands me a bill and I'm off running, down the stairs, up the street, as fast as I can. I run down the main street, toward the crossroad where I've noticed buses coming up and down on the way to bigger places. I need to find out more about those buses. I can't run all the way to Yana Urku, but maybe I can take a bus.

I pass the intersection, and by the time I reach the store, I'm breathing so hard that when Doña Mercedes greets me and asks what I need, I can barely say "milk."

She counts out my change. "Your name is Virginia, right?"

I nod. She's seen me here with the Doctorita before, and asked me questions then, but I was too scared to answer because of the Doctorita's rules.

"So, how do you like living here?" Doña Mercedes asks, smiling gently.

I hesitate. If I say something, will the Doctorita find out? I don't want to give her another excuse to beat me, like she did in the diaper incident. Almost every week I do a new chore wrong and her fists come flying at me.

Doña Mercedes is waiting for my answer with kind eyes. She wears a soft cream sweater that makes me think of a baby lamb, and her hair falls loose and wavy over her shoulders.

"Fine," I lie.

"You know, I have two girls about your age. Marina and Marlenny." She hands me the milk in a plastic bag along with some coins. "You could play with them sometime."

"Thank you," I whisper. I feel the coins in my hand and

34

wonder if they're enough to get to my village. I look into her eyes, which are hazy brown with the tiniest hint of green. "Do you know which bus could take a person to Yana Urku?"

"Yana Urku?" She looks at me sadly. "I'm sorry, Virginia. I've never heard of that place. Is it very small? Where is it? Is that where you're from?"

Before the tears come, I dash out of the shop, down the street, past the bus turnoff, past our neighbors' houses and up the stairs. My lungs burning, I bang on the door, praying I've made it in time. The Doctorita opens the door and takes the milk and the coins from me without a word. She doesn't yell at me, so I guess I've made it under five minutes. I breathe out in relief. She'll trust me to run errands alone again, and when she does, I'll keep my eyes and ears alert and find a way to escape.

The Doctorita does trust me to go out alone, more and more often. If I come back late because of a long line at the shop, she hits me with whatever weapon is within her reach—books or shoes or just her fists—and yells, "You should have been back five minutes ago, *longa!*" Even though running errands by myself means risking another beating, it's worth it.

Sometimes when I'm late, Niño Carlitos stands outside on the corner, watching for me. Maybe he's still afraid I'll run away, or maybe he cares about me. Either way, he pretends not to be watching for me. "Oh," he says casually, "I'm just getting air, *m'hija.*" My daughter. I can't help smiling at this. Maybe he worries about me the way he'd worry about his own daughter. Maybe he knows he's my protector, that the Doctorita would never hit me for being late with him at my side.

After a while, I grow more daring, and sometimes, when the

35

Doctorita tells me to get eggs, instead of buying them from Doña Mercedes, I run all the way to a store at the edge of the town square. That way I can see the giant cathedral and the water spouting from the fountain and the happy people strolling under the trees. Carrying the eggs, I run back home, breathless, dripping with sweat. The Doctorita looks at me suspiciously. "What took you so long?"

"I went to the store by the square." I hand her the eggs and take a step back, in case she tries to smack me. "Doña Mercedes was out of eggs," I lie.

"Humph."

The store owners like me, especially Doña Mercedes. One day when the Doctorita and I go together to buy milk, Doña Mercedes gushes, "Oh, this little Virginia is so cute! So pretty. So smart. And she's so fast. Always running!"

I smile.

"And so obedient. Look at her!"

The Doctorita gives a satisfied grin. "That's because *yo la machuco*."

Silence, thick and heavy. Doña Mercedes flicks her mossy eyes at me. They're watery, like little ponds. Then she goes back to counting out the Doctorita's change.

Machucar. Pound, crush, bruise. Nearly the same word as *machacar*—what the Doctorita does to raw, tough beef before she fries it. She pounds it with a hammer until it's soft and full of holes. So that's what she thinks she's doing to me. That's what her punches and slaps are for. To make me soft and weak, to crush my spirit, to pound every last bit of *vivísima* spark out of me.

No! My word is silent, but it thunders inside me. My word gives me power. She might beat my body down, but my spirit will stand tall. I shut my eyes and make myself a promise: I will defy the Doctorita, every day, every chance I get, in my own secret *vivísima* way.

chapter 6

"VIRGINIA," the Doctorita says one evening after dinner, "you're going to learn how to knit so you can make sweaters for Jaimito." That very night, she forces me to start knitting a poncho, and every time the rows turn out uneven or I don't do a knot right, she snatches the knitting away from me. "*Longa estúpida,*" she mutters. She shakes her head and sometimes adds a thunk on my head for good measure.

The Doctorita loves knitting. Her favorite things to knit are dresses for the Baby Jesus doll that lies in a cradle on top of the wardrobe. She says that every year she makes him a new outfit to bring her good luck.

Since she loves knitting, I decide I hate it. I make mistakes on purpose, taking her blows as I shout *No!* inside. Knitting is something she can't force me to do.

And to my joy, I win. The Doctorita gives up on making me knit. But she hatches another plan to make me a more useful servant.

One day, as we're watching TV in her bedroom—me on the floor on my sheepskin, and Niño Carlitos and Jaimito and the Doctorita on the bed—she announces, "I've decided you'll go to elementary school to get the diploma you need for sewing school. Then you'll learn to sew clothes for me and Jaimito and Carlitos!" She looks delighted with her plan.

Fuming, I stare at the TV, at a commercial with happy blond children drinking red juice. I think carefully before I give her an answer.

You see, I've been to school before. For six terrible weeks. I was about five years old, and, against my mother's wishes, I went to school instead of pasturing the sheep. That first morning, with high hopes, I tromped down the dusty, pebbled dirt road toward the school, a low cement building. Inside the classroom, everything smelled of chalk dust and pencil shavings and disinfectant. I started out the morning with my most charming smile, hoping the teacher would notice how my eyes danced, how irresistibly *vivísima* I was.

I learned quickly that this *mestiza* teacher ruled her little kingdom with a cruel hand. Three times that first morning she pinched my ear with her sharp fingernails. Four times she called me a stupid *longa*. "How many fingers?" she demanded during math time, stabbing the air with her pointy nails.

I knew my numbers in Quichua from playing market so much; I could even add and subtract and make change. But in Spanish I was speechless.

"Stupid *longa*," she said, hitting the side of my head.

Over the next six weeks, my ears had permanent red marks from the teacher's nails, as did the other indigenous students'.

Whenever I whispered to my classmates in Quichua to ask what letter comes after *c* or how to make a lowercase *f*, there came the nails again.

I blinked hard, over and over, and bit my tongue and thought of Cheetah, waiting for me outside the classroom. Cheetah, who believed I was the smartest girl in the world. For six weeks I suffered through this, and here is why.

Mamita gave me a few riales every day to buy a snack at school. But I decided to save my riales for my first pair of shoes, because my bare feet looked ugly next to all my classmates' shoes and boots. At snack time, while the other children bought little plastic bags of popcorn, I cuddled with Cheetah. I hung on to my riales in my sweaty fist, my stomach growling as I pictured the little pile of riales growing in a cloth bag at the bottom of my cardboard clothes box.

Once I had enough money, my sister brought me to the market to spend it. And that afternoon, back at home, I stood tall in my brand-new black rubber boots and jutted out my chin and announced to Mamita, "I am never going back to school again."

"Fine." She shrugged. "Now you can make yourself useful and pasture the animals."

This was one of the few things we agreed on. School was a waste of time.

"No," I finally say to the Doctorita. "I'm not going to school." My muscles tense instinctively, preparing for her fists.

At first her eyes flash with anger, as though she'd hit me if my bodyguard Niño Carlitos weren't nearby. But a sour smile creeps over her face. "Fine. No school for you. You'll stay an ignorant *longa* all your life. You'll never know how to read or write."

Something about her words stings more than a slap. I turn away from her smug face and look at the TV. The commercial has ended and the show is back on. There's a beautiful lady in a glittering dress onstage, belting out a romantic song. Her sequins flash in the spotlight like thousands of little mirrors.

An idea forms inside me, an idea that gives me happy shivers. Maybe I can be a famous singer when I grow up. That way it won't matter if I can't read or write—except for my name, of course, to give autographs. I imagine myself onstage, my fans going wild. After my last song, they stand up and cheer and shower me with rose petals and flowers and everyone is begging for my autograph, even the Doctorita. Niño Carlitos gives me a giant bouquet, the biggest of all, so big I can barely carry it. *I am proud of you, my daughter,* he says, and kisses the top of my head.

Now, in the mornings, while the Doctorita and Niño Carlitos are gone, I practice being a famous singer. I turn up the stereo and let my hair loose and swing it around and clutch an invisible microphone and dance and sing in front of the mirror. Jaimito dances with me, bouncing up and down, wobbling his head and clapping and laughing. He sings too, opening his mouth wide, sticking out his tongue and shouting *Yayayayaya.*

I love watching my reflection, how my face gets shiny and sweaty like I'm under hot spotlights. But there's a nagging problem. It doesn't look right to see a famous singer in *indígena* clothes. Indigenous women cook and clean and work in fields and take care of children; they don't sing in the spotlight on TV to thousands of fans. I need a sequined dress, or at the very least, regular *mestiza* clothes.

It's been almost a year since I left home, and the few clothes I brought with me have worn out and gotten too small. One afternoon, the Doctorita comes home with three blouses. They are ugly *indígena* blouses, used and grayish white, the color of dirty laundry water. I can tell just by looking that they're way too big for me.

"Try one on," the Doctorita says.

The neck is so large it slides off my shoulders. The stitches of the embroidered flowers are big and sloppy and all wrong. The thread's cheap dye bleeds into the fabric. Without a word, I fold the blouses and stuff them in my cardboard box where I don't have to see them.

A few days later, in the kitchen, the Doctorita demands, "Why aren't you wearing those new blouses?"

I shrug.

"Tell me."

I stare at the potato I'm peeling. "I don't want to wear them."

The Doctorita slaps my face. "Tomorrow you'll start wearing them."

"No," I say, bracing myself for the next blow.

Another slap. *"Longa tonta,"* she spits. Fool *longa.*

With trembling hands, I set down the knife. At my sides, my fists tighten. I look at her beady eyes lined with smudged mascara. "I want to wear clothes like other girls around here."

"You're a *longa,* and you have to dress like a *longa.*" And she turns and walks away.

42

The next day, once again, I refuse to wear the new blouses. She hits me. "Ungrateful *longa*."

But I hold my ground. I *will* become a star someday. And I will *not* wear indigenous clothes.

Once, when I was about four, I pretended to be a *mestiza*. I remember it clearly, like a vivid photo that stands out from all the other, blurred ones. I was in the giant cornfield, helping Mamita pull weeds from the still-short plants, scratching at the lice on my head, feeling my sun-warmed hair, tangled as a bird's nest, and squinting into the dry wind to see if anything more interesting was happening outside the edge of the cornfield. Just other workers, mostly women with *fachalinas* folded on their heads to keep off the sun, some with babies strapped to their backs, all bent over, faces close to the earth. A few rows over, my cousins Zoyla and Gregoria were pulling weeds and wiping the sweat from their foreheads, crisscrossing their faces with streaks of dirt. Beyond them stretched more cornfields, a few whitewashed houses with red tile roofs, and, towering in the distance, mountains.

I picked at some flea-bite scabs on my calves, which were split and caked with dried mud and hardened blood. At the sound of voices speaking Spanish, I straightened up, alert.

Alfonso and his wife, Mariana, were walking by. Alfonso wore snakeskin cowboy boots with heels that made him look taller than he really was, and an expensive leather hat. His hand rested just above Mariana's rump, which swished in a short skirt that revealed doughy legs teetering on spiky heels. The cloth of her shirt seemed stuck to her rolls of fat, and her hair was long and spiraled into a large ball pinned to her head.

Once they moved on, I hitched my *anaco* up to my knees, tucking it into the *faja* at my waist. I smoothed my loose blouse close to my belly and tied it in back. Then I twirled my hair into a knot. Grinning, I put my hands on my hips and cut through the rows of corn to Zoyla and Gregoria. "Get to work, you *indias*," I scolded them in a shrill voice, strutting around just like Mariana. My cousins shrieked with laughter.

At that moment, Mamita looked up. She dropped her machete and stormed over to me. She snatched the fabric of my *anaco* from the *faja* and tore my hair loose. Then she slapped me and said in a low, dangerous voice, "Virginia. Never do that again. Never. You hear? We are *indígena*. We will always be *indígena*. Nothing will change that."

Well, Mamita was wrong.

A few weeks later the Doctorita comes back from her relatives' house with a little pile of used clothes. *Mestizo* clothes.

She drops them on my sheepskin. "Are these good enough for you?"

I pick them up and grin. "Thank you, Doctorita." I've won again, and she knows it.

Later, at night, waiting for sleep to come, Cheetah doesn't have to lick any tears off my face because I'm so busy picturing how beautiful I'll look in *mestizo* clothes.

The next morning, after the Doctorita and Niño Carlitos leave for school, and while Jaimito is still asleep, I tear off my *anaco* and blouse. Which to try on first? There's a blue dress that looks a few sizes too big, a green shirt with short sleeves and a stain on the hem, a gray sweater with two buttons missing, a white dress with frayed lace, and a pink skirt with tiny flowers.

I put on the skirt and the green shirt. With the shirt tucked in, you can't see the stain. In front of the mirror, I let my hair loose and stare at the strange girl facing me. I smile a tentative, excited smile. The mole at the corner of my mouth is no longer a mole; now it's a beauty mark, just like a movie star's. When I squint my eyes so that everything looks blurry, I can almost believe that the skirt is fancy leather and the shirt has sequins and my skin is fair.

I can almost believe that I am backstage, after a performance, eating mangoes and drinking Inca Kola. Then Mamita, who was in the audience, comes up to me and says, *Forgive me, daughter. Forgive me for telling you I'd be happy if you left forever. I have done nothing but cry since you've been gone.* I open my mouth to speak Quichua to her, but only Spanish comes out, and she stares at me, not understanding.

That's the true part of my daydream. More and more lately, Quichua words have been burying themselves deeper and deeper in dark places in my memory. Sometimes I look at the carrots or tomatoes I'm cutting and try to remember the Quichua words. When I whisper them, they feel strange and clumsy in my mouth.

My body is starting to feel different too, like a soft white roll or mushy white rice, from all the *mestizo* food I eat. My skin has grown pale and smooth from staying inside most of the day. My body is no longer made of dirty potatoes just pulled out of the earth and wild, weedy herbs.

I ask the girl in the mirror: *How long until people forget you were ever a* longa?

chapter 7

WHENEVER NIÑO CARLITOS calls me *my daughter*, a cozy warmth spreads through me. He is kind to me, kind to all children, one of the favorite teachers at the *colegio*, the junior high and high school. He teaches social studies, grades seven to twelve, and he never tires of talking about the Seven Wonders of the Ancient World. *"M'hija,"* he says, "let me tell you about the Seven Wonders of the Ancient World."

I pause in my sweeping and sit down beside him on the sofa, listening to his words slip out, soft and thoughtful, painting pictures of temples and pyramids.

Sometimes, when he's nervous, his words get stuck in an endearing stutter. He blends into the background, the same way his features blend into each other—pale skin and hair and teeth and shirt—all yellowed shades of white. I like watching him sit on the sofa, staring into space, quiet and nearly invisible, while inside his mind ideas for fun projects whirl around like sparks and colors.

When the rainy season comes, Niño Carlitos spends weeks building a very tiny pyramid. The Doctorita frowns at the pyramid pieces stacked on the table. "I can't believe you're playing with toys while I run our household and feed our family."

"It's not a toy," he says, looking hurt. "It's a perfectly proportioned replica of the Great Pyramid of Giza in Egypt. The only one of the Seven Wonders of the Ancient World still in existence."

But the Doctorita's words must shame him because he decides to use his spare time making extra cash. One day he comes up with the idea of creating wooden puzzles to sell at school. So the whole family starts spending afternoons in Niño Carlitos's workshop. Jaimito sits on the ground playing with piles of sawdust while we work. My job is to sand the puzzle pieces with scratchy paper.

"Good work, *m'hija*," Niño Carlitos says. "Very smooth edges."

Meanwhile, the Doctorita glues pictures of Bugs Bunny and Mickey Mouse onto the wood. Every once in a while, she rolls her eyes and mutters, "Here I am, a trained dentist and a teacher, gluing puzzles."

"But you're so good at it, Negra," Niño Carlitos says as he dumps a new batch of puzzle pieces on the table. "So precise."

After three or four months, Niño Carlitos grows bored with making puzzles and starts building a wooden airplane that will be big enough for Jaimito to ride around in. I perch beside Niño Carlitos on a bench, watching him work, bouncing with anticipation. A new toy for Jaimito means a new toy for me. Once it's finished and painted red and white, I ride around in it too.

"You're too big for that," the Doctorita snaps. "It's for toddlers, not eight-year-old girls. I forbid you to ride in it." But it's the most popular toy in the neighborhood, and when she isn't nearby, I roll around in it proudly as the other children watch in awe.

At the top of the dirt hill, I tell Jaimito that I am a pilot flying us far from here, to Yana Urku to pick up Cheetah and Hermelinda and Manuelito, and then we'll all soar down to the beach and play all day. Jaimito squeals and giggles at my plan, clapping his pudgy little hands together. I kiss his pink cheek, despite its coating of smeared snot. Together, we whoosh down the hill.

The Doctorita is always complaining about how little money they have, ranting about their debts and bad investments, moaning about their pitiful teacher salaries, nagging Niño Carlitos to find other ways to make money for the family.

Since people will pay a lot of money to eat roasted guinea pigs during celebrations, Niño Carlitos decides to raise them. He says once they're plump and grown, he'll sell them to restaurants. I help him by gathering alfalfa from the field behind our apartment and feeding the quickly growing pile of guinea pigs. Listening to them squeak reminds me of my life at home, of lying on my scratchy woven mat at night and listening to our guinea pigs rustle in the corner.

In Yana Urku, Mamita used to cure sick people with our guinea pigs. When a relative was feeling bad, Mamita would grab one of the little creatures and stuff it in a sack. I trailed along behind her as she barreled straight to the patient's house, on a mission. Inside the house, she prayed to the gods of the mountains and the God in heaven, all the while rubbing the live guinea pig over the sick person's skin. The guinea pig soaked up the person's evil air like a sponge, until its squeaking grew weak and its fat little body was limp as wilted lettuce from all the sickness inside it. Then Mamita drew her knife.

I put my hands over my face, but left a space between my fingers to peek through. Mamita sliced the guinea pig's belly from its neck down to its rear legs, then spread apart the furry, bloody flesh. She examined the guts closely, as though she were reading a book, and diagnosed the person's sickness. She told whether they had gotten a fright from a snake or whether a witch had put a curse on them or whatever. Then she told them what they had to do to be completely cured.

What would the Doctorita and Niño Carlitos say if they knew that even after a year of living with them, I still have these memories inside me? These images of fresh guinea-pig blood and heathen Indian things? These dirty, devil things that would give the sweet Baby Jesus doll nightmares in his cradle? I keep these memories to myself, tucked away in a dark, secret place in my mind.

Soon after the guinea pigs comes the cow, white with black spots. Every afternoon, I take the two-minute walk down the dusty dirt side street to our cow pen. I let the cow out and lead her by a frayed rope down another dusty road to the *colegio* grounds, where she grazes on the grass near the avocado trees. This way the grass stays short and the cow gets fed and it works out for everyone.

The cow reminds me of Josefa, my family's cow in Yana Urku, and like Josefa, she quickly becomes my friend, flicking her tail happily when I rub the space between her enormous eyes.

Niño Carlitos also starts buying crates of eggs from people in the countryside and then selling them in town. "Listen, Negra. Listen, *m'hija*," he says. "These eggs are for selling, not eating."

We store the eggs in a musty, falling-down wooden shed next to the cow pen. Some of the eggs are huge and extra delicious, with two yolks. The Doctorita likes those eggs too. "Virginia," she says in a conspiratorial voice, "go to the storehouse and tell Carlitos to give you some eggs. He can never say no to you."

So I run to the shed. "Niño Carlitos," I say, flashing a smile and letting my eyes dance, "please be nice and let me pick out some eggs."

He hesitates for a moment, runs his hand over his face, then says, "Of course, *m'hija*." Grinning, I pick out the biggest eggs, satisfied that being *vivísima* has its rewards.

We're taking one of our evening walks around town—the Doctorita and Niño Carlitos and Jaimito in his stroller and me. The sun is gentle and golden at this time of day, melting like butter behind the mountains. Our shadows stretch long in front of us and crisscross with the shadows of other people strolling along. On the outskirts of town, when we pass an orchard, I scamper up a tree to pick guavas, eating the sweetest, prettiest ones myself and tossing down the worm-eaten, half-rotted ones to the Doctorita. From the treetop, I hear her grumble to Niño Carlitos, "I know she's up there eating the best."

He just laughs. "Oh, this Virginia! We're lucky to have her."

I grin, smug in another tiny victory against the Doctorita.

I like these walks. They're a chance for me to figure out what other people think of the Doctorita. The more I know, the more power I have. So I'm always listening, watching, thinking in secret.

Passersby say hello to the Doctorita, often with exaggerated respect. I'm beginning to realize that their respect isn't as simple as it seems. They *have* to be nice to her. She teaches their children science at the *colegio*. She's known for her temper, and no one wants her to unleash it on their children. Most of all, people know they might need the Doctorita to fill a painful cavity or pull a tooth someday. If she likes them, she'll help them, and even if they can't pay her money, she'll accept a bag of fruit or a box of eggs instead. They, too, see the value in staying on her good side. Or at least appearing to.

Every now and then, I overhear women talking about her in hushed tones. *It's too bad she's put on so much weight, but of course, she works so much she can't exercise,* pobrecita. *She wears the pants in the family, you know, but her poor son, he has to survive without a mother all day,* pobrecito. *She makes more than her husband, you know, so we'll see how well the marriage fares—what a shame. She's so much darker than her husband, but lucky for her he doesn't seem to mind—of course who knows how long that will last.*

There is a certain wistful, almost jealous, look in the ladies' eyes as they gossip. It occurs to me that maybe the Doctorita makes them feel bad about their lives as homemakers, mournful they don't have their own careers.

As much as I hate the Doctorita, I wonder if one day I could be like her, only not as fat and mean. Maybe I could graduate from college and get a professional job. Maybe I could make more money than my husband so he couldn't boss me around. Maybe everyone would have to treat me with respect.

Many people on the street recognize me by now and know that I'm the Doctorita's servant. Sometimes they say, "What a pretty little girl," or "Such a fast little girl," or "This little girl is *vivísima*," and my heart swells and I wonder: if a new person came to town, would she see me strolling and think I was part of the family, like a daughter?

Hello, Doctorita, hello, Carlos, this newcomer would say. *Oh, your daughter is getting prettier by the day. Why, I saw her on TV last night singing in a gorgeous sparkly dress. You're so lucky to have such a talented daughter. All my daughter does is go to school and play.*

Oh, yes, Niño Carlitos would say. *Virginia is our treasure.*

chapter 8

IT'S DURING THIS TIME, my second year with the Doctorita and Niño Carlitos, that their big troubles begin. And against all logic, I find myself caring about them. In another attempt to make money to pay off their debts, they buy a bus with a brother-in-law. The idea is to hire a driver to take passengers around Otavalo, and then divide the profits. "We'll be swimming in money soon," Niño Carlitos says. So they take out loans to pay for the bus, claiming they'll earn the money back in no time. But the bus is a lemon, always breaking down, and after they've poured heaps of money into repairs, some thieves steal it.

"Oh, my nerves!" the Doctorita whines. She's become a disaster herself, ever since the theft of the bus. For months now she can barely drag herself from bed in the mornings, and after school she flops right back in, frantically knitting Baby Jesus dresses and ranting about thieves. She fears that criminals are lurking around every corner, plotting to steal more of her things.

"Just thinking about those horrible thieves makes my heart race," she moans, pressing her hand to her chest. "Maybe I'm having a heart attack. Open the window, Virginia! I'm suffocating!"

I climb onto a chair and open the window. Fresh, cool air blows into the room. "Everything will be all right, Doctorita."

"No, it won't," she says, her knitting needles flying and clicking. "We're in debt up to our ears. We'll all starve."

She has a point. The cupboard is bare except for a bag of dried rice, some sugar, and spices. Inside the refrigerator sits a lonely pitcher of our cow's milk. "What should I make for lunch?" I ask the Doctorita hesitantly.

"Go find something," she calls from her bed. "Stop bothering me."

I cook sweet rice pudding with milk and cinnamon for lunch, which at least makes Jaimito happy. That evening, when Niño Carlitos comes home and plops on the sofa, I say, "Excuse me. Niño Carlitos?"

He waves his hand in the air, flicking me away. "Not now, not now, *m'hija*. I'm busy thinking." He's been spending more time away from the house, staying later at school, going out to the bar in the evenings. And always a distracted look clouds his face.

"But there's no food to cook," I say.

"Oh, you'll think of something," he mumbles. "You're a clever girl."

A clever girl. *Clever for stealing food* was what Mamita always said.

I begin to hatch my plan.

* * *

That afternoon, with two-year-old Jaimito at my side, I lead the cow to pasture in the *colegio* yard, near the clump of avocado trees. I glance around. No one in sight. "Wait here, Jaimito. Keep a lookout."

I climb the tree and gather avocadoes, dropping them furtively into the bag slung over my shoulder.

Next, we take the cow farther down the dirt road, to the groves of fruit trees on Don Arturo's property.

"Stand guard," I tell Jaimito, who is staring at a bee and sucking on his thumb. The Doctorita is always yelling at me about his thumb sucking, a habit which she insists could mess up his teeth for life. "And take your thumb out of your mouth," I add.

I scamper up a tree and quickly pluck a dozen guavas. Then we make our way farther down the path to Don Gerardo's vegetable fields. This will be trickier; they're surrounded by a barbed-wire fence, and rumor has it Don Gerardo pulls a gun on anyone who trespasses.

But surely he won't shoot at a two-year-old. "Jaimito," I whisper, "when I say go, crawl under the fence and take some fat red tomatoes. And the biggest cucumbers you can find. And some green peppers. You'll have to pull really hard. Can you do that?" I wish I'd brought disguises, so if someone spots us, we could run fast around a corner and then rip off our masks and act like we were innocently strolling. I take one last look up and down the dirt road and squint at the field. Not a soul in sight. "Now, Jaimito. Go!"

He toddles to the fence and wriggles underneath like a worm. If Don Gerardo catches us, I'll say that Jaimito is just a little boy who doesn't know what he's doing. Jaimito wanders through plants taller than he is, tugging with all his might at the vegetables and dropping them, with clumsy toddler hands, into the sack. Finally, he crawls back under the fence, dragging his loot and grinning. I kiss his forehead and brush the dirt off his shirt and pants so the Doctorita won't get mad.

"Let's go, little friend!" I say, taking the heavy sack from him.

On the way back, we pass Doña Juliana's chicken coop. By this time, Niño Carlitos's egg-buying business has fizzled. I pause in front of the coop. Doña Juliana won't miss a few eggs. I sneak inside and snatch six eggs, still warm from the hens, and put them carefully into the bag of fruit and vegetables.

"Now remember, Jaimito," I said. "Don't breathe a word about this. Not to anyone. Especially not your mother. All right?"

He nods, slurping at his thumb, happy to share a secret that involves getting dirty. As a reward, I let him suck his thumb in peace all the way home.

That night I make a big, colorful dinner, a *cortido* salad of fresh tomatoes and cucumber and peppers, rice, eggs, and guavas in sugary syrup for dessert, with enough guavas left over for the next day's juice. I heap the plates with food and set them on the table. "Time for dinner!" I call out.

The Doctorita wanders to the table in her bathrobe, still clutching her knitting needles, half a yellow Baby Jesus dress draped over her arm. She stares at the food, dazed at first and then suspicious. "Where did you get all this?"

"Oh," I say mysteriously, motioning with my chin, "over there."

The Doctorita raises her eyebrows at Niño Carlitos. The corners of her mouth turn up. "Well, let's eat."

As usual, I haven't set a place for myself, since I don't eat dinner until after they've finished. So it's a surprise when the Doctorita says, "Why don't you join us tonight, Virginia?"

Food tastes better when you're eating with other people, much better than scarfing down leftovers alone in the kitchen. After we've stuffed ourselves, I collect the dirty dishes, their china ones and my metal ones.

Niño Carlitos pats his gut. "*Rrriquísimo, m'hija*. And just the perfect amount of salt." He winks.

The Doctorita nods, her chin jiggling. "Virginia, I don't know how you do it, but thank you. You've cooked food when there was nothing to cook."

What would they do without me? I feel like one of those saints the Doctorita is always praying to, like the Virgin of Baños in elegant robes and a giant crown who does miracles for desperate people. I imagine being carried through town on a golden throne, smiling and waving to my fans. *Thank you, Virginia*, everyone shouts. *You are a worker of miracles! You make food out of nothing!* People shower me with applause and confetti and candy, especially caramel squares and purple lollipops.

chapter 9

DURING MY FIRST YEAR IN KUNU YAKU, my mind was always plotting how to escape, but as the first year has slipped into the second, something inside me has shifted, settled. Oh, I can still see opportunities to run away. I could use the grocery money to pay my bus fare, or sneak out on the days the Doctorita forgets to lock me in the house. My plan to make them trust me has worked.

But I don't take the next leap. I give myself the same excuses—that I wouldn't know where to go, that someone could steal me, that I'd get lost, that Mamita and Papito don't want me anyway. I tell myself that the Doctorita's beatings aren't as bad or as frequent as when I first arrived. Although she still calls me hurtful names and whacks me for one thing or another every day, she usually doesn't leave bruises or draw blood. Niño Carlitos is always telling her to treat me more kindly, reminding her that I'm a little girl, yelling at her if he sees me

58

with a black eye or split-open lip. Now a whole month might pass between beatings, the bad beatings when she pounds me until I'm sobbing, until my legs collapse and I curl up, stinging and throbbing and aching, on the floor.

Sometimes I wonder: *What would you do if they took you with them to visit Niño Carlitos's parents? How could you resist escaping then?* But as soon as I ask the questions, I push them from my head. They scare me. And exhaust me. It's hard work to be miserable all the time.

At some point, I decide to dwell in the bright moments. And there are some. Moments when Jaimito wakes up babbling to himself and then, when he sees me, lights up with a smile. Moments when I'm tickling him and he's laughing, breathlessly, and rolling around, and I can't help laughing too. Moments when I come home from an errand and he runs to me and throws his arms around my waist like I'm the most important thing in the world.

Sometimes I try to remember what my little brother Manuelito looks like. I close my eyes and see light brown eyes framed by curly dark lashes and wispy brown hair. It's not Manuelito's face I see, but Jaimito's.

It's early Saturday morning and the Doctorita is dashing around the house, packing for a weekend visit to Niño Carlitos's parents in Yana Urku. Whenever they go on these visits, they refuse to take me, locking me inside the house all weekend, which isn't so bad because I can secretly watch all the TV I want and sleep in their pink bed and dress up in the Doctorita's clothes.

I'm folding Jaimito's little pajamas and outfits and arranging them in his knapsack, when the Doctorita says, "Pack a change of clothes for yourself, Virginia. You're coming, too."

"I am?"

"We'll be at a wedding tonight, there in Yana Urku, and we need someone to take care of Jaimito."

For a moment, I'm frozen in shock. Then, trembling, I change into my favorite blue dress and brush my hair back into a braid. I'm so excited I can barely finish my papaya juice. I imagine walking along Alfonso's cornfield. Mamita and Papito—who will be working in his fields—will spot me. They'll watch with open mouths as the breeze ripples over my blue dress and the sunlight shines on the lace trim; I'll look like an angel. *Oh, my daughter, you're beautiful! Please come to live with us again. We'll always give you the biggest potato of the soup, always.*

It's been a long time since I let myself think about Mamita and Papito, and it feels good, like sneaking cookies. But I usually don't let myself think too long, because then the good thoughts veer into bad thoughts that leave my stomach aching and my eyes burning.

As I pack my bag, I think of Mamita. I try to find a memory of her smiling at me, but in every memory she's frowning. Now I'm remembering how she used to frown at me when I begged her to take me to work in the fields. I wanted desperately to start making money to make my dreams come true.

"Take me, please, Mamita," I'd beg. "Let me be your partner."

Everyone needed a partner to plant: one person made a hole with a stick and dropped in three corn kernels, and the other person dropped in three beans and covered up the hole with dirt. That way the bean vines could wrap around the corn plants like necklaces and dangle their pods like earrings.

Alfonso paid his workers in cash, not in sacks of beans or corn, but real silver coins and paper bills. I'd been dreaming of buying a lamb who would be my cute, cuddly friend and grow up to be a sheep who would have lots of babies that I could raise and sell—my first step to being rich.

One morning, annoyed by my whining and begging, Mamita snapped, "Fine." She strapped my brother to my back and my sister to hers and headed to Alfonso's field. I ran alongside her, breathless from Manuelito's weight tugging down my shoulders.

The brown field stretched out, the remains of last year's crop plowed into the soil. Mamita tied a cloth around my shoulder and made a sling where she put a few handfuls of beans. She walked ahead, digging a hole with her stick and dropping in three corn kernels from her own sling. I followed, carefully counting out three smooth beans and letting them fall into each hole and patting dirt on top.

As the morning wore on, the sun blazed and wind blew dirt into our eyes, our mouths, our noses. Soon I grew tired of walking and planting and started dumping beans by the handful, quickly covering them with dirt so Mamita couldn't see. When I announced that my sack was empty, she frowned at me, suspicious, but didn't say anything.

When the sun was directly overhead and everyone was ready to have lunch, Alfonso emerged from his big white hacienda with its red tile roof and sauntered by, checking on the progress. All the workers lowered their heads, mumbling, "Good afternoon, Amo Alfonso," or "Good afternoon, *patrón.*"

Alfonso stopped near me, very close. I tilted my head back to look up at him. He was so tall my neck got a crick in it, and I had to squint into the sun behind him.

"You are a very pretty girl," he said, "and very smart, and I like how you're working."

"Thank you, Taita Alfonso." I jutted out my chin stubbornly, calling him *Taita*, the title I'd use for any indigenous man in our village.

He didn't seem to care. "Now, how old are you, *guagua*? Five? Six?"

I shrugged. "Who knows."

He grinned the way a man grins at a pig when he's deciding whether to buy it—admiring it and imagining how good it will taste or how much money it will make him.

I smiled the most charming smile I could muster up, letting my eyes dance. "Taita Alfonso, if you like my work, we can make a deal." I paused, searching for the right words in Spanish. "I can work more days for you. And you can pay me a lamb."

He chuckled and pushed up the rim of his hat.

I stretched my smile even bigger, proud that he understood my rough Spanish. "You don't need to pay me money. A lamb will do."

"All right," he said. "If you work hard and plant all the beans today, you'll get a lamb."

As he moved away to talk with other workers, I felt rich and important already, just like a business lady must feel after making an especially good deal.

But Alfonso broke his promise. He never paid me my lamb.

A month later, huge, chaotic clumps of plants sprouted from

the holes where I'd thrown handfuls of beans. The vines crowded each other in a twirling mass, winding desperately around each other's stems, suffocating the tender corn shoots. A furious, red-faced Alfonso asked his workers who was responsible, while at his side, Mariana pinched her lips together as if she'd just eaten a green berry.

I said nothing.

But Mamita knew. "You're the one," she said, frowning at me like I was soup with too much salt. Or corn with worms.

Once I was sure she wasn't going to hit me with a eucalyptus stick as punishment, I smiled inside, because that rotten, lying thief Alfonso and his wife got what they deserved.

In the truck, on the road out of Kunu Yaku, the Doctorita opens a crinkly bag of fried plantain chips. "Have some, Virginia."

"Thank you, Doctorita," I say, pouring some chips into my palm. I'm watching the roads carefully, in case I ever do decide to make this journey alone, by foot or by bus. But I may not need to. What if I run back to my family today and refuse to leave? My insides leap wildly at the idea.

"Now, Virginia," the Doctorita says sternly, as if she can hear my thoughts, "you know if you try to go home to your parents, they're going to sell you to other people. To a family that won't treat you as well as we do."

I grit my teeth. She might be lying . . . but maybe she's telling the truth. After all, Mamita had said, *I'd be happy if one day you left and never came back*. If only I could forget those words. Thinking about them makes me blink and blink to keep from crying.

I eat the chips slowly. The salt stings my tongue, makes me thirsty. I'm quiet during the ride, watching the fields and canyons out the window, memorizing landmarks and turnoffs. The two Virginias inside me argue—the brave one and the scared one, the one who wants to leave the Doctorita and the one who wants to stay.

The brave Virginia says, *Stop thinking about Mamita's bad words to you. She said some good words, too. Think of them.*

So I think and think and when I spot a *chilca* tree out the window, I finally come up with something. A memory where Mamita is not frowning at me. A memory where she has something close to a smile on her face. *My daughter, she can do it.* Words that glisten with a kind of tender reverence.

Whenever a neighbor had *mal viento*—evil air—or *espanto*—fright—Mamita would walk me over to the sick person's house, and announce, "My daughter, she can cure you. She can do it."

Mamita would take a warm, fresh egg from beneath one of our hens, then break off a bunch of small branches from the *chilca* tree. I carried the heap of leaves, pressing them to my nose in anticipation, breathing in their strong scent, a scent that seemed sweet at one moment and pungent the next. At the house of the sick person, usually a cousin or aunt or uncle of ours, I put a holy look on my face. At those moments I forgot the itch of my flea bites and the sting of my cracked cheeks; I felt pure, like a scrubbed-clean angel dropped straight from heaven.

First, I knelt on the woven mat and prayed: "My God, give me the power to cure." Then I rolled the whole, smooth egg over the patient's arms and legs and neck and stomach and back and head, to soak up all the evil air. I patted the *chilca* leaves vigorously over the sick person's body to clean his spirit. Within moments my breath quickened, and soon I was nearly gasping for air, my arms aching, heavy and weighted down. The more evil air a person had, the more my body turned into a limp rag afterward.

But it was worth it. The patients and their families paid me a few riales and thanked me with respect, as though I weren't a little girl but a wise, grown-up healer. And best of all, Mamita nodded proudly, saying, "My daughter, she can do it."

Finally, after six hours in the truck, when my legs are stiff and cramped, we turn onto the dusty, pebbled road to Alfonso's house. In the distance, my parents' shack perches on a small hill, looking a little lopsided. Gray smoke streams from the chimney. They must be home. Mamita must be cooking potato soup. My brother and sister are probably playing together. I close my eyes to keep the tears in.

Behind my eyelids, I imagine little Manuelito crawling under the bed and discovering my box of old clothes. *What are these?* he asks. Hermelinda shrugs. Mamita frowns. *Once there was a girl named Virginia*, she says. *But she was bad and she hit her sister and stole food and always got into trouble. So we gave her away and we hope she never comes back. She is dead to us now.* Manuelito grows bored playing with the clothes and starts banging on pots with Hermelinda and laughing. They forget all about the bad girl named Virginia.

My eyes open and I strain to catch a glimpse of someone in my family, but the yard remains deserted. I struggle to remember the good words—*My daughter, she can do it*—but they feel flimsy and light, as though they could blow away in a gust of wind. No, the other words, heavy as mountains, are the ones that stick. *I'd be happy if one day you left and never came back.*

The Doctorita follows my gaze. "There you have nothing. It's filthy and there's not enough food to eat. And it will always be that way. With us you have good food and shelter. With us you live like a civilized person."

I try to ignore her, try to find some Quichua words to use as shields or weapons. How to say *Hello! I'm home!* How to secretly insult the Doctorita in Quichua—*ugly* mestiza, *mean* mestiza, mestiza *whose chin jiggles!* But the words stay hidden.

As we pull up the dirt driveway to Alfonso's house, the Doctorita asks, "Virginia, do you want to leave us? We can take you back to your parents right now."

"No," I say softly.

The Doctorita pats my knee. "Good, Virginia."

Niño Carlitos smiles his bland smile. "You're making the right decision, *m'hija.*"

We climb out of the truck and unload the bags. I clutch Jaimito's hand as we walk toward Alfonso's house. I take one last look back at my old home, the flat tin roof flashing in the afternoon sunlight, the column of smoke fading and drifting away.

The weekend passes quickly. Sunday afternoon, under clouds heavy with rain, we head back to Kunu Yaku. My parents' house looks sad and abandoned and swallowed by the mist. As we pass it, I shiver and wrap my sweater tightly around me. I peer at the valleys and pastures and red tile roofs spread out below us, dissolving into fog, and then up at the Imbabura mountain disappearing into a stony white sky.

I tell myself that the next time I come here I will be a famous singer in a sequined dress, and these sights and sounds will mean nothing to me. I will breathe in the smells of wood smoke and cows and potato fields and there won't be an ocean of tears in my throat and it won't matter if my parents don't want me, because I will be famous and loved by all and no one will ever know that I came from this place.

PART 2

chapter 10

THREE YEARS HAVE PASSED, and I'm settled into the rhythm of life in Kunu Yaku. I've learned how to do all my chores perfectly. I no longer burn the rice or add too much salt or forget to sweep under the sofa. Only once in a while, when I slip up, or when the Doctorita is in a bad mood, does she beat me. And this happens only when my bodyguard, Niño Carlitos, isn't around. Afterward, when he notices my face bruised and swollen, he whispers something sternly to the Doctorita, who hollers, "Well, why is this *longa* my burden?"

I understand the Doctorita better now. Even though she often treats me cruelly, I see that she is not all evil. Her students seem to like her, even joke around with her, although only to a point. She's known for her temper and impatience and strictness, which make her students cautiously friendly with her. She works hard, waking up early to finish planning lessons and grading papers, going to bed late after squeezing in some dental exams in the evening. There's even a playful side to her when she's in a good mood, the side that laughs at Jaimito's and my antics and cracks jokes with Niño Carlitos.

I understand her marriage better now, maybe from all the soap operas I've watched with her while lying on the floor beside her bed. Not to mention all the talk shows I've watched in secret, while she and Niño Carlitos are at work and Jaimito is at preschool. I often watch television while doing my chores, making sure to turn off the set fifteen minutes before they come home, so it has time to cool off. And all day long, I think.

I think about this family I'm stuck with, about my place with them, about their places with each other, their places in our town. I see that part of Niño Carlitos is proud of how smart and accomplished his wife is, yet part wishes she would be a simple mother and housewife. Part of him feels bad that she makes more money than he does. Part wishes that she would worry about staying slim and pretty and pleasing him, rather than lying like a bulging sack of potatoes on the sofa, exhausted from her two jobs, bossing me and him around.

I see from their wedding photo that the Doctorita and Niño Carlitos were once in love, and that back then, he didn't care that his mother didn't like her. Back then, the Doctorita's education probably impressed him more than threatened him. Back then, he probably liked the way her fat bottom pressed at the seams of her skirt. Over the past three years, there have been times when they fought so much, I was sure they were on the verge of divorce.

Lately, though, life has flowed smoothly. Niño Carlitos seems to have a new appreciation for his wife, as though he's remembering how he used to feel. They've paid their debts and made better investments and saved enough money to rent a new apartment down the street, bigger than the last, with two floors, separate bedrooms, and space for a dentist's office downstairs. I sleep on a narrow bed in the room where they keep the ironing board and sewing machine and mops and brooms and buckets. Nothing purple or frilly, but my own bed in my own room.

Jaimito is five years old now and has a two-year-old brother. While the Doctorita was pregnant, she glowed, all pink and round and happy because she had an excuse to eat a lot. As her belly popped out, I grew more and more furious that I'd have to wash heaps of diapers again, just when Jaimito had gotten potty trained. But it turned out Andrecito was such a sweet cherub of a baby that his diapers didn't bother me. He's always called me Mamá, since he spent most of his first year strapped to my back with a shawl as I washed dishes and made meals and cleaned the apartment. Now that he can walk, we dance together to *cumbia* tunes on the stereo—which, like the television, I'm not supposed to touch, but could operate blindfolded.

I've made friends, students my own age from the *colegio*, and when I walk down the street, they talk to me as if I'm a normal kid, not a servant, not a former indigenous girl. I understand my place better, in this family, in this town, in this country. I am the only *indígena* maid in town. Some other people have maids, but they are poor *mestiza* girls from tiny farm communities. In bigger cities, like Otavalo and Quito, there must be lots of indigenous maids. I remember Matilde saying that she would see other maids like her at the markets in Quito or on the street running errands.

Here, there is no one like me. Sometimes I wonder what it would feel like to have a girl like myself to talk to, a girl who

73

used to be indigenous, a girl who doesn't know what she is now. I would ask her if she, too, feels an empty space inside her.

It's a space I'm always trying to fill. It's like the open beak of a baby bird squawking to its mother, *Feed me, feed me, love me, love me*. A gaping, hungry, dark space. The smiles from my friends and Jaimito and Andrecito and Niño Carlitos fill part of it, and my fantasies fill another part, but sometimes I wake up in the middle of the night afraid that the emptiness has swallowed everything.

Often in the afternoons, while I pasture the cow or gather alfalfa for the guinea pigs, I run into Doña Mercedes's daughters, Marina and Marlenny. They have crushes on a sexy singer named Chayanne and always carry little folded-up magazine pictures of him in their pockets. "Ohhh! Isn't Chayanne gorgeous?" they moan. "Look at those muscles. Look at that chest."

I nod. "He's good-looking. But he's not as smart as MacGyver."

My heart belongs to MacGyver, the star of my favorite television show. He's a handsome special agent, always solving mysteries and saving people and getting trapped in deadly situations and figuring a way out at the last second. He's a genius. Even if he has only a match and a can of Coca-Cola and a stick of mint gum, he can use them to booby-trap the bad guys and escape. All the women on the show fall in love with him. When he kisses them, I pretend it's me he's kissing. *Oh, Virginia, mi amor,* he whispers, caressing my face. *You're so beautiful, so smart, such a fast runner. Will you be my secret-agent partner? For as long as we both shall live?*

"One day I'll marry Chayanne," Marina sighs.

"One day I'll marry MacGyver," I sigh.

Marina is twelve years old, and she figures that in six years she can find Chayanne and make him fall in love with her. And she just might: she has shiny, wavy hair that she wears back in glittery barrettes, and thick, naturally curly eyelashes, and full, pouty lips. "Don't worry, Virginia," she assures me. "You'll have no problem making MacGyver fall in love with you. You have bright eyes and a quick mind. That's how he likes his women."

I agree. I'd be the ideal girl for him if I were a few years older. I still don't know exactly how old I am, but I figure I must be around Marina's age.

Sometimes Doña Mercedes and the Doctorita speculate on my age. "Well," Doña Mercedes says, eyeing her daughter and me, "my daughter is taller than Virginia, but look into their eyes. Marina has the eyes of a child, but Virginia has the eyes of someone much older."

The Doctorita shakes her head. "Oh, no, my Virginia is younger."

I flinch whenever she says *my Virginia*, as though I'm her pet. She laughs. "Look, my Virginia barely has breasts."

I blush and fold my arms over my chest.

"I still say Virginia's older," Doña Mercedes says, unconvinced.

"Well"—the Doctorita shrugs—"either way, she's definitely becoming a teenager, the way she primps in front of a mirror for an hour before she goes out. Even to buy a bag of eggs!"

My face flushes hotter still. It's true. Before I go on errands, I brush and smooth my hair into a perfect waist-long ponytail and try on three outfits before I find the right one. Once I tried to leave my hair loose, like some of the ninth-grade girls I'd seen at the *colegio*, but on my way out the door, the Doctorita snapped, "What do you think you're doing?" and made me pull my hair back.

Sunday mornings are best, because the Doctorita and Niño Carlitos sleep late and Jaimito watches cartoons with Andrecito. I can leave to buy the milk and bread without them knowing what time I've left. I get up early and put on my favorite pea green jacket. My other clothes are all a little too big or too small, but this jacket fits me as though I went to the store and bought it just for myself. I slip out of the house around eight o'clock and head toward the town square.

Life feels as quivery-new as the morning air. I walk around the sparkling fountain slowly, taking my time, wandering through the crowds, past the people lined up to buy warm popcorn and steaming potato tortillas. *Cumbia* music floats out of the shops and fills me up, makes me feel part of the thrilling buzz of families and couples who've come from the villages to spend the day shopping and talking and strolling.

I imagine MacGyver walking next to me, his arm around me, his hand resting comfortably on my hip. He brushes a strand of hair from my face and whispers words of love in my ear. We sit on a bench and munch popcorn while I tell him my secrets: how my family is fading from my memory, except for the words Mamita told me, that she would be happy if I left. Those words will never fade. MacGyver's jaw clenches. Mi amor, *if you want, I'll booby-trap her house to get revenge. Just say the word.*

After my walk, when I slip back inside the house an hour later, my heart beating fast, Niño Carlitos and the Doctorita are still in their bedroom and the boys' eyes are still glued to

76

the TV. My body vibrates with the rhythms of the *cumbias*, as though my blood and bones have absorbed the music and my insides are dancing.

One bright afternoon, while I'm walking down the street to our house, swinging a bag of sugar and dried lentils, I see MacGyver.

In the flesh.

He's talking to some teachers from the *colegio*. The breeze whips through his hair—the same caramel-candy brown as MacGyver's, a little feathered and longer in the back. His shoulders stretch broad and muscular beneath his shirt.

The closer I walk, the more convinced I am. He has MacGyver's eyes, piercing and intelligent, and the same strong jaw and gentle lips. Even his fingers, twirling a key chain, are precise and nimble, ready to defuse a bomb or pick a lock at a moment's notice.

What is MacGyver doing in Kunu Yaku? My knees grow weak. Very slowly, I walk by him, staring and glancing back over my shoulder.

Later, while making dinner with the Doctorita, I muster up a casual voice. "So, I saw a new señor in town today. He was talking to some teachers from the *colegio*."

"Oh, the new teacher." She moves her head closer to mine so Niño Carlitos can't hear. "A handsome young man?"

I nod. "What's his name?"

"Roberto, I think."

Roberto. Maybe that's MacGyver's code name. Maybe he's scoping out our town to see if they should shoot an episode here. Of course he'd be using a fake name and job so he wouldn't be

77

bombarded by fans. This way he'll fit better into small-town life in rural Ecuador. Maybe the episode is about some evil people plotting to blow up Kunu Yaku, and his assignment is to find the bomb and save us all. He'll need a helper for the mission, someone who knows the town inside and out, who knows all the people, their habits and personalities. Someone fast and smart and good at looking innocent. I wonder if they've found an actress to play that part yet.

On Saturday the Doctorita and Niño Carlitos invite some teachers over to our house. I answer the door and greet them, one by one, and lead them to the living room. At the third knock, I answer the door, and there he is, twirling his key chain.

"Good afternoon," he says, glancing around with intense brown eyes, as though he's surveying the room in case he needs materials to build a last-minute booby trap.

"I'm Roberto," he says to me.

I nod and smile, too nervous to talk. *Don't worry*, my eyes say silently, *I won't blow your cover*. I lead him to the red velvet sofa.

"Bring us some juice, Virginia," the Doctorita says.

I take the pitcher of sugary cantaloupe water from the refrigerator and pour five foaming glasses. I bring out MacGyver's first. My hands are shaking and I worry I might spill some, or worse, trip on the walk across the living room. My cheeks hot, I hand him the glass. Our fingers brush as he takes it.

"Thank you," he says.

I try to make my mouth move to say *you're welcome*, but it stays shut, so I give a little smile.

I hover at the edge of the living room, listening and watching.

"I can't believe you haven't heard los Kjarkas," MacGyver is telling the teachers as he pulls out a cassette from his jacket pocket. He sticks the tape in the stereo and turns the volume loud, the way I like it. Then he sits down on the red velvet sofa and leans his head back and closes his eyes and listens.

The music is different from anything I've ever heard. First there's guitar music strumming fast and passionate, then flute music trilling and waving and rising and falling like the mountains and rivers.

I imagine MacGyver and me dancing at the end of the episode. He spins me and dips me and runs his fingers through my long, loose hair. And then, like a gust of wind, the music picks us up and we are flying in hang gliders like birds over the mountains, swooping in valleys and rising over peaks. Over rich earth and sun-warmed stone and sparkling, sunlit streams.

After the song ends, he turns down the volume a little. "Well, what do you think?"

Niño Carlitos and the Doctorita and the other teachers nod politely. "Oh, very nice." But I can tell that it hasn't reached in and grabbed their souls the way it has for me and MacGyver.

"Where's this group from?" Niño Carlitos asks.

"An Indian village in the Andes," MacGyver says. "It's *indígena* music."

Indigenous music.

And just like that, the music turns dirty. Ugly and cheap and coated with mud. Barefoot and ridden with lice and fleas. Something you want to hide in a cardboard box, something to stamp out of your mind.

MacGyver passes around the tape case, and I catch a peek of it over Niño Carlitos's shoulder. There are three men with long hair in braids, wearing wool ponchos and hats, the same as the men from my village. The same as my father. A sick feeling spreads through my insides. The music fills the room, something haunting now, like a ghost that echoes and rattles in my bones. I look at the tile floor and wish the music would stop.

After one more song, MacGyver tucks the tape back into his shirt pocket. They chat a little more, and then the Doctorita gives little bags of guavas to MacGyver and the other teachers and says goodbye.

I run upstairs to the balcony to spy on them leaving. Below, the door opens and MacGyver emerges, chewing on his guava, shaking hands with the other teachers. Then he spits the skin onto the ground and heads down the street. After he disappears around the corner, I race downstairs and out of the house and snatch up the guava skin.

Back in my room, I sit on my bed and brush the sticky skin on my cheek, touch it to my lips. His mouth touched this skin, and now it's touching mine, and it's almost as if he's kissing me. And I don't care if he's really just a regular man, a normal teacher instead of a TV star or secret agent; still I hear him say, *Oh, Virginia, my beautiful spy, come with me on my next mission, far from the Andes, north, to America.*

That night I sleep with the guava skin beside me on my pillow. As I drift off, I hear that indigenous music and try to make it stop, but it scoops me up like the winds of the Andes and makes me fly. And again, I struggle against it, but in the end it is too strong, and it carries me away.

chapter 11

I'M WALKING BESIDE THE COW on the *colegio's* grounds in a gray drizzle. I like the cow's company. She moves slowly and munches on the grass and looks at me once in a while with her gigantic eyes. Now that Jaimito is in kindergarten and Andrecito is in preschool, I'm alone more during the day. The house feels strange with no little boy babbling or laughing or whining or crying or shouting or tugging on my skirt or reaching his arms up to me. More and more, I find myself hovering at the edge of the schoolyard, always with an excuse, like picking avocadoes from the trees by the fence, or pasturing the cow.

The Doctorita's science class is about to start, but she hasn't arrived yet. The clouds hang heavy over the low, flat roof of the *colegio*, hiding the mountains, giving everything a dull metallic sheen. A bunch of seventh and eighth graders in wine-colored uniforms are crowded outside the building, beneath the overhang, trying to stay dry. They're holding their books open and talking with animated gestures. They seem wound up about something—maybe the rain, maybe an exam, maybe a dance coming up.

If I were in school, I'd probably be in eighth grade now. I imagine that I'm huddled over there with them, wearing a burgundy skirt that grazes my knees and white socks pulled up my calves and an ironed white shirt and neat vest and sparkly barrettes.

Voices break into my daydreaming; a couple of boys are calling me over. "Virginia! Come out of the rain!"

The boys are friends of Marina and Marlenny who always greet me and chat politely whenever they see me. One is tall and pimply-faced and the other short and baby-faced, and they're both smiling and gesturing at me. I tie the cow to an avocado tree and walk over, shaking the water droplets from my hair. A few other kids say hi and smile and then go back to studying. The tall boy, Leo, says, "Hey, will you help us study, Virginia?" Before I can refuse, he hands me his book.

I hold it awkwardly in the crooks of my elbows. It's heavier than a sack of flour.

"Quiz us. Ask us the practice questions."

I look at the page and beg my eyes to see whatever it is their eyes see.

"Come on, Virginia. Please?" Leo points to the bottom of the page. "Right there. The questions on page one twenty-seven. Right next to the photosynthesis diagram. Ask away."

There's a column of tiny black circles and lines that mean nothing to me. Next to the letters is a picture of clouds, rain, sun, plants, roots, and soil, with red arrows pointing from one thing to another, like symbols on a treasure map. I stare at the letters until my vision grows watery. Something must be wrong with my eyes.

"Sorry," I say finally. "I just don't feel like reading now." I thrust the book back into his hands, and half running, lead the cow away in the rain. The fields shine green and wet, and tree leaves drip, and I can almost see, hovering in the air, those mysterious red arrows and black letters hiding a world from me.

That's it. I wipe the salt water and rain from my face, determined. *I'm fixing my eyes.*

Later in the afternoon, before the Doctorita gets home from school, I sneak a book off the shelf and stare at the words, waiting to see what other people see, waiting for some meaning to pop out from the ink, rubbing my eyes and blinking and moving them in and out of focus. What do everyone else's eyes have that mine don't? Frustrated, I slam the book shut and stash it back in the bookcase, glaring at the shelves of books like locked boxes holding secrets.

After dinner, as I'm clearing dishes and the Doctorita is grading papers at the table, I say, "Doctorita, I want to go to school."

She glances up and makes a laughing sound that's more like a snort or a bark. "What for?"

"I want to learn to read."

She shakes her head and goes back to grading the exams, red checks or Xs next to each question. "Remember," she says in an I-told-you-so voice, "I asked you years ago if you wanted to go to school and you said no."

"But now I want to."

"Well, you missed your chance." She's checking and X-ing an exam, her eyebrows furrowed. "There's too much work for you to do around here now. No time for school. You're too old, anyway. It's too late."

I feel like hurling the dishes at the wall, one by one. *Bam. Bam. Bam.* I clench my fists around the plate rims. "But I want to go to school and college and have a real career when I grow up."

She chuckles and shuffles to a fresh exam. "You're going to work for us your whole life. You're a *longa*. You don't need to read to clean and cook, now, do you?"

I glare, too furious to form words.

Without looking up, she says, "There's a pile of dishes waiting to be washed. Get to it."

In bed I toss and turn and watch the dark shadows of the broom and mop looming in the corner like monsters. I'm awake, but my thoughts are nightmarish. I see myself as an old lady, about fifty years old. Marlenny and Marina and all the students from the *colegio* have finished university and gotten jobs—as doctors and lawyers and teachers—and here I am, hunched-over and gray-haired, washing dishes for the Doctorita and Niño Carlitos and their children and grandchildren and great-grandchildren. The kids tell me, Viejita—*old lady*—*help us study*. And the Doctorita—ancient, nearly blind, and wrinkled like a raisin—laughs. *Hehehe! Virginia is a* longa, she creaks. *Virginia can't read. She'll die here, washing dishes, washing the diapers of my great-great-great-grandchildren. Hehehe!*

* * *

84

The next day I stare at the Doctorita across the living room, my face fixed hard and determined as stone. "I want to read."

"You're a *longa*. *Longas* don't need to read."

The next day, I say again: "I want to read."

She ignores me.

And the next day: "I want to read." I plan to tell her over and over, until one day, at a weak moment, she will say yes.

And sure enough, finally, one night she slams down her pen and says, "Stop bothering me! Ask Carlos to teach you if you want to read so badly. I don't have time for this."

So I ask Niño Carlitos, who's out front playing ball with the boys in the street. "Will you teach me to read?"

"Of course, *m'hijita*. I'll teach you sometime." And he rolls the ball to Andrecito.

Days pass and he doesn't say anything more about it. Every trip I make to the store is pure torture now. Everywhere I look, letters are taunting me, letters on signs and in ads and news-papers and magazines, and still my eyes can't see the secrets.

A few days later, I ask in a quivering voice, "Niño Carlitos, when will you teach me to read?"

He looks at me for a long moment. "This is important to you, isn't it, *m'hija?*"

I bite my lip and nod.

"How about tonight?" he asks, resting his hand on my shoulder.

"Yes! Thank you!"

After I race through washing the dinner dishes, Niño Carlitos and I sit down at the dining room table with a small notebook and pencil. The pages smell woody and fresh and magical, treasure maps waiting to be made. He writes the letters of the alphabet and says their names and has me repeat. Under each letter he draws a funny picture. For *a*, he draws a chicken's wing. "A," he says. *"Ala de pollo."* Wing of a chicken. And I repeat. First *a, e, i, o, u*, and then the other letters, all the way to *z*. If I dig deep into my mind, way back into my past, I see flashes of these letters from my six weeks of school in Yana Urku. It's as if those letters stayed there on purpose, knowing they'd come in handy someday.

Soon it's late and the TV is quiet and the Doctorita is putting the boys to bed. But I'm not tired at all. I'm humming like a bee's wings, never more awake, more alive. I copy the letters, one by one. My circles are shaky and my lines not as straight as Niño Carlitos's, but he says, "Good, *m'hija*," and touches my shoulder. "You're *vivísima*, Virginia. Really bright."

I *feel* bright, glowing like the sun, bursting with light and sparks and fire.

Then Niño Carlitos shows me how to combine letters. *Ba, bi, be, bo, bu*. And I repeat and copy the letters. By the time we get to *za, zi, ze, zo, zu*, it's very late. Outside the window, the night sleeps in silence, not a car sound, not a voice, not a note of music. It's as though we're in a secret middle-of-the-night hideout, deciphering a top-secret code. He writes some short words and has me sound them out. M-A-M-A. *Ma. Ma. Mamá!* And I do it, as easy as that.

Finally, when Niño Carlitos is yawning and his eyes are starting to close, he says, "That's enough for tonight, *m'hija*." He hands me the notebook and gives me a hug.

I run upstairs and lie in bed, embracing my notebook, breathing in the new paper smell, feeling the smooth cardboard cover against my cheek, seeing the letters in my head, moving my lips with the sounds. *Ma-má. Pa-pá. Be-bé.* I lie awake all night, waiting for tomorrow, when I will see the world with brand-new eyes.

I read slowly at first, very slowly, sound by sound, my finger crawling along the page like a potato bug. It takes me a whole morning to finish a single paragraph. After many weeks, I make it through two entire chapters of the science textbook *Understanding Our Universe*. And during these weeks, the world transforms into a different place, a pulsing, breathing ball, swirled with blue and green and revolving around the fiery sun that is really a star. Plants aren't just clusters of green leaves; they're living beings that started as seeds in the ground, then broke open and reached through the soil toward the light. And their roots stretch out and drink water that moves up through the stems and leaves, and the plants breathe in carbon dioxide and breathe out oxygen and soak up sunlight for energy to grow.

Pho-to-syn-the-sis, I sound out, my finger moving from letter to letter. My new favorite word. I have to ask Niño Carlitos for help with that one, but most of the others I eventually figure out on my own.

When I pasture the cow, passing fruit trees and vegetable fields, I stop to peer into flowers, at their stamens and pistils. I watch how bees crawl between petals and drink nectar and become coated with pollen that they bring to another flower. While the flowers are happy they're being fertilized, the bees are happy they're eating sweet nectar. The world shimmers, as if everything is coated with magical golden pollen.

I don't read around the Doctorita, fearful she'll punish me, because *longas* are supposed to spend their time sweeping and mopping and cooking and serving, not reading. She doesn't know that when she's at school, I race to finish the housework so I can dive into her science book, copying beautiful new words into my notebook. *Respiration. Chlorophyll. Pollination.* When her key scrapes in the lock, I quickly slide my notebook under the refrigerator, where no one will find it, and grab a broom and pretend to sweep.

chapter 12

I'M SITTING AT THE TABLE, eating my favorite dinner—fried potatoes and rice topped with an egg and lentils—on a forbidden ceramic plate with a forbidden silver spoon whose vines twirl up the handle. I am all alone. The Doctorita and Niño Carlitos and the boys have gone to visit relatives for the weekend. Niño Carlitos, as always, seemed a little guilty leaving me, asking me over and over if I was sure I'd be all right by myself. Now that I'm a teenager, he has this idea that every boy in the neighborhood will be crawling through the windows to find me. But I'm thrilled to be alone—two days of watching TV and reading and dancing around the house.

After dinner, I watch *MacGyver*. It's a good episode. A tiny airplane drops him off in a jungle thick with green leaves and palm and banana trees—what I imagine the Ecuadorian rain forest must look like. He meets the local villagers and discovers that an evil man with a machine gun has enslaved them, forcing them to grow poppy flowers that he turns into drugs. So

MacGyver makes booby traps using pulleys and levers that drop coconuts on the evil man's head.

Once the evil man is knocked out, MacGyver smiles and my heart turns to honey. He proclaims to the slaves, "You're free now!"

The slaves stare at him, motionless, in front of their bamboo huts. It's not that they don't understand Spanish. Anywhere in the world MacGyver goes, everyone speaks Spanish with a little accent, although their words don't exactly match the movements of their lips, I've noticed. These slaves understand his words, but still they stand and stare.

"Go! Do what you want now!" MacGyver says, motioning with his hands. "You're free!"

They keep staring until one man says, "There are more bad men above him. Now they will be angry and get us. We will always be enslaved."

Then creepy music plays and a commercial for cornflakes comes on. A blue-eyed family is crunching cereal together and smiling. The mother's voice sounds as smooth and soft as her creamy curtains and her skin glows as white as the milk she pours into the cereal. She finishes the last spoonful, grabs her briefcase, and laughing, kisses her children and husband on the nose one by one, then clicks out the door on her high heels.

I can see the life I want: to go to school and be a professional and have money and my own family and a house and a briefcase. Just like the lady in the commercial. But how do I get there? What would happen if one day I were free? Would I stand there and stare?

After a commercial for gum and another for laundry soap,

MacGyver comes back on and makes a plan with all the villagers to defeat the higher-up bad guys. They use an inflatable raft and a Jeep and a rope and more coconuts and some special chemicals. One by one, all the bad guys get bashed on the head by coconuts and knocked out. The villagers cheer. They realize that saving themselves is as easy as using basic scientific principles to build lots of booby traps.

Now they are free. For real this time. With their new confidence, they start making plans, and my chest swells with pride for them.

Later that night, after I turn off the TV, I notice music—loud *cumbia* rhythms—coming from outside. It's pounding, shaking the walls. The *colegio* students must be having a dance tonight. I consider sneaking out and watching from the shadows. But the Doctorita often warns me that the whole neighborhood is watching me when she and Niño Carlitos leave. "I have eyes and ears everywhere," she likes to remind me. It's true, gossip travels swiftly in Kunu Yaku. If even one person saw me and told the Doctorita, I'd be dead.

MacGyver would find a way to watch the dance. My eyes scan the room, eagle eyes, narrowed and focused.

I find a board left over from one of Niño Carlitos's projects and carry it out the window and onto the roof. The night is cool, with a sweet, light breeze. I lay the board across the gap between houses, to the roof of our neighbors' apartment, where I'll have a perfect view of the dance. I wait, peering at the two stories of darkness below, gathering up the nerve to crawl across.

Once, in Yana Urku, when I was about five years old, my sister Matilde was playing with her friend in the green canyon as I tagged along. They jumped across an irrigation ditch with their long, nine-year-old legs. I stopped in front of the water, afraid to cross. "Matilde!" I whined. "Help me across." But she and her friend were absorbed in a game and didn't pay attention. "Matilde, Matilde!" I shrieked, eyeing the deep, murky water. "Help me across."

She rolled her eyes. "Cross it yourself if you want to so badly." And she went back to her game. No one was going to help me. I'd have to do it myself. I wiped my tears and got a running start and leapt across the water to the other side, landing safely in the squishy mud. I grinned, stunned, and glanced toward Matilde. That's when I saw the flash of relief in her face. She'd been watching me out of the corner of her eye the whole time, ready to save me if I fell.

Now Matilde is a faint, faraway memory, so faint I can barely recall the features of her face. But remembering her watching me gives me courage. With my heart pounding, my body shaking, the rough board scraping my bare knees, I begin to cross. Halfway there, I look down, into the blackness stretching below, and I am paralyzed. I take a deep breath and feel the music vibrate my bones and focus on the roof just an arm's length in front of me. I move toward my destination, centimeter by centimeter.

Once I reach the clay tiles, I lean back on my elbows, lightheaded and reveling at my small feat. The dance spreads out below in a circle of spotlights; beyond it, the shadows of fields and mountains melt into darkness. A group of boys huddle on one side of the basketball court, near the giant speakers, and the girls on the other. As the night goes on, the boys grow braver, daring to approach the girls and ask them to dance. Soon almost everyone is dancing, spinning. Skirts swirl, hips sway. When the slow, romantic songs come on, the girls nestle their heads on the boys' shoulders and my heart skips along with theirs.

For a long time I sit, watching them and staring at the sky, full of zillions of stars. In *Understanding Our Universe* I read that stars are really distant suns. Each star is the center of its own solar system, planets encircling it, and moons encircling each planet. This makes my problems on Earth seem small. Maybe far across the universe, on another planet, the *indígenas* are the powerful ones, the ones who go to school in burgundy uniforms. Maybe the *mestizos* are their servants.

Why was I born on this planet? Why was I born to people who don't love me? Why, out of all the zillions of possibilities, have I ended up a servant? I try to let the secondhand music and the distant blazing suns and the far-off happiness fill me, but it is not enough.

Something else begins to fill me, though, an energy like the flaming heat of the sun—all 5,600 degrees Celsius of it—and I make a pact with myself. One day, when I am free, I will not stand and stare. I will take the leap. And in the meantime, I'll get a running start.

I become a secret-agent student.

Every day after Niño Carlitos and the Doctorita leave for work, I race through my chores in a whirlwind, then plop down at the dining room table to study exactly what the Doctorita's and Niño Carlitos's eighth-grade students are studying. I shuffle

93

through their stacks of ungraded homework and make myself do the same assignments in my little notebook. When a fresh batch of blank exams sits piled on the table, I steal a copy for myself and slip it under the refrigerator. The next day I take the test and then check my answers with the key.

When I pasture the cow near the *colegio*, I time it so I can talk to the students, like an infiltrating spy, to pump them for information.

"Hi!" I say to Leo, the tall guy who asked me to read months earlier.

"Hi, Virginia," he says, almost shyly. I've noticed lately that when I'm around boys my age, they tend to get nervous, with flickery eyes and dry mouths.

"Want some help studying?" I ask. "I can quiz you."

"Sure." He hands me the book, and this time it feels light and comfortable in my hands, as though it belongs there.

And as the words roll off my tongue, I discover what the students are studying. Static electricity. Ions and electrons and nuclei. The chemical elements.

"So," I ask casually, "what lab experiments have you been doing lately?"

"This one on page two fifty-six." His face is turning pink, which makes his pimples redder. He seems flustered by my attention. "That one was fun," he said. "Rubbing a balloon on your hair and making it stick to the wall." His voice cracks and he swallows hard. "Oh, and this one on page two seventy-five. It was so exciting, everyone was screaming. The Doctorita got mad."

"What was the experiment?"

"Building a volcano."

Building a volcano!

The next day, Saturday, the Doctorita and Niño Carlitos plan to go with the boys to Ibarra to shop all day. Now that they're out of debt, they've been wiser with their investments and have even saved extra money to spend on clothes and toys for the children. They want me to come, but I say, "I'm not feeling well. I think I'll stay here."

Niño Carlitos eyes me suspiciously. "No boys in the house, Virginia."

"Of course not!" I say, indignant. Niño Carlitos's worries about boys have been getting out of hand lately. Even the Doctorita rolls her eyes at him.

"Maybe we should lock her in," Niño Carlitos says quietly to the Doctorita, thinking I can't hear him.

I hold my breath. They haven't locked me in for at least a year now. That would completely ruin my plan.

"Oh, come on, Carlos," she says. "Don't be ridiculous."

While the Doctorita is gathering a bag of food for the trip, I take the key to the science lab off her key chain.

Once their truck has disappeared, I walk nonchalantly down the road toward the school. If anyone catches me, I'll say that the Doctorita forgot some important things in the lab and asked me to get them. Still, if she finds out, I'll be beaten for sure. I glance around. No one in sight. I open the door, slip inside, and click the lock behind me. Quickly, I close the blinds. It's dark, but little lines of light creep around the windows' edges.

I imagine I'm a world-famous scientist who was brutally

kidnapped but managed to use her brilliance to escape to perform this vital experiment. If I can complete the volcano without anyone catching me, I will be free and the world will be saved.

In the dim light, I open *Understanding Our Universe* to page two seventy-five and squint at the diagram, then search the cabinets for the ingredients. Perfect. They're all in a single cabinet, neatly arranged and labeled in the Doctorita's tiny, cramped handwriting.

My pulse racing, I mix the flour and salt and oil and water to make the dough, kneading it with my hands like bread. Then I put a plastic Inca Kola bottle in a pan and shape the dough around it, just like in the picture. Only I make mine more realistic, so it really looks like a mountain, with crags and nooks and rock outcroppings. If I had more time, I would shape little goats from the dough, and children and cows and houses and potato fields. But I stick to the instructions, and fill the bottle with warm water and some drops of food dye and detergent and baking soda to make the lava.

And then, the final step. The book warns to jump back from the volcano after this step. I can almost hear the suspenseful music playing, just like in a *MacGyver* episode right before something explodes. What if I blow up the whole lab?

I pour in the vinegar and jump back.

Slowly, it starts rising—the vinegar reacting with the baking soda and making carbon dioxide—and now bloodred lava is bubbling over the sides of the volcano, spilling down the slopes. I move closer and sink onto a plastic chair, a little disappointed there's no explosion, but mostly amazed that you can mix together simple, innocent kitchen ingredients and come up with a frothing volcano.

How will it feel when, one day, I am free? A giant explosion? Or a slow, bubbling transformation? I watch the oozing lava and wish that other students were crowded around me oohing and ahhing and giggling. I put the materials back into the cabinet, wipe off the table, raise the blinds, stuff my soggy volcano in a garbage bag, and go home to scrub the floors.

chapter 13

"WHAT ARE YOU SMILING ABOUT?" the Doctorita asks, suspicious.

We're taking an evening walk along the fields and orchards with Niño Carlitos and the boys. The school year has just ended, and on my top-secret final exams I scored the second highest in social studies and the highest in science, out of the entire eighth grade.

"Oh, nothing." I try to make my face solemn, but the sky is too pink, the clouds too silver, the light too golden. And the crickets and frogs are too enthusiastic, chirping and cheering for my success. Jaimito is running ahead, kicking up dust. Andrecito's pudgy hand clutches mine, and the other hand clutches his father's. Every few steps, we swing Andrecito in the air and he squeals with delight.

"You don't have a boyfriend, do you, *m'hija?*" Niño Carlitos asks quietly.

"No!" I blush. Of course, I still have a lingering crush on

MacGyver. Not on Roberto the MacGyver look-alike—he's engaged to be married to another teacher—but the original MacGyver, the one on TV. Marlenny and Marina know all about my devotion to him, but I'd never admit it to Niño Carlitos or the Doctorita.

"You're forbidden to have a boyfriend," the Doctorita warns.

"I don't have a boyfriend. I'm just . . . happy." I turn to Andrecito. "One, two, three, swing!" And we laugh together.

"Humph," the Doctorita says, screwing up her face into a half frown, half laugh. "We better not find out you have a boyfriend."

I'm in the truck, breathing in smells of sunshine on plastic and the pungent sweat pouring from my armpits. I'm nervous. We're on our way to Yana Urku, my old village. For some reason, they've decided to bring me along to visit Niño Carlitos's parents for the weekend. They were probably afraid something crazy would happen if they left me alone in the house with all my mysterious happiness.

All five of us have been squeezed on one seat for three hours, Andrecito asleep on my skinny lap and Jaimito on the Doctorita's wide lap, and Niño Carlitos driving. Andrecito's face is damp and smells sweet and sticks to my arm. His cheeks are rosy and his little lips parted and his chest rising and falling. Meanwhile, Jaimito is bouncing and shifting as the Doctorita tries to hold him still. He's going through a phase where he talks and asks questions nonstop.

"What are those plants?" he asks, staring out the window at fields of tall stalks. I can't help smiling at the way he still can't pronounce his *s*'s.

"Cane," Niño Carlitos answers, since the Doctorita has no patience.

"Why did they plant cane?"

"To make sugar and liquor."

"Why?"

"For money."

"What's that smoke?"

"Part of the sugarcane-making process. They distill it."

"What's distill?"

The Doctorita rolls her eyes while Niño Carlitos explains distillation. I listen for a while, recognizing some words from *Understanding Our Universe*—evaporation, pressure, water vapor.

As the mountain Imbabura grows bigger and closer, I try to remember my mother's and father's faces. My sisters' and brother's. They are frozen in time, and fading, like old photos in an album. Do they remember my face? Do they wonder how I might look now? Would I recognize them if I passed them on the street? What did we used to talk about? Definitely not distillation and evaporation. What, then? Potatoes? Corn? What would we talk about if we saw each other again?

With a damp handkerchief, the Doctorita dabs at the sweat trickling down her face. She shifts Jaimito, who has finally quieted down and fallen asleep in her lap. Now she and Niño Carlitos are talking about their plans to move to Ibarra, a nearby city, much bigger and busier than Kunu Yaku.

"I'm sick of our backwater town," she snorts. "I can't wait to live in Ibarra. Civilization."

Niño Carlitos looks straight ahead. Light pours through the window, illuminating his bald spot. "Well, if our job transfers go through, then we can move there. But for now be patient, Negra."

A couple of years ago, when they first started talking about moving, I felt fluttery with nervous excitement. A new place filled with new people. Something different, something big. But after years of hearing about the move, I began to accept that it would never actually happen. Complaining about Kunu Yaku was just another of the Doctorita's little fixations, I realized, like knitting Baby Jesus dresses and fretting about thieves and worrying about her boys catching germs.

"It better be soon," the Doctorita says, just like she always says. Her chins jiggle extra hard with every bump in the road. She never lost the weight from her last pregnancy, and now she has two fleshy chins.

She wipes her forehead again and turns to me. "Virginia, I know you want to go to school. So I'll pull some strings and get you a diploma from the elementary school, and with that you'll be able to go to sewing school in Ibarra."

"Really?" I say, trying not to show any emotion, reminding myself that this will probably never come to pass. I press my lips to the top of Andrecito's head, onto his wispy hairs. The thought of getting a diploma gives me tingles; it's the next step toward my dream. With a diploma, I'd be able to enter the *colegio*. The sewing school part, though, makes my stomach queasy. Maybe I can just take the diploma and then refuse to go to sewing school, or run away if I have to.

I blow on Andrecito's neck, cooling him off, and wonder why the Doctorita is bringing up school now. Then I realize: she's afraid I'll run away to my parents. She wants to give me a reason to stay with her family. This annoys me a little, that she

101

thinks she can manipulate me. At the same time, it touches me that she cares enough that she's scared to lose me. It gives me a backward kind of power.

In the midafternoon, when the sun is high overhead—the earth's equator close to the ball of burning fire, just like the diagram in *Understanding Our Universe*—we turn onto the dirt road to Yana Urku.

Nothing has changed. The giant blue sky, the fields of potatoes and corn, the white houses with red tile roofs, the rocky canyons, the mountains towering overhead. Quichua words come back to me in tiny pieces that smell like wood smoke and people sweating in fields and rain-soaked wool. *Urku*—mountain. *Api*—soup. *Kiya*—moon. The words float by, flecks of ash, seeds on the breeze, remnants of another life that hasn't quite vanished. I try to snatch at the words, hold them in my hand and remember their textures, feel their shapes on my tongue.

Mariana, Niño Carlitos's mother, emerges from the house to greet us and fuss over her grandchildren. Jumbled memories return—Mariana stealing the sweetest *choclos* from our cornfield, Mariana scolding indigenous workers, Mariana and Alfonso sitting with my parents and Niño Carlitos and the Doctorita the first time I met them. As Mariana hugs Andrecito, I notice the graying hair wound tightly at the back of her head, and remember what we used to call her: *misha copetona. Mestiza* with the ridiculous bun.

After she hugs the boys, she greets me with forced warmth. "Virginia! My, you're looking beautiful. What a lovely young

102

lady." Her words seemed sugarcoated, hiding dark intentions, and as she ushers us inside, I feel a chill. Is she also being nice to me so that I won't take this opportunity to run back to my parents?

A little while later I'm watching the boys play with sticks in a patch of grass at the edge of the driveway, when Mariana approaches me. "Virginia, I want you to leave Romelia and Carlitos and come to work for my daughter in Quito." When she says the Doctorita's name, her lip curls, as though she's tasted something rotten. I remember that Mariana doesn't like the Doctorita, that she's often told her son his wife is too fat, too dark-skinned, too bossy—far from the slim, fair, gentle wife he deserves. "Well? What do you say, Virginia?"

I stare at the profile of her giant bun and shrug, thinking it best to keep my mouth shut.

She goes on. "Quito is a big, beautiful city, so much prettier than those boondocks where you live now. And my daughter needs a maid desperately. She's an angel. She'll treat you well." She looks at me expectantly. When I stay silent, she says, "Think about it," and goes inside.

Of course I won't go. I don't trust a word she says. Still, I can't help considering it. Later, as I'm cleaning up after dinner with the maids I mention Mariana's offer. They exchange looks. "Go to Quito, Virginia," they urge. "The Doctorita beats you and treats you terribly. How could you want to stay with her?" They push and push so much I realize Mariana must have told them to convince me to go.

"I'll think about it," I say, and step outside into the cool dusk, thick with the scent of fresh earth and cows. I feel all mixed up, the way soil must feel after the oxen come through, plowing it, turning it inside out, getting it ready for planting. And when a seed is dropped in, it can easily germinate and take root and push its tender new leaves toward the sun and begin the marvelous process of photosynthesis. When I think about it, the seed has been inside me for years—the idea of leaving the Doctorita. Every time she yells at me or hits me or reminds me of my place as a lowly *longa* maid, she's watering the seed. And now Mariana's offer is like cow manure, fertilizing it, nourishing it, reminding me of my power, my options.

But Quito is not where I'll go. I'll go home to my family.

Sunlight shines on the green cornstalks and makes my eyes scrunch up. The corn is taller than me, a forest of leaves whispering along with the breeze. Corncobs poke out everywhere, ripe and wrapped in green, ready to be picked and opened up and grilled. It's late Sunday morning, and everyone has gone to Otavalo except me and the other maids, who are pasturing the cows in the valley. They were supposed to keep an eye on me, but I insisted I had a headache and wanted to stay behind to rest.

I walk along the cornfield, toward my family's house, framed by mountains. I squint into the sun, looking at the house, trying to tell if my mother or father is in the yard. No one. Strangely relieved, I walk closer and closer, my eyes glued to the house, spots from the sun swimming in my vision. Still no one. My heart's racing now, and I slip inside a row of corn. Here in the cool shadows I feel protected, as though I'm undercover in the jungle, a secret agent, spying on my own family.

As I walk, I remember the Doctorita's words from the last

time she brought me here. *If you go back to your family, they'll give you to another family, a family that won't treat you as well.* And my mother's words. *I'd be happy if one day you left forever.*

I creep around the house, sticking close to the shadows of the corn. There's my father's *soga* hanging on the wall, his farm tools, my mother's broom, the eucalyptus stick she smacked me with when I misbehaved. Two huge pigs are asleep in their pen, and two sheep are rooting around in the weeds by the tree where they're tied. Chickens peck at corn kernels scattered across the dirt. No Cheetah the goat. She's probably been eaten by now.

I take a deep breath, then run across the clearing to the house, ducking a little, as though at any moment someone could open fire. Instead of bullets, dogs skid around the corner of the house and descend on me—a whole new set of scrawny, half-starved dogs, barking and growling. From my pocket I tear my weapon—a plastic bag of stale bread I thought to bring at the last minute—and hurl pieces at the dogs like hand grenades.

After that, they follow me eagerly, wagging their tails, drooling. I make it to the wooden door and knock softly.

No answer.

I knock harder.

Still no answer. I push at the door. It's open. I slip inside and close the door behind me.

Inside it's quiet and heavy and dark, and my eyes take a moment to adjust. A thousand memories press on me all at once, nearly suffocating me. There's the lingering odor of kerosene, woodsmoke, dirt, guinea pigs, wool. I wander around the room, opening drawers, poking in cardboard boxes, peering at the guinea pigs huddled in a corner, feeling the thick fabric

105

of my mother's *anacos*, sitting for a moment on the bed and touching the woven grass mat that serves as a mattress, patting the musty pillow stuffed with rags and hay, picking up a wooden spoon, running my hand over a blackened iron pot. I kneel at the fire pit, hold my hand over the ashes still warm from breakfast. *Nina*—fire. *Uchufa*—ash. *Chushac*—empty. My family must have been here earlier this morning. Maybe they left to spend the day in Otavalo.

My heart is pounding so hard I'm afraid it will burst through my chest. I'm praying no one will come home and find me spying. And I *am* spying. This is not my house. This is the house—no, the run-down shack—of poor people, Indian people. It's dirty and ugly, no decorations like crocheted table runners, or framed cross-stitched roses on the walls, no red sofas or plush chairs. All gray and brown and dark and hard. Packed-dirt floors, dull wood rafters, crumbling clay walls. Filthy clothes and blankets heaped in piles on the ground. Flea-ridden guinea pigs squeaking and humping and scratching, living in the same room as the entire family.

How could I have come from this place? What was I hoping to find here? Love? Love that never even existed?

I wouldn't have learned to read if I'd stayed here. I'd be working in the fields all day, right in the midst of so much photosynthesis, yet without any idea of what photosynthesis was. I wouldn't have shelves of books waiting to be read. I wouldn't speak Spanish perfectly.

I'm heading toward the door when I spot something strange.

At the foot of the bed, on a shelf, is a book. There were never books in my parents' house before. They can't read. I pick up the book, brush off the thin layer of dust. *The Holy Bible* is written in swirly gold lettering on black vinyl. I open it and press my nose in the pages, like I secretly do with all books. It smells new, of paper and plastic and glue, as though it's hardly been touched.

What is this Bible doing here? My parents pay more attention to the gods of the mountains and sun and rain than to the Christian God. Maybe a door-to-door missionary gave it to them, or maybe Matilde brought it from the house where she worked. I flip through the pages, whispery thin and edged with gold paint. And then, on the first page, marked by a red ribbon, I notice something written, lightly, in pencil, and a phone number underneath it.

> *Mi Hermanita* Virginia,
>   I do not know if you even exist anymore,
> but if one day you find this, call me.
>   Love,
>   Your Sister Matilde

I read the message again and again. My heart feels like it's cracking in two. *Hermanita*, little sister. Someone loves me, someone misses me and thinks about me. I am someone's beloved little sister. Tears stream down my face.

I tear out the page and clutch it in my hand, press it to my lips. Gently, I lay the book back down and walk out the door, into the sunshine. Who knows when Matilde wrote these magical words, or what made her write them, or how she guessed I would find them. It's a mysterious miracle. Like a TV sound track, that flute music wells up inside me, the *indígena* music, the music I hate and love with all my soul.

* * *

When I was a little girl, my love for Matilde was as thorny and tangled as a blackberry bush. Somewhere in there were sweet berries, but my legs got scratched with so many spines and branches along the way. Once in a long while, buried somewhere in all the brambles, I caught glimpses of some pure, deep blackberry love—like when she helped me buy my first pair of shoes at the market. But most of the time her sweet smile and beautiful clothes and perfect skin filled me with rage. Most of the time, I wished she would go away and let me be the oldest, best-loved daughter. Most of the time, I thought I hated her.

The last memory I have of her is this.

It was nighttime, and I'd just returned from a two-week trip high into the mountains, where, at about seven years old, I was the youngest person harvesting potatoes. Mamita and Papito stayed at home, and I went with my good-natured aunt and uncle and cousin, who laughed at everything. At night we slept with dozens of other workers in a single hut, shivering and trying to get the spot closest to the hot ashes of the fire pit. During the days we dug up delicious fat purple potatoes, chatting and joking all the while. We handed most of the potatoes over to the landowner in exchange for our wages, but some we boiled into soup, which we ate every night for dinner.

The best part was that we could each gather a free sackful of potatoes to take home. I filled my sack to the brim; I could hardly budge it, so people helped me carry it, marveling over how *vivísima* I was.

After a long, bumpy, windy ride in the bed of a pickup back to Yana Urku, I was still buzzing with excitement, eager to show

108

off the purple potatoes to Mamita. At first, it was just how I imagined. I showed her all the delicious fat potatoes and she said, "Oh, my poor little Virginia, *pobregulla,* look what you brought back all by yourself."

I soaked up her kind words like a thirsty sponge and felt like an angel, basking in my purple-potato glory.

Then she gave the bad news: "Your sister's visiting. You better be nice to her this time."

The next morning, Matilde was already dressed in her nice *anacos*: two layers, cream underneath and deep blue on top. She was wearing a bright white embroidered blouse and shoes made of black velvet with square toes and a dainty string tying them to her ankles. Her skin was shining, clean and soft, almost as fair as a *mestiza*'s, as though her boss's whiteness had magically oozed into her, as though all that fancy rice and fluffy bread had seeped into her skin.

I grew conscious of the dried mud splattered on my legs, the thick coating of dust and grime, the cracked, reddened web of skin on my cheeks from ten days out in the sun and wind. It had been more than two weeks since I'd washed myself. I tucked in my filthy blouse and tied my *faja* around my waist and ran my fingers through my tangle of hair.

Mamita was sitting next to Matilde and stroking her smooth hair in its painfully tight-looking ponytail wrapped with a ribbon. "Ah, how I missed you," she told Matilde. "My oldest daughter, my pretty daughter."

"Good morning, Guagua Zapalla," Matilde said to me in her light, happy way. *Zapalla* means "pumpkin," and it was also the name of my grumpy old grandmother, and the last thing I wanted to be called was Pumpkin Kid.

All morning, Matilde and I pastured the cows and sheep together, with Cheetah close at my side. While the animals munched on grass, we went to a *capulí* tree to see if any little fruits were ripe. All the lower branches had been picked clean, but I spotted ripe, red *capulís* higher up. Matilde was no good at climbing trees since she lived in the city. And her soft padding of fat made her slow and clumsy. Anyway, she didn't like to get her blouse dirty or risk tearing her *anacos*.

"I'll do this," I told her smugly. I scrambled up and picked handfuls of *capulís*, then leaned over to hand them to her, and she made a little pile of berries at the base of the tree. After a while, I noticed that as I was busy picking the *capulís*, Matilde was choosing the ripest, reddest, biggest ones from the pile and popping them into her mouth.

"Stop!" I shouted.

"What's wrong, Guagua Zapalla?" She smiled sweetly.

"I worked for those *capulís*!" I shrieked. "They're mine. You can't take the best ones!"

She plunked another big red one on her tongue. "Be quiet, crybaby." She chewed contentedly.

I barely restrained myself from pouncing on her and slapping and clawing at her. Last time she'd stolen fruit from me, that was exactly what I did, and I got a beating from Mamita as a result.

Matilde popped another *capulí* in her mouth, grinning. To her, the world was one happy joke. She smiled at everything. I'd bet she could fall off a cliff and then, bleeding and broken, still laugh about it. It was always like this with her. I was the one who did all the work; I was the one who had to put up with Papito's beatings and Mamita's harsh words, while Matilde just

110

breezed in and out of our lives like a plump, pretty princess, always getting the best of everything.

Back at the house, at lunch, things got worse when Mamita was about to serve the purple potato soup.

"I got these potatoes," I reminded Mamita. "I brought them for everybody, but I don't want you to give Matilde the biggest ones. Those are for me."

Mamita looked at me like I was a rat that she wanted to hit with a broom. She turned her head away so I could only see the angry whites of her eyes. Papito didn't say anything, just sat on the stool, staring at the hot coals with his stony expression.

Matilde laughed, a tinkling bell sound. Her cheeks were pink and merry from our walk, her lips stained red from the *capulís* she had stolen from me.

My voice rose to a piercing pitch. "Mamita! Don't give her the biggest potatoes. Give *me* the biggest ones."

Mamita's mouth formed a tense, thin line. "Your sister only comes from Quito once in a while. Treat her well."

"But I worked for these potatoes. They're mine."

"You're a selfish brat," Mamita said. "You don't deserve any potatoes."

"Yes, I do!"

Mamita gave me a long, cold look. "Know what? I'd be happy if one day you left and never came back."

Her words froze my insides. *Fine*, I said to myself. *I will leave, and after I'm gone you will cry and cry and cry over me.*

When the soup was ready, Mamita served the biggest, best potato to Matilde.

I glared at Matilde across the ashes, my skin prickling with rage. *If I never see you again*, I silently told her, *I'll be very happy.*

111

* * *

Have you noticed that if you really want something, you can make it happen? But you need to be sure it's what you really want, because sometimes, when it comes true, you realize too late that it's not what you wanted.

Not at all.

chapter 14

Back in Kunu Yaku, I keep the paper under my mattress. Every night, I take it out and read the word *Hermanita*. Little sister. A cozy word, like sweet, warm bread. I imagine Matilde and me giggling over our crushes like Marina and Marlenny do. I imagine telling her about the volcano I made, and eating popcorn and dressing up and pretending to be famous singers together.

The phone number she wrote has an area code from Quito, the capital, just a few hours away. It's bewildering to know that if I call her, she could be here within hours.

We don't have a phone in the house, so I can't call her easily. I could go to a phone booth at one of the nearby stores, but all the store owners know the Doctorita and are prone to gossiping. And what would I tell Matilde anyway? To come visit me? To take me away from these people? And then what would I do? Where would I live? I'm afraid if I call her without a plan, she might try to convince me to go back to our parents' little shack. For the moment, I decide to just hold on to the paper while I think of a plan, and let its kindness ooze into me.

For the past week, the Doctorita has been in a bad mood. It started the day after we got back from Yana Urku, when we ran into Niño Carlitos's slim, pretty ex-girlfriend on our evening walk. He was quiet the rest of the evening, and then, the next day, when the Doctorita criticized him for spending too much time building tiny spaceship models, he accused her of being fat and lazy. "*¡Plastona!*" he said. "Stuck to the couch all the time!" She yelled back, "Well, who's the breadwinner in this house? Who has two jobs? Who deserves to relax at the end of the day?" He grumbled under his breath that he should have married the ex-girlfriend instead of the Doctorita. When she heard that, for days she lay in bed crying and knitting dresses for her Baby Jesus doll.

After a few days, Niño Carlitos apologized and bought her an aerobics book full of photos of thin, fair women in shiny leotards and leg warmers. She used the book once, gasping and sweating for ten minutes, then stuck it angrily on the bookshelf and flopped on the sofa.

She hasn't touched the book since. She's barely talked to Niño Carlitos all week. Instead, she's been taking her rage out on me.

I'm on the roof in the glaring sunshine, cleaning the Doctorita's dental instruments with soapy water in the cement washbasin. With my fingernail, I scrape at the dried blood and bits of crushed tooth and gum stuck to the metal. This is my least favorite task, almost as disgusting as washing diapers. Once all the gunk is off, I carry the tools down two flights of stairs in a plastic bin, to the Doctorita's dentist office, just off the entrance hallway that serves as a waiting room. I plunk the tools into the sterilizing machine, which will kill the germs so the tools will be ready to use on the next patient.

At that moment, Jaimito bursts in the room, his eyes wide and excited. "Virginia! Come outside! I found a dead snake!"

I run out the door after him, reminding myself I'll have to return to arrange the tools and press the Start button, but soon I'm caught up in examining the snake's shiny skin and entrails. I wish I had a lab notebook to write my observations in, the kind with graph paper like the *colegio* students have. This is like a dissection, seeing the inside parts that let the snake eat and breathe and make energy and waste. I explain to Jaimito that snakes are cold-blooded reptiles, that they need the sun to warm them, which is why sometimes you come across them sunbathing on rocks. He listens and asks question after question, and most of them I can answer scientifically. I hope he won't tell the Doctorita what I've told him, or she might suspect I've been reading *Understanding Our Universe*.

The next day, Niño Carlitos is out playing basketball with a friend and I'm in the living room making Play-Doh monsters with the boys. The Doctorita is with a patient in her office, and I'm not expecting her to be done for an hour or so. But after a few minutes, she storms into the room and, without warning, punches me in the face.

Jaimito screams. Andrecito cries. And the Doctorita beats

me with a handful of wire hangers from the hall closet. "¡*Longa tonta!* You fool! You didn't sterilize my tools! One simple task, and you mess it up. ¡*Longa estúpida!*"

I cover my face with my hands, clutching my nose. Sticky liquid spreads over my face, my hands. Blood drips to the tile floor. The hangers cut into my arms, sting my shoulders and back. Out of the corner of my eye I see Jaimito kicking his mother, trying to pull her away from me. "Stop, Mamá," he cries. "Stop! Leave her alone!"

Finally, the Doctorita pushes me toward the bathroom. "Clean yourself up."

I rinse the blood from my face, but more keeps pouring out, like water from a broken faucet. I give up and go back to the living room with blood still trickling from my nose. The Doctorita throws a kitchen rag at me. "Hold your nose and put your head back."

I do what she says, sitting cross-legged on the floor. It's been a while since she's beaten me this badly in front of the children. This has shaken them up as much as me, maybe more. Andrecito hugs me and Jaimito snuggles against me, stroking my hair. "It's all right, Virginia," he whispers. "We love you." For once, he is quiet. He holds me fiercely, like a little lion cub, so tightly that I have to loosen his grip.

When I notice he's crying, I wipe his tears and rock him, one hand holding him, the other at my nose, and say, "It's all right, *mi amor*, it's all right." He's so sensitive, he probably won't be able to sleep tonight; he'll call for me to stroke his head and sing to him.

When Niño Carlitos comes home and sees the bloody rag at my nose and my puffy, tear-streaked face, he kneels down beside me. "What happened, *m'hija?*" His voice is hoarse and tender, as it always is in the aftermath of the Doctorita's beatings. And this one is especially bad. The bleeding won't stop, no matter how hard I press the rag against my nose.

I don't say anything, only glance at the Doctorita, who is shuffling through school papers at the table. By now Andrecito has gotten distracted with a wooden Bugs Bunny puzzle, but Jaimito has not left my side. He points a little finger at his mother.

Niño Carlitos turns to her, his eyes hard. "What happened to la Virginia?"

"Nothing," the Doctorita says defensively.

"Then why is her nose bleeding?" He's yelling now. He hardly ever yells. "After the last time, you said you'd be easier on her."

At the sound of his father's raised voice, Andrecito drops the puzzle pieces and runs over to me, burying his face in my shoulder.

The Doctorita slams down her pen. "She didn't sterilize the instruments. And a patient came and I had nothing to use. She humiliated me."

Niño Carlitos's lip curls in disgust. "My God, Romelia, she's a child. The Baby Jesus incident nearly put her in the hospital."

He's talking about the time I was dusting her Baby Jesus doll, when I dropped Him and His arm broke. I tried to hide the damage under His crocheted green dress, but when the Doctorita discovered it, she erupted in a rage. Luckily the boys didn't witness that beating—they would have had nightmares for weeks.

The Doctorita glares at me, then says, "Don't make me out to be the bad guy again, Carlos."

117

He clenches his fists at his sides. "This has got to stop. You'd better not hurt her again. Not under my roof."

"Not under my roof," echo Jaimito and then Andrecito, their arms loyally around my shoulders.

It feels good that Niño Carlitos cares about me and protects me like a father. I have not told you much about my father yet. I would like to say it's because he wasn't around much. It's true he was often working for weeks at a time on construction projects in Quito. And when he was home, he was usually in the fields all day with Alfonso's oxen, plowing or planting or harvesting. In the evenings, he went out to drink *puro* with other men. When Papito was with us, he was mostly silent and stony-faced, communicating through grunts and orders.

But I must force myself to shine a flashlight into the darkest places, to admit the real reason I've avoided mentioning Papito. You see, Papito ignited worse than fire. If someone—man, woman, or child—provoked him, the cold, quiet man disappeared and the fire inside him flared up like a rag doused with kerosene, all flames and flying fists.

There are so many moments I've tried to forget.

There was the moment Papito discovered that the dogs had snuck into a hole in our house's clay wall and stolen the meat. He blamed it on me, strung me up to the rafters by a rope looped around my neck. As I dangled there, gagging, he beat me with a dried leather whip until my hands stopped struggling to pull the rope from my neck, and I could no longer breathe, and blackness swallowed the world. Then he released me and I fell to the ground in a gasping heap of snot and tears and blood.

There was the moment when, at a drunken party, Papito accused Mamita of sleeping with the man who bought pigs door-to-door. I watched him punch and kick her unconscious and then drag her home by her hair, her face scraping and bouncing over the rocks. The next morning, I watched her wince as she spread a bright green herbal remedy on her face, which had been bruised to black, one eye swollen shut.

There were the moments when Papito beat Mamita, even though her belly was big with a baby inside. There were the moments she lost her babies. I was a little girl, and vague on the details of pregnancy and miscarriage, but I remember that for a long time after the last baby died, Mamita cried and screamed and told me to leave her alone. "I wish I'd given you away, brat." But this only made me plead for more attention, to whine at a higher pitch, to beg extra hard to work in the fields with her. The more I pleaded, the more she seemed to hate me.

The worst was that Papito kept beating her, and as he did, he glared at me with beady eyes, reddened and drooping from liquor, and yelled in her face, "That brat is the pig trader's daughter, admit it. Admit you lay down with him." Which was not true, because when Papito was gone, Mamita worked in the fields and fed the animals and sold pigs, always with Manuelito strapped to her back. She was never alone, ever, especially not with a man, and especially not lying down. Anyway, the pig man was fat and ugly, and I didn't look anything like him. And Papito and I had the same feet, with extra-long toes, proof that I was his daughter. As a little girl, despite everything, I wanted Papito to want me, to feel proud I was his daughter.

* * *

Now I've found a kind of father in Niño Carlitos. He calls me daughter, and defends me, and says he's proud of me, and calls me pretty and smart—all the things I always wanted to hear from my own father. How can I leave Niño Carlitos? And how can I leave the boys, who love me more than anything? But my nose is throbbing, and as much as I love Niño Carlitos and the boys, I hate the Doctorita.

Hours later, I'm in my room, nursing my wounds and clutching the paper with my sister's number. Niño Carlitos and the boys have left to pasture the cow, and the Doctorita has sterilized the tools and is now filling the patient's cavity. I stare at Matilde's message, the neat, round letters and numbers that I already know by heart. And then, quickly, before I can change my mind, I take some coins from the Doctorita's purse and walk to the shop with a phone booth. My face is hot and angry, my nose pulsing, my head aching. The fabric of my shirt rubs at the raw scratches all over my torso. I walk like an old lady, every step painful.

When I reach Don Luciano's store, I hesitate outside. A sick feeling spreads out from my stomach. I can guess what will happen next. Don Luciano will have me write the number on his notepad, then he'll dial, and when someone answers, he'll tell me to pick up the phone in the booth, and then he'll hang up. He'll eavesdrop on my conversation through the thin wood door, and within an hour, word will spread all over town that I've called my sister because I can't stand living with the Doctorita anymore. What will she do to me then?

I think of the elementary school diploma the Doctorita promised. How can I throw that away? And what if my parents don't even want me back? Or what if they do, and I never see

Jaimito and Andrecito and Niño Carlitos again? What if my parents force me to live in their dirty house without rice or meat or books or a TV? What if Papito still beats my mother? What if he tries to beat me? He's much stronger than the Doctorita. I look at the scars on my legs from when Papito whipped me as I dangled from the rafters. The scars have faded a little, but I doubt they'll ever disappear.

I take one last look at the phone booth through the window of Don Luciano's store. My nose isn't throbbing as much now, and the swelling will probably go down in a few days, and the welts from the hangers will fade in a week—a small price to pay for a diploma and a house full of books and weekly *MacGyver* access. I fold the worn paper with Matilde's phone number on it, turn away from the shop, and trudge home.

A scene flashes in my head: MacGyver telling the slaves, "Go! You're free!" and the slaves just standing and staring. I understand why. Fear feels familiar. And freedom feels terrifying.

chapter 15

INSTEAD OF ESCAPE, my mind turns to revenge. In the meantime, I keep the paper under my mattress, in case I really need it one day, although I'm not sure how I'll know when that day comes.

It's Saturday morning and silvery rain is pouring outside, trickling down the windowpanes, making it cozy inside the house. My wounds from the Doctorita's hanger rage have nearly disappeared, but my anger at her has lingered. She's gone now, along with Niño Carlitos and the boys, to spend the weekend with her family, while I've stayed here to feed the guinea pigs and pasture the cow.

I consider starting the long list of chores she made me memorize. She still doesn't know I can read, which is a good thing, because then she'd probably write me an extralong list of chores. I pick up the mop and bucket, and then, on second thought, let them clatter to the floor.

I have the house to myself and I will do what I want. *¡Viva* *la libertad!* I snatch the Doctorita's favorite green polka-dot dress from her wardrobe. It barely fits her anymore, clinging to her bottom so tightly the seams have almost split. I put it on, loving how it skims my new curves and hangs gracefully at my ankles. I slip on her high heels and let my hair loose and admire myself in the mirror.

The swelling in my nose has gone down. Now there are only faint purple-blue marks beneath my eyes. My friend Marina said she'd read in a fashion magazine that if you have a pimple on your face, you should wear lots of eye makeup and lipstick to distract people. My puffy nose isn't exactly a pimple, but maybe the same strategy will work. I put on the Doctorita's bright red, special-occasion lipstick and gold eye shadow. Pleased at my reflection, I dance in front of the mirror and sing along with the *cumbia* music blasting on the stereo.

Still wearing the high heels, I sweep and mop until my feet hurt, then I change into my regular clothes and put on fresh lipstick and run out to feed the guinea pigs and pasture the cow. Later, back home, I read for a while. When my stomach growls, I make myself a mountain of greasy potatoes and fried steak for dinner and papaya and mangoes for dessert and lounge on the Doctorita's pink llama blanket watching TV until I nod off.

Sunday morning, I wake up late in the Doctorita's bed, to watery gray light and more rain pattering on the windows. My gaze rests on her wardrobe, on the drawer she forbade me to open my first morning here, a rule she continues to remind me of regularly. She keeps the key in a secret place, and I've never seen her open the drawer. It must hold something very, very secret if she's managed to hide it from me all these years. I tug on the drawer, hard, but the lock is too strong.

I eat breakfast and read for a while, then feed the animals and do my other chores. In the afternoon, as I'm dusting the Doctorita's room and making the bed, I catch a glimpse of myself in the wardrobe's mirror, at the two blue-yellow crescents beneath my eyes. When I was younger and the Doctorita beat me, I thought that when I was big I'd get revenge. But I am big now, nearly as tall as her, nearly grown up. Thirteen years old and she's still beating me.

Revenge. I stare at the drawer. I'll find a way to open it. I take a knife from the kitchen and wiggle it around in the keyhole, the way I've seen MacGyver do. I imagine him at my side. The clock is ticking. Sixty, fifty-nine, fifty-eight . . . only one minute to open the drawer and defuse the bomb. The evil, jiggly-chinned thief is plotting to blow up the world, and I am the only hope to unlock the drawer in time. Me, María Virginia Farinango, world-famous lock picker, the expert who flies around the globe, opening locks in the nick of time. Nine, eight, seven . . . almost there. MacGyver leans over me, whispers in my ear, his breath warm. *If anyone can do this, you can, Virginia, my love.* Three, two, one . . .

There is a click and the drawer opens. I pull the drawer out and set it on the floor, my hands shaking with excitement. I shuffle through the papers—birth certificates, a marriage license, diplomas. Boring, boring, boring. A few pieces of jewelry—clunky earrings and bracelets I've seen the Doctorita wearing to weddings and baptisms. And that's it. All these years of wondering about the forbidden drawer, and it's just a bunch of junk.

Deflated, I shove the drawer back into the wardrobe. But it won't shut all the way. The metal lock is sticking up. I try to push it down, but it's stuck. I jam the knife in the keyhole and wiggle and twist it, with no luck. Frantically, I grab a handful of knives from the kitchen and try each one in the keyhole. One of them has to work! I try scissors and hairpins and knitting needles, but nothing will budge the lock.

Just thinking about what the Doctorita will do when she sees the drawer makes me shudder. If she gave me a bloody nose for forgetting to sterilize her instruments, what will she do to me now? My thoughts bang around, frantic and crazy, until I think my head will explode.

I could call my sister. She could come and take me away from here. But it's Sunday afternoon. Don Luciano closes his shop on Sunday afternoon to have lunch with his family. And what about the elementary school diploma? And meat and books and TV?

Then, in the midst of my panic, an idea shines through, clear and bright. An idea that makes me wipe my eyes and sit up straight. I am stronger and smarter than the Doctorita. I can think of a way out of this. MacGyver always identifies his enemy's big weakness first. What is the Doctorita's weakness? What is she most afraid of?

I mentally flip through her large, strange collection of fears, fears that make her break out in a sweat, make her moan about feeling suffocated. Germs, gas leaks, bad traffic, volcanic eruptions, kidnappings, thieves. When Niño Carlitos rolls his eyes at her ridiculous fears, she insists it's not her fault. Supposedly, according to her doctor, it's *nervios* from working two demanding jobs, and she should drink lots of lemon balm tea to calm her nerves.

I try to narrow down her fears to the very worst one.

Thieves.

Years ago, the theft of the bus traumatized her. Ever since, she's ranted about thieves, double- and triple-checking to make sure our doors are locked, worrying that someone will steal the truck, clutching her purse against her chest in crowded markets. Yes, thieves it is.

So thieves she will get.

But it will have to be convincing; I can't just go halfway. I glance at the clock. Three o'clock. That gives me about two hours until they come back. They usually return before dark because the Doctorita frets that a gang of bandits will jump out in the darkness and hijack the truck.

I turn the drawer upside down, dump the papers and jewelry on the floor, kick them around. In a mad whirlwind, I tear the curtains from the rods, gather the pink bedspread in a ball and hurl it at the wall, knock over the lamp, push the trinkets and doilies off the chest, throw magazines and pillows around the room. This feels delicious!

Gathering momentum, I run into the living room, swipe the photos off the table, rip the framed cross-stitched roses off the wall. I consider knocking over some flowerpots, but that wouldn't be fair to the innocent plants, who are only trying to lead a peaceful existence of photosynthesis and respiration. Instead, I grab the cushions from the couch, toss them around the floor, pull out drawers and scatter clothes in heaps, jump on her favorite polka-dot dress. Room by room, I terrorize their belongings, just like a thief on a TV show.

But the best part is still coming. Breathless and full of wild energy, I take a ball of rope from the kitchen drawer and run upstairs. To make it really convincing, I'll have to tie myself up.

Thieves always tie up their victims. I stand with my back to the bedpost and wind the rope around myself, feet first. In almost every *MacGyver* episode, someone gets tied up, so I know how to do it. I wrap the rope around the post and my body, all the way up to my neck, and knot it tightly.

Then I stand there, waiting, feeling my heartbeat slow a little. The alarm clock is lying on the floor, facedown, so I'm not sure how much time has passed. With the rain, I can't tell where the sun is.

I wait and wait. After a while I get thirsty. And then hungry. And then I have to go to the bathroom. And then my legs grow tired. I watch a fly buzz around the room, land on the overturned lamp and then on the naked curtain rod. I listen to the raindrops drumming on the windows. My nose itches, but I can't scratch it with my hands bound.

I have plenty of time to think of everything that could go wrong with my plan. What if they figure out I'm lying? That I've done all this myself? Nervous sweat trickles down my sides. She'll kill me, that's what she'll do. She'll beat me to death. And my family will never find out, because according to Matilde's note, they don't even know if I exist anymore.

I can almost see myself looking down from heaven, watching the Doctorita bury my battered body in a cornfield in the dead of night. Later, when Marlenny and Marina and Doña Mercedes and Niño Carlitos and the boys ask, *Where's our beloved Virginia?* she'll only say, *Oh, that* longa *must have run away.* And everyone will cry and cry for me. *Why didn't she say goodbye to us? Oh, how we'll miss her.* Meanwhile, the Doctorita will grin her evil grin, knowing she got away with murder.

Now I really, really have to go to the bathroom. Finally, I untie myself, which takes a while, and dash to the bathroom and pee for a full minute. Ah, sweet relief.

And then, while I'm on the toilet, I hear the truck pull into the driveway. They're home!

I run back to the bedroom and frantically wrap the rope around myself, wind it around and around, and tie it to the bedpost.

The door clanks open.

"Virginia?" the Doctorita's shrill voice calls out. "I thought I told you to lock the door. Didn't I—" And then a scream and a thump. She must have just seen the giant mess and dropped her bags in horror.

Niño Carlitos's voice calls up: "Virginia! *M'hija!* Are you all right? Where are you?"

I muster up my most traumatized voice. "Help me! Up here! In your bedroom!"

They run up the stairs. The Doctorita's face is white, the color drained away, her mouth open. She clutches the door frame, looking about ready to collapse. "Wh-wh-wh-wh-what happened?"

"Thieves!" I cry. And on command, the tears start gushing from my eyes. "Th-th-they came into the house! I-i-it was h-h-h-horrible, Doctorita."

Her pudgy fingers tremble as she unties me. "Are you all right?"

I snivel and sniff and give a weak nod.

Niño Carlitos turns to the boys. "Go to your room and close the door and stay there." He comes up to me, touches my cheek. "*M'hija*, did they hurt you?"

I shake my head. "They just—they just scared me really badly."

"Because if they touched you, I'll kill them." A vein pops out on his forehead. "I mean it, I'll kill them."

I whimper some more as he strokes my hair.

"Virginia, what did they look like?"

"I-i-it was two thieves," I say. "O-o-one was short and light-haired. A-a-and the other was tall and dark-haired. A-a-and they wore baseball caps."

"I'm going to go look for them, Virginia," he says, jogging out of the room. He turns back, his face pained. "Are you sure they didn't touch you?"

I nod, miserably. "They just t-t-tied me up."

The Doctorita finishes untying me, her hands still shaking, her chins trembling. "Virginia, go take a shower to calm down. I'll fix you a cup of tea." I leave her sitting with her hand over her heart as though it could jump right out of her body. After my shower I come back to her bed and lie there, watching TV like a princess. She brings me lemon balm tea to settle my nerves and starts cleaning up the mess, breathing hard with effort and fear, muttering about how she knew it, that thieves are lurking around every corner. How the world is a dangerous place, even in a little town like Kunu Yaku.

Suddenly, she pauses and looks up at me. "Why didn't they steal anything?"

I shrug.

She tilts her head. "Are you sure thieves broke in?"

"Yes," I say, indignant.

"Did you do all this?"

"How could you think that, Doctorita!" I say, letting tears

leak from my eyes again. A whole lake of tears has been under the surface for years, waiting to come out. "How could I tie myself up? Why would I do that?"

"To scare me," she says slowly. "You know my nerves are bad. You did this, didn't you?"

"That's not true." I stare into her eyes, as though I believe it with every cell in my body. As though I'm a famous actress on a soap opera.

A cloud of doubt passes over her face. "It's true," she says weakly, then sinks down on her hands and knees to gather the spilled trinkets.

The boys come in and cuddle with me, one on either side. Soon Niño Carlitos pokes his head in the room. "More tea, m'hija?"

"Yes please," I say, sweetly. "Thank you." And I let a few more tears fall for good measure.

He pats my shoulder. "It's all right, m'hija. We're here."

The Doctorita continues cleaning on her hands and knees, eyeing me suspiciously. She watches me as though I am not a child servant, but a real, grown-up woman with thoughts and schemes of my own. She watches me almost cautiously, as though I am unpredictable and not to be trusted. She doesn't say anything more about it, only watches me with different eyes.

Meanwhile, the boys and Niño Carlitos are fussing over me, gushing love and warmth and concern. I soak it up eagerly. Maybe I should consider a career in acting. What else can I do with the rest of these stored-up tears?

Niño Carlitos keeps patting my shoulder. "Don't worry, m'hija. You're safe now."

chapter 16

I WOULD MAKE A GOOD SOAP-OPERA STAR, but I'm starting to suspect it's an impossible dream. Nearly everyone on TV is either *mestizo* or American. Only once in a while, on the soap operas, is there an *indígena*, and she's usually a fat, middle-aged maid who never speaks except for *yes, señora*. She does nothing but sweep, open doors, and serve food. I hate watching those fat indigenous maids. As much as I want to be an actress, I don't want to play a fat servant.

One of my favorite programs features singers performing music. The women are always slender and smooth and beautiful, no bulges on their stomachs, no jiggly fat on their thighs. Only the curve of their firm breasts and hips and bottoms.

From what I remember, none of the women in my village looked like that—they waddled like round hens and thought they were pretty. If a girl was thin in Yana Urku, people said she looked as sickly and ugly as a dying tree. But now I see they were wrong. That's just another thing that makes them ignorant *indígenas*. They don't understand what it means to have a beautiful body.

Everyone knows that *mestizo* men like their women slim with fair skin. As I've witnessed when Niño Carlitos gets angry, he tells the Doctorita she's ugly and fat, which makes her cry and knit Baby Jesus dresses for days on end. I smile on the inside because if I can't get vengeance on her, at least she's getting it from someone else. I feel a little sorry for her, but mostly it feels good to see her hurt the way I hurt when she calls me names.

And here's another thing that makes me secretly happy. Niño Carlitos is always telling me, "Oh, *m'hija*, you look pretty today." Or, "I like your hair that way, *hija*." Or, "That skirt looks nice on you, *hija*." So when he insults the Doctorita, I smile to myself, knowing that he thinks I'm pretty.

But most of the time, I don't feel pretty.

Most of the time, I worry that any day now I could turn into a fat, ugly *indígena*.

The Doctorita has forgotten about the aerobics book that Niño Carlitos gave her, but I haven't. Every day, I race through the cleaning, then look at the color pictures of beautiful *mestiza* women in skintight leotards with flat stomachs and narrow thighs. I imitate their exercises, jogging in place, moving my arms in tiny circles, lying on my back and moving my legs around like I'm riding an upside-down bicycle. My muscles ache and burn, but it feels good knowing my body is that much closer to looking like theirs.

Lately my breasts are swelling more, little by little, which is fine, but my belly and thighs and hips and bottom are also getting a padding of fat, which is not fine. If this keeps up, soon I'll be waddling around like the *indígena* servants on TV. What's worse, little ugly hairs are sprouting up in hidden places—under my arms, between my legs. The women in the exercise book only have glossy, long hair pulled in high ponytails, no other, ugly hairs as far as I can tell. Every day, I wish harder and harder for a body like the exercise ladies', like the singers' on TV.

The harder I wish, the less I eat.

I feel proud when I get through a whole day with only a bite of beef and a few spoonfuls of rice and a glass of melon juice. My stomach rumbles all the time, but I embrace it as a sign I'm getting thinner.

No one notices but Niño Carlitos. He notices me much more than the Doctorita does. He notices how my breasts have been growing. Sometimes, when he thinks I'm not looking, he stares at them. After dinner one night, as I'm washing the dishes, he studies me with concern. "Are you all right, daughter? You seem so thin. And pale. Do you feel sick?"

"I'm fine," I say, pleased he can tell I'm thinner. And the pale skin is an added bonus. "Just fine."

There was another time, years ago, back in Yana Urku, when I felt the thrill of turning white. It happened when I got my first pair of shoes, when I was about six. Matilde brought me to the market with the riales I'd saved from my snack money during those six torturous weeks in first grade. The vendor handed me the boots—black rubber with zigzag soles, just like Papito's—and I was the happiest girl in the universe.

That afternoon, I wore my shoes to pasture the cow and sheep. With abandon, I ran and skipped and kicked big rocks and stomped through mud puddles. I showed off my boots to every child I passed. My feet sweated and slid around inside them; when I reached the pasture, I discovered that two blisters had formed on the thin skin over my anklebones. By the time I came home, the blisters had popped and their water mixed with the sweat in the boots; even this, somehow, seemed beautiful to me.

All week I wore the boots. Every evening I cleaned them, using a stick to remove any last trace of mud from the zigzag soles. After I took off my boots, my feet looked wrinkled and tender and white. That's when I realized that these were magic shoes. Mixed with sweat, they had the power to turn me white!

The next morning I woke up early, excited. Inside the kitchen, I poured water from the pot into my boots, filling them up, then carefully wedged my feet back inside. Some of the water spilled over the sides, but the remaining water still reached the rims. Now my ankles and calves would turn white too. And then the whiteness would spread to the rest of me. This was my deepest, secret hope.

All day in the pastures, I sloshed around in my boots with my goat, Cheetah, and Josefa and the other cows and sheep. People I passed gave me strange looks. "What's wrong with you, girl? Why are you walking like that?" I didn't tell them my secret. They would see, tomorrow.

At home that evening, I took off my shoes outside and dumped out the water. I examined my feet. White! All the way past my ankles! White and very wrinkled.

I sipped my soup in bliss.

When I finished, I examined my feet again.

Brown and pink.

The same feet as always.

Tears welled up first and then rage, a deep sense of injustice. It stung like Mamita's slap when she'd told me, "We will always be *indígena*. Nothing will change that."

After a few months of eating nearly nothing, it takes every bit of strength I can muster to do the little arm circles. When I stand up after doing sit-ups, I feel dizzy and steady myself with the wall. As I sweep, the joints of my shoulders and elbows ache. Sometimes a sharp pain, like a needle, shoots up my arm while I scrub the bathroom. Climbing the stairs, my knees hurt, as though they're tired of carrying me everywhere. I doze on the red velvet sofa whenever I get a chance, too exhausted to follow Jaimito and Andrecito around. It's the price of beauty.

And then one day, I can't hold the broom.

It falls from my hand and whacks the floor.

"What's wrong with you?" the Doctorita demands.

"My arm hurts."

"Why?"

I shrug. "It just does."

"Pick up the broom."

I bend down, and my body aches, but I muster up all my strength and manage to pick up the broom. I am like an old lady.

This scares me.

Still, I eat even less and exercise even more.

From time to time, the Doctorita piles us all in the truck for a trip to her relatives' house in Santa Rosa, a couple of hours away. I love these trips. Unbelievably, her mother, Anita, and niece, Silvia, and nephew, José, are sweet and dote on me, giving me hand-me-down clothes and telling me how beautiful I

135

am. They treat me like a niece, or a granddaughter. Whenever they're around, the Doctorita hardly ever hits me or calls me *longa*. If she slips up and yells or orders me around, Anita scolds her. "Treat our Virginia with respect, *hija*. And be easy on her. She's just a young girl."

Silvia always looks at me deeply, with kind eyes that really see me, that really look, and when she asks, "How are you, Virginia?" I feel like she means it, like she truly wants to know.

A week after dropping the broom, I'm at Anita's house, eating dinner with the whole extended family. They never ask me to serve them, and they let me eat off china plates and use good silverware with the rest of them. I'm casually rearranging the food on my pretty flowered plate, pushing the meat around, wondering if I can slip any into my pockets and throw it out later. Today I'm too tired to enjoy their conversation and kindness. I can only think about resisting food and sleep, which is hard with a permanently rumbling stomach and eyelids that hang heavy as stones.

"Virginia," Silvia says, her forehead wrinkled in concern, "you don't seem like yourself. Have you been sick?"

I shake my head, too exhausted to form words.

Anita turns to José. "Why don't you take a look at la Virginia, dear."

José is a doctor, young and handsome. He studies my face, and I feel self-conscious, wondering if they've noticed I've only had two bites of meat and a quarter of a potato, and worrying I'll somehow get in trouble. "Virginia, are you sure you feel all right?"

Dully, I nod.

After lunch, José brings me to his office in the clinic and sits me on a little bed covered in a tight white sheet. The room smells like disinfectant and bleach and a hint of his cologne. Normally this would thrill me, to be alone with this handsome doctor paying attention to me, but all I want to do is lie down on the bed and slip into sleep. He listens to my heartbeat with a stethoscope. "Pretty fast." He takes my blood pressure. "A little low." He feels my face with the back of his hand. "Cold." He studies my face.

"Do you always breathe so fast, Virginia?"

I shrug.

He rubs his hand over his eyes. "Has Romelia been feeding you well?"

I shrug again.

"You're thin and pale," he says.

Good. Thin and pale is exactly how I want to be.

"Too thin, Virginia. You're malnourished and anemic." He looks sad, or angry, or some other feeling he's trying very hard to hold in. He takes a deep breath and presses his lips together, then says, "Let's go."

I set a slow pace back to the house. Walking makes me short of breath. A block seems like ten kilometers. "Will I get in trouble, José?"

"What?"

"With the Doctorita. She'll get mad at me, I know it."

His mouth tightens into a hard line. "I'll talk to her. Don't worry, Virginia."

Inside, the Doctorita is watching TV and talking with her mother. José tells me to wait in the kitchen, but I peek out and listen. His face is red and he's talking to the Doctorita in a low voice that makes me think of opening the lid of a pot just a little so steam can pour out, so it won't explode. "This girl's starving, Tía—how can you keep her malnourished like this? Don't you feed her?"

"What are you talking about?"

"Virginia has anemia and vitamin deficiencies."

Anita looks at the Doctorita in horror. "How could you do this to our Virginia?"

The Doctorita blinks. "I give her plenty of food." She turns to Niño Carlitos. "Don't I?"

He says nothing, just looks thoughtful.

Anita and José eye her suspiciously. "Admit it. You've never treated her well."

"I give her lots of food!" the Doctorita shouts.

And then Silvia comes in and when she hears what's happened, she's yelling too, and then the Doctorita is crying. She snivels and sniffs and finally calls me out of the kitchen and glares at me. "Don't I feed you?"

I nod.

"Then why is she malnourished?" José demands.

I have to tell the truth. "I wanted to be thin."

The Doctorita has that look in her eyes like she wants to smack me, and she would if there weren't people around.

José closes his eyes and shakes his head. "Look, Virginia, I'll give you vitamins and shots to help you build back your strength. But you have to eat. *Bruta*, you have to eat if you want to grow. You'll stay short forever if you don't eat. Your bones are growing. You need to eat. How can you grow up if you don't eat?"

These are the magic words. The one thing I want more than anything is to grow up so the Doctorita can't hurt me, so I can leave and start my own life. I want this more than being thin.

For the rest of the afternoon, José and I sit in the kitchen. He explains how my body is growing and all the nutrients it needs. Vitamin A from carrots for my eyes. Calcium from cheese for my bones. Iron from meat for my blood.

"Virginia, promise me you'll start eating again."

"I will. I promise." I pause. "José?" I don't know what I want to ask exactly. "Do you think it's my fault? Do you think I'm bad?"

"Oh, Virginia, of course not. Your life isn't easy. We know this. Just remember, you're beautiful how you are."

When it's time to go home, Niño Carlitos puts his arm around my waist and helps me into the truck, fussing over me. The boys cuddle with me, sensing something is wrong. On the way home, the Doctorita doesn't look at me. "Doesn't matter to me if you get sicker and sicker," she says, looking out the window. "I should just let you die instead of spending this money on shots and vitamins. Don't eat. See if I care."

But at home, she watches me at mealtimes like a hawk, mumbling, "*Longa estúpida*, how could you think you could stop eating?" She watches me and makes sure I eat every last grain of rice, every last crumb of bread, every piece of gristle on the meat.

Niño Carlitos buys chocolates for me on the way home from work. "Here, *m'hija*," he says, rubbing my back. "Eat. You need to fatten up." He does this when the Doctorita isn't around. He doesn't want to make her jealous that I can eat lots of candy and she can't.

At first, all this food makes me nauseous, but after a couple of months, I feel strong again. My joints stop aching and I gain weight and I grow taller. My body isn't turning out like the exercise ladies', but it's growing, and the more it grows, the sooner I'll be grown up and the sooner I'll leave this place forever.

In the meantime, while I watch the thin, beautiful *mestizas* living glamorous lives on TV, and the fat, ugly *indígenas* serving them, I try hard, very hard, to hang on to José's slippery words. *Just remember, you're beautiful how you are.*

chapter 17

I UNDERSTAND, more or less, how flowers reproduce—with fruit and seeds and pollen—but the sexual parts of the human body baffle me. I study the diagrams of naked people in *Understanding Our Universe*, all pink and red and yellow, networks of tubes and veins and arteries and organs. The words are long and hard to pronounce, like *fal-lo-pi-an tubes*. I can't figure out how these pictures correspond to what's inside me.

And the diagrams leave important things out. They don't show ugly dark hairs under ladies' arms. Or blood trickling between their legs.

One day I'm chopping carrots, when suddenly I feel like I'm peeing. I drop the carrots and run to the bathroom. There's a big red spot on my underwear. A terrible, sinking feeling comes over me. Sometimes, washing the Doctorita's huge, stretched-out underwear, I've noticed bloodstains, which I soak in soapy water with my nose wrinkled in disgust and horror. I never let myself think it would actually happen to me.

Oh, Dios, I'm turning into her. First the ugly hairs and now this.

I stay in the bathroom, wrapped up in panic. I suspect this blood has something to do with becoming a woman.

Oh, Dios, I don't want to become a woman. Why can't I be a man instead?

I wipe away the blood with toilet paper and pray it won't come back, but it keeps coming, and for days I'm running to the bathroom to wipe more away. After a few days, thankfully, it stops, as though my wish has come true.

But then, just when I've nearly put it behind me, a month later, the blood comes back.

Of course, I can't tell the Doctorita. Even thinking about it turns my face hot with shame. Once, a few months ago, I was cleaning the waiting room of her dental office and discovered a small comic book that had fallen behind the chair. A patient must have left it behind. I opened it and saw drawings of naked ladies with gigantic breasts and legs spread wide and I got a funny feeling. I put down my broom and sat on the chair and flipped through the book, curious and excited, sensing this was something very forbidden.

I was so absorbed in the book, I didn't notice the Doctorita until she was standing above me. "What are you looking at?"

I jumped and shut the book fast, tucking it under my arm. "Nothing."

She snatched it from me.

My face burned.

She smacked me with the book. "Dirty *longa*, dirty girl!" She smacked me again. "I never want to catch you with this trash again, understand?"

And now, if I tell her about this blood, she'll somehow find a way to blame me, make it my fault, make me feel like a dirty *longa*.

One day, after a few episodes of this bleeding that comes for four or five days, then disappears for a month, the Doctorita's mother, Anita, comes to visit.

"Oh, my," she says. "You've grown, Virginia! You get prettier by the day. You look so lovely now that you gained some weight back, dear."

I give a weak smile. I don't feel pretty—I feel stained by all the blood, always anxious it might soak through my skirt.

Later that day, I'm dusting the Baby Jesus doll, when I feel liquid trickling out of me, wetting my underwear. My tears come; I can't help it.

At that moment, Anita breezes into the room. She throws her arms around me, as though I'm her granddaughter. "What's wrong, Virginia? Did my daughter hit you? Did she yell at you?"

I shake my head and let the truth stammer out. "It's just that . . . I'm bleeding . . . between my legs . . . and—and . . . I don't understand why it's happening and I don't want it to happen." I bury my face in her shoulder. "I don't want it to happen."

She smooths my hair. "Oh, Virginia, dear, that's normal. You're turning into a woman. It's all right, Virginia."

For a long time, I sob into her shoulder. She doesn't seem to care that her pink blouse is damp with tears and snot. Once I calm down, she moves a few wet strands of hair from my cheeks. "Do you mean to tell me Romelia hasn't told you anything about this?"

I shake my head.

"When did you first start bleeding, dear?"

"A few months ago."

"And what have you been using?"

"Toilet paper. Lots and lots of toilet paper."

"Oh, my poor, dear girl."

When the Doctorita comes home from work, Anita doesn't greet her. She just says, "¡*Grosera!* How can you not think about this girl? How can you ignore her like this?"

"What are you talking about?"

"She's been having her period for months and she's scared to death about it."

The Doctorita looks at me, annoyed. "*Longa tonta,* stupid *longa,* why didn't you tell me?"

Anita puts her arm around my shoulders. "Don't talk to Virginia like that."

The Doctorita is quiet. She opens her change purse and dumps out a few coins. "Go buy some pads at the pharmacy."

That evening, Anita shows me how to put the pads on my underwear. I hate using them. They feel like diapers. I can't forget they're there, while I'm walking and talking and cleaning and reading.

Later, the next time we go to Santa Rosa, José shows me a diagram in one of his doctor books. He explains the fallopian tubes and ovaries and follicles and uterine lining. Now the diagram in *Understanding Our Universe* makes more sense.

"This is a nice, special thing," José says. "You're a woman now. It's nice."

It is not nice. "I wish I were a man," I say.

He smiles. "Now, Virginia, you have to be careful because this means you could become a mother, and you're not ready for that yet. So if boys want to touch you, don't let them. All right?"

I nod, blushing.

"Any more questions, Virginia?" he asks, shutting his book. "Anything else?"

I shake my head. But there is something else, something I can't bring myself to tell him, or anyone. I'm starting to suspect that the danger will come not from boys but from someone else.

chapter 18

THEY SAY THAT on the Day of the Dead, the veil between the living and dead is lifted, and the spirits of dead relatives come back to Earth for a night. This is not my favorite holiday. Back in Yana Urku, on the Day of the Dead, we all went to the grave-yard and my mother got drunk and cried about her dead babies and then everyone started yelling and punching each other. At least, that's how I remember it.

On my last Day of the Dead in Yana Urku, everyone gath-ered in the cemetery, as they did every year, among lopsided, blue wooden crosses on dirt mounds, where the dead people slept. The noon sun beat down on us as Mamita spread a cloth over the tiny hill of my dead baby brothers and sister. On the cloth altar, she arranged baskets of food—quinoa and cheese and hard-boiled eggs, and as a special treat for the most recently dead baby, chocolate ice cream and a bottle of Inca Kola. The ice cream melted quickly, and Mamita said, "My poor little son. Look how thirsty he was."

In a brief moment of sympathy, I thought, *Yes, these poor dead babies. They must be thirsty.* Then I thought how thirsty *I* was, and how *I* wanted a bottle of Inca Kola and chocolate ice cream.

Mamita looked sad, and I guessed she was worried that the babies were still *yumbo*—savage creatures in the darkness— since they'd never been baptized. Whenever Mamita was drunk, she moaned about her poor, wild, *yumbo* babies.

My mouth watered at the food spread out on their graves. It had been forever since I'd eaten anything besides beans, corn, and potatoes. Mamita knew my thoughts. "Don't even think about eating this, Virginia," she said through her teeth, and then went back to her mourning.

Some of the food was for the dead babies, some to exchange with other families, and some to give to the *rezadores*—the people who prayed. The *rezadores* walked solemnly to Mamita and asked if they could pray for any dead relatives of hers. She nodded and thanked them, and they prayed and prayed in their singsong voices as I drooled over the food. Finally, they stopped and she offered them cheese and eggs, my favorite. Every fiber of my body wanted that creamy cheese and those eggs and the ice cream that had already melted. *I am alive*, I wanted to scream. *I am alive and the babies are dead. Give me the food.*

Later that day, once all the grown-ups were drunk on *puro*, Papito started accusing Mamita of sleeping with the pig man. At first Mamita rolled her eyes, but then he clenched his fist and punched her in the face. That was the night he dragged her home by her hair through the cornfield, her face bouncing and bashing against rocks and dirt.

He beat her because of me, because he thought I was the daughter of the fat, ugly pig man.

No wonder Mamita couldn't love me. I was the cause of so much hatred.

No wonder, not long after that, she gave me away to the Doctorita and Niño Carlitos.

On this year's Day of the Dead, I'm staring at myself in a full-length mirror and trying not to think about the terrible graveyard celebrations of my childhood. I'm all dressed up in a new hand-me-down outfit—a rosebud-embroidered skirt and a cream blouse with little plastic pearl buttons. This gold-edged mirror is hanging in the guest room of the home of Don Joaquim, a friend of Niño Carlitos and the Doctorita's. He has invited them to this big, echoey house in Riobamba, a city famous for its festivities and dances. And they've brought me along to watch the boys at the fiesta tonight.

Don Joaquim is the friend who is supposedly helping them get transferred to the school system in Ibarra, where the Doctorita wants to live, more desperately by the day. Almost daily, she continues to harp on this idea of moving to civilization, and I continue to doubt it will ever happen, just like I doubt she'll ever get me that primary school diploma she promised.

I put on a pair of earrings, tiny gold hoops that Anita gave me for Christmas last year. I smile at my reflection, vaguely wishing that the mole near my lip would disappear. But overall, I like how I look, although I wouldn't mind if my calves were a little more slender and my belly a little flatter. I do aerobics, but just a few times a week now, and I let myself eat until I'm full, and don't worry so much about getting fat. José was right—I feel stronger and better and clearheaded now that I'm eating again.

I glance eagerly at the clock. Nine-thirty p.m. The fiesta starts around ten, and I'm giddy with the thrill of being in a different place, a place where something exciting might happen. Andrecito and Jaimito run down the hall toward the room, their little feet pounding like wild-horse hooves. They've been wound up for hours, dashing around the house, thrilled to be awake so late.

I poke my head out the door. "How do I look, boys?"

They skid to a stop. Jaimito grins shyly. "Prettier than a TV star," he says, touching the plastic pearls. Then he launches into a million questions about where pearls come from.

I tell him all about pearls and oysters. I actually know about them from a magazine article I read in the Doctorita's waiting room. I was dusting when I saw the picture: a rough shell holding slippery, slimy innards and, right in the middle, a perfect, iridescent white pearl. I stared at it for a while, in love with the idea that something so ugly could be hiding something so beautiful in its center. It took me all day to read the article, a few sentences at a time, dashing up and down stairs to do more chores in between.

Ten minutes later, on the way out the door, Jaimito is still asking me questions about oysters, when Niño Carlitos looks me over from head to toe, and says, "Virginia stays in the house."

"Why?" the Doctorita says, impatient. "She needs to watch the boys at the fiesta so we can enjoy ourselves. That's the whole reason we brought her along."

Don Joaquim and his wife are outside, waiting for us in a pool of streetlight. Jaimito and Andrecito run to them, their chubby legs and arms flailing.

"I'll keep an eye on the boys," Niño Carlitos says. "Virginia stays here."

"No, Carlos." She's growing exasperated. "You'll be wanting to drink, so we need her to watch the boys."

"But there will be guys there, and they'll—they'll be looking at her."

"Oh, don't be ridiculous. What's going to happen to her? We'll be there." She gazes at me, almost fondly. "When I was fourteen, I loved going out at night. It's a treat at her age."

Unbelievable. For once the Doctorita is taking my side, sticking up for me. For once I'm glad she can be so stubborn and bossy. She tugs on his arm.

He doesn't budge. "I want her to stay here." The look in his eyes is bordering on crazy. I glance nervously at the others waiting for us outside.

"Why are you being like this, Carlos? Virginia is coming with us. And that's that."

He looks at his feet and his face hardens. But he doesn't stop me as I breeze past him out the door.

We walk in the darkness, only a few streetlamps lighting the way. When we reach downtown, people dressed in black are parading solemnly through the streets: nuns carrying crosses; men and women holding candles, the tiny flames lighting up their faces eerily. We follow the procession to the cemetery, which glows with thousands of candles and smells of dripping beeswax. I shiver, and keep glancing behind me into the shadows, as though my mother and father are trailing me like ghosts. I wonder if I feel dead to them, too. I wonder if Mamita went to the graveyard today and left Inca Kola and melting ice cream for me along with her other dead children.

Now people are trickling out of the graveyard and moving to the streets. We turn a corner and suddenly the atmosphere changes. Bright lights illuminate the street like a stage. Smells of roasted guinea pig and potatoes and chicken and corn fill the air. Food stands line the street, with blue and orange awnings and wooden stools and plastic chairs and heaps of salads and steaming meats on display. Music blasts from giant speakers— my favorite *cumbias*—and soon a crowd is dancing in the street.

It's amazing how around the corner, the world can change so drastically. I wish my life would turn a corner. With Andrecito on one side of me and Jaimito on the other, we sit in a section of chairs at the street's edge and watch women and men swirl and dip and spin and move to the rhythms. The women's faces are radiant, their jewelry flashing, hair flowing. I smooth my skirt and wonder how it would feel if someone was spinning me around, how the silky fabric would fly out around me.

And then a boy who looks about fifteen or sixteen comes up to me and holds out his hand and shyly asks, "Excuse me, señorita. Will you dance with me?"

My heart flutters. He's handsome, wearing polished black shoes and a neat orange button-down shirt tucked into his ironed pants. Tiny beads of sweat glisten on his upper lip. I look at the Doctorita hopefully. She smiles and nods, a wistful look in her eyes, as though she is reliving her first dance through me. "Go ahead. I'll watch the boys for a while. Enjoy yourself."

I want to laugh from pure happiness, but I bite my lip and offer the boy my hand. He pulls me into the crowd and we dance a *cumbia* with plenty of spinning, just like the students at the *colegio* do during school dances. I let the melody carry me and move my feet and sway my body. I love how his hand feels in my hand, warm and damp, and how his other hand feels resting on my hip. My face grows moist and my ponytail swings and my skirt billows out. I am flying and floating, light as a petal.

At the end of the song, the boy says, "Thank you, señorita."

"Thank you," I say, hoping he'll ask me to dance the next song. He's still holding my hand when I hear my name.

"Virginia!" Niño Carlitos cries out. "Virginia!" With drunken, angry gestures, he motions for me to come.

I smile an apology at the boy, then reluctantly pull my hand away and walk to Niño Carlitos.

Up close, his face is red, the vein on his forehead popping out. "No more dancing for you," he says.

The Doctorita rolls her eyes. "That's silly, Carlos. We're all here watching her. Nothing can happen."

"No. Look at all these guys. They only have one thing on their mind."

As they argue, Niño Carlitos's face grows redder, nearly purple, and his voice louder and angrier.

I sit on the plastic chair and watch everyone else laughing and dancing. My eyes narrow and my jaw sticks out. I do not play with Jaimito or Andrecito or smile or joke or say one word. Meanwhile, the Doctorita gossips with her friend and Niño Carlitos drinks liquor with his friend, his eyes glued to me. He does not leave me for a second. He refuses to dance with the Doctorita. When I stand up to stretch my legs and get my sweater out of the bag, he follows me, reeking of liquor.

More boys ask me to dance, but before I can answer, Niño Carlitos barks, "No." And then the Doctorita says how silly he's being and then he yells at her and she says he's embarrassing her and they argue some more.

Under Niño Carlitos's gaze, I fume. This is my life: waiting and watching other people have fun and go to school and dance together. Always watching, but never allowed to join in. Reading and dancing in secret, alone in the house, living a life in dreams and fantasies. Around me, the music and lights and colors whirl and pulse. Inside me, dark shadows gather, like the somber procession of the dead.

I've heard that some fathers can be overprotective, that this is how they show love. Is this Niño Carlitos's idea of fatherly love? But there's something more, a crazy intensity to his gaze. Something like jealousy.

chapter 19

FOR HIS FOURTH BIRTHDAY, Andrecito gets a set of colored letter magnets that you can arrange on the refrigerator to spell words. If the magnets come close to metal, they stick and won't let go until you pry them off. But if you try to move two magnets close together, they jump away from each other. In *Understanding Our Universe*, I read that a magnet's north pole attracts another magnet's south pole, but it repels another magnet's north pole.

Slowly, I begin to notice that whenever Niño Carlitos and I are alone in the house, a magnetic force seems to pull his hands toward my body. At first he begins touching my shoulder more often, and then lets his hand linger there, longer each time. Then he starts finding any excuse to hug me. *Oh,* m'hija, *you're such a good cook.* M'hija, *thank you for cleaning up so well. You're so smart,* m'hija. *So beautiful. I'm so lucky to have you. . . .* Words I've always dreamed of hearing from my own father. For a little while, I glow in his attention.

But then he starts coming home from school earlier than the Doctorita, creeping up behind me and wrapping his arms around my shoulders and pressing against my back. And I feel myself moving away, as though his north pole is approaching my north pole.

I squirm out of his grasp, laughing nervously. "I have to work, Niño Carlitos," I say. "I'm busy." I whiz around the kitchen with fast, jumpy movements, avoiding his hands.

He doesn't want the Doctorita to see him touching me, that is obvious. When he hears her key in the lock, he jumps away and walks quickly into the living room. Is he afraid she'll feel jealous of him treating me like a daughter? *Is* he treating me like a daughter? Is this how fathers treat their daughters? On TV, daughters sometimes sit on their fathers' laps and the fathers pat their backs and kiss their cheeks. Maybe this is what Niño Carlitos is trying to do, to treat me like a daughter. Maybe the reason it makes me nervous is that I'm not used to it. Maybe I just have to get used to it.

There's a full moon, and it's late at night, and I'm peering out my window at Niño Carlitos, who is drunk and banging on the front door. He hardly ever drinks, only at fiestas, or sometimes with his friends at a bar, like tonight. The rule is that I have to answer the door if the Doctorita is asleep, so I pad down the hallway in my nightgown, groggy. On the way downstairs, the shock of the cold tile on my feet wakes me up, makes me suddenly scared. I rub my goose-bumped arms and open the door.

Niño Carlitos sways there, his eyes droopy and red, giving me a strange look. It's the look of a hungry dog salivating over food. His voice creeps out, low and guttural. "Come here, *m'hija*."

I turn to run back upstairs but he grabs my arm, pushes me hard against the wall. He presses his body close to mine and rubs his hands over my bare arms. His face moves toward mine. I turn my head and he kisses my cheek, leaving a slobbery wet spot. I try to push him away but he's too strong. Finally, I manage to duck beneath his arms and run outside, into the shadows behind the truck in the driveway. The yard is thick with trees and bushes, and surrounded by a tall metal fence. The gate at the end of the driveway is always locked with a key at night.

"Virginia!" Niño Carlitos yells. Luckily, he's drunk enough that it takes him a moment to follow me. "Come here! I order you to come here."

Terrified, I crouch behind the truck's tire. Maybe he forgot to lock the gate tonight. Maybe I can make a run for it.

"Virginia," he says, his voice growing closer. He's on the other side of the truck, just a few meters away. I see his shoes. I can either run for the gate and hope it's unlocked, or try to stay hidden.

"The gate's locked," he calls out, as if he's read my mind. "I know you're here somewhere."

I slide underneath the truck, shaking, my face pressed to the concrete driveway that smells of motor oil. I try not to make any noise as I cry. Even as drunk as he is, it's only a matter of time before he looks under the truck.

"Virginia!" he shouts. "I want a glass of water! I order you to serve me water!"

I press my hand to my mouth and bite my thumb, stifling my sobs.

Then the Doctorita's voice breaks the night, faint, from inside the house. "What's going on?"

Niño Carlitos's voice is slurred. "This *longa* doesn't want to serve me water."

He has never called me a *longa* before.

"Virginia!" the Doctorita yells. "Get Carlos his water."

Reluctantly, I emerge from under the truck, into the moonlight. Niño Carlitos watches me, furious. I dart past him. He follows me inside, and to my relief, the Doctorita is standing in the hallway, hands on her hips. "Come to bed, you drunk!" she says, pushing Niño Carlitos up the stairs. "Get him his water," she calls to me over her shoulder.

I grab a glass of water from the kitchen and carry it to their room. Niño Carlitos watches me through squinty, half-closed eyelids as I place the glass on the bedside table. I hurry down the hall and close my door, then scan the room for the heaviest piece of furniture I can move. There's the sewing machine table that they store in here. I push it in front of the door and sit on the edge of the bed, gripping the mattress.

In fifteen minutes he's knocking on my door. "Open up!" he growls in a loud whisper.

I stand up, ready to hurl all my weight against the table. What will the Doctorita say if she wakes up and sees this? Somehow, she'll blame me.

More knocking. "Open the door! I order you."

The knob turns and the door inches forward. I push on the table with every last bit of strength.

After what feels like forever, he stops, and I hear his uneven footsteps as he staggers down the hall to his bedroom. All night

I lie awake with my body tensed, ready to leap up at the slightest noise.

If this is how fathers treat their daughters, I don't want one after all.

"Can I please have some more eggs, *m'hija?*" Niño Carlitos asks the next morning at breakfast.

I scoop more eggs onto his plate, keeping as far from him as possible.

"Thank you, *m'hija. Rrriquísimo.* Really delicious." He looks tired and worn, yet he's treating me as if last night never happened. Have I overreacted? Am I the crazy one?

A few days later, on the way to cut alfalfa for the guinea pigs, I spot Doña Mercedes feeding her chickens. Seeing her always lifts my spirits. "Hello, Doña Mercedes."

"Hello, Virginia." She speaks in a mild, pleasant way and smells like rose-scented soap. She's the one person in town who never gossips or says bad things about people. "Pretty day, isn't it, dear?"

I nod. We talk a bit about the weather and the chickens and Marina's crush on Chayanne.

Doña Mercedes scatters the last of the corn kernels and then studies my face. "Are you all right, Virginia?"

"Mmm," I say.

"You look . . . troubled about something." If only she were my mother.

I take a deep breath, still staring at the chickens, unable to meet her eyes. "Doña Mercedes, tell me, how do fathers show love for their daughters?"

"What do you mean, dear?"

"Well, for example, can fathers grab their daughters here? Or here? Can they touch them like this?"

Doña Mercedes sinks down onto a tree stump, puts her hand over her mouth.

I keep talking, because once I start talking, it feels good. "Can fathers hug them a lot and press against them a lot?"

Doña Mercedes stares at me long and hard. "Who's doing this to you, Virginia?"

"Oh, no one," I say casually, keeping my gaze on the chickens. "I was just wondering."

"Virginia?" She takes my hand. "Don Carlos isn't doing this to you, is he?"

I hesitate. Finally, I say, "No. No, no, no. No, he's not doing this to me."

"Why don't you talk with the Doctorita about this?"

"No!" I loosen my hand from hers. "Please, Doña Mercedes, just answer my question." My lip is quivering. "Tell me how fathers show love to their daughters."

She sighs. "Well, fathers love them and respect them. But fathers can't touch them like that. Don't let anyone touch you like that, Virginia. Understand?"

"Yes, well, I was just wondering. Thank you, Doña Mercedes." And off I run at top speed.

The next time Niño Carlitos comes up behind me like a magnet, I duck away and run to my room and shut the door. Again, I think about telling the Doctorita, but I know she'll find a way to make it my fault. I'm the one with something to lose. Not Niño Carlitos.

I'll have to handle this on my own.

* * *

Whenever you're in a tricky situation, it's a good idea to ask yourself, *What would MacGyver do?*

I'm pondering this question as I sweep the Doctorita's waiting room, near the front door, where dirt from patients' shoes always builds up.

The answer is easy: he would carefully observe his environment to see what materials he could use to make a simple machine, like a pulley or a lever. For instance, in rocky terrain, he would wedge a branch under a heavy stone and make it roll down a mountain toward his enemies. In the jungle, he'd rig up vines to drop coconuts on his enemies' heads.

And just like that, I see the solution play out in my mind, complete with the *MacGyver* sound track: Niño Carlitos walks through the doorway, eager to press against me, but this time I'm ready. I pull a rope and—*bam!*—a rock falls onto his head, smack onto his bald spot. He staggers, dizzy, and then falls, right onto his face. When he comes to, I say, *Try to touch me again, buddy, and there's another rock with your name on it.* He rubs his head and begs, *Forgive me,* m'hija. *I'll never bother you again.* After that, he transforms back into the old Niño Carlitos, the simple, sweet, stuttering one who used to build toys for Jaimito and me.

Perfect plan. But a rock could get me in trouble. It might even kill him. And no coconuts grow in Kunu Yaku. I look around the room for a substitute. Spider plants and rhododendrons hang from the ceiling, dangling their leaves. Conveniently, one plant hangs just inside the doorway, its vines trailing all around the room.

I glance at the clock: 12:45. He'll be home in fifteen minutes. Excited, I toss aside the broom and run to the kitchen for some twine that will blend in with the vines. I stand on a chair and tie the twine to the plant's hook. Then I lay the rope over the ceiling hook, pull it taut, and fasten it to the leg of a nearby chair. I survey my work. The plant is in a plastic pot, not a ceramic one, and only medium-sized, not so heavy that it will actually kill Niño Carlitos. Hopefully it will just knock him out for a little while.

I sit on the waiting-room chair with the twine tied onto its leg, watching the clock. The broom, my alibi, leans against my knees. When footsteps sound on the path and a key rattles in the lock, I untie the twine from the chair and hold it, the weight of the plant pulling at it. The door swings open and I let go of the rope. The plant crashes to the floor.

Just behind Niño Carlitos.

I jump.

He jumps. "What the—!"

I drop the broom and act shocked, which isn't hard because the crash was very loud and sent my heart racing. "Oh no!"

He stands by his schoolbag, shaken and confused, looking up at the ceiling and down at the overturned plant in a pile of dirt. "La Negra and her stupid houseplants! What if I'd been a patient?" And he stomps upstairs, cursing the Doctorita.

Not exactly what I envisioned, but not bad. Not bad at all. With a secret, smug smile, I remove the rope from the scene of the crime and clean up the dirt, patting it carefully around the plant. Only a few leaves were crushed, and the roots are fine. No injuries serious enough to interfere with photosynthesis and respiration, I hope. I give the plant some water and whisper it an apology.

That afternoon Niño Carlitos does not try to hug me or

161

touch me. Even though the plant didn't crash onto his bald spot, I consider my plan a success. And there's an unexpected bonus: when the Doctorita comes home from school with the boys, he yells at her about her stupid houseplants.

Later, after our chicken and lentil dinner, Niño Carlitos says, "Thank you, *m'hija*. That was *rrriquísimo*."

The Doctorita pushes away her empty plate and eyes me suspiciously. "Did you make that plant fall, Virginia?"

"Of course not."

"Then it was just a coincidence you were there when it happened?"

"I guess." I start clearing the table. She is on to me. And although this fact dampens my armpits with nervous sweat, it feels good to know she realizes I'm more than just a simple servant girl.

Niño Carlitos steps to my defense, just like the old days, when he was my bodyguard. "Negra, don't try to blame this on la Virginia. It was your dumb idea to hang a plant over the door. An accident waiting to happen. Any fool could have seen that."

Once he leaves the table, the Doctorita looks at me doubtfully. "No more *MacGyver* for you," she hisses. "That's where you get these ideas, isn't it?"

Standing straight, keeping my chin high, I meet her gaze. For a stretched-out moment, our eyes lock. Hers are wary, almost nervous, and finally flicker away to the window. There's the tiniest tremble in her voice as she says, "You're not the innocent little victim that Carlos makes you out to be."

* * *

Now I can only watch *MacGyver* in secret, when the Doctorita isn't around. And now that the show is forbidden, an extra thrill runs through me at the theme song. Triumphant music that assures you MacGyver will always win in the end. All along you know this, but still, in the middle of the show when he's tied up and a bomb is about to explode, you hold your breath and dig your fingernails into your palms. Then, just before the bomb explodes, he cuts himself loose and dives for cover, and you breathe out and nearly cry with relief.

Then he is happy and everything is good . . . until next week.

The flowerpot incident doesn't exactly solve the problem of Niño Carlitos, but it does make me feel stronger and smarter. I become an expert at finding ways to avoid being alone with him. In the afternoons, I watch for him through the window, and if I see him walking home alone from school, I dash out on an errand. If the Doctorita goes to bed early, leaving me by myself to wash the dishes, I just pile them in the sink for the next morning and go straight to my room and shut the door.

Still, it's tiring to always be on guard, always peering out the window, looking over my shoulder. How much longer can I keep this up? It's only a matter of time before he catches me alone, before he comes home late at night drunk again. But as any *MacGyver* episode will show you, when things look bleakest, that's about the time you turn a corner.

chapter 20

ONE AFTERNOON, I'm pasturing the cow on the *colegio* grounds, walking along the concrete wall of the school. I turn the corner, and suddenly I'm face to face with a boy.

"Ay!" I jump back.

He has brown eyes, not as dark as mine. The color of coffee with a little cream swirled in. Or those delicious caramel milk candies. He looks surprised, in a happy way. He tucks a strand of wavy hair behind his ear, only to have it slip out again and hang over his cheek. I smile a little at that, and then he smiles a little, and then I keep walking, my heart pounding. I feel him watch me go.

After that, I notice him whenever I pasture the cow or cut grass for the guinea pigs near the *colegio*. He hangs out there, under the avocado trees, with a group of guys my age. Most of them are students who have chatted with the Doctorita and Niño Carlitos and me before. When I pass them, I blush, but I don't change my route.

I notice that he's usually talking with Leo, one of the Doctorita's students, a lanky, friendly guy. But I don't recognize this boy as a student at the *colegio*. As I pass, I watch him out of the corner of my eye. He's always watching me, too.

I walk slowly, memorizing his slim waist, his muscled arms, the small, charming ponytail at the base of his neck. I like the way he moves, kind of swaying along like a branch in the breeze, at ease in the world. Sometimes he picks a piece of grass and sticks it in his mouth and chews on it thoughtfully as he looks at me. When I come close, he sits up straighter and tucks loose strands of hair behind his ears.

As I pass him, I grow very conscious of the frayed rope in my hand leading the cow, and the rhythm of my ponytail swinging back and forth behind me. I start sneaking a little gel into my hair before my walks, making it smooth and shiny, and secretly wearing the Doctorita's lip gloss.

I hope we run into each other again, because next time, maybe I won't pull back. Maybe I'll let myself fall into him.

A few weeks after running into the boy, I'm on my way to the store to buy eggs, walking quickly, weaving around slower people crowding the sidewalk. As always, the Doctorita has given me the same warning. "Five minutes. Don't talk with anyone. If you see someone you know, *buenos días*, and come right back."

I'm zipping along when I spot him half a block in front of me, heading my way. I slow my pace and move my eyes straight ahead so he won't think I'm staring.

"*Hola, guapa*," he says as he draws nearer. *Hello, beautiful.* No boy has ever called me beautiful before. His eyes dance and

I can't help smiling. Heat rises to my face, and suddenly I feel embarrassed. I force my feet to keep walking.

Again, I feel him watch me go. He whistles through his teeth, a low whispery whistle. Tickles spread over my skin, feathery light.

I buy the eggs, flustered, and on the way back I see him again, leaning against a wall, waiting for me.

He straightens up and asks, "May I walk with you, señorita?"

I laugh. Then, unsure what else to do, I run back to the house as fast as I can.

A few days later, at the *colegio*, some students are talking to the Doctorita after science class. I'm standing beside her, holding hands with Jaimito and Andrecito. The boy who called me beautiful walks over with Leo and some other friends. Immediately my heart starts hammering.

"Good afternoon, Doctorita," he says.

"Good afternoon," she replies.

He looks at me with singing eyes. "Good afternoon."

"Good afternoon," I say softly.

"I'm Antonio." He extends his hand. "What's your name?"

"Virginia."

His hand feels rough and calloused, but his grip is gentle. Muscles and veins ripple his forearm, like the arm of someone who works in fields all day.

I glance at the Doctorita to see if she notices my flushed face. But now she's talking to him and I barely hear what she's saying because the rush of blood has filled my ears. It sounds like they're having a normal conversation about the weather and the crops. Then Antonio starts talking to Jaimito and

166

Andrecito; after a while, he says goodbye and looks at me for a long moment. "Nice to meet you, Virginia."

"Nice to meet you, Antonio."

On the way back from the *colegio*, the Doctorita says, "What a nice young man. Such good manners. And handsome, isn't he?"

"Yes, I think so," I say casually.

"He was a good student," the Doctorita says. "He had to stop school at eighth grade to help his family work in the fields. What a shame."

"Yes, what a shame," I say, already feeling a bond with him. "A real shame."

The boys are asleep and Niño Carlitos is out with his friends, and the Doctorita and I are watching the latest episode of *The Slave Isaura*. It's the Doctorita's and my favorite soap opera, about a beautiful slave from Brazil in the 1800s. Like me, Isaura is a servant. Like me, she sometimes buries her face in her arms and sobs over her cruel destiny. But also like me, she knows how to read and write and dreams of freedom.

And like me, she's forbidden to have a boyfriend.

But Isaura escapes to be with her true love, and together, they start leading a normal life in a town where no one knows she was ever a slave.

This episode is an exciting one. Isaura's evil master, Leoncio, has hunted her down and announced to her neighbors that she's really his runaway slave. I keep wishing that MacGyver would make a guest appearance, but I figure he wouldn't have been alive back then. He really would have come in handy, though. Isaura's true love tries to defend her, but without

167

knowledge of booby-trapping, he fails, and Leoncio drags her back to his mansion.

"You pig!" the Doctorita shouts at the TV. "Let the poor girl live in peace, Leoncio!"

Strange how the Doctorita always calls Isaura's evil master a pig, yet she doesn't think of herself as a pig. She claims it's wrong he keeps poor Isaura as a slave, yet she doesn't think it's wrong she keeps me.

Am I a slave? A place beneath my ribs hurts when I think about this. She doesn't pay me. She acts as though she owns me. I'm unclear whether she bought me or stole me or whether my parents gave me away. She never shackles me with chains, but she beats me. And Niño Carlitos acts as though he has certain rights with me, the way the slave masters think they have rights with the girls on their plantation.

The masters on *The Slave Isaura* think it's perfectly normal to own slaves. Maybe the Doctorita thinks it's perfectly normal to keep an unpaid *longa* servant. Maybe she doesn't see that really, it's the same terrible thing—trying to own another person. And maybe, like those slave masters, Niño Carlitos thinks it's natural for a boss to put his hands all over a *longa* servant.

The Doctorita sniffs and snorts, her eyes spilling over with tears for Isaura. "What a pig, that Leoncio. How could he do this to poor, sweet Isaura? We can only pray that one day she'll be free." And she blows her nose loudly in her cross-stitched handkerchief, freshly washed and ironed by me, the unpaid servant, sitting on the floor below her.

* * *

168

I'm leading the cow to the *colegio* grounds, my hair shining, my lips glossed, my flowered skirt swishing around my knees. And when I spot Antonio there, waiting for me, my heart melts.

"*Hola,* Virginia," he says.

"*Hola,* Antonio."

"So, how've you been?"

"Good."

"What have you been up to?"

"Same as always," I say. "Cleaning the house and taking care of the boys and pasturing the cow."

"Oh." He nods enthusiastically, as though I've said something fascinating. "Do you like pasturing the cow?"

"It's all right."

He takes a deep breath. "Virginia, would you—would you like to go out with me sometime? Maybe for a walk? There's a pretty stream not far from here. Sometimes you can even see fish in it. And there are pebbles that look really pretty underwater. And once I saw a deer drinking there."

As he's talking, I'm realizing how impossible this is. I'm forbidden to go out with boys. If anyone saw us walking together, word would spread quickly. The Doctorita would kill me and Niño Carlitos would kill poor Antonio.

"I'm sorry," I say. "I can't." I feel my eyes glisten like Isaura's. Her true love is an abolitionist who fights for the freedom of slaves. Their love is impossible too. Of course, the impossibility of love makes it all the more exciting.

Antonio's eyes grow wet with tears. He clears his throat. "You don't like . . . streams?"

"I do, Antonio, but I'm not allowed to go out with a boy."

He looks at me for a long time, until I say, "I should go," and lead the cow away. As always, I feel him watch me leave. On *The Slave Isaura*, when Isaura and her true love cry together, it means they are bound to one another, no matter what happens.

The next evening, I'm upstairs making the bed, folding the sheet back one, two, three times, when I hear music blaring on the street. It's one of my favorite romantic songs, *"Estrellita de la tarde"*—Little Evening Star. The singer has a passionate voice that reaches right inside your chest and clutches your heart. I smooth the sheet, then walk down the hallway to see where the music's coming from. It's too early for a school dance—the sun is barely setting over the mountains, its rays still long and angled through the windows.

I step onto the balcony, and there he is, Antonio, across the street from my house, with a boom box at his feet. A smile spreads across his face when he sees me. I smile back and let the music wrap around me. *You rise to the window and give light to my life. . . .*

As the song ends, he points to me and mouths *you* and then points to his ear—*listen*. The next song is a string of all the golden words I've ever wished someone would tell me—*I love you, I want you, I need you*. Oooy! My heart is flipping and dancing around and I laugh from sheer joy. People are passing by on the street, and they glance at Antonio and his boom box, thinking he's just some kid blasting music.

But for me the sky is parting and a piece of heaven is pouring through, all liquid gold and papaya pink, shining on

Antonio and me, and my heart opens and our spirits rise up and swirl together and it is the most magical, miraculous thing that has ever happened in the history of the universe.

"You don't have a boyfriend, do you, Virginia?" the Doctorita demands as I wash the dishes.

"Why do you think that?" I ask, rinsing the last plate.

"Because you've been smiling nonstop the past two days."

"I'm just happy is all." I arrange the plate in the rack.

"You'd better not be seeing anyone. If Carlos found out, that would be the end of you and the boy, you hear?"

I nod and dry my hands on the dish towel, but even the Doctorita's threats can't wipe the smile off my face.

chapter 21

WHEN THE WEEKEND COMES, the Doctorita and Niño Carlitos and the boys plan to go to Quito to stay with relatives, leaving me alone in the house. The Doctorita gives the usual warnings: "Don't leave the house, Virginia. You know we have the whole neighborhood watching you. I don't want to hear that you went out except to feed the guinea pigs and pasture the cow."

Niño Carlitos looks at me for a moment. "Be good, *m'hija*," is all he says. But the edge to his voice makes clear this is a warning. Be good *or else*.

Later in the morning, there's a knock on the door. It's Leo.

"*Hola*," I say nervously, hoping no neighbors are looking.

"*Hola*." He looks as nervous as I am. "Antonio wants to talk to you."

"About what?" I ask.

He shrugs. "When can he come?"

"This evening," I say. "When it's getting dark. That way no one will see him."

I do my chores, dancing around with the stereo blasting romantic *cumbias*. I play *"Estrellita de la tarde"*—which I managed to record from the radio—over and over again all afternoon. The ball of excitement in my stomach won't let me eat much lunch. I let my hair fall long and loose around my face, which I can never do when the Doctorita is around. I dab on her lip gloss and silver eye shadow and a touch of blush. And I sit by the door, too giddy to read, just waiting in the fading light. I keep the lamps off so that no one will see Antonio's shadow through the curtains when he comes.

I imagine his visit, see him taking me in his strong arms and kissing me, a long, passionate kiss. *Virginia, my beautiful little evening star, you are the girl of my dreams. You give light to my life. I love you, I want you, I need you.*

At dusk, a soft knock. I swing open the door, let Antonio in, and close the door quickly behind him, praying no one has seen. And here we stand, alone. A faint scent of cologne hovers around him, the kind they sell at the corner drugstore. His just-ironed shirt looks light blue, though it's hard to tell in the dim light. His work boots smell of fresh polish.

I rub my lips together, feeling the gloss, smooth and sticky. "Hi, Antonio." I search for simple small-talk words, but none come to mind, so I ask, "Um, what did you want to talk to me about?"

He pushes a loose strand of hair behind his ear and it falls right out again, over his eyes. "From the first time I saw you, Virginia, I liked you a lot." The words sound rehearsed, as though he was practicing the whole way over here. "I really like you and I'd really like it if you could be my girlfriend." He looks at me hopefully.

173

I feel flooded with something—joy and fear all gushing together. I say nothing, thinking of the Doctorita's threats, thinking of Niño Carlitos's jealous gaze, of how dangerous it is for Antonio to be here.

He keeps talking, rambling, his words flowing more naturally now. "The first time I saw you, you looked like a princess leading around that cow. Like those stories where a princess has to live in disguise as a peasant. You know? I saw you and I wanted to touch your hair. It's the longest hair I've ever seen, a princess's hair. Have you ever cut it? And every day when I watched you, I said to myself, *This girl has a light inside her.* Do you know that? Everyone else has just a tiny candle flame, but you have a giant sun inside. From the first time I saw you, I knew this."

My face is hot. I don't know what to say. I fiddle with a plastic pearl button on my blouse.

He takes a step toward me. "We're old enough, Virginia. How old are you?"

"I—I don't know."

He gives me a strange look. "Well, when were you born?"

"I don't know. What about you?"

"I'm fifteen," he says.

"Well, I think I'm about fourteen," I say. "I don't know my exact age. See, I was born . . . on a farm."

"Me too! I was born on a farm. And now I work in the fields with my family."

I keep talking. "My parents, well, I don't even know if they have my birth certificate because they don't really read—"

"Neither do my parents!"

"Then I came here to work for the Doctorita when I was a

little girl." I look at his face in the near-darkness, made of tiny points of blue and purple. It makes me feel safe, this time between day and night, as though we're floating together in an in-between place where anything is possible. "Antonio, do you know the soap opera *The Slave Isaura?*"

"I've seen it at Leo's. I like that guy who fights the slave owners, you know, Isaura's boyfriend."

"See, Antonio, that's kind of like my life." My story tumbles out, gaining momentum like a boulder rolling down a mountain. Well, most of my story falls out. Not the part about being born a *longa*. But that's easy to hide, since I don't dress in *indígena* blouses and *anacos* or speak Quichua anymore. And my dark complexion doesn't necessarily mean anything; Antonio's *mestizo* skin is even darker than mine from working in the fields all day. The only possible giveaway is my long, long hair, but in Antonio's eyes, this just lends me a royal presence.

I don't say anything about how my parents don't want me either. Or about what's going on with Niño Carlitos. But I tell him the rest—studying in secret and watching the students walk by in their uniforms and longing to go to school and dreaming of leaving the Doctorita one day.

"Virginia," he says, "we're perfect for each other! What do you say? About being my girlfriend? The Doctorita doesn't have to find out. I'll just come to see you in secret."

Keeping a secret in this town isn't easy. It would be just a matter of time before Niño Carlitos and the Doctorita killed us both. "No, Antonio. No, no, no, no, I can't. It's too risky. You should go."

Sometimes dreams do come true, exactly how you want them to. In the blue twilight, he reaches out and touches my

175

hair, then takes me in his arms and lightly presses his lips to mine. The kiss lasts only a second, a fleeting feeling of his lips soft yet a little chapped. My knees go rubbery and we look at each other like we share an incredible secret. Then I giggle. "You have to go," I whisper, pushing him out the door.

"¡Gracias, mi amor!" he says.

"Go, Antonio, go!"

He leaves and I lean against the door and feel every electron in my body vibrating, alive. I move my fingers to where he kissed my lips. In a happy daze I float upstairs and lie on the red sofa feeling soft as *gelatina*, playing the scene over and over and over again in the darkness.

Being a secret-agent student has been good training for having a secret boyfriend. It comes naturally to me. Leo knocks on our door almost daily, claiming he has a question for the Doctorita about schoolwork. "Excuse me, Doctorita. I didn't understand this part of the lesson today. Could you go over it one more time?"

And as the Doctorita explains—with patience the first time, and exasperation by the fifth time—I hang around, sweeping or mopping nearby. When I walk nonchalantly behind Leo, he presses a note into my hand. The notes are always tiny and folded up, and I clutch each one so tightly it's damp with sweat by the time I open it.

The first one reads:

> Dear Virginia,
> I ♥ you!
> Love, Antonio

The next:

> Dear Virginia,
>> When can I see you?
>>> Love,
>>> Antonio

And the one after that:

> Dear Virginia,
>> You're the girl of my dreams!
>>> Love,
>>> Antonio

Soon everyday life becomes more thrilling than an episode of *The Slave Isaura*. When I run errands, Antonio always seems to be nearby, waiting for me, smiling at me. I smile back, our secret smile, and keep walking along, feeling like an undercover princess with my shiny long ponytail swinging behind me.

One perfect Sunday afternoon—not too hot, not too cold, just blue-skied and brilliant—the Doctorita and Jaimito and Andrecito and I are walking back from feeding the guinea pigs, passing a soccer game on the field. I strain my eyes to see if Antonio is playing, and yes, there he is, the goalie, looking handsome in his bright white jersey. He's pacing back and forth in the goal, ready to throw his body in front of the ball. His legs are even more muscular than his arms. Pieces of hair fall loose from his ponytail and he brushes them behind his ear in that little movement that makes me feel all liquidy.

And then, unbelievably, the Doctorita says, "Why don't we

177

stay and watch the game a while? Some of my students are play-ing. There's that pesky string bean Leo who always bothers me about his homework. See?"

We settle down in the grass on the sidelines, near midfield. By this time Antonio has spotted me and keeps glancing over. I smile and raise my hand just a little, so the Doctorita won't notice.

I whisper to Jaimito, "Run over there." He's used to being an accomplice in my plans, so he doesn't question me, just starts running along the sidelines toward the goal.

"I'll keep an eye on him," I tell the Doctorita. So I chase after him, and when I get close, I whisper, "Keep running Jaim-ito, all the way to the goal."

I run after him. Luckily the ball is on the other side of the field, so no one's looking in our direction.

"*Mi amor*," Antonio says. "You've come to see me!"

"Yes, Antonio, but pretend you're not talking to me. Just look straight ahead." Meanwhile, I pretend to play with Jaimito.

"All right, but I want to look at you so badly. I want to hold you, *mi amor*. When can we be together?"

"We can't. The Doctorita would kill me." I sneak a look at him. "But I want to tell you how much I love your notes. And I want to tell you . . ." I hesitate. I want to tell him a million things. Finally I settle on, "Good luck in your game."

"I'm dedicating this game to you, *mi amor*. I'm going to win." Then he looks at me.

"Don't look!" I laugh.

"Please, *mi amor*, escape from the house some night and I'll come to meet you."

"I can't. The Doctorita locks the door every night." I glance over at her. She's looking the other way, busy talking to a student's mother.

"Please," Antonio begs. "Somehow, find a way to escape!"

"Antonio, she's like a wild dog when she's mad. And I don't even want to think what Niño Carlitos would do to you."

He looks at me again. "Remember that I love you, wherever you are, even if we can't be together."

"I love you too, Antonio." Then, shyly, I add, "Something inside me feels so happy when I see you. Even when I just think about seeing you."

"That kiss I gave you," he says. "It was my first kiss."

"It was my first kiss, too!"

And then the ball flies down to our end of the field and he blows me my second kiss.

The next day, when I come back from pasturing the cow, the Doctorita is in an unusually good mood, listening to music, waltzing around the house, her cheeks rosy. She almost looks pretty, the way she does in her wedding photos.

"Listen, Virginia!" she says. "Those fools finally gave us the jobs! We're going to live in Ibarra!"

I blink.

"One more week! Soon we'll be living in civilization! Can you believe it?"

I feel numb.

"Well?" she says. "Aren't you happy?"

"That's great," I say, and barely make it to my room before the tears come. I muffle my sobs in my damp pillow. The slave Isaura often cries over being apart from her freedom-fighter boyfriend, only she wears an enormous hoopskirt, so when she sinks to the floor in anguish she looks graceful in her pool of satin and lace, overflowing with angst and beauty. I am not as graceful. My face grows sticky from mucus and tears, and I punch my pillow, hard, over and over again, until finally I throw it against the wall.

chapter 22

WITH A GIANT LUMP IN MY THROAT, I trudge around the *colegio* grounds beside the cow, through sunny clumps of weeds and wildflowers. We'll be getting rid of the cow since Ibarra is a big city. A bee flies from one blossom to another, burying half its body in the petals, emerging coated with pollen, intent on its task. Will there be wildflower pollination in Ibarra? All I've seen of the city are concrete buildings, cement sidewalks. Not a single bee. Will I be able to see the stars and remember how small my problems really are? And will I meet anyone there who cares about me as much as Antonio does?

I turn the corner, and there he is, Antonio, standing by the avocado trees with his friends. When he spots me, he jogs over. The sun lights him up from behind like a saint, illuminating his hair and the tips of the grass and leaves. "*¡Mi amor!*" he says.

Before I can say anything, my lip quivers out of control and the tears leak out. "Antonio, I have to leave." I wipe my face with my sleeve. "The Doctorita and Niño Carlitos got jobs in Ibarra and we have to leave in a week and—and—"

Antonio looks at me, his eyes wet. "Do you want to go?"

"No! But I don't have a choice."

"You always have a choice." His voice grows determined. "Why not tell them you're staying here, with me?"

"Because the Doctorita would put me in the cemetery." I wish we were alone so that I could touch him. I can tell his friends are watching us, curious. Instead, I run my hands over the cow's coarse fur, over the black spot between her ears where she likes being scratched.

"But I love you, Virginia. What about me?"

"I don't know." I stare at the cow's black spot. "Maybe you can come to the city and find me."

He looks at the mountains, then closes his eyes for a long moment. "Escape with me, Virginia. I'm serious. Stay with me here. With me and my family. We can get married. There's a parcel of land my father will give me when I'm married. We can farm it together."

His eyes are so full of passion, that suddenly anything seems possible. "Really, Antonio? You mean it?"

"Yes, *mi amor*."

"Then let's do it."

He takes a step closer. "I want to hold you so badly right now. Can I hug you?"

"No, people might see." I glance around anxiously. "So how should I escape?"

He thinks for a moment. "I could ask my older sister to come for you. Maybe at night when the Doctorita and Don Carlos are asleep?"

"I think the daytime's better." I consider their schedule. "How about Friday, in four days? Their last day of school. The day before we leave. At eleven o'clock. They're always at the *colegio* until one. And Andrecito and Jaimito will be at school."

"All right. Eleven on Friday. I'll tell my sister to wait for you across the street from your house." He looks at me like he wants to kiss me again. "We're really going to do this, aren't we?"

I nod, excited.

Antonio lets his hand graze mine, as if by accident. "I love you, Virginia."

I take hold of his hand for a second, then let go. "I love you, Antonio."

Over the next few days, we pack boxes and bags and load them into the school bus that the *colegio* has loaned to the Doctorita and Niño Carlitos to use for the move. We can barely cram in all their things—the red velvet furniture and lamps and clothes and kitchen utensils and crocheted doilies.

Before the photo albums are packed away, I take my favorite picture of Jaimito, sitting in his wooden airplane, a giant smile on his face. And for Andrecito, who still calls me Mamá, even at age four, I take a photo from his first birthday party, cake smeared everywhere. I play with the boys as much as I can now, trying to memorize the smell of their freshly shampooed hair.

I pack my notebooks that have been hidden underneath the refrigerator for two years, along with all my clothes into a big plastic garbage bag. Before the books are stacked into boxes, I press *Understanding Our Universe* to my chest, as though it's a best friend I'm leaving. I consider stuffing it into my bag, but that would really infuriate the Doctorita, and anyway, I have it nearly memorized.

By Thursday night, only mattresses and a few clothes and toiletries remain in the echoey house. I lie on my mattress, with the orange and turquoise blanket pulled under my chin, unable to sleep. I try to relax and imagine my life free of Niño Carlitos's groping and the Doctorita's beatings and insults.

A movie plays out in my head: myself in the future, married to Antonio, living with him and his family. We sleep in a narrow bed in the corner of the room that we share with his brothers and sisters. We wake up before dawn to start working in the fields. All day I work, my back bent, just like my mother's, and even when I try to stand tall, my shoulders hunch over with invisible weight. Antonio plows with the oxen and a *soga*, just like my father. Soon we start having children, one after the other, every two years, and they work with us in the fields. In the evenings we're too tired to do anything but fall into bed. There is not a single book to read, but it doesn't matter—we wouldn't be able to waste the lamp's kerosene on something as useless as a book.

Now my eyes are wide open and I'm sweating in a panic. I've traveled this far—how can I go back to living the humble life of a farming family? I try to calm down and focus on Antonio's eyes and the music he played to me while I stood on the balcony and the notes he sent me and him saying, *I love you, Virginia*, and tucking the adorable strand of hair behind his ear. But it's as if there's a grown-up woman deep inside me—an older, wiser Virginia from the future—and she's steering me toward some other destiny, calling out, *You're making a mistake, Virginia! Don't do it!*

* * *

After a night of struggling in my head, the purple light of dawn comes, and I've made a decision. I will escape with Antonio, and once I'm free, I'll call my sister and visit my parents and look at all my options. I don't have to marry Antonio right away. Or live a farming life with him. Like he said, I'll always have a choice. And if he truly loves me, he'll understand. He'll help me reach my dreams. The most important first step is to not stand and stare at the chance to be free, but to do something.

In the morning, as the Doctorita shuffles around in her bathrobe and Niño Carlitos shaves with his buzzing razor, I wonder if I'll miss them. We've had some good times together, walking in the fields, picking fruit, strolling in the park. If only I could erase the Doctorita's beatings and insults and keep the tender moments. And erase Niño Carlitos's groping and just remember him calling me his daughter and making toys for me and the boys.

I hug Jaimito and Andrecito extra long before they leave for school. "I love you," I whisper, and finally force myself to pull away. As they tromp off with the Doctorita and Niño Carlitos, unaware that this is the last time they'll see me, I stand at the door, waving. "Goodbye! Have a nice day!"

"Bye, Virginia!"

Teary-eyed, I watch them leave, the Doctorita waddling quickly, Niño Carlitos taking long, slow strides, the boys half running to keep up, backpacks bouncing.

Now I have more than three hours to wait. I walk through the empty house, pausing in each room, remembering all that has happened to me here. I feel like an empty house myself,

185

about to start a new life filled with new things. Finally, at ten-thirty, I settle cross-legged on the floor inside the entrance and wait for eleven o'clock to come.

Within a few minutes, the metal gate clanks. Is it Antonio's sister, coming early? But she's supposed to meet me across the street. My insides tighten. It can't be the Doctorita; she's never come home before one o'clock before.

A key scrapes in the lock. What if it's Niño Carlitos, sneaking home early to try to press against me?

I pick up my bag, frantically searching for a place to hide it, but the room is completely bare.

And then the door opens.

The Doctorita steps inside.

She jumps, seeing me right here in front of her. "Virginia, you scared me! What are you—?" She spots my bag. "What's this? What's going on?"

"I—I—" But I can't think of a lie fast enough. "I'm leaving. I don't want to live with you anymore."

After a moment of shock, she asks, "Where are you going?"

"I'm—I'm just going." There's no way I can tell her about Antonio. "I'm going to my parents.'"

"And how will you get there?" She drops her schoolbag on the floor and stands still, a lumpy mountain blocking the door.

"I don't know. I'll get help."

"Who will help you?" She raises an eyebrow.

"A—a woman."

"Tell me who."

"Just a woman."

Her eyes fill with tears. "You ungrateful *longa*! I've cared for

186

you. I've given you food and drink, and shelter, and clothes, and this is how you pay me? With this ingratitude?"

I take a step back, but she grabs my arm and pulls me toward her and punches me in the nose. My head snaps back. Pain shoots out over my face.

"Ungrateful *longa*," she spits.

Tears are streaming from her eyes now. "How could you want to leave us? How?" She pushes me toward the stairs. My nose is bleeding, my hands covered in blood. I tilt my head back and walk upstairs as she follows.

She leans against the bare living room wall and puts her face in her hands, as though I've hurt her. As though *she's* the hurt one. "Go clean yourself up," she whispers.

I wash off the blood and then tiptoe down the hall, to the balcony overlooking the street. I peek outside. It's a sunny morning like any other, neighbors walking with bags of groceries, talking to each other, whistling and sweeping in front of their houses. And then I spot her, a teenage girl in a simple white shirt and blue skirt, pacing back and forth on the street, watching our house, waiting patiently.

Now I can really sympathize with how the slave Isaura felt after she was caught by the evil Leoncio. In my empty room, I lean against the bare wall next to the plastic garbage bag filled with my possessions. Tucking my legs up, I balance my notebook on my knees and write, in slow, careful letters.

> Dear Antonio,
> The Doctorita caught me, I can't live with
> you, I have to go to Ibarra. Thank you for

187

liking me and caring about me, you don't
know how much it means to me.

I love you,
Virginia

The Doctorita spends most of the afternoon by the door as
neighbors come to say farewell. She keeps one eye on me the
whole time to make sure I don't run. Meanwhile, Niño Carlitos has stayed late at school to do paperwork. It turns out they
weren't teaching today, only finishing up grade reports and doc-
uments, which is why the Doctorita came home early.

Leo stops by under the pretense of saying farewell to the
Doctorita. As he speaks with her, I creep closer and closer. He
stares at my swollen nose, at the circles starting to darken under
my bloodshot eyes.

The Doctorita frowns at me. "Virginia, why don't you go
back upstairs and sweep the living room."

"I want to say goodbye to Leo," I tell her firmly, and before
she can send me upstairs, I shake hands with him. "Goodbye,
Leo," I say, pressing the note into his palm.

In the early-morning sunshine, teachers and students help
load the last few things into the school bus as Niño Carlitos
and the Doctorita watch me like hawks. Yesterday afternoon,
when Niño Carlitos saw my wounds, he started yelling at the
Doctorita, until she told him she suspected there was a boy in-
volved in my plan. Then he turned pink and furious and
shouted at me, demanding that I tell him who this boy was.
I kept my lips pressed tight together and swallowed my tears.

All morning, as people have been loading the bus, I've been

188

scrubbing the apartment clean, finding excuses to walk past the window to glimpse Antonio outside. For hours, he's been sitting on the ground, leaning against the wall of the building across the street, the place where he played me the music that magical evening. He's just sitting and staring with the saddest look in the universe.

Once the bus is loaded, the Doctorita and Niño Carlitos make one last sweep of the house to be sure they haven't forgotten anything, and then we climb into the bus. The teachers and students wave and their farewells float through the open windows. Among them are Marlenny and Marina and Doña Mercedes and Leo and Roberto-MacGyver and his new wife, all shouting, "¡Adiós, Doctorita! ¡Adiós, Don Carlos! ¡Adiós, Jaimito! ¡Adiós, Andrecito! ¡Adiós, Virginia!"

I crawl through the maze of boxes and bags and furniture to a space in the back of the bus where I can be alone. The engine turns on, rumbles. I watch Antonio from the back window, then push it open and raise my palm, mouthing the words *Adiós, Antonio*. And he mouths *Adiós, Virginia*, and waves a mournful wave. The bus chugs down our street, and I watch him grow smaller, and then the bus turns the corner and he is gone.

chapter 23

Without you,
my soul dies, though my body lives.
Without you,
I no longer dream of a beautiful future.
This world is a valley of tears.
This world is a valley of tears.
This world is a valley of tears.

I FILL MY NOTEBOOK WITH POETRY, always hiding it under
the refrigerator, where no one but me looks. Back in Kunu Yaku,
Antonio told me I walked like royalty, like a princess in disguise. But in Ibarra, I am dazed and dull and stooped over while
the world happens around me. I trudge through the days, as
though walking through wet cement. And sometimes in the
middle of my chores, I feel so heavy I sink to the ground and
stare at nothing.

In Ibarra, the sky seems shrunken. You can still see the

mountains, but only over the rooftops. And you have to search for glimpses of green. Our neighborhood is gray and white and black cement; you have to peek through metal gates into hidden courtyards to find trees and flowers.

In our new house, my room is on the roof. From the second floor, I have to climb an extra flight of stairs to the flat cement roof. It's mostly a big terrace with some sinks for washing clothes and crisscrossed clotheslines. My room and the guest room are small, with single windows and metal doors that open onto the terrace. Across a low cement wall is the upper level of our neighbor's apartment, whose glass doors also open onto the terrace.

Sometimes the daughter, Blanca, who looks a few years younger than me, plays there with her little brother. They wave, but haven't invited me over, maybe because I'm about fifteen by now, nearly a woman, and usually busy washing clothes and hanging them to dry. At night, I peer through the glass doors and see Blanca and her parents and brother watching TV or talking together in the soft yellow light. Or I gaze at the stars, even though it's disappointing because I can only see half as many stars as in Kunu Yaku.

The Doctorita is happy in civilization. And on top of that, she's pregnant again, which pleases her because it gives her an excuse to get fat and grow another chin. She says, "After this next one, I'm going to do aerobics and get my girlish figure back." Niño Carlitos rubs her back and doesn't call her lazy when she spends evenings with her feet up on the sofa eating an entire bag of sugary orange wafers.

Whenever she falls asleep on the sofa or takes naps on weekend afternoons, Niño Carlitos slips into the kitchen to talk to me. I barely answer his questions about how my day was or how I like Ibarra. But he's not interested in my answers anyway. His hands are always touching me, stroking my hair, my neck, my cheek, my shoulder; when they creep lower and his body moves closer, I duck away, find an excuse to leave. It's tiring to be on guard all the time, to keep my muscles tense and wary.

As I watch the Doctorita's belly swell, I think about the diapers I'll have to wash now that Andrecito is out of his. My life, endlessly washing diapers. Recently, Niño Carlitos suggested buying a washing machine, but the Doctorita said, "Humph. What do we need that for? We've got Virginia." That's what I am, an appliance, a multipurpose appliance that cooks and cleans and washes and babysits.

I imagine what the commercial for me would be like. The Doctorita's on TV, her teeth bleached white, a giant fake smile stuck to her face. *Hi*, she says in a voice as slick as motor oil. *I want to tell you about my favorite new appliance, the ultimate time-saving device, My Virginia!* The camera zooms in on me holding a broom—a zombified me with wide saucer eyes—then swings back to the Doctorita. *It cooks*, she says, *and it cleans*, and *it takes care of your children!* Niño Carlitos walks into the room, exclaiming, *Is there anything it doesn't do?* He rests his hand on my shoulder and squeezes. The Doctorita assures him, *My Virginia does* everything. *And the best part? It's free! No strings attached! And easy maintenance! Just pound My Virginia once a month and you're set! Don't wait! Get one today!*

After dinner one evening, as I'm collecting the dirty plates, the Doctorita rubs her giant belly. "Virginia, sit down for a moment before you do the dishes."

I sit down. It must have scared her when I tried to run away. She must have realized she couldn't take me completely for granted. Here in Ibarra she doesn't hit me as much, although that could be because of her pregnancy, or because now they're making more money, living more comfortably.

"What's wrong with you?" she demands. "Why don't you talk anymore? Or smile?"

I shrug.

"Why don't you play with the boys anymore?"

I shrug.

She pastes a kind expression on her face. "Now that we're all settled in the city, I can get you that elementary school diploma you've been wanting."

"When?"

"Soon."

"All right," I say dully. Soon might never happen.

She must sense my doubt, because she tries a different tactic. "You know that Carlos and I are earning more in our jobs here. In a few years we'll build another, small house on this property. A house for you. Your own house."

My own house? I perk up. If she really gave me a house one day, I'd paint it purple with white trim. I'd invite Antonio and my friends from Kunu Yaku to come over for parties, and we'd blast *cumbias* and dance into the night. But then the Doctorita intrudes on my fantasy, barging into my dream house and flipping off the stereo. The room goes silent. *Longa,* she shouts with all three chins jiggling, *you have a pile of diapers to wash. Your friends had better leave and you'd better get started. Now!*

Later that night, the moon is a sliver in the sky, shining like a luminescent potato peel. On the roof, I lean against the cement wall and think about my options.

Stay with the Doctorita and Niño Carlitos and get my diploma and my house—if she ever keeps those promises. And in return, be their maid forever.

Run away to my family and live with them in their dirty house with fleas and put up with my father's beatings. And turn back into an *indígena*.

Run away to my sister and see if she can find me a maid job with another family that might let me go to school. Or might not.

Run away to Kunu Yaku and marry Antonio and live life as a poor farmer's wife and have lots of kids. And no books.

Something else. And until I figure out what that is, write poetry.

Number five seems like the best option at the moment. I open my notebook and, by the glow of our neighbors' yellow living room, write:

> *This world is a valley of tears.*
> *This world is a valley of tears.*
> *This world is a valley of tears.*

* * *

When the Doctorita is seven months pregnant—her belly nearly the size of a basketball—her doctor finds a problem with the baby and tells her that whenever she isn't working she should be resting in bed. This means I'm often alone in the kitchen, cooking and cleaning up. Which means that Niño Carlitos has even more opportunities to come up behind me at the sink and press against me and move his hands over me like magnets as I squirm away. At night I cry, feeling ashamed, as though his hands have left prints on my skin, like marks in drying clay.

When I was little, back in Yana Urku, the wind and sun would burn my cheeks and calves and feet, crack my flesh, make spidery red lines of blood that would fill with dirt and sting and ache. Despite this, I couldn't resist scratching the flea bites clustered at my ankles, making the skin more and more raw, oozing blood and pus. Seeing this, Mamita had me pee in a cup and then she poured my warm urine over the cracked flesh, gently rubbing it in. My eyes watered at the hot sting, but within a few days, my skin was healed, whole again. I ran my fingers over my smooth legs, brushed my hands on my soft cheeks, feeling as brand-new as a freshly laid egg.

This is what I long for now, something to make Niño Carlitos's touch disappear, something to make me good and complete and pure again. More and more now, I think about telling the Doctorita. Then, one day, something happens that makes me realize that she would blame me without a doubt.

I'm in the storeroom ironing Niño Carlitos's button-down work shirts, when the Doctorita storms through the door, waving my notebook and shouting, "Why are you writing love poems? Who is this you're writing about? What's his name? I thought I forbid you to have a boyfriend!"

Oh, no. She must have looked under the refrigerator for some reason. "I don't. I never did," I lie. "It's all from my imagination."

"And did he teach you to read, too? So he could send you love letters?"

I watch my notebook as she swings it around. I hate seeing her fat hands on this thing that is sacred to me.

195

"Ha!" she snorts. "You know, *longa,* if you ever left here and went after this guy, you know what would happen?"

I say nothing and keep ironing.

"You *longas* are like dogs, dogs that we spend a lot of time training. It wasn't easy for me—you were wild when I got you. I fed you and gave you shelter, and you've had a good life. But you know what happens when a dog gets in heat?"

I stare at the shirt on the ironing board, half wrinkled, half smooth.

"Answer me!"

I shrug.

"It doesn't matter if it's tamed or not. Within a month the dog is knocked up. It lives on the street scrounging for scraps. And then one day it shows up, back at its owner's door."

I bite the inside of my cheek in humiliation. The iron hisses and spews an angry cloud of steam.

"Don't even think about running," she yells. "Because in three months you'd be knocking at my door, pregnant and begging for your job back. Because that's how you *longas* are."

I set down the iron, shaking now.

"Well? What do you have to say for yourself?"

What I want to say is this: *You and your husband are the animals. You and your husband are the dogs, dangerous dogs, frothing-at-the-mouth, rabid dogs. But me, I'm the poetess. I'm the scientist. I'm the singer. I'm the secret agent. I'm the dancer. I'm the human.*

Instead, I say flatly, "Can I have my notebook back?"

She throws the notebook on the floor on her way out. I pick it up and hug it to my chest. Then I ball up Niño Carlitos's half-ironed shirt and hurl it against the wall. In my room, I open my notebook and read, *This world is a valley of tears.*

chapter 24

THE DOCTORITA RETURNS from her eight-month prenatal appointment pale and terrified. The doctor has said there's a major problem, that she has to go immediately to the big hospital in Quito.

In a panic, Niño Carlitos packs her bag and drives her to the hospital, over an hour away. That evening, when he comes home, dark circles hang beneath his eyes, and he sinks into a velvet chair. "Can you get me some lemonade, *m'hija?*"

I pour his lemonade. "How's the Doctorita?" I ask nervously. "Will she be coming home soon?"

He shakes his head. "She has to stay there until the baby's born."

"How long?"

"A week. A month. Depends when the baby comes."

My muscles tense. That means a week or more in the house with just him and the boys. No amount of booby-trapping will stop him from getting what he wants. I'll have to do something else. In the meantime, until I make a plan, I hope he's so exhausted he'll just go to bed and sleep all evening until the next day.

After dinner, he goes to his room to rest. The boys are in their room, playing with their dump trucks. I can hear faint *bbbrrrs* and *vvvrrrmmms* and plastic truck crashes through the door. I start washing the dishes, praying Niño Carlitos will just fall asleep and sleep until morning.

His voice calls out. "Virginia!"

"Yes?"

"Bring me some water."

I pour a glass of water and take a deep breath. The water shivers in its glass. Upstairs, I knock on his door softly.

"Come in."

I push the door open. Niño Carlitos is lying on the pink llama bedspread, his head propped on fluffy pillows, watching me with colorless eyes, the lids half closed. His face looks gray and pasty and eager, his thin hair combed pathetically over the growing bald spot. How could I ever have wished this man was my father? How could this man ever have been my protector?

I set the glass on a doily on the bedside table and turn to leave. *"M'hijita,"* he says, his voice greasy. "How nice you are. How pretty."

"Thanks," I mumble, and head out the door.

"Come here," he says. "Come sit down on the bed."

I keep walking. "I need to wash the dishes now," I call over my shoulder, and run downstairs to the kitchen. With trembling hands, I finish washing the dishes. As I'm drying my hands, his footsteps sound on the stairs. He presses up behind me, same as always, but this time is different. This time I know

198

I can defend myself for only so long. Even if I run out on an errand, he'll be waiting for me, alone, when I come back.

I duck away. "I'm going to clean the floor now," I say, and dash upstairs.

He follows me.

I run up the next flight of stairs to the terrace, where I keep the bucket and mop.

Thankfully he doesn't chase me up here. "Bring me more water," he calls.

I lean against the wall, feeling nauseated. Orange light pools at the horizon, like heaps of glowing silk. I think about *Understanding Our Universe*, of its diagram of the sun's rays angled in the evenings. Air molecules scatter the short wavelength colors, so only soft, warm pinks and yellows and oranges shine through. Knowing this comforts me. I want to stay out here, beneath the sky where things feel safer and simpler, where I understand things.

"Virginia!" he shouts. "Now!"

Every cell in my body dreads going downstairs. Clutching the bucket and mop, I force myself to walk down to the kitchen and pour another glass of water. This time, as I put it on the bedside table, his hand shoots out and grabs my wrist. He pulls me onto the bed, on top of him.

"No," I cry, struggling with all my strength. His grip is firm, but I manage to untangle myself. I stagger back, away from the bed. Once I catch my balance, I run upstairs to my room. I lock the door and sit on my bed, my heart hammering.

And then, with a drowning feeling, I realize: he has an extra set of keys to all the rooms of the house.

* * *

Later that night, after the boys are asleep and the city is dark and quiet, Niño Carlitos bangs on my door. "Open up!" His voice is slurred. He must have been drinking. "Open up, Virginia!"

¡Dios mío! It's only a matter of time before he goes downstairs for the extra set of keys. *What to do? What to do?* I sit on the edge of my bed and hug my pillow tight.

Even if I push furniture in front of the door, that will only keep him out for so long, and this time there's no Doctorita down the hall. I look around for a weapon. Nothing. My room is stark—a narrow bed, a small table, a bare lightbulb, an old chest of drawers for my clothes. Not even a lamp or a pocketknife.

Eventually the banging stops. Niño Carlitos curses and stumbles down the metal stairs. I take a deep breath and open the door a crack, peering out. All clear. Now's my chance. I run across the dark terrace, climb over the wall, and head toward the neighbor's glass doors. The lights are on, but no one's in the room.

Niño Carlitos's shouts rise from below and his footsteps start clanking up the metal steps. I hear the keys jangling.

No time to knock. I open their door, slip inside, and lock the door behind me. I wander down the hallway and run into Blanca in a sky blue nightgown and fluffy pink slippers.

She jumps. "Virginia! What are you doing here?"

I try to think of a good reason. "I—I—I—" And then I break down into tears. "Blanquita, please don't make me leave. Please let me stay, please."

Her mother comes into the hallway. She has a sweet,

worried face and a frilly blue and white checked apron, just like a TV mother's. She takes my hand and leads me to the kitchen table. Everything is blue and white checked in the kitchen—the towels and napkins and curtains and tablecloth. A neat, cozy place. "What happened, honey?" she asks in an angel's voice.

"It's that—it's that"—I can't cover it up any longer—"it's that my boss, he's drunk, and he's trying to come into my room, and the Doctorita is in Quito, and I'm scared. I'm really, really scared, señora."

She pats my shoulder. "It's all right, Virginia, you can stay here. Calm down, honey. You'll spend the night here. He's not going to touch you. We'll take care of you."

She boils water and serves us lemon balm tea in dainty yellow cups. She takes the chipped cup for herself and gives me the perfect one, as though I'm a real guest. As I sip, she looks at me with concern. "Is there anyone you can call, honey? We have a phone. You could call your parents."

I shake my head.

"Brothers or sisters?"

I hesitate. "I think my sister lives in Quito. I know her phone number." If it *is* still her number. It's been years since I found her note in the Bible, and who knows how many years earlier that Matilde had written it there.

"Well, honey, Quito's not far at all. Just a bus ride away. Now, why don't you get a good night's sleep and tomorrow you can call your sister."

I nod. "Thank you, señora."

That night, I sleep with Blanca in her bed. We stay awake

talking for a long time, and she tells me about her boyfriend and makes jokes and giggles a lot. "I'm glad you're here, Virginia," she confides. "I've always wanted a big sister."

I stay awake most of the night, wondering what will happen when I call my sister the next day. I can't imagine what she's like now. I've always pictured her the same age she was when I left—probably about twelve. Younger than I am now. Blanca's age. Which means Matilde must be a grown woman.

This realization makes a new round of tears soak my pillow. What I want is to go back in time—to a childhood I didn't have—and be a carefree girl like Blanca, giggling with her big sister, sharing jokes and dreams. I want this simple sweetness, this innocence. I want it so badly. I ache with wanting something that never existed, something that never can exist.

The next morning, I wake up early, after just a few hours of broken sleep. The señora is up already, wearing her blue checked apron. "Good morning, honey," she says, and serves me chamomile tea and bread with blackberry jam, while the morning news blares on the TV. "Your boss hasn't come for you," she assures me as she whirls around the kitchen. "I don't think he even knows you're here, dear. You're safe with us. You just take all the time you need."

I thank her and try to force down the bread and tea. It's good, but my insides feel too fluttery to eat. After breakfast, she shows me the phone and then, with an encouraging smile, leaves the room to give me privacy.

I put my hand on the receiver, feel the cool plastic. Will Matilde try to make me go back to our parents? Will they give me away again? Is my sister even at this number anymore?

Hundreds of questions bang around in my mind while my stomach leaps wildly. Finally, I dial the number that I've known by heart for years and press the receiver to my ear.

After three rings, a woman's voice answers. "Hello?"

"Hello," I say, sweat trickling from my armpits. My voice sounds strange, outside of my body. My life is about to leap into an unknown place. Here at the edge, it feels like a dream. "May I speak with Matilde, please?"

PART 3

chapter 25

"THIS IS MATILDE," she answers in a grown-up voice, smooth as cream. As children, I realize, we always spoke Quichua, and now her Spanish words make her sound like a stranger, even though I no longer speak Quichua myself.

I try to steady my voice, but it squeaks out with an edge of desperation. "This is Virginia."

A pause. "Virginia?" Another pause. "Virginia who?"

I go numb. Then, suddenly, I want to cry, scream, throw the phone against the wall. I grip the edge of the table until my knuckles turn white. "This is your sister."

A silence. Then a whisper. "Virginia? It's really you?"

Within seconds, I'm blubbering like a little girl. "You forgot about me, all of you, didn't you?"

"Oh, Virginia, no, little sister. It's just that it's—it's been so many years."

"But how could you—" And then my sobs take over.

"Virginia." Her words are soft. "Shhh, it's all right."

I wipe my nose and try to breathe. "Matilde, I want—I want to go home."

"Of course. Of course, little sister. Where are you? I'll come get you."

An old, familiar feeling washes over me, Matilde's tenderness when I least deserved it. I remember the time when I was little and ventured alone to the market in Otavalo to buy boots with my saved-up snack money. I got hopelessly lost. As punishment, Mamita beat me with a eucalyptus stick, but later, when I told Matilde about it, teary and embarrassed, she held my hand and used that same soothing voice. *I'll help you, little sister. I'll take you to the market myself.* As though she'd forgotten about all the times I'd hit her and refused to share fruit and yelled at her in a jealous rage over who would get the biggest potato.

"Thank you, Matilde," I say.

After she copies down my address and assures me it's not far from her home in Quito, she says, "Virginia," her voice full of concern, "can you wait until tomorrow? The señora isn't here now and I can't leave her children alone."

How will I survive one more night of Niño Carlitos? Maybe I can sleep at Blanca's again if things get bad. I take a deep, wavery breath. "All right. Can you come around eleven tomorrow morning, Matilde, when my boss is at work?"

"Of course, little sister. There are plenty of buses from Quito to Ibarra. I'll see you at eleven o'clock."

My tears finally stop and I feel a strange sense of calm, the glassy surface of a lake once the wind stops. Now that we're older, maybe I can let go of the last lingering envious feelings. Maybe it isn't too late to giggle together and tell each other secrets. I rub my fingers along the edge of the blue checked tablecloth, feeling the crisp, fresh fabric. A new beginning.

And then, with excitement creeping into her voice, Matilde says, "I have some news."

"What?"

"I'm getting married."

Married. A punch in the stomach. Matilde will live with her husband and start having babies and have no time for a little sister. A new batch of tears and mucus streams down my face.

"Virginia, are you still there?"

"Yes," I manage to say between gasps.

"*Hermanita*," she says. Little sister. The word comforted me for so long whenever I read it on my precious piece of paper. Now it stabs at me. "Tomorrow I'll bring my fiancé with me so you can meet him."

"All right," I whisper.

"See you tomorrow, little sister."

"Bye." I hang up and cradle my head in my arms and bawl all over the freshly ironed tablecloth.

An hour later, I'm standing on the terrace in a gray drizzle, watching Niño Carlitos leave for school, his widening bald spot exposed, followed by the boys, who are hunched under big backpacks that make them look like turtles. I'm not sure what Niño Carlitos thinks about my leaving last night. I wonder whether he looked for me, or whether he's worried about me. I wonder what he told the boys this morning when I wasn't there to make their breakfast and get them ready for school.

Once they disappear around the corner, I shiver, then

209

breathe out slowly. I poke my head inside to thank Blanca's mother.

"Oh, honey, are you sure you don't want to stay here until your sister comes?" she asks for the tenth time.

"I'll be all right, señora." I walk slowly across the terrace toward our house, not caring that the rain is soaking me, vaguely wondering why I refused Blanca's mother's offer. And the only answer I come up with, unbelievably, is that I don't feel ready to leave the Doctorita's family, as flawed as it is. Inside, I sit on the red velvet sofa, my skin damp and goose-bumped, my feet tucked under me. I stare at everything I might never see again: the dangling plants, the crocheted doilies, the cross-stitched roses that I know so well.

Do I really want to go with Matilde tomorrow? I remember the elementary school diploma and the house the Doctorita has promised me. My rewards for putting up with them for eight years. But if I leave now, I'll have nothing. Absolutely nothing. After all these years.

I've already survived the worst. Now the Doctorita only beats me once in a while; maybe after this next baby she'll get a fourth chin and be so fat, she won't be able to muster the strength to hit me. Besides, a small part of her appreciates me, respects me even, a part she tries to hide but that springs out sometimes.

A few years ago, when she and Niño Carlitos were in their biggest fight ever, on the verge of divorce, I decided it was up to me to save their marriage. I cooked them a special candlelit dinner, complete with blackberries and cilantro sprigs as garnishes, and rice molded to the shape of an upside-down cup like I'd seen in a magazine. I played a tape of old, romantic music from the years when they were dating, the kind that always gave the Doctorita a far-off, dreamy look in her eyes. Then, despite their protests, I lured them to the table and made a speech. "We are a family. Jaimito and Andrecito and I want our home to be peaceful and happy. So we're asking you to make up. Now apologize and hug each other." They smiled hesitantly, then laughed, then really looked at each other for the first time in weeks. And as they said they were sorry, their voices softened, and they melted into a hug.

Later, after dinner, I served them liquor in fancy crystal glasses and they insisted I join them. The Doctorita hummed along with the songs, her hand in Niño Carlitos's. "The music is a nice touch, Virginia," she said, "but I thought you didn't know how to work the stereo." Feeling brave, I said, "Well, actually, I listen to it every day when you leave the house." She grinned. "Virginia, what would we do without you?" And Niño Carlitos pulled his wife closer and looked at me with pride. "Thank you, my daughter. You're tremendous."

They need me.

Now, in the watery light, I shift on the sofa, move my gaze to the framed photos on the coffee table that I dust every day— Jaimito and Andrecito looking adorable in their school uniforms; the Doctorita and Niño Carlitos walking down the aisle amidst flowers and rice, just married; all four of them together at Christmas, crowded around the Baby Jesus doll in its new lime green outfit. And more frames hold relatives at balloon-filled birthdays and First Communions and baptisms—parents and sisters and brothers and nieces and nephews, all arm in arm, fitting together perfectly.

Their favorite nephew, Raúl, with curly hair and a charming

smirk, has a frame all to himself. The Doctorita loves to brag that he's at the top of his class in the most prestigious *colegio* in Otavalo, República de Ecuador, the *colegio* where her own smart boys would surely go one day. I wonder, does she ever brag about me?

And then it hits me, I am not in a single photo. I am the behind-the-scenes person, the invisible one who makes their lives run smoothly, the one outside the camera frame, the one in the kitchen cooking food or on the patio washing diapers. As much as I want to be part of this family, I am not. And I never will be.

Still, it seems impossible to unravel myself from their lives. Like it or not, we're crocheted together as tightly as the yarn of a Baby Jesus dress.

The clock says twelve o'clock. An hour until the boys and Niño Carlitos return from school. Maybe if he's nice to me, if he apologizes, if he promises to go back to how things were before . . . maybe then I'll give him one last small chance.

Around one o'clock the door opens and, with a burst of color and noise and raindrops, the boys tumble in and throw their slippery arms around me. Andrecito makes a beeline for his favorite dump truck and starts zooming it around the living-room-table legs. Jaimito shrugs off his backpack and asks, "Where were you this morning, Virginia?"

I glance at Niño Carlitos. Now is his chance to apologize, to make everything better. But no. He's glaring at me, his face turning red. "Go upstairs to your room, boys."

They start to protest. "But—"

"Now!"

Groaning, the boys disappear upstairs. Niño Carlitos moves closer. "Where were you last night?"

"In my room." I stand up, bracing my muscles to run.

He takes a step toward me. "You're lying."

I edge away, toward the door, my heart pounding.

He blocks my path. "What's going on with you?"

I force myself to look at his eyes, searching for a remnant of the soft-spoken man who once thanked me for saving his marriage. But there's only this crazy-eyed man cornering me like a rabid dog, acting as if he wants to tear me to pieces.

For a tense moment, we stare at each other as the rain drums against the windows. Finally, he barks, "Make the boys their lunch," and stomps upstairs.

I heat up chicken and potato soup and rice, crying. At the table, my stomach is too jittery for me to eat. Niño Carlitos doesn't touch his food, either. Jaimito and Andrecito keep putting down their spoons to reach over and hug me. Andrecito offers me his dump truck for comfort, placing it gently on my napkin. Jaimito rests his head on my arm. "Why are you sad, Virginia?"

I look at Niño Carlitos.

In a flat voice, he demands, "Why *are* your eyes puffy, Virginia?"

For a moment I stare at him in disbelief, and then my voice shoots out, hard and cold. "Maybe I'm sick."

He shakes his head and pushes his plate away, as though I'm the unreasonable one. "I have to go back to Quito for a few days to check on la Negra. You'll stay here to take care of the boys."

I look out the front window, past the dripping pink bougainvillea bush to the street, wishing Matilde would appear now and snip every last tie I have with these people.

He moves his head close to mine and whispers low enough that the children won't hear, "You wouldn't leave the boys, Virginia." His words are smug. "Would you?"

I hand Andrecito back his dump truck, whisper thanks, then collect our dishes, letting their clatter fill the silence, and head toward the kitchen without a word.

chapter 26

Niño Carlitos's leaving is a relief. But having the children stay with me puts a glitch in the plan. He's right; I can't leave them alone. Yet that's a relief, too—an excuse to stay a bit longer, at least for now. The boys and I spend the evening watching TV on their parents' bed, Jaimito on one side of me, Andrecito and his dump truck on the other, all cuddled together, our arms warm around each other.

The next morning, while the boys are at school, I wait for Matilde, peering out the window in case she comes early. I wonder if I'll recognize her. Every few minutes, I run to the hallway mirror to see how I look, to make sure my lips are still glossed, trying to guess what she'll think of me.

Bangs frame my face now, and permed hair cascades down my back in waves that turn frizzy if I don't use plenty of gel. But all the gel is worth it; on good days the hairstyle makes me look a little like a rock star. I've chosen a safari outfit look for today—a white T-shirt and my favorite green jean jacket and a tan skirt that just skims my knees. My socks are neatly folded over and my loafers polished a deep shiny brown, like roasted coffee beans. Spread over my eyelids is a touch of the Doctorita's violet eye shadow.

At ten-fifty, there's a knock at the door. With sweaty hands I open it. A pretty indigenous woman is standing before me, smiling. She's a grown-up. She's about twenty years old, dressed in a long, straight wraparound skirt and a puffy white blouse that glimmers in the morning light. Flowers of pink and yellow and orange trail around the neckline, and her face looks like a flower itself, with petal-smooth, rosy cheeks. Soft, dimpled elbows poke out from her lacy sleeves, and red beads wind up her wrists. With the spray of pink bougainvillea behind her, she looks as though she's just emerged from a garden, dusted with golden pollen.

Behind her stands a skinny indigenous man in jeans and a white button-down shirt, his hair in a long braid. He looks younger, a boy still, about eighteen, with wide, friendly eyes.

Matilde wraps her arms around me, pressing me into her pillowy body. Beneath the smell of flowery soap is the deeper smell of Matilde. A sweet smell of ripe blackberries, with a hint of heat, like just-fried onions and sun-warmed rock. A smell I thought I forgot, but which must have lived in a secret nook inside me all these years.

She takes a step back and stares, studying my face. Suddenly, I see what she sees: a confused girl in safari clothes with rock-star hair and purple eye shadow and cherry red lip gloss. A girl who is no longer *indígena*. A girl who doesn't know what

216

she is. I twirl a strand of wavy-frizzy hair around my finger and search for words.

Finally Matilde speaks, in her grown-up voice. "Virginia, this is Santiago. My fiancé."

I extend my hand, glad to have something to do with it. "Nice to meet you."

"A pleasure, Virginia."

I stand for another moment, feeling the breeze on my calves. "Uh, come in, sit down."

I bring them lemonade, and we sip it awkwardly, me sitting on the red velvet chair, and Matilde and Santiago perched side by side on the sofa, two lovebirds.

"Tell us what's going on, Virginia," Santiago says. His lips are big and soft and never seem to close all the way, which makes him seem like a child, his mouth open in wonder. As much as I want to hate him, I can see why Matilde feels tenderness for him.

I start explaining, first in clumsy stutters, and then letting everything tumble out—how the Doctorita hits me and Niño Carlitos tries to hug me a lot and, finally, what happened the night before I called her.

Santiago sits through it silently, his eyebrows furrowed, mouth parted in rapt attention, holding Matilde's hand as she grasps his more and more tightly. Afterward, she shakes her head and rests her hand over her chest. "Virginia, little sister, I don't understand." She leans forward. "Why didn't you ever come home?"

I swallow hard. "The Doctorita said our parents didn't want me anymore. That they'd sold me." Saying these words makes my blood burn, but I force myself to go on. "That if I ran away, they'd sell me to someone else."

Matilde leans closer, across the coffee table, reaching out her hands.

I don't take them. Instead, I keep my fingers wrapped around the glass of lemonade balanced on my knee. The surface feels cold and slippery, the tiny droplets of water in the air condensing onto the glass.

Matilde is crying now. "Oh, little sister, our parents did everything they could to look for you. Mariana and Alfonso said you didn't want to see them again, that you wanted to forget about your poor family. We didn't know if they were lying or not. Mamita and Papito searched and searched for you; as the years passed without a word, they thought you must be dead."

"They gave up on me?" I'm clutching my glass so hard it might shatter in my hand.

"Oh, little sister, it's not like that. For years, Mamita slept with your old *anaco* and blouse. She put them to her face and cried into them."

I blink. "She cried for me?"

"She cried nearly every day for you, *hermanita*. For years."

"But she never acted like she loved me." Anger is rising inside me, pure, fiery anger. "She told me she'd be happy if I left forever."

Matilde moves from the sofa and crouches beside me, holding my limp hand. "Virginia, Mamita started having children when she was your age. And many of them died. She was always mourning her dead babies. She drank to forget them. And remember how Papito beat her? Remember how there was never

218

enough food? She was a young woman, in over her head. She never should've let you go. She made a bad decision. Now she's older and understands that. You'll see. If you come home, trust me, it will be the happiest day of her life."

I take a sip of tart lemonade. It's too tart, not nearly enough sugar. Like me. Matilde is all white sugar—sweet and forgiving—while I'm pure acidic lemon. Why can't I find any sympathy for Mamita? Why do I feel only rage?

Matilde stands up, and Santiago follows. "Get your bags, Virginia," she says. "Let's go, little sister."

"I—I can't."

"What?"

"I can't go," I say, almost defiantly. "I can't leave the children. They're at school and Niño Carlitos is in Quito for two days."

Matilde looks at me doubtfully.

I go on. "And anyway, I'm scared of what my bosses will do to me."

She and Santiago glance at each other out of the corner of their eyes, as though they have their own secret language.

It's not supposed to be like this. I'm supposed to have the secret sister language with Matilde, and Santiago is supposed to be the outsider. "And—and more than that," I say. "Matilde, we never laughed together as teenagers or told each other secrets or talked about crushes on guys." I glare at Santiago. "You're all grown up and getting married—and—and it's too late now."

Matilde throws her pudgy arms around me. "Oh, come on. Just because I'm getting married doesn't mean I'm dying. I'm here! We can still share things."

I push her away. It's as if no time has passed, as if we're girls and she's made me so angry I want to pounce on her and hit her. My voice grows shrill. "No, we can't! You don't understand. There's more to it, there's the price I've paid to live here with these people. I have no money. I have nothing to show! Sure, my body has grown taller, but my spirit—my spirit has grown small and bitter."

Matilde puts a hand to her mouth and steps toward me.

I move away. "The Doctorita said she'd give me a diploma. And my own house. And I don't think it's worth it to leave after so many years of suffering and—"

"Virginia!" Matilde yells. "You're crazy! Now that you can finally go, you're choosing to stay? And for what? A house?"

She's shaking, and Santiago's holding her elbow to steady her. I don't remember her ever yelling before; she always seemed as soft and mushy as overcooked potatoes.

"I swear to you, Virginia, they will never give you a house! Look at all the other *indígenas* who spend their lives serving, without being given anything in return. That's all they do. They serve the *mestizos*. And that's how you want to live? That's how you choose to live your whole life?"

I'm speechless, standing in the middle of the living room. The door of my prison is open and I'm too scared to leave. I bury my face in my hands. "I don't know. I'm so confused. I tried to leave before and they wouldn't let me."

Matilde's face is blazing. "Virginia, listen to me. What are they going to do to us? We're your family. We have every right to claim you."

"But you don't understand. They're going to punish me, beat me."

"Listen, little sister. I'll come with our parents the day after tomorrow. Your bosses can't hurt you if we all come."

I'm still not convinced, but I say, "Fine."

After they leave, I wash the lemonade glasses to hide evidence that they've been here. My mind feels like a thick, swampy cesspool, a muddled mess. I was always the strong one, and Matilde weak. Now Matilde is the one who wants to stand up and fight, while I'm ready to roll over, belly-up, like a frightened puppy. I don't even know who I am anymore.

chapter 27

THE NEXT DAY, Niño Carlitos comes home looking haggard, with dark crescents beneath his eyes. He plunks down at the kitchen table and I bring him lemonade before he even asks. "Are you hungry?" I ask, biting my cuticle.

He shakes his head and sips the lemonade.

"How's the Doctorita?"

"Fine. Bored. Knitting a lot."

I stand in the kitchen doorway, watching him, trying to force the words out.

He glances up. "What is it?"

"I have to tell you something."

"What?" His voice is wary.

"My family is coming tomorrow."

He stops sipping. "H-h-how did they find out you're here?" He's stuttering. He must be scared.

"I called my sister."

The vein in his forehead pops out. "Where did you call from?" he booms. "And with what money? Did you steal from us?"

You *stole from* me! I want to shout. *You stole my childhood.*

Instead, I say, "Blanca's mother let me use her phone."

"And what did you tell her?"

"Nothing. Just that I wanted to talk with my sister. And she came here and we talked."

"So you were plotting together in secret? Remember what happened last time you tried this?"

"I'm used to bloody noses," I say quietly. "One more won't matter."

He slams back his chair. There's splashing and clattering as he dumps the lemonade in the sink, pours a cup of liquor, downs it, and pours a second cup. Then he storms over to Blanca's house, banging on her door. "Don't let Virginia use your phone!" His shouts sound through the walls. "I forbid it. And stay out of our business."

That night, I barely sleep, my muscles tensed, watching my locked bedroom door. With dread, I wait for the knob to turn, the banging to start. But all is quiet, eerily quiet, except for the tick-tick-tick of my clock. The room feels small and suffocating, and I begin to worry that he might lock me in here. He could tell my family I went away. Or that I changed my mind. And keep me prisoner. But I'm too scared to open the door to check. He might be there, waiting. All I can do is watch the patch of black night through my window turn to blue and then yellow, ever so slowly, with the light of morning.

* * *

Niño Carlitos and I do not talk at breakfast. I sweep the floors, even though they don't need sweeping, to give my hands something to do. Every few minutes, I peek anxiously out the window. Niño Carlitos has sent the boys to their room to play and now he sits on the red sofa holding his origami instruction book—his latest project—with little squares of colored paper spread on the table in front of him. His eyes stare at the print, unmoving, his fingers motionless on the pages. He looks old and worn, like the red velvet sofa that's frayed and faded over the years. The first time I saw all that velvet, eight years earlier, I thought of berries and blood. Sweetness and fear. And now I see that my life with these people has been a confusing mixture of both.

The doorbell rings.

Niño Carlitos puts down the origami book, takes a long breath, and stands up. I make it to the door first, and open it.

Two strangers face me. They look small and old and dark. There is a man who must be my father. He barely reaches Niño Carlitos's shoulder. The sour smells of wood smoke and wool and cows cling to him, saturating his poncho, his rough skin. He's not the scary, big man I remember from my childhood. No, he stands crookedly, like a humble farmer, out of place in this city, out of place on the milk-white tile floor. His feet look like animal paws in sandals, heavily calloused with thick nail-claws and coated with dirt. His worn hat keeps his eyes shadowed.

And the woman who is my mother stands behind him, shorter than me, her shoulders hunched, a black shawl knotted at her neck over her blouse. Fake gold earrings and fat plastic beads loop around her neck, framing a face that might have once been pretty but is now deeply lined with exhaustion.

Beside them, Matilde and Santiago are smiling expectantly, Matilde with her apple cheeks and Santiago with a wide gap between his front teeth. Maybe I'm supposed to hug my mother, the way Matilde hugged me before. But Mamita never held me or comforted me as a child. Anyway, how can I touch this strange *indígena*? She's no different from the ones begging for coins on the street with outstretched hands—the ones who make guilt creep over you like tiny, biting fleas.

"Come in," Niño Carlitos says gruffly, and ushers them into the room.

My father removes his hat and holds it in his thick, farmer's hands, the palms caked with grime, soil caught beneath the fingernails. Teary-eyed, my mother takes a step toward me and pats my back lightly, murmuring words in Quichua.

I cringe at her touch. I have no idea what she's saying. She could be a guinea pig, chattering in incomprehensible squeaks.

Seeing my blank face, my father speaks in broken Spanish, choppy and slow. "Are you all right? Where have you been all these years? Why didn't you come back? Why did you leave us?"

The words stick in my throat. Finally I whisper, "They said you didn't want me anymore."

"*Tonta!* Fool! How could you believe what they say? You know how the *mishus* are."

I stare at my father, unable to speak. *Then why did you let them take me?*

Niño Carlitos clears his throat and says, "Sit down," motioning to the sofa. My parents perch on the red velvet, their feet not quite reaching the ground, dangling like children's feet. Matilde and Santiago sit in the armchairs and I drag in two dining room chairs for Niño Carlitos and me to sit on. There's room for me on the sofa, but I don't want my mother to try to touch me again.

"So, how is the corn harvest this year?" Niño Carlitos asks, as though they're normal visitors.

"Fine," my father says.

"N-n-not much rain, though." Niño Carlitos shuffles the origami papers nervously. Red, yellow, blue, green, gold.

My father shakes his head.

"How was the p-p-potato crop?"

My father scoots forward on the sofa, so that his sandaled feet skim the floor. "Why did you take my daughter? Why? Why didn't you ever bring her to visit?"

I flush at his directness.

Niño Carlitos is caught off guard. "W-w-well, she's the one who didn't want to go. A-a-and also, you know, we've been really busy."

"Busy for eight years?" my father says. "She's my daughter. You had no right to keep her here." I strain to understand his thick accent. It's like trying to understand a two-year-old. He can't pronounce his r's properly, and his vowels come out all wrong.

Niño Carlitos turns to me. "*M'hijita*, you haven't wanted to leave, isn't that right? You've been happy with us, learning all kinds of things. Isn't that right, my daughter?"

I press my lips together, tasting the cherry gloss, and stay silent.

My father says, "We've come to take Virginia back."

226

"But Miguelito," Niño Carlitos says, his voice suddenly hard, "what do you have to offer her? You live in filth. In a place like that, anything could happen to a young woman. Here with us, she's safe."

"We're bringing her home."

Then my sister speaks, eyes flashing with anger. "Virginia, tell this man! Isn't it true that you want to come with us?"

I hesitate. I don't know what I want. Suddenly, the thought of leaving forever terrifies me. Leaving and starting a new life with these strangers who are supposed to be my family. Maybe I could just go for a little while and see how I feel with them. And if I don't like it, I can come back to live here, where life isn't perfect, but at least I know what to expect. At least I know who I am.

I swallow hard. "Well, Niño Carlitos, it's just that I want to go to my sister's wedding. That's all." My voice sounds small and timid. "A few days. Just for the wedding."

Matilde widens her eyes. "Virginia—"

"And when is the wedding?" Niño Carlitos interrupts.

"In a week."

He turns to my sister. "So you're only taking her for the wedding, then bringing her back?"

"Yes," I say quickly. "Of course."

Niño Carlitos weighs my words. "Fine," he says, turning to my father. "I'll send Virginia to Yana Urku in a week."

My father stands up and my mother follows, hanging her head like a submissive *indígena* wife, and then Santiago and Matilde stride to the door, hand in hand, glaring at Niño Carlitos. Mamita pats me on the shoulder and says some things in Quichua. I give her a weak smile.

227

"We'll be waiting for you there, Daughter," my father says. "On Friday."

"And on Monday, she returns here," Niño Carlitos says harshly. "Right, my daughter?"

I nod, even though from what I remember, weddings in Yana Urku seemed to go on for days, maybe even weeks. But I'll deal with that later. I'm too overwhelmed to argue. For now I want these people to leave so I can think about what I'm going to do.

"Goodbye, my daughter," Papito says, and Mamita says something in Quichua.

Matilde holds my hand tightly. She narrows her eyes at Niño Carlitos. "You promise you'll let her come?"

"I always keep my promises," he says, smoothing the few strands of hair over his bald spot.

"Promise you won't touch her?" she presses. "You won't hurt her?"

He pats my shoulder. "I've never hurt you before, have I, my daughter?"

I step away.

Matilde hugs me, whispering in my ear, "You're not really coming back here, are you?"

"I don't know, Matilde. I don't know."

After they leave, Niño Carlitos slouches on the sofa, folding origami and then balling the paper up and throwing it against the wall. After three throws, he seems to come to a decision, and calmly picks up a bright green square. With precise movements, he folds a perfect origami frog. "For you, my daughter," he says, offering it to me. Then he calls upstairs, "Come on, kids! Get in the truck. I have a surprise."

The boys run downstairs and bounce into the truck. I follow warily.

He drives us to Yaguarcocha Lake, nestled between green mountains, a place where we've come only a few times before for special treats. The water in this lake is supposed to be sacred. If you throw an orange peel into the lake, it passes through long underground tunnels and mysteriously reappears kilometers away, at the Peguche waterfall, a place where wishes come true.

At a restaurant at the lake's edge, we eat our fill of fried fish and share a giant bottle of Coca-Cola, which the Doctorita never lets us have for fear of cavities. Afterward, we buy a bag of tangerines for dessert, and as the boys play chase on the shore, Niño Carlitos walks with me. Sunlight glints off the water, off the tips of tall grasses and reeds.

"You like the origami frog, *m'hija?*" he asks.

"Yes." I squint up at him, the sunlight so dazzling it's hard to see.

"I can make you a penguin next."

"All right." I pop the last section of tangerine in my mouth. I like the juicy, sweet part, but have to force the white, stringy part down my throat. I toss the peel into the lake, watching the waves lick at it, carrying it farther from shore. How long it will take it to travel to the place where wishes come true? Weeks? Months? Years? Will it really ever get there?

I try to make a decision. It was easier to feel strong when Niño Carlitos was attacking me. Then I *knew* I had to leave.

I had no choice. But now that he's showing his sweet side, I feel weak. Staying with him might not be so bad after all.

Niño Carlitos holds out his hand, midair, on the path to touching my cheek, then he snatches it back and rubs it over his face. "Virginia, I don't know what I'd do without you."

chapter 28

OVER THE NEXT WEEK, Niño Carlitos gushes compliments about my potato and chicken soup, brings me blackberry jam pastries, and takes me and the boys walking in the park. He makes me an origami penguin, crane, cow, and caterpillar. He does not try to come into my room all week. He does not try to touch me or hug me or cling to me like a magnet. The memories of the scary Niño Carlitos slide from my grasp like a wet bar of soap, and all I see is a thoughtful, generous man who is skilled at origami.

"Are you sure you want to go to this wedding?" he asks on Thursday night.

"Yes. But I'll come back." I can't meet his eyes as I say this.

On Friday morning, I put on my best dress, long and flowered with narrow lace trim around the neckline and a fitted waist. I brush my hair and pull it into a ponytail with a little of the Doctorita's gel.

At the bus station, Niño Carlitos stares at me a long time and says, "Goodbye, my daughter."

I hug the boys tightly, one in each arm, and whisper, "You are my favorite little boys in the whole world. Remember that." I don't want to let go. What if this is the last time I see them? With a lump in my throat, I kiss their noses. "Take care of each other while I'm gone."

When the bus pulls away, I let my tears fall. After an hour, the bus parks at the station in Otavalo. Once I step off the bus and look around, trying to orient myself, everything seems unfamiliar. I remember the day a decade ago when I came alone to go to the market for my boots. I feel exactly like that little lost girl again.

After hours of wandering, asking for directions and getting conflicting answers, I find the side street where the buses to Yana Urku pass. When I climb on the bus, people stare. I want to think it's because I look beautiful in my dress. But the truth is, I'm one of the only girls on the bus not dressed in *indígena* clothes. I sit toward the back and look out the window, at the fields and white houses with red roofs and cows and pigs in the yards, the hills and scattered trees, and beyond them, lush mountains topped with jagged peaks. I push the window open and breathe in the soil and farm smells and woodsmoke. I reach up and let my hair loose from my ponytail, let it fall over my shoulders and run my fingers through it.

I am free. I can wear my hair how I want. I can dress how I want. I can go wherever I want. I can say whatever I want. I can do anything. The breeze blows in, lifting my hair up as though it has a life all its own, and I try to embrace my freedom. It's not easy with this giant nervous ball gnawing at my stomach.

At the elementary school, I get off the bus. After just a few steps, my good shoes are coated in dust. I pass the low concrete building that brings back the feeling of the teacher's sharp fingernails and the dreaded smell of chalk dust. It's as if I fell asleep ages ago and had a long, strange dream and now I'm waking up. Nothing has changed—the school, the pink corner store, the crooked barbed-wire fences covered with drying clothes.

I drift along, and just before the turnoff to my parents' house, I spot Papito at the edge of a field, by the road, fixing the fence. I pick up my pace, trying not to turn my ankles in the potholes. As I draw near, he looks up at me with a blank expression, then returns his gaze to the fence.

About fifteen paces away from him, I stop and stare, willing him to greet me. He looks up again for a longer moment, then goes back to hammering the fence post.

He doesn't remember me. He's forgotten me all over again, after only a week.

"Papi," I say in a hurt voice.

He stares blankly.

"Papi, it's me, Virginia."

He keeps staring. "That's you, Virginia?"

"Yes," I say, struggling to hold back my tears.

"Your hair's different." He sticks his hammer in his belt and says in Quichua, *"Venipe,"* motioning for me to come.

I walk toward him.

"How are you?" he asks.

"Fine."

We look at each other for another awkward moment and then he says, "Mamá is in the house."

"And Matilde?"

233

"In Quito. We'll all go there tomorrow."

I give a light nod. "All right."

"The wedding will last a week," he says, watching me.

"I know." ·

"You're not going back to the *mishus*, are you, Daughter?" His voice is low, rough with emotion.

I stare at the ground. "I don't know."

He pauses, then says, "After the wedding, we can go get your things. You can live with us."

I don't answer. In silence, we walk up the wide, weedy path, past the chickens pecking at trash at the side of the field, past the dogs that growl at me until my father waves a stick at them.

The yard and house haven't changed except for the walls, which are now made of cement block instead of earth. The door is the same, a heavy wooden plank, and I push it open. Inside, my eyes take a moment to adjust to the dimness. There is the same dirt floor; a cooking fire to the left, with a pot of mint tea bubbling over it; pots and pans on rickety shelves; homemade wooden beds to the right, with old clothes piled up in falling-apart cardboard boxes; guinea pigs squeaking in the corner.

Mamita looks up from the simmering tea and stares at me, her wooden spoon frozen in midair.

Before she has a chance to not recognize me, Papito says, "It's Virginia."

"*Ñuka guagua*," she murmurs, like a birdcall. "*Ñuka guagua.*" In a flash, the meaning comes to me—*my daughter, my girl*; it's what she would say with pride when I gave neighbors a spiritual cleaning with herbs. *My daughter, she can do it.* "*Ñuka guagua*," she says, in tears.

Five children kneel on the floor near the cooking pot,

looking at me with big, scared eyes. When I smile at them, they
cover their faces with their hands and run to the corner, where
they huddle as far from me as possible. They're filthy, barefoot,
their skin caked in dirt, their hair a wild mess.

"*Buenas tardes,*" I say.

They say nothing, just peek at me between fingers.

My father says in Spanish, "These are your cousins and
brother and sister, Virginia."

The two oldest must be Hermelinda and Manuelito. They
would be the right ages. I swallow hard, searching their eyes for
some glimmer of recognition. Nothing.

Mamita clears off a space on a bed and motions for me to sit
down. I hesitate, sure there are fleas or bedbugs crawling around
in the wool and woven reeds. But there is nowhere else to sit,
no sofa, no chair. If I were an *indígena* guest, they would spread
an *estera* of woven grass on the ground and offer me a seat there.
But I'm not one of them. I perch on the edge of the bed.

Mamita motions to her stomach and mimes eating.

I shake my head. "I'm not hungry."

She goes outside, gesturing for me to follow her. At the side
of the house, she grabs one of the chickens rooting around in
the torn paper wrappers and cracked plastic bottles and dirty
diapers strewn in the weeds. Unceremoniously, she snaps the
chicken's neck. When I was little, we ate meat only on special
occasions. I tell myself I should feel happy she considers my arrival worthy of a chicken sacrifice.

Back inside, she makes chicken and potato soup and speaks
to me in Quichua. I try to decipher the words, but they run together like a gurgling stream, and when she asks me a question,
I shake my head and shrug. *Api*—soup—is the only word I

remember. Slowly, the children approach me, asking me questions in Quichua, which I can't answer. They dare each other to touch me. One after another scurries forward and pokes at my loose hair and then scampers off to the others, giggling.

Mamita serves me first, giving me the biggest piece of chicken and the biggest potato from the soup, what I yearned for so much as a little girl. We sit around the fire and eat, the children kneeling on the floor, my father on one stool, and me on the other. As a little girl, I longed to be given the honor of the stool, but now I just feel too tall and awkward, with these children staring and whispering about me from below. I can only pick out the word *mishu* in their whispers. *Mestiza*. My siblings and cousins think I am a *mestiza*. And why wouldn't they? I'm dressed as a *mestiza* and I don't speak their language and they have to notice how uncomfortable I feel in this dirty house.

Mamita has given up on making conversation with me, and she slurps her soup in silence. Papito asks me a few questions in his broken Spanish, which I answer with a few words. I wish I had a spoon and knife and fork. They sip their soup directly from the bowl and eat the chicken with their hands. I want a napkin for my greasy fingers, or a table to put the bowl on so I won't have to balance it clumsily on my knees. The hem of my best dress is already coated in dust and grime.

Earlier, my mother gave me a glass of water, but I didn't touch it, worried she hadn't boiled the water first. Under a microscope, a drop of it would probably look worse than the swamp water I secretly examined in the Doctorita's lab. The water in my glass has to be swimming with microbes, judging by the children's skinny limbs and swollen bellies, signs of amoebic infections.

After the soup, I offer to help wash the dishes, but Mamita says no, motioning that she and the children will do it. She says something to my father in Quichua and he translates: "Why don't you walk around the pastures, where you used to go with the cows?"

I nod, a little hurt that they want me out of the house already, but mostly relieved to have a break from them. I grab my notebook and a pen and head down the road. On the way to the pasture, my good shoes become completely coated with mud. Everyone I pass stares at me from a distance and then, as we grow closer, looks down at their feet and mumbles *buenas tardes, señorita* in heavily accented Spanish. After they pass, I feel them sneak glimpses back at me and whisper to each other.

I veer off the road, onto a path through the eucalyptus grove, down into the green canyon, to the little stream where I used to look for watercress when I was hungry. I sit on a rock at the water's edge, listen to its murmuring and the insects' humming, feeling utterly alone. What would I do in this place?

I open my notebook and begin writing a story about a girl named Soledad. Her name means Aloneness.

The heart-wrenching story of Soledad starts one year before she was born, when her mother—a poor, beautiful woman—was seduced in the moonlight by a rich, handsome man. Later, when she told him she was pregnant with their child, he abandoned her, tossing her away like a picked-clean chicken bone. The baby was born with a coating of moonlight stuck to her skin, and she was named Soledad. As her mother slaved away as a servant, little Soledad wandered the pastures, trailing moon glimmer, side by side with her only friend, the cow. Without so much as a sister to keep her company, Soledad felt as though she were the only girl in the universe, leaving behind tears like comets, much as her beloved cow left behind trails of manure as part of the carbon cycle. . . .

I'm deep into Soledad's story, which is going to be juicier than any soap opera, when Manuelito appears at the edge of the eucalyptus grove, shouts something in Quichua, and then runs away. That's when I realize it's already dusk and the crickets are chirping and the air is growing chilly. With heavy feet, I walk uphill to my family's shack.

My parents sleep on one bed and I sleep on the other, along with my brother and sister. In and out of sleep I drift, wakened every so often by Manuelito's and Hermelinda's snoring, by the biting fleas, by the scuttling of little creatures beneath the bed, which I hope are guinea pigs but suspect are rats. I ask myself: *Where do you want to live? Do you want to live free and poor and covered in flea welts? Or enslaved, with your own clean room and a shower with hot water? Who are you, Virginia? Who are you, really?* And as I fade in and out of dreams, that wind music carries me through memories and valleys and over mountains and then it changes into my own voice, my spunky, five-year-old voice belting out, *Stand tall, little radish flower. Stand tall.*

When I was a little girl, I would go to the bakery, and the owners—two sisters—would tell me to sing for them. I sang the *Rabanito* song, about a purple radish flower standing tall and proud in the wind. They laughed and clapped and said, *How* vivísima *this girl is!* and gave me a free warm roll as a reward.

Maybe that's what I need to do now, muster up everything that was ever *vivísima* about me and somehow find a way to stand tall.

238

chapter 29

ON SATURDAY MORNING, I leave with my whole family for Quito by bus, along with cousins and aunts and uncles and grandparents. We're loaded down with sacks of food for Matilde's wedding feast—corn and potatoes and squirming guinea pigs, their squeaking barely muffled by the bag. Santiago's family lives just outside of Quito, and their house is full of activity, people preparing for the wedding.

In the yard, small groups of *indígena* women are stirring steaming pots of beans and chicken broth over fires, and peeling an enormous mountain of potatoes. I help peel, waving the stinging smoke from my eyes as the women talk and joke in Quichua, ignoring me. Mamita is busy butchering guinea pigs in a swarm of flies under a tree. After slitting the creatures' throats, she lowers the barely dead carcasses into boiling water, then tears off their fur. With deft hands, she slices open their bellies, pulls out their goopy organs, and washes their flesh in a bucket so they're ready for roasting. Meanwhile, Matilde is overseeing the arrangement of balloons and flowers. I've hardly seen her all day. I retreat into the imaginary world of Soledad, inventing more twists and turns to her story, eager to write it all down before I forget.

The next day, the wedding day, I wear my other favorite dress, a light blue one with pleats that fall just below my knees and narrow sleeves that stop at my elbows. I polish my good shoes as best I can; although they're scuffed from my walk to the pasture, most of the dried mud comes off. Outside the church, I'm adrift in a sea of *anacos* and gold beads and blue ponchos; only a few other people are dressed like *mestizos*. I follow Mamita and Papito around as they speak with guests. When people glance at me curiously and question Mamita in Quichua, she motions to me and explains, I suppose, that I'm her long-lost daughter. Then they smile sympathetically and nod while I fiddle nervously with the sash of my dress.

Inside the church, pink and white flowers and balloons abound. My sister looks like a big cloud in her white gown with poufy sleeves and long train. Santiago wears white pants, a white shirt, blue poncho, and a stiff new sombrero. I can see only their backs as the pastor speaks to them, in Spanish, for which I am grateful.

"Today," he booms, "you will leave your families and form a new family of your own." He turns to my parents and siblings and me. "Best of wishes to you. Your daughter and sister—a part of you—will go far from you. She will be yours but no longer yours."

And I start bawling, because she never really was mine, was she? None of them were, and none of them are now.

* * *

After the ceremony, we take buses to the reception hall and wait outside as the banquet food is laid out. I lean against a tree, wishing I could climb it and hide in the branches. Even the Doctorita's house would be better than here. Her family needs me; her boys love me. There I'm useful. There I can speak the language. I look at the crowd gathered around Matilde and Santiago, talking excitedly in Quichua. Santiago catches my eye, excuses himself, and walks over to me.

"How do you feel, Virginia? Now that you're finally home with your family?" He looks at me with his mouth half-open in concern, as though he really wants to know.

"To tell the truth, Santiago, I feel out of place." There, I've said it, what's already obvious. "I want to go home. To the Doctorita's home. And I'm dreading the next few days, when everyone gets drunk and fights. That's what I remember about fiestas when I was a little girl. My father getting drunk and angry and hitting us."

Santiago plucks a leaf from the tree, turns it over in his fingers. "Did you know that your father's father was a slave to the *mestizos*? His boss could whip him with a leather *soga* for something as simple as not addressing him with enough respect. Your father watched his own father be punished this way. He was probably whipped this way himself."

"I didn't know," I say, conscious of the scars from the time my father hung me from the rafters and beat me with a *soga*. Every day I see the scars when I sit on the edge of my bed after my shower and rub cream on my legs. The lines crisscross my calves, shiny, a different texture from the rest of my skin. Now I can feel them, an old, throbbing ache.

I wonder, could a man feel so powerless in the world that he

241

looks in smaller places for power . . . power over his children and wife? Could a man do to his children what the *mestizos* did to him? And could this go on and on in a chain, like baking soda and carbon dioxide reacting in my volcano, bubbling over with bloodred dye?

Matilde's voice rings across the grass. "Santiago! Come on!"

He squeezes my hand and jogs over to her. I spot my father, waiting in a line to enter the hall, and I slip my hand in his.

"I'm glad you're home, *m'hijita*," Papito says. He seems more tender than I remembered. Still gruff, still a man of few words, but now I see flickers of something like love. He's a jagged rock worn smooth by years of water currents, and if the light is right, hidden bits of goodness glint like mica. I lean against his wool poncho. "Papito, can I come inside your poncho?" As a little girl, I secretly wanted to do this.

He nods, and I lift the poncho and duck underneath and lean my head against his chest, and it feels cozy and dark and warm. I like blocking out the rest of the world, muffling all the chatter I can't understand. I like the smell of wool and wood smoke. He holds me against him. I think of Niño Carlitos and how when he touches me it feels terrible, even though he calls me daughter too. But my father's touch, his hug, feels right. As though I could forgive everything and dwell in this singular moment, in the warmth he's offering me now, the warmth of a father who loves his daughter.

"Are you all right, *m'hijita*?"

"Yes." I feel his heart beat against my ear. "Papi, if I leave the Doctorita's house, will you always protect me? Will you make sure that no one hurts me? Will you always love me?"

242

He pats my back. "You're my daughter. Of course I'll protect you."

And these words make me feel warm, even though I know that really, I'm the one who will have to protect myself. But here under this poncho, for this moment, I let myself sink into this feeling.

It is inside this safe space that I decide I will try.

I will try to leave the Doctorita and Niño Carlitos forever. I will try to build a new life for myself in Yana Urku with my family. And even though part of me still aches and rages over the way my parents carelessly gave away my childhood, I will try, somehow, to love them again. Most of all, I will try to figure out who I am and who I might someday become.

At Niño Carlitos and the Doctorita's house, with my family standing behind me, I take a breath and ring the bell. It's Thursday. Niño Carlitos was expecting me to return on Monday. But Monday slipped away and I stayed with my family in Quito, eating my fill of guinea pig stew with Santiago's family and the other guests. Mamita and Papito drank plenty of *puro*, but thankfully stopped before the fighting started. And then Tuesday passed, and on Wednesday we took a bus back to Yana Urku.

And now it is Thursday, and here I am, three days late. Niño Carlitos will be furious. I tell myself it doesn't matter. I'm not coming back here to stay; that's my decision, and I have to stick to it. *Unless*, a little voice in me says. *Unless he apologizes and begs me to stay, then maybe.*

I quiet that voice, wondering if I should have come here at

all today. My parents and Matilde and Santiago wanted to come without me and pick up my things and tell Niño Carlitos I would never return. But I insisted on coming, too. I want to see the boys one last time and say goodbye properly and make sure I get all my clothes and other belongings. That's my excuse, at least, but secretly I've felt reassured knowing that at the last minute I can still change my mind.

Niño Carlitos answers the door. He doesn't greet us, just demands, "Why weren't you here three days ago?"

"Good afternoon," I say. I wait for him to invite us in, but he stands blocking the door.

"So, where were you?" Niño Carlitos asks, barely glancing at my family.

"The party lasted all week."

"Well, I hope you're happy. There was no one here to cook or look after the boys. And meanwhile, la Negra had the baby. Now say goodbye to these people and get inside."

And suddenly, my last flecks of doubt disappear. Suddenly, I believe in my decision with absolute certainty, a certainty that thrums through every cell in my body. "I'm leaving with my parents."

He hesitates. "Come inside. We'll talk." But he does not invite us to sit down, so we stand awkwardly in the living room.

The Doctorita is lying on the sofa. Her belly is still swollen from childbirth and her hair disheveled and her face weary without makeup. "Well? What took you so long?" She doesn't even acknowledge my family, just gives me a sour look.

"I'm leaving with my parents. Forever."

If she had the strength to throw something at me, I'm sure

she would. "Ungrateful *longa*! After all these years we've taken care of you, given you food, raised you. I offered you that school diploma. You're a fool to give that up."

I speak softly. "For many years you've offered to get me the diploma. I don't think you'll ever give it to me."

"It's just that I was too busy, but now it's all set. If you stay I can get it for you right away. Next week."

I stare at her. "I don't think so."

"What are you going to do there anyway, in that pigsty? Live with the animals? It's filthy there."

I say nothing.

"Fine, get your things. And take your blanket and sheets with you. Now that a *longa's* used them all these years, they're contaminated. I'd just throw them out. Go now, quickly, so I don't have to look at you anymore."

I walk out of the room. *Stand tall, little radish flower.* I keep my head high. I stop by the kitchen and get a garbage bag from under the sink, then head upstairs and stuff my clothes and the blanket and sheets in the bag, not bothering to fold anything.

Back downstairs, the Doctorita is writing something on a piece of paper. "Before you leave, sign this."

"Why?"

"Just sign it, before you make me angrier."

I read the paper.

> I, María Virginia Farinango, am leaving this house of my own will, feeling very grateful, be-cause my bosses have treated me very well, and I was very happy living with them all

these years. They gave me food and clothes and an education and I'm very grateful and have nothing bad to say about them.

I look up. "But this isn't true."

She folds her arms. "Sign the paper."

"But—"

"You're not leaving until you sign."

"I don't think—"

"Sign it!"

Reluctantly, I sign my name.

She snatches the paper. "What terrible handwriting you have. Is that your sorry excuse for a signature?"

"That's my signature," I say between clenched teeth.

"Now go," she says, "and take those rags with you."

Niño Carlitos nearly pushes us out the door. When I'm on the threshold, the Doctorita calls out in a wild, shrill voice, "You know what? In three months, you'll be at this door, knocked up and begging me for work. Just like all *longas*. Once they get on the street, they breed like dogs and then when they're pregnant they come back pleading, 'Oh, help me.' And when you come back on your knees, I'm not going to help you. I'm going to tell you to get the hell away. Don't even try to come back saying, 'Oh, but Doctorita, please, *por favorcito* . . .'"

We leave through the gate and walk down the street. I am shaking and burning with humiliation. *One day she will be sorry,* I tell myself. *She will come to me, asking for my forgiveness.* For two blocks I say nothing to my family because if I open my mouth, red-hot flames might shoot out.

Finally, at the bus station, Santiago says, "What they did to you was illegal, Virginia. A crime. Even though you signed that paper, you might be able to press charges and sue them."

Anger is fire that can burn you up, the way it made my father hurt his family. Or it can shine like the sun and provide energy for photosynthesis. I will use my fire as fuel to live the life I want to lead. Whether I'm a *longa* or *mestiza* or whatever, Antonio was right, I have a blazing sun inside me and I will use it.

"I just want to live my life now," I say.

"You don't want revenge?" Santiago asks.

"My revenge will be getting an education and having my own career. One day she'll see that she's wrong. One day she'll ask for my forgiveness. In the end, I'll win."

chapter 30

IT'S THE MORNING OF MY FIRST DAY OF SCHOOL, and I'm sitting on the stool by the fire pit, trying to keep the hem of my best dress off the dirt floor. I sip at my soup, almost too excited to eat.

Papito gives me a doubtful look. "I don't see why you have to go to school."

"It's my dream, Papi," I say firmly. During my first week of living with my family, I heard about an opportunity for older, uneducated kids to attend school. I signed up immediately. When I told Mamita about it, she frowned and muttered something in Quichua. Papito grunted that school was a waste of time and money.

Now he pokes at the ashes with a stick, shaking his head. "You could be working in the fields instead."

I counter with the answer I've prepared. "In the long run I'll make more money with an education." I'm not arguing with him, just stating the facts. We both know that whether he approves or not, I'm going forward with my plans.

He and Mamita have been treating me like a houseguest over the past week, an important outsider to politely accommodate. This distance feels wrong, awkward, yet in some ways it seems easier than acting as though we have a bond. It makes my chest ache, wondering if we might be too different to ever make any real connection.

It seems hopeless, since even our thoughts have nothing in common. My mind is filled with ideas and plans and information I've read. I'm always inventing stories to write in my notebook or imagining I'm traveling to the Seven Wonders of the World. I don't want to forget what I've learned, so I make mental diagrams of the respiratory system, the process of condensation, meiosis and mitosis. I look at the mountains and imagine the geological movements of plates beneath Earth's crust over millenia. I love letting my mind leap from microscopic things to immense things and back again. It reminds me that the universe is full of possibility.

And what goes on in my parents' minds? I'm guessing they must be practical things, rooted in the small world of a farming community: when to harvest the potatoes and radishes and onions; whether to butcher the chicken for lunch or keep it longer for its eggs; how to stop mice from getting into the sacks of corn in the rafters; how many days until the pregnant sheep births her lambs.

Our differences aren't the only obstacles to forming a bond. Sometimes, when my parents look at me, I catch glimpses of shame or regret, what must be lingering guilt about giving me away. I wish I could hug them and tell them it's all right, that I'm letting go and moving on. Instead, I look away. As much as I want to reach out, my hurt feels too raw. It's not a simple thing to forgive such a huge betrayal.

Papito breaks the silence. "You're too old for school."

"I'll be good at it," I say evenly. "I'll like it."

But on my way to school, weaving around mud patches and potholes, I feel less certain. What if the other students shun me because I'm so much older than them? As part of the continuing education program, the elementary school principal said he'd let me enter sixth grade, even though I'm about fifteen, and let the teacher decide whether that's the right level. Which brings me to another fear: what if that terrible teacher with the sharp fingernails is still there?

Inside the classroom, I discover I'm the tallest student by at least a head or two. The desks are too small for me; my knees push up into the wood. The first class is Spanish, all about subjects and predicates. I haven't studied those before, but as soon as the teacher explains, it makes sense and I raise my hand high to answer every question. This teacher, Maestra Eva, is a young, pretty woman with a bright red blouse and gold hoop earrings and short, clipped fingernails, which she doesn't inflict on any students. When I'm wrong, she says, "Good try, Virginia," but most of the time I'm right, and she says, "Excellent, Virginia."

Then there's science, and of all things, they're studying plants. I answer every question correctly and Maestra Eva looks impressed at how the words *chlorophyll* and *respiration* and *nitrogen-fixing cycle* roll off my tongue. Next is math, fractions,

which is a little more difficult. I have to think hard and con-
centrate so much my head hurts. At recess, I sit beneath a tree
with my notebook and review subjects and predicates and fractions while the other children play.

Three days later, Principal Marcelo sends for me to come
to his office. I like him. He smiles often and really looks in your
eyes and listens when you talk, smoothing his mustache and
waiting a thoughtful beat before answering. "I've spoken with
your teacher, Virginia. She says you're very advanced in most
areas, that you're more at a *colegio* level."

I can't help smiling and telling him how I was a secret-agent
student. I've told my parents about it and they weren't impressed, but I have a feeling this man will appreciate it. "See, I
used to study in secret. My bosses were *colegio* teachers, and I
read their textbooks and did the students' homework and took
their tests." Since Principal Marcelo looks interested, I ramble
on a bit about the science experiments I did without the Doctorita knowing.

Once I finish, he's quiet, and then he says, "You, Virginia,
are an extraordinary girl. You will go far."

My heart swells. "Thank you."

"We think you should stay for three months, until the end
of the school year. I'll pull some strings and get you your
diploma so you can enter *colegio* in the fall."

I fly out of his office like a bird taking off from a tree. I wish
I could run home to a mother and father who would hug me
and congratulate me. Instead, I bring the cows and sheep to the
pasture and write more of Soledad's story.

251

*The lovely Soledad proved herself to be the most
brilliant student in the whole school. The teachers
loved her and gave her medals and scholarships for
being the best at everything. One day, when
Soledad came home to show her mother her latest
prize, her mother embraced her warmly, as usual.
"M'hija, I'm so proud of you." But then her
mother grew dizzy and collapsed and, through
sobs, revealed to her something terrible beyond
words. "M'hija, I am dying of cancer."*

*Soledad was sad, but brave. She asked for
help from passersby and swept the streets and
washed clothes in exchange for money, but one
tragic evening, in a pool of moonlight, her mother
died in her arms.*

As I finish Soledad's story, I know that despite her tragedies,
she will go far in life, even though she will have to live with
this piece of sadness inside her forever. She will have to make
her way alone in the world, but she is smart enough to do it.

The next week at school, Maestra Eva announces that some
important visitors—foreigners—will be coming, and they're
considering making a big donation to fund the construction of
a science lab at the school. They will come on Mother's Day,
and the sixth graders will put on a play in honor of our mothers and the foreigners. The performance will have to be really
good, she says, in order to win the hearts of these rich foreigners.

When I find out we're supposed to invite our families,

especially our mothers, an anxious knot forms inside me. Mamita would feel utterly out of place in a school auditorium. I wonder if she's even heard of Mother's Day, or if she'd agree to come to a school event. Even if I do invite her, I doubt she'd come.

After waffling over it late into the night, I fall asleep, still undecided. The next morning, over breakfast, it's on an impulse that I ask her, maybe from a sense of obligation, or maybe from a small hope that she'll enjoy seeing this piece of my world. I extend the invitation in Spanish, slowly, using gestures, feeling flushed with embarrassment. Through the steam of my soup, I watch her wrinkle her eyebrows in response, looking uncertain. She doesn't say whether or not she will come.

I'm determined to make the Mother's Day performance spectactular, not for my mother but for my teacher and principal, so they'll be proud of me. And I want to impress the foreigners, so they'll give my school the donation. All day, ideas for the show are brewing in my head. After school, I run to Maestra Eva's desk and tell her about my Soledad story. "It would make a perfect play for Mother's Day," I say, nearly bouncing with eagerness.

"Wonderful, Virginia!" she says, and puts me in charge of the whole production—writing, directing, casting, everything.

At home, in the kitchen with my family, as the children chatter in Quichua and my parents slurp tea, I consider telling them about this honor. But the words stick in my throat. They probably don't know what a play is, much less the different roles in producing one. I'm guessing that the words *director* and *playwright* don't even exist in Quichua. And even if I explained it slowly and simply, Papito would most likely brush off plays as a huge waste of time and grunt that I should be doing real work in the fields. So, as always, I stay quiet, sipping my tea and keeping my thoughts to myself.

For a week, while I'm pasturing the animals after school, I write the story out in script form in my notebook. Then, by hand, I copy a script for each student. There are twenty-two roles total, one for each student in the class. At the end of the week, my hand is aching as I assign students their roles. I am the lead, Soledad, because no other girl is able to cry on command, and that is essential to the part. During rehearsals, we laugh and have fun and, little by little, become friends.

On the day of the performance, all the students' parents and aunts and uncles and cousins and siblings have come, enough to fill the auditorium to overflowing. The important foreigners and school officials sit in the front rows in their suits and fancy dresses. Out in the audience, the *mestizos* and *indígenas* are all mixed together. From the wings, I spot my mother, with Manuelito and Hermelinda and my little cousins crowded around her. She looks just as confused and uncertain now as she did when I invited her.

Swallowing hard, I smooth the skirt of my favorite dress, the flowered one, and rub together my lipsticked lips. Maestra Eva has put some of her makeup on my face and pronounced me prettier than any movie star.

Onstage, in the spotlight, everything feels right. The audience is rapt. At the part where Soledad's mother dies and I have to cry, I draw on the valley of tears inside me. I think of the saddest moments of my life. I think of Antonio watching me leave on the bus. I think of Papito whipping my legs, the Doctorita beating me with hangers, Mamita saying she'd be happy if I left.

I think of watching the students from the balcony back in Kunu Yaku, wishing I could be one of them.

The tears pour out. I sob and moan and clutch my hair, pulling it in utter agony, pounding my fists on the wooden stage, consumed with grief, looking up toward the heavens, asking, *Why, why, why* . . . and finally I collapse on top of my dead mother.

The End.

As I stand up, I look at the audience and see that they're crying too, the women wiping their tears with their shawls, even the men catching their tears on shirt cuffs. Some are sniffling and tearing up silently, and some are sobbing openly. It feels as though they are crying for me, for all that I've suffered. The whole community is crying for my sorrows.

The rest of the cast streams onto the stage and we hold each others' hands. I bow first and they all follow. The audience is standing up, clapping and smiling and whistling. After a long time, the applause finally fades, and I hear people asking each other, *Who is that girl? Who are that girl's parents? Where did that girl come from? She's like a soap-opera star!*

Principal Marcelo comes onstage and says, "Thank you, sixth graders, for the brilliant performance. Well done! Now it's time for the students to present cards they've made to their mothers."

This is the moment I've been dreading. I look at all the other mothers and wish that any of them were mine instead of Mamita. My insides sink into a puddle of shame. My mother looks so small and poor and bewildered. She is entirely out of place here. I wish I could slip away and mysteriously disappear into the night.

After about eight kids, Principal Marcelo turns to me. "María Virginia Farinango," he says, with an encouraging smile. I feel myself flush at all the eyes following me as I weave through the crowd to my mother. And when I stop in front of her, I feel their confusion and hear their whispers. *But she is* mestiza *and her mother is* indígena. *How is that possible? How is it possible that her mother is so* humilde, *so poor and humble?*

My mother stares, baffled, as I present her with a red construction-paper heart, with writing on it that she has no idea how to read. In front of all these people, I am supposed to hug her, just like the other students hugged their mothers. I put my arms around her shoulders—for the first time I can remember—and she stiffens in my arms.

A week later, when Principal Marcelo gives me the good news, he hugs me, a natural joyful hug, the kind of hug he probably gives to his children every day. "Thank you so much for what you've done for our school. It's a great thing, Virginia. The school owes you a lot." It turns out that the foreigners were so impressed with the performance, they decided to pay the entire cost of the school's new science lab, even more than Principal Marcelo had hoped for. During the last two months of school, everyone buzzes about the mysterious actress who brought the whole village—even rich foreigners—to tears.

chapter 31

EVER SINCE THE MOTHER'S DAY PLAY, Mamita hasn't complained about my attending school. Sometimes, when she's talking to neighbors in Quichua, I overhear her say my name with an expression of pride. The one person in Yana Urku who is not at all impressed with my newly discovered ability to write, direct, act, and get good grades is Papito.

One night, as I'm doing homework by the light of the kerosene lamp, he says, "You know, you live here and eat our food." He pauses. "And that's fine because you're our daughter. But the rest of us work for this food. We plant corn and beans and we clear the fields of weeds and we harvest the crops. You spend all day at school, and what do you have to show for it?"

"But I will have a lot to show for it, Papi. Just wait. I'll get my diploma and then go to *colegio* and then to university."

"With what money, *m'hija?*"

He's got a point. Even though I'm only in elementary school, I can barely scrape together money to pay for notebooks and pens and pencils. And since this school is in a poor community, we don't have to pay for uniforms. But if I go to the *colegio* of my dreams—República de Ecuador, the one that the Doctorita's nephew Raúl went to—I'll have to pay for two sets of school uniforms and a gym uniform and outfits for special events, which cost hundreds of sucres.

To make money, I spend weekends planting for Alfonso and Mariana, who pay me a few sucres, a tiny fraction of what I need. I'm clumsy in the fields, holding the shovel awkwardly, my movements jerky and full of effort. All the other workers have spent their lives working in fields, and their hands move quickly, automatically. But I'm even slower at planting than the little children. When I drop the seeds in, I count them out, unable to feel, on instinct, how many are in my hands. And I'm out of place in my *mestiza* pants and T-shirt, when all the other women wear *anacos* and blouses.

What's more, when Mariana and Alfonso pass me, I notice a certain smugness in their gaze, as if they're thinking, *See, here you are working in the fields like the* longa *you are. You'd have been better off with Carlos and the Doctorita.* I imagine them telling the Doctorita how I work in the fields, and the Doctorita assuming it's a matter of time before I come begging for my job back. But they're some of the only landowners who pay in money, and there don't seem to be other part-time job opportunities here, so I swallow my pride and work for them.

As I work, I remember when I was a little girl pretending to be a rich *indígena*. Now I understand that these people I admired weren't exactly rich, simply better-off than the people of my village, one of the poorest in Ecuador. These middle-class *indígenas* came from Otavalo or less impoverished communities, and owned shops or market stands or export businesses. Even now, years later, whenever I go to the market with my mother, my eyes linger on their beautiful clothes and jewelry. They have enough money to educate their children and live comfortably, owning land, a car, a two-story house, a TV.

The *mestizos* treat them with more respect than the poor ones, which is not to say they're friendly. I've noticed that when a middle-class *indígena* buys something from a *mestizo's* shop, he's treated with only superficial politeness. If there are both an *indígena* and a *mestizo* waiting for assistance, nearly always the *mestizo* will be attended to first. There's so much broiling beneath the surface. The *mestizos* can barely disguise their prejudice; the *indígenas* can barely suppress their resentment. So the two groups exist in separate realms—the *mestizos* in theirs and the middle-class *indígenas* in theirs—and rarely do they mix.

It's obvious that the poor *indígenas*—the *longos*, as the Doctorita would call them—get the worst of it. They're scorned by *mestizos* and middle-class *indígenas* alike. The shopkeepers openly disdain them, not even bothering to use the polite *usted* form. This is how people treat my parents. When my mother and I are together at the market in Otavalo—me dressed in my regular clothes, and her in poor indigenous clothes—people assume I'm a *mestiza* girl with her maid.

Where do I fit in? I study these groups carefully, looking for clues, watching how they interact. Soon I realize that my in-between position could offer me freedom to move among them as I wish. I start wondering how the middle-class *indígenas* got that way. They—or their parents or grandparents—must have started out poor at some point. They must have been clever and

259

determined and somehow found a way to make money from nothing.

Again, I think back to when I was a little girl, practicing at being a rich *indígena* in the pasture. The worn scraps of fabric felt deliciously soft in my hands as I folded them in neat squares, transformed by my imagination into fine clothes for sale. I plucked leaves to use as money, which I stashed in my shirt, just like the *indígena* ladies at the market. Kneeling in the grass with my fabric-scrap clothes spread before me, I imitated the rhythmic tones I'd heard at the market.

"Look, señora, buy this, it's cheap. Buy this, buy this, señora. How much will you give me?"

"Two sucres," my cousin Zoyla said, holding forth two leaves, grudgingly playing along.

"Five," I countered, my voice even and confident.

"Three," she said.

I shook my head, holding my ground. "Five. Look at the fine cloth. Here, feel it. Not a sucre less than five."

She reluctantly picked a few more leaves from the tree and counted five into my outstretched palms. I tucked them into my shirt, then gathered my fabric scraps in a sack, slung it over my shoulder, and scampered up the tree. I shouted to Josefa the cow and the scattered sheep, my voice echoing off the canyon walls. "I am a rich lady with my own business and I am traveling far away from here!" The tree transformed into my truck, full of merchandise—piles of blouses and skirts and shoes, and I bounced on the limb, beeping and roaring my engine to far-off places like Quito and Colombia. I closed my eyes and felt the wind in my hair and the thrill of traveling into a dazzling, bright future, certain that one day I would be old enough to do this for real.

And now that I'm old enough and resourceful enough, what's stopping me?

One sunny, windy morning, on a day off from school, I'm on the way to Alfonso's field with Mamita. We pass through our own field first, where, just beyond the outhouse, big green pumpkins are growing like weeds. Mamita uses these *sambos* to make dessert on special occasions, but this year has been a particularly good year for *sambos*, and there are more than we could possibly use.

"Mamita," I say, swinging my machete as I walk, "what are you going to do with all those *sambos*?" I speak slowly in Spanish, gesturing and using simple words, the only way we can communicate.

"Who knows," she says in Quichua, which I'm understanding more of, little by little. "Probably feed them to the pigs."

"Can I have them?"

She gives me a strange look and shrugs. "Take them." Most of the time, she doesn't know what to make of me, so she lets me have my way. She still has no idea what kinds of places I go to in my head, and I don't try to explain. It's like I'm an extraterrestrial who landed in Yana Urku from another planet. The advantage to this, I realize, is it lets me see things from a fresh, entrepreneurial perspective.

My plan is to make *sambo* jelly, which I've made before, with the Doctorita. I spend all evening cutting up the pumpkins, and boiling them for hours with sugar to make a sweet paste, and then I use my last sucres to buy loaves of bread from the bakery. I spread the paste onto thick slices of bread and cut the sandwiches in half on a diagonal and put a stack of them in a plastic bag. Monday at recess, I sell them to the students and teachers for two sucres apiece. Within fifteen minutes, I'm sold out, and I go home that afternoon with a heavy pocketful of change. That evening, dancing and singing to myself in the kitchen, I make twice as many *sambo* jelly sandwiches.

The next day at recess, as I'm taking coins from the kids who are lined up, two old *mestizo* men walk past, ever so slowly. I catch one of them say, "This *guaguita* here, now, she shows us all how to work hard if you want to get ahead. This *guaguita* will go far in life."

These words nourish me, these words I wish my parents would tell me. I decide the old man is right. And Principal Marcelo is right. I will choose to listen to their encouragement rather than my parents' doubt. I *will* go far.

With my profits I buy lollipops and bananas from Otavalo and spend weekends at soccer and basketball games in nearby communities selling my sandwiches and candy and bananas. They're a hit. Every weekend I come home with more money than I could make after a month of working in the fields for Mariana and Alfonso.

My little cousins and siblings love my new business, since it means free sweets for them. Sometimes, when I give Manuelito a spoonful of *sambo* jelly, he smacks his lips with delight just like Jaimito did when I'd sneak him a spoonful of honey. These treats bring me a little closer to the children, but they still keep their distance. I miss the warmth of my relationship with

Andrecito and Jaimito, but I try not to wallow in memories. Instead, I focus on now, on expanding my business, selling snacks at dances and festivals.

My best customers are teenage boys. They buy a sandwich and say, "Delicious!" and then, "What's your name?" and then, "You're really pretty," and then, "Would you like to go for a walk?" or "Would you like to go out sometime?" I just smile and let my eyes dance and say, "If you like my sandwiches so much, why don't you buy some more for your family and friends?" They eagerly hand over more money and I smile and thank them and come home rich.

Sometimes a boy reminds me of Antonio, the way he used to gaze at me, like I was a miracle, like I was giving him a gift just by talking with him. After a moment of wistfulness, I try to let go of these memories, let go of my friends from Kunu Yaku, my beautiful cow, all the other sweet parts of my old life. And I move on, letting myself become swept along in the momentum of my new life.

I end up earning enough to pay for school supplies and contribute money to my family for food. Papito doesn't exactly congratulate me on my success, but at least he no longer complains that I'm leeching off them. Best of all, I can even buy a few luxuries for myself. The biggest luxury is books, and my first book is the most magical one of all. This book is the key that will open the lock to the door to a new life.

The shop is small and dark and musty and filled with books from floor to ceiling. All these books together in one place— the jumble of colors and letters and pictures—make my heart thud. At first I just stand and soak up their papery presence.

"Feel free to browse," the shopkeeper says, pushing up her glasses, then looking back at her own book.

"Thank you!" I just ducked into this store impulsively, while running errands for Mamita in downtown Otavalo, and now I feel as though I've stumbled onto a gold mine.

I run my hands over the spines, reading the titles wistfully. I miss the Doctorita's shelves of books. It only took me a couple of weeks to read my sixth-grade textbooks cover to cover, and now I'm hungry for more.

One title catches my eye. *Secrets to a Happy Life*. On the cover is a garden bursting with flowers, and a silver key and keyhole. I wipe my hands on my skirt to make sure they're clean and then flip through the book, careful not to hurt any pages. It's all about how to reach your dreams. And the key idea is *Querer es poder*. *To want is to be able to*. *To want is power*. If you want something enough, you'll find a way to get it. You have to be creative, think outside the box. You have to repeat your dream to yourself, with complete faith that you will get it. You have to envision your dreams as if they're already real.

It's as if the book is breathing and pulsing in my hand, buzzing with its own vibrant energy. It's the feeling I got when I learned to read, like discovering a doorway to another world. It's as if deep inside I've known these things already, these secrets to a happy life, but here they are, written out so that I won't ever forget or doubt.

I buy the book and carry it with me everywhere. Within weeks it's worn and soft. I start repeating to myself, *Querer es poder*, as I walk, in rhythm with my footsteps. The words become an undercurrent in my life, like music that sticks in your head, a constant background to every thought.

After elementary school graduation, when I tell my classmates I plan to attend the prestigious República de Ecuador in Otavalo, some of them laugh. "Only *la gente que puede* can go to that *colegio*. Not you." *La gente que puede*. The people who can, people of means, wealthy people, high-class people. Instead of responding, I whisper to myself, *Querer es poder*.

Years ago, when I told the Doctorita I would one day graduate from the República de Ecuador, the same *colegio* as her beloved nephew, she said with scorn, "That school is for the *gente de clase*." *Gente de clase*. The people of a certain class. Meaning *mestizos* with money, not poor indigenous kids.

Querer es poder, I repeat silently.

Over the summer, I take the entrance exam to the República de Ecuador and pass it with a score high enough that the head of admissions wants to interview me.

The next step is to a find an adult representative to sign the paperwork. Papito, of course, thinks the whole idea is ridiculous, especially after he finds out how much it costs. "That's more money than I make in a month," he snorts.

I remind him how much I've made from my little business, but he flicks that aside. "And how will you keep your business while you're studying? While you're on the bus two hours a day to and from school? And what about uniforms? And books?"

"I'll find a way," I say, gritting my teeth.

Mamita simply shakes her head at my request. When I push, I realize she's intimidated by the thought of just walking through the school's imposing gate, past its security guard, through its neatly manicured gardens. She won't inflict such humiliation on herself. She won't expose herself to the shame of not being able to speak to the administrators in Spanish, or read the paperwork, or even write her name on the form.

In frustration, I run out of our cramped, dark shack, down to the pasture, where I flop on my back and stare at the enormous blue sky. I repeat to myself *yo puedo, yo puedo. I can do it, I can do it.* The next morning, I start asking other adults in my village to be my representative, and by the afternoon, I've found a kind young woman who will do me the favor.

During my interview, I let my eyes dance. I talk about how much I love science, how it opened my eyes to the world around me. I talk about how reading is a doorway to another world, about how hungry I am to learn as much as they can teach me. I talk about the notebooks of poetry I keep, the stories about Soledad I've written.

The interviewer is a middle-aged woman with gentle eyes who asks me questions and listens carefully to my responses, taking notes on a pad of paper. At the end of the interview, she shakes my hand. "Señorita, even though you're a few years older than the other entering students, we'd love you to attend our school." She raises an eyebrow. "On one condition."

I swallow hard and smooth the skirt of my dress. What if she asks me for some kind of proof that I'm *gente de clase, gente que puede?* What if there's a secret certificate that those people have that I can never get no matter how hard I try? "What's the condition, *maestra?*" I ask with dread.

"No chasing boys."

I breathe out and smile. "No problem."

"And no makeup."

I am smiling so big I'm practically laughing. "I promise." And then, "Thank you. Thank you, *maestra.*"

* * *

The first day of school I get up at four a.m. Mamita gets up early too, and heats up my soup and watches me eat, which is maybe her way of saying good luck. I put on my uniform last thing before I leave the house so it doesn't get dirty as I eat breakfast by the fire pit. I ride the bus downtown—an hour's trip—and quickly walk the rest of the way in the cool morning air.

I arrive a full hour early, just as the guard is opening the iron gates. I half expect him to turn me away, to tell me that only *gente de clase* can enter, not people like me. He only smiles and says, *"Buenos días, señorita,"* as I breeze past. A few other students are gathered inside the grounds, joking and talking nervously. I don't stand too close, worried they'll smell the wood smoke and kerosene and farm-animal stench clinging to me, even though I've dabbed on perfume to cover it up.

But everyone is friendly. "What's your name? What year are you? What elementary school did you go to? Where do you live?"

I tell them, with pleasant vagueness, that I live on the outskirts of town, where I recently moved from Ibarra. I don't mention the name of my community, in case they know it's indigenous and impoverished. I'm careful to paint a picture of myself as *gente de clase*, a middle-class *mestiza* girl from a nice family with a rustic home in the country.

No one questions my story or acts like I don't belong. The teachers seem to like me too, especially the social studies and science ones. I know the answer to every question already, since I've studied the seventh- and eighth-grade curricula in Kunu Yaku. By the end of the morning, I've made three

267

friends—Esperanza and Carmen and Sonia—who are already inviting me to hang out and study together after school. They've been best friends for years, and for some reason, they invite me to sit with them at lunch. Within minutes, I'm laughing and joking with them as though I've been a part of their group for ages.

Esperanza is big, a little fat but in a muscular, athletic way. I get the feeling her family is wealthy from some things she's mentioned, like her country club and her trips to Disneyland in California. She's always cracking jokes, making everyone laugh. During recess, when she catches me examining a flower I'd never seen before up close, and I explain I'm counting the stamens, she starts calling me Virginia the Esteemed Scientist. Carmen and Sonia laugh and throw their arms over my shoulders. It makes me feel part of things.

Sonia is quiet and fair-skinned with light brown hair. Freckles spot her nose. She has a gentle, graceful way of floating around, from years of ballet lessons. Boys are always staring at her, trying to talk to her, but she's too shy and instead retreats into our little group of girls. She's sincere and thoughtful and observant and asks unexpected questions, like "What do dogs dream about?" or "Would you rather be able to fly or read minds?" or "Have you noticed that the snack vendor on the corner always wears purple pants?"

And then there's Carmen, who's always smiling and arranging her barrettes or refolding her socks or retucking her shirt. She's extremely neat, with a perfect, smooth bobbed haircut—not a strand out of place. She organizes her colored pencils in their tin case according to the colors of the light spectrum and has an eraser and six writing utensils on her desk at all times—a black pen, a freshly sharpened pencil, a highlighter, and backups of each. When, in her earnest voice, Sonia asks Carmen why she does this, she laughs, "In case of emergency!" She gets along with everyone; she's from a big family. They're well-off, but since she has seven brothers and sisters, she has to wear their hand-me-downs and guard her possessions so no siblings will snatch them.

Even after just a few days, I adore my new friends and teachers, and they adore me. But these precious relationships seem tender, vulnerable, at the risk of disappearing with one wrong word from my mouth. I resolve to do everything I can to protect them. Not a single student or teacher at this school will ever discover that I come from a poor, indigenous family. Never.

For weeks, I follow the same pattern: wake up before dawn, catch the bus to Otavalo, walk to school, attend classes, study and hang out with my friends after school, and ride the bus back home at night. Thankfully, my friends don't think it's odd I live outside of town. They assume my family owns a big hacienda with plenty of land, that we simply prefer the country to the bustle of the city. Thankfully, too, they show no interest in seeing my home, content with having me visit their houses, just a convenient couple of kilometers from school.

And really, my family and home are the only things I have to hide in order to keep my heritage a secret. It's true my skin is dark, but plenty of *mestizos* have skin just as dark as mine. I don't speak Quichua. I don't dress as an *indígena*. And even though *Farinango* sounds more indigenous than Spanish, I have heard of *mestizos* with the same last name.

On Fridays, I stay up late making *sambo* sandwiches to sell at parties and games over the weekend. Here and there, I find

269

snatches of time to read *Secrets to a Happy Life*, flipping it open to random sections.

Close your eyes and visualize how you want your life to be. How does it feel? Who is there? What is your job? Where do you live?

I love these visualizations. In a way, I've been doing them all my life, assuming they were only fantasies, when actually, they were much more.

I let my tired eyelids fall shut and see myself as a star student, receiving awards. And an actress, who makes people cry and smile. And an elegant, beautiful young businesswoman, who people regard with respect. I imagine the Doctorita and Niño Carlitos asking my forgiveness. I imagine Andrecito and Jaimito giving me big hugs. I imagine eating rice and meat and fruit and cakes and pies. I imagine living in a purple house like a mansion from *The Slave Isaura*, with high ceilings and lots of windows, and gardens outside, and tiled floors and a stove instead of a wood fire, and shiny bathrooms, everything sparkling clean.

I whisper, *"Querer es poder,"* and open my eyes.

chapter 32

IT WORKS!

Three days later, I discover the house from my fantasy, only it's yellow instead of purple, and more like a palace than a house. It makes me think of a giant daisy, with its fresh, white trim like petals. And best of all, it's real, just a few blocks from the Plaza de Ponchos in downtown Otavalo. I peek inside and actually gasp. The ceilings are high, higher than a cathedral. And at the top of the ceiling is a window that lets sunlight pour over a lush indoor garden, spilling over with orange bird-of-paradise and pink bougainvillea and giant deep green tropical leaves with red flowers. There is so much photosynthesis happening right here in this house that the air must be extra rich with oxygen. Every single breath fills me up, makes my head swim.

Carmen is at my side. We take a step into the entryway, our mouths hanging open. A minute earlier, walking along the sidewalk, we noticed the sign on the door that read PART-TIME HELP

271

WANTED. CLEAN, POLITE GIRLS TO WORK IN KITCHEN. An after-school job would be perfect for both of us, we agreed. Carmen lives in a nice big apartment in Otavalo, but because of all her brothers and sisters, her family won't buy her new clothes. She wants her own pocket money. And I'm tired of traveling to different communities to sell *sambo* sandwiches and candy and fruit every weekend.

"This must be the home of someone important, like the mayor," Carmen says, refolding her socks.

"Or the president," I say.

"Or Chayanne," she says. Like Marlenny and Marina, and every other teenage girl, Chayanne is her favorite singer.

"Or MacGyver," I say, giggling. I love giggling with Carmen. It makes me feel like a normal teenage student, like the ones in Kunu Yaku I watched with envy for years.

A very short man, about my height, with a stocky square build and a gold tooth grins at us. "How can I help you ladies?"

"We're interested in the kitchen jobs," I say.

"Right this way, please," he says with a twinkle in his eye.

He leads us past dainty tables, like white iron lace, each holding a small vase of carnations. A few people are sipping coffee and eating yellow and white pie—lemon meringue or banana cream—that matches the building. Most of them are foreign-looking people in shorts and jeans with light hair and glasses and fair skin burnt pink, some chatting, some poring over books.

We walk over wooden floors, polished to a sheen with pine-scented wax, past stairs that curve up to a wraparound balcony that overlooks the gardens. Finally, we arrive at the far end of

272

the enormous room, stopping before a cluster of elegant blue velvet chairs.

"Please wait here and make yourselves comfortable," the man says.

Carmen and I perch on the edge of the chairs, staring at each other, speechless, listening to the parakeets chirping in the indoor garden.

Moments later, the short man returns with a very tall man with light skin and a mustache that has a few crumbs stuck in it. "Walter Blanco Morales," he says, extending his hand. And I can tell from the smile crinkles at the corners of his eyes and his gentle way of moving that I want to work for him. This is where I want to be.

"I'm Virginia. And this is Carmen."

He shakes our hands and launches into a tour of the palace. There are dozens of rooms, so many he has to number each one. And each with its own TV! Twelve bedrooms on the first floor alone. This man must have hundreds of friends who come visit him. The second floor has its own kitchen, and more tables, and a formal dining room lined with wrought-iron rails and floor-to-ceiling doors of glass. The tables are already set for the next meal: napkins folded in a fancy way; three different kinds of forks, two spoons, all shining and brilliant; two glasses with stems at each setting; flowers at the center of the table—white buds floating in glass globes. Airy music is playing, classical piano, floating from speakers in the walls.

Don Walter is speaking in his low, calm voice, and I'm try-ing to listen, but all these beautiful things are bombarding my senses. "After school, you can come to help prep for dinner, and then after dinner, help clear the tables and wash dishes. And can you do Saturday and Sunday brunches as well?"

We both nod. "When do we start?" I ask, feeling like a firework just set off, rising and rising and full of brilliant anticipation.

After a few days of work, I realize this isn't Don Walter's private palace, but his hotel. The Hotel Otavalo, the best one in town. The foreigners who sit drinking coffee with their noses in books aren't his friends and family, but paying guests, many of them *gringuitos*.

Carmen thinks these pale foreigners are funny and strange, but I feel a bond with them, because like me, they don't exactly belong here. Yet that doesn't stop them. They are bold and adventurous, and even though many of them don't speak much Spanish, they brazenly find a way to communicate. And best of all, they don't seem to have much idea about the distinctions of *mestizos* and *indígenas*, or rich and poor—it's as if we're all just Ecuadorians to them. They're blissfully ignorant of the invisible lines that separate one group from another.

I especially like the *gringuitos* whose faces are buried in books. When I ask them eagerly, "What are you reading?" they let me flip through their books, mostly guidebooks with little maps of Otavalo and information about the markets and Quichua culture. The books are filled with glossy photos of indigenous women, showing close-ups of their thick strands of gold necklaces, the coral beads winding up their wrists, the lace and embroidery of their blouses, the woolen *fachalinas* folded intricately on their heads or knotted around their shoulers, their proud profiles against the Andes.

Sometimes these tourists ask me about indigenous customs—

a topic that fascinates them. I shrug and say, "I wouldn't know," and hope they don't notice me flushing. If they ask where I'm from, I give vague answers, saying I used to live with my family in Ibarra. I would die if my coworkers overheard me admit the truth, if they discovered my secret. So I keep my roots hidden.

It's astonishing to me, the curiosity these foreigners have about indigenous culture. It's the very reason they come to Otavalo, sometimes from all the way across the world. With gushing admiration, they photograph indigenous clothes, pay money to watch traditional dances, marvel over everything about Quichua celebrations, crafts, folktales, rituals, gods and goddesses.

Talking to the tourists, I realize that if it weren't for the indigenous culture here, these foreigners wouldn't have much reason to come to Otavalo. Which means that Don Walter's hotel might not be in business without *indígenas*. This gets me thinking. The *mestizo* business owners in town must realize that *indígenas* are important to our town's economy. Which leads to the slippery conclusion: despite their prejudice against *indígenas*, especially poor ones, the *mestizos* value Quichua culture. It's what makes their town special. This is a contradiction I can barely grasp.

Spending my days in Otavalo, I notice that whenever there's an indigenous holiday, like Inti Raymi—the Festival of the Sun—the hotels and streets and squares overflow with tourists. The city spotlights Quichua parades and rituals, like the pilgrimage to the Peguche waterfall, promoting them as tourist attractions. Incredibly, it never occurred to me before that indigenous culture might be the heart of this city, maybe even the heart of the entire province of Imbabura.

Still, it seems safest to guard the secret of my roots. The well-off *indígenas* may be valued in some ways, but they keep to their own circles. If my coworkers or friends discovered who I was, they'd treat me differently, I'm sure of it. They'd expect me to hang out with other *indígenas*, people I have nothing in common with.

And I don't want to give up the fun I have with my coworkers, especially Don Lucho with his gold tooth. He's the doorman and security guard, and he's always cracking jokes while he's waiting to carry suitcases up and down the stairs. My other coworkers, too, like to joke around, and I find myself laughing and dancing around the kitchen and happily flying up and down the stairs.

After I do my homework in the lobby, I take the last bus back to Yana Urku at about eleven o'clock, arriving so exhausted I can barely drag myself home from the bus stop. It is strange, after the tinkling crystal luxury of the hotel, to lie on a woven mat on a wooden bed frame with Manuelito and Hermelinda pressed against me as I itch my flea bites for a few idle moments before falling asleep.

I sleep for about five hours, then get up before dawn to take the bus to school. Even on weekend mornings, I have to leave early to work the breakfast shift at the hotel. After I get off work, I stay in the hotel café, doing my homework, which is easier than doing it at home. At the hotel, there's better lighting, and tables and chairs, and plenty of people nearby to help with hard math problems.

I barely see my parents anymore. My mother always wakes up early to heat up soup and eat with me while the rest of the family sleeps. Sometimes she stares at me as though she wants to ask me something, but then looks down at the ashes of the fire pit. Beyond the language divide, she probably has no idea what questions to ask me about my life. She's never even been inside a *colegio* or a fancy hotel, places where I spend nearly all my time now. And I still don't know our neighbors or relatives well enough to attempt to chat about the goings-on in our village. So, most of the time, we sip soup in silence.

Papito occasionally asks me questions when I come home late at night. "Do you eat decent food for lunch and dinner? Do they treat you well at the hotel? Do you have enough money?" But he doesn't ask me about what I'm learning, or what my research papers are about, or what books I'm reading. And I don't know what questions to ask him about his world of farming and pasturing animals.

My siblings and little cousins continue to act shy around me, huddling together and whispering with each other in Quichua. I'm too busy with school and work to try to draw them out of their shells, beyond giving them treats here and there.

It's painfully clear that I don't fit into the world of my family. My world now is with my new friends in Otavalo.

One morning at dawn, I'm in the dark bus, bumping down the steep, dusty dirt road to Otavalo. *Cumbia* music is blasting, too loud for me to sleep, and the driver is swerving around potholes, jerking me this way and that. I returned from the hotel last night around midnight; now, six hours later, I'm heading back again. I glimpse my reflection in the window. My face looks heavy, weary.

I catch a whiff of woodsmoke, coming from my hair, and my stomach sinks. Earlier this morning, in the pitch black, I bathed and washed my hair in the wooden shack out back, crouching, shivering, wincing beneath buckets of frigid water. Afterward, over breakfast, my freshly washed hair must have absorbed the smoke from the fire pit. I sniff my school uniform, smelling traces of smoke saturating it, too, mingled with an animal smell—the reek of guinea pigs. Bending over to scratch the flea bites on my calves, I smell something else—manure—and notice a clump clinging to my shoe. Groaning, I make a mental note to scrape it off with a stick right when I get to town.

I can't do this anymore. If I keep this up, it's only a matter of time before my classmates and coworkers discover my family's poverty. I lean my forehead against the cold windowpane and shut my eyes. Under my breath, I whisper, *"Querer es poder."* Over and over, I whisper my mantra. And then, gathering my last wisps of strength, I pull out *Secrets to a Happy Life*, flip to a random section, and reread it in the dim light.

An hour later, by the end of the bus ride, I've come up with a plan.

After school, I walk straight into the hotel, pausing only briefly to talk with Don Lucho. Before I lose my nerve, I find Don Walter. He's sitting in a blue velvet chair in the lobby, going over an accounting notebook. He greets me warmly, as always, and when he sees my face, so hopeful and nervous, he asks, "What can I do for you, Virginia?"

I take a deep breath. "Don Walter, is there a little space in this hotel where I can sleep for the nights?"

Soft crinkles form at the corners of his eyes. "Your long commute's been hard on you, hasn't it?" He pauses, thinking. "Yes, I can find a place for you, Virginia. I'd be happy to."

I breathe out in relief.

"You know," he says, smiling, "our guests would be thrilled if you lived here. They love talking to you." He closes his notebook and stands up. "Come on."

I'm walking on air as he leads me past the indoor garden, down the stairs, to a small, windowless room in the basement. It's the ironing room, tucked in between a storage room and the laundry room. "This is the best I can do, Virginia. We'll move a bed in here for you, and a dresser. Not luxurious, but I won't charge you for it."

"Oh, this is perfect, Don Walter!" I want to cry, just thinking about the extra hours of sleep, the clean mattress, warm showers, indoor toilets, electric lights. "Thank you!"

My parents don't seem to mind me leaving. I suspect they may even be relieved. I'm certainly relieved, although a small part of me wishes we'd discovered something to talk about, some common ground, some way to connect. It might feel good to be able to forgive them, respect them, maybe even love them. But that hasn't happened, and I'm beginning to doubt it ever will. I plan on making a token visit to my family every few months, for Sunday lunch, and then returning to the comfort of the Hotel Otavalo.

And so, once again, I have a new home, and a new family.

Don Walter becomes like a father to me. Every day, we talk about what I'm doing in school, and he asks about my projects and homework and tests. When I tell him about getting the highest grade in the class on my science exam, he says, "I'm proud of you, *m'hija*." And when I tell him I'm having problems with my math homework, he sits down at the table and says, "Now let's see if I can help you with that, *m'hija*."

279

I am inside my vision of how I've always wanted my life to be, living in a gorgeous home with people who like me, who care about me, who laugh with me, who read books.

Still, there is a piece of me that worries I'll be caught impersonating a *mestiza* girl, pretending to be one of the *gente que puede, gente de clase*. I'm walking a tightrope, careful with my words, hoping my friends and classmates and teachers and coworkers won't discover my secret, because if they do, I will fall and crash. This scared piece of me gnaws at my stomach, makes it burn so badly that sometimes I can't even eat; sometimes I double over, gasping in pain.

Carmen and Sonia and I are at Esperanza's house, sitting at the dining room table with our social studies books and notes spread out. We're mostly talking about cute boys in our class, and only here and there studying for our exam on the ancient Incan empire.

"Are you thirsty?" Esperanza asks. "Want some lemonade?"

We nod, and I start to stand up, to help her make the drinks.

But she stays seated and calls out, "Rosita!"

An indigenous girl a couple of years younger than me—maybe twelve or thirteen—appears at the door to the patio, her hands red and wet, probably from washing clothes. She wipes them on her *anaco* and says, "Yes, Esperanza? What can I get you?"

"Lemonade for me and my friends," Esperanza says, not even looking at her. "And extra sugar."

When the girl places the lemonade in front of me, I mumble, "Thank you, Rosita," and try to avoid her eyes, because there is a place inside me that aches when I look at her. Rosita is the same age as Esperanza, yet Rosita is serving and Esperanza is ordering, and no one seems to think this is strange or terrible or unfair. No one makes the connection that the ancient Incans we're studying—a civilization respected throughout the world for its technology and art and architecture—are Rosita's ancestors.

I try to make sense of this, just as I've tried to make sense of the other contradictions I've been noticing more and more lately. How can people boast of Quichua culture in guidebooks and textbooks while overlooking the fact that their maids are Quichua? Maybe it's similar to the way, while watching our favorite soap opera, the Doctorita sobbed over the cruelty of Isaura's enslavement while failing to see that she herself had enslaved me.

Later, Rosita collects our empty glasses, slipping her arms between our piles of books and papers, unnoticed, well practiced at being invisible. I glance up and watch her walking to the sink, her hair wrapped in a ribbon hanging down to the small of her back. My stomach starts hurting and I push my thoughts away, hoping Rosita doesn't realize that I am a traitor.

Every day, I feel lucky it doesn't occur to the other students that I might be from a poor indigenous family. Thank God they assume I'm *gente de clase* like them. They seem to truly like me. I become known as the girl to turn to when you need advice. I listen carefully and ask questions and give them suggestions. A lot of my advice comes from *Secrets to a Happy Life*, but some of it comes from things I've figured out on my own. I draw on what I've learned over three lifetimes—one in Yana Urku, one in Kunu Yaku, and the one I'm living now in Otavalo.

After our talks, the girls always say they feel better. "Thank you, Virginia! You're an angel." And I smile, satisfied, like I did as a small child, after I gave *limpiezas* to troubled people to clean their spirits with eggs and fresh herbs. I remember when people exclaimed to my mother, "My, your daughter is a natural healer, isn't she?" and Mamita said, "My daughter, she can do it."

I also become renowned in school for imitating famous singers, using an imaginary microphone, flinging my hair around and dancing and singing and pursing my lips. Carmen and Esperanza and Sonia clap, squealing with delight. All that time dressing up in the Doctorita's clothes and blasting her stereo and dancing has paid off. My friends and I teach each other dance moves—salsa and *cumbia*—and talk about boys we wish we could dance with. Finally, I'm living like a normal teenage girl, making up for the years that were stolen from me. Being a little older than my classmates adds to my allure; they look up to me, admire me even.

"You're so lucky, Virginia!" they say when they visit me at the hotel, ogling the indoor garden and skylight and elegant furniture. "It's so cool to hang out here with all these *gringuitos*." Don Walter lets us study and practice dances there, and the *gringuitos* watch and clap for us. With my friends over, I notice how fluidly I move around my home, weaving through tables, greeting our foreign guests by name and even dropping some hellos in English or French or German. Sometimes, when students come over to work on group assignments, they assume that Don Walter is my father, that this is my family's hotel. "Your father is so nice!" they say, and I just smile and nod.

I almost begin to believe that he *is* my father. On my occasional visits home, when I catch sight of Papito—usually from a distance, when he's off in a field—he looks like a stranger. Every time I see him, it's startling to remember that he's my real father. When he takes off his boots, I stare at his feet, with their long toes—bigger and older echoes of my own—and I wonder how I could be related to this man. To him or Mamita. I help her cook soup, chopping the potatoes and onions, just wanting to get the visit over with so I can go back to the hotel and school, places where I'm comfortable.

But if I'm honest with myself, maybe I'm not really comfortable there, either. At nights, in my little room in the basement, I lie awake with my stomach aching and wonder what would happen if my friends found out who I really am. Which makes me ask myself, *Who are you, really?*

chapter 33

ONE SUNNY DAY AFTER SCHOOL, Sonia and I are outside the *colegio* gates, eating popcorn and waiting for Esperanza and Carmen. Cars and buses pass in clouds of exhaust, and clusters of students walk by carrying steaming food bought from vendors along the street. I'm in the middle of a story about our cute math teacher when Sonia reaches out and touches my hair, which hangs loose to my waist.

All the other girls' hair is shoulder length, or chin length, or down to midback; no one's hair is anywhere near as long as mine. This is the last remnant of indigenousness I've hung on to. And somehow, even though I've cut bangs and permed my hair over the years, I haven't been able to chop it off.

Sonia runs her fingers through my hair. "Your hair is so pretty, Virginia! It's so long!"

"Thanks," I say, stiffening a little. Something in her voice puts me on guard.

"Virginia"—she tilts her head and studies my face—"are you *indígena?*" She says it as though it can't possibly be true, but maybe, just maybe, it is.

Nervous sweat trickles from my armpits. "Why do you ask?" I manage to say through my closed-up throat.

"*Mestizas* don't have such long hair. Only *indígenas.*"

Why didn't I just cut off my hair before school started? Is this the one tiny thing that will give me away and ruin the rest of my life?

Finally, in a soft voice, I say, "Yes. I'm *indígena.*"

Sonia stares at me, stunned. It takes her a while to find words. The silence is torturous. "Then why do you dress like a *mestiza?*"

I shrug. "I just—I don't know. I just like to dress this way."

"Oh."

Suddenly, Esperanza and Carmen run up and steal our popcorn, giggling. Sonia tries to grab it back and soon they're all squealing and I force myself to laugh with them, but really I feel like crying. And before I have to listen to Sonia tell the others my secret, I mumble something about having promised one of the *gringuitas* I'd help her with her Spanish. I walk away, sure that will be the last time we'll ever laugh together.

It's dark and the clock says three-thirty a.m. and it feels like someone is stabbing a sword through my stomach. I toss and turn, desperately trying to sleep, but I can't stop imagining Sonia telling everyone I'm a dirty Indian. Tomorrow in school no one will want to come near me for fear of catching *indígena* germs. My friends will no longer invite me to their houses and let me sit on their sofas and eat off their plates. They will order me to bring them lemonade. The teachers will tell me I have no right to study there, that *longas* aren't allowed in their school.

Of course, if I think about it rationally, they'd probably assume I was one of the middle-class *indígenas*, not a poor *longa*. Still, my mind can't help spiraling into fear. It's as if the thousands of times the Doctorita called me a dirty *longa* are being stirred up into a whirlwind of old, painful insults. It all comes back to me: how she made me use separate dishes, and wouldn't let me sit on the bed and watch TV with the rest of the family, how she said with disgust that I'd contaminated the blankets, and told me I was no better than a stray dog in heat. No matter how much I tell myself that my friends would never call me dirty names, I feel buried under the Doctorita's insults.

The next morning, in the bathroom, I hold a pair of scissors to my hair, right at chin level. My plan is to cut it and say I was just joking about being *indígena*. *See*, I'll say, *I'm mestiza or else I wouldn't have cut my hair*. Not a great plan, but my only hope to keep my life from being ruined. I squeeze the scissors and cut off one thin strand. It's long, longer than my arm. My science book says that hair grows at a rate of one centimeter per month. I have five years of hair in my hand. Where was I when those strands of hair were first sprouting from my head? What was I doing at that precise moment?

Five years ago I would have been about eleven years old, living in Kunu Yaku, with Niño Carlitos and the Doctorita. Maybe I was being beaten or insulted. Maybe I was stealing food with Jaimito. Maybe I was washing Andrecito's diapers. Maybe I was running as fast as I could around the fountain and through the town square with a bag of eggs to deliver to the Doctorita.

Somehow, it feels sad to cut off all those years. They're a part of me; they made me what I am now.

I think of my dreams when I was a little girl, dreams of becoming a rich *indígena* with long hair wrapped in a fancy ribbon. I think of the tourists at the hotel, who tell me I'm beautiful. What if my hair is the thing that makes me beautiful? What if this piece of me that is still *indígena* is actually a good thing?

I put down the scissors and start working the comb through my damp hair, untangling the knots, a process that takes a long time.

At school, I walk through the gates, conscious of my hair swinging behind me and, despite reason, bracing myself for a crowd to begin taunting, *Longa, dirty Indian*. But by the pink rosebushes where we always meet, Carmen spots me and calls out, "Virginia! ¡Hola!" and Esperanza and Sonia wave hi too, all bright and smiling. Esperanza drapes her arm around my shoulder, saying, "¡Hola, *chica!* Cool bracelet!" and Sonia says, "Hey! Can you help me with this science homework?" No one says a word about me being *indígena*. Has Sonia told them? Do they just not care? Or did Sonia somehow miraculously forget about it?

Later, in homeroom, Sonia passes me a tightly folded note, and I think, *This is it*. She's going to say we can't be friends anymore. My hands shaking, I open the note.

> Hola, chica! I need your advice. Jorge's been
> flirting with me like crazy, but I only like him
> as a friend! Help!!! Can we hang together
> after school???
>
> Hugs!!!
> Sonia

287

I glance over at her. She smiles, and I search for a trace of sarcasm or scorn or disgust, but as hard as I look, I find none. Beyond all comprehension, she doesn't seem to care if I am a *mestiza* or an *indígena*. She sees only Virginia.

Eventually, Sonia mentions my secret to Carmen and Esperanza. They're full of questions. I become their personal *indígena* expert, their window into a foreign world. They ask how to say things in Quichua, and are disappointed when I explain I know only a few words. They're disappointed, too, that I don't have any *indígena* clothes to let them dress up in, not even a gold-painted bead necklace. After a few days, the novelty wears off, and they seem to forget about it. I go back to being the same old Virginia.

My friends love me for being me. To them, I am Virginia the scientist and singer and dancer and star student and advice giver. To them, the *indígena* piece is just another part of me, something that even seems to add a little allure.

But not everyone in Ecuador sees it that way. Everywhere are reminders of this.

The next week, at the Parque Bolívar, I'm sitting on a bench in the shade, watching some children play by the fountain. I'm ten minutes early to meet Sonia for a study session, and as I wait, I can't help but overhear the boisterous laughter of two men. A man with a big red nose is telling the jokes and two younger men are laughing at them.

"When a *mestizo* is drowning," he says, "you throw a life preserver at him. When a *longo* is drowning, you throw stones at him."

I swallow hard and try to let the kids' shouts stomp out the men's voices.

The other men laugh and slap their knees. "Good one."

The big-nosed man smiles, gathering fuel for the next joke. "If a *mestizo* goes to a brothel, he's looking for pleasure. If a *longo* goes, he's looking for his sister."

More laughter.

My face burns.

He keeps going. "If a *mestizo* is running, he's an athlete. If a *longo* is running, he's a thief."

I am shaking now, shaking and sweating, and the tears are sizzling off my eyes. I stand up and walk away, as tall as I can, even though my legs are quivering. Behind me, as much as I don't want to hear, their voices travel over the water's pounding.

"If a *mestizo* is coughing, he has a cold. If a *longo* is coughing, he has tuberculosis."

They laugh in loud, violent barks. On the other side of the fountain, I sit on a bench and bite my lip and dig my fingernails into my palms. I try not to care, but even though the men are out of sight, their words are everywhere, in the chatter of everyone, in the tumbling water.

For her birthday, Esperanza invites me and Sonia and Carmen to her family's country club. She loves going to the club, even though she makes fun of the snobs who go there by sneering and strutting around with her nose twitching high in the air. At her house, I've seen framed pictures of other birthdays she's had at the club. There's a big, beautiful pool with turquoise water surrounded by trees with huge orange and red flowers like upside-down bells. White lounge chairs encircle the pool, and people wear sunglasses and sip Coca-Cola in their bathing suits.

I beg Walter for extra hours of work so I can afford a bathing suit. A week before the party, I find one—red with white flowers—on sale. I try it on in my room in the hotel basement and stand on the bed so I can see myself in the small mirror. My thighs don't look fat. They look muscular, from dance practice. I actually look good. I put my hand on the curve of my waist and feel the smooth, stretchy fabric and imagine us girls sipping our Coca-Colas in lounge chairs and then dipping our toes in the water and floating around luxuriously.

I buy Carmen a gold hair clip with little fake diamonds. It sits on top of my folded bathing suit, wrapped in shiny pink paper topped with a silver bow. Just looking at it gives me tingles.

After school on Friday, the day before the party, Esperanza rolls her eyes and says, "Just to warn you, *chicas*, my obnoxious little sister will be there. And my mother says we have to let her hang out with us. So watch what you say in front of her."

Esperanza can't stand her little sister. She's like a short, bratty spy. Everything we talk about in front of her goes straight back to their parents. Last month, after Esperanza's mother found out about her crush on the neighbor's son, she wouldn't leave them alone together for two seconds.

Carmen groans. "Can't your maid keep your sister entertained?"

"Maids aren't allowed in the club."

"Why not?"

"Some dumb rule. The idiots in charge think the *indígenas* don't have good hygiene or something. Like they'll make the pool dirty."

I want to die.

I want to melt and disappear into the sidewalk.

I want to dissolve into a zillion particles and float far, far away.

"Idiots," Carmen says.

Sonia looks at me. I see in her eyes that she's just remembered who I really am. One of the *indígenas* who might have bad hygiene. Who might make the pool dirty. She reaches out and strokes my long, long hair, then links her elbow in mine.

"Idiots," she says.

All night my stomach aches. I look at the present and the bathing suit on the chair in the corner. Now they give me a sick, panicked feeling. What if the people at the club can tell I'm *indígena*? What if they let all the other girls in but send me home? Or what if I'm swimming and they realize I'm *indígena* and they clear out the pool and empty out all the water because I made it dirty? What if Esperanza's family gets kicked out of the club because of me? Or what if people just laugh at me and crack jokes about throwing stones?

The next morning, bleary-eyed and doubled over in pain, I call Esperanza. I don't know if she's made the connection between me being *indígena* and her maid being *indígena* and the club's rules. All I know is that there's no way I can go to this party.

"Esperanza, I have a terrible stomachache today. I can't come."

"But Virginia, it won't be any fun without you."

"I'm sorry."

"Can't you take some medicine?"

"No, *chica*. Medicine won't fix this."

A long sigh. Some sniffs. Is she crying? "We'll miss you," she says finally. "Call me later and tell me how you're doing, okay?"

"Okay. Happy birthday." And I hang up fast because now the tears are coming. I walk downstairs, slowly, a little bent over from the pain, and go into my dark room. I change into the bathing suit and lie on my bed, staring at the ceiling.

chapter 34

I'M IN THE KITCHEN, washing dishes and joking around with my coworkers, when Don Lucho pokes his head through the doorway. "You have some visitors, Virginia," he says with a twinkle of the eye and a flash of his gold tooth.

I dry my hands and smooth my hair back and wipe the sweat off my forehead and hope I don't smell too much like dish soap and grease. Unexpected visitors make me nervous. Even though my friends still like me, I can't help worrying that someone from my past will appear and spill out all the ugly details of my life.

A short, round *mestizo* man and a pretty *indígena* woman are waiting for me on the blue velvet chairs in the lobby. When they see me, they hop up. "Finally!" the man says. "You're a hard girl to track down."

I stare for a moment, wary, then say, "Please sit down." I show them to a table in the café. "Would you like a drink?"

They shake their heads politely, and the woman says, "I'm just so glad we found you!"

Are they undercover police of some kind, patrolling Otavalo to expose poor *indígena* girls disguised as *gente de clase?* Once we're seated, I ask, squeezing my hands in my lap, "How can I help you?"

The man introduces himself as José and the woman as Susana, then leans forward eagerly. "I know you from your community, Yana Urku."

My heart jumps. "Oh, really?" I am careful not to admit to anything.

"I saw you star in that marvelous play, and you brought me to tears, Virginia! I haven't been able to forget it. So when our organization started looking for a beautiful and talented girl to represent us, I thought of you! It's for the competition of Sara Ñusta. To choose the *indígena* queens of corn, water, and sky."

I flush at being called beautiful and talented, but when he says *indígena*, I freeze, then glance around to make sure none of my coworkers are close enough to hear. "Thank you, señor."

Susana continues, talking quickly and breathlessly. "First, we went to Yana Urku and asked around about you, and your parents couldn't remember where you live, but finally someone at the school told us you were here in the Hotel Otavalo."

I am speechless. I can't help but feel flattered that they would take this time to look for me, when the town is full of indigenous girls who would love to compete for queen. I study Susana. The beads around her neck are small and expensive, glass coated with real gold paint, and her blouse shimmers with flowers of finely stitched gold and pink thread. She is one of the wealthy *indígenas*, I can tell. One of the *indígenas* I wished to be when I was a girl. One of the *indígenas* respected by *mestizos*. And she speaks Spanish perfectly, an educated Spanish, enunciating all her words delicately. They are waiting for me to say something, so I say, "Oh, and what is your organization?"

Susana smiles proudly. "We collect funds to help children in *indígena* communities study in preschool. If you represent us, you'll compete against girls from organizations all over the Ecuadorian Andes for one of the three queen crowns. This is based on an old tradition, dating from Incan times. They stopped doing the competition about twelve years ago, and now we're reviving it!"

"Sounds wonderful," I say politely. I have to admit, I do like the idea of being a queen. "What are the requirements?"

"Oh, that's easy," Susana says. "You just need to be *indígena* and speak Quichua."

I hesitate. First, I'm not exactly *indígena* anymore, and second, my Quichua is at the level of a three-year-old's.

"We really hope you can do this!" José says. "It took us so long to find you, and the rehearsals start soon."

"Well," I begin, slowly. "It seems fun. But—"

Their faces fall.

I lower my voice so that Don Lucho and the others won't hear. "But I don't dress as an *indígena* anymore." Suddenly, I realize how tired I am of hiding and keeping secrets. "See, the truth is I lived with *mestizos* for years as a servant. And they thought *indígenas* were stupid and dirty and only good for serving them, and . . . well, I didn't want to be *indígena* anymore. I threw out my old clothes and dressed in regular skirts and shirts. And I don't have enough money to buy new *indígena* clothes, especially fancy ones like yours. And—and—really, I don't know if I'm even *indígena* anymore." I stop there because my voice is quavering and if I say another word, I might cry.

Susana takes in what I tell her, nodding sympathetically. "Of course you're still *indígena*, Virginia. Don't worry. We'll make sure you have clothes. We'll take care of everything."

"But I don't speak much Quichua either, señora. I used to, but now the words feel strange coming out of my mouth."

"No problem," Susana says. "We'll help you remember. So what do you say?"

I twist my hair around my finger, stalling.

"Sorry to rush you, Virginia," José says. "But we do need to know your decision now."

"Well, then." I take a deep breath. "All right. I guess."

Their faces light up. "Oh, good!" Susana says, clasping her hands together. "You'll need to go to rehearsals, and the first is this afternoon. Can you do that?"

"I need to talk with my boss," I say, realizing it's too late to change my mind now, wondering how I'll manage school and work and friends and these rehearsals.

"We'll talk to him." José stands up and shakes my hand. "You just get ready to go."

Susana extends both her hands and gives mine a squeeze. "We'll stop by my house to get you the clothes."

In a daze, I go downstairs to my room to brush my hair and spray on some perfume to hide the kitchen grease smells. I half wish Don Walter will say I can't have time off work, that we're too busy. But upstairs he puts his hand on my shoulder, and says, "What an honor, Virginia! I'm proud of you. Of course you can miss some work."

Then, in a whirlwind, Susana whisks me off in her car.

* * *

"Pick out whatever you want, Virginia." We're standing in Susana's bedroom, in front of her open wardrobe, a treasure chest of expensive *anacos* and blouses. I choose a blouse with flowers of all colors embroidered around the neck and delicate lace ruffles at the elbows. The *anacos* are a soft wool blend with fine zigzags along the bottom, a cream *anaco* underneath and a dark one on top. I pick out a purple *faja* for around the waist, in honor of the *rabanito* flowers standing tall in the song I sang for fresh rolls as a little girl. This would have been a dream come true for me then. Susana plucks some dangly earrings and a heap of gold and red beads and a long ribbon from her jewelry box and sets them on top of the wardrobe.

"All right," she says, glancing at her watch. "Try them on!" She turns away as I take off my skirt and shirt and fold them up, and slip on the blouse. It feels different than the blouses I wore as a child. Not only is the fabric much silkier and shinier than the plain cotton ones I used to wear, but now my breasts fill the space inside. I wrap the *anacos* around my waist. Then, with clumsy movements, I take the long *faja*, wrapping it around and around the top of the *anacos*.

It isn't easy. I wish I had another hand. But I'm too embarrassed to admit to Susana that I can't handle wrapping my own *anacos*. It would be like asking her to zip up my fly or hook my bra.

"Everything all right?" Susana asks, still looking away to give me privacy.

"Oh, yes," I say, struggling to hold up the fabric with one hand, while wrapping the *faja* around my waist with the other, pulling it extra tight. It's the only thing holding up the *anaco*;

297

it would be disastrous if it came loose. Finally, I tuck the end of the *faja* in and try to breathe. It's suffocating, pressing on my ribs and constricting my lungs, so I can only breathe halfway. But there's something secure-feeling about it too, familiar and almost comforting, a kind of hug.

I wrap the ribbon around my ponytail and tie it at the ends, then put on the necklace of dozens of thin golden strands and the dangly earrings. Susana drapes a cream wool *fachalina* over my left shoulder and knots it. Last, I slip on her black velvet shoes—which fit me perfectly—and tie the dainty strings around my ankles.

I turn to study myself in the mirror.

I look beautiful.

There is no other way to say it. I look exactly how, during my childhood in Yana Urku, I dreamed of myself looking as a young woman. "I'm ready, señora," I say hesitantly.

Susana's eyes widen. "Gorgeous! Simply gorgeous. A true queen." She grabs her keys. "All right, let's go."

"Just give me a minute to change back into my regular clothes."

"Why? Just come like this."

"But—" I close my mouth. The truth is, this feels like a costume, like I'm playing dress-up. It's not the kind of thing I could wear on the street. What if I run into someone I know? What if one of my classmates or teachers sees me dressed like an *indígena*?

Susana is waiting, jingling her keys.

"All right," I say, leaving her room with my regular clothes draped over my arm. In the car on the way over, I keep my hand near my face, trying to hide myself, hoping no one will recognize me.

"Now, Virginia," Susana says, "I'll just drop you off here and be back in two hours to pick you up. All right?"

I nod and get ready to race across the sidewalk and into the building. "Thanks, señora. Bye." Luckily, in front of the rehearsal building, a stream of teenage girls in *indígena* clothes are moving from their cars to the doorway. I try to blend in with them.

Inside, there's a giant auditorium with a stage at the far end and hundreds of seats. About fifty girls, all dressed in *indígena* clothes, sit in the first few rows. Five minutes after I arrive, the organizers—three excited ladies onstage—introduce each girl, who stands up and smiles and then sits down again.

The lesson for our first rehearsal is how to walk across the stage like models. "Heads high! Like a golden string is attached to the top of your head!" one of the ladies keeps shouting. Our feet have to walk lightly, almost tiptoe, while our hips sway a little, swishing in our *anacos*, and our shoulders have to be held back and our chests thrust forward. I observe the woman closely, eager to walk like a model, grinning at the idea of myself strutting gracefully around the hotel, picking dirty dishes up off the tables with extra flair, slinking into the kitchen as if down a runway.

As we wait for our turn to cross the stage, we girls whisper together, getting to know each other. Luckily, the girls speak in Spanish, not Quichua, and I can understand. They seem mostly friendly, but with an edge of competitiveness. The undercurrent of every conversation is the knowledge we'll be competing against each other. Only three out of fifty girls will be queen: the Queen of Corn, of Sky, and of Water.

The other girls are, without a doubt, the wealthiest, most educated class of *indígenas* I've ever encountered. I catch intimidating snippets of the conversations floating around the auditorium.

"Oh, we live downtown, just next to the restaurant we own, Restaurante El Pájaro. What about you?"

"We own Andes Exports."

"Oh, really? We have another restaurant just down the street from there."

"What did you do over summer break?"

"France, Germany, and Italy."

"Cool. We did Europe the year before last. We were in Japan this past summer."

One of the girls—Elsa—turns to me, her face open and friendly, assuming that I'm one of them. "What about you? Where do you live?"

"The Hotel Otavalo," I say, and watch their eyes grow big.

"Wow! That's a nice place! I pass it on my way to school."

I find myself going on. "My father owns the place and I help him out."

"Cool. Where do you go to school?"

Most of them have graduated already, and some go to Santa Juana de Chantal, which I guess must be the *colegio* for indigenous students. "República de Ecuador."

"I've heard that's a good school. But isn't it more for *mestizos?*"

I shrug. "I love it there." And quickly, desperate to change the subject, I ask, "Where did you get that pretty barrette?"

* * *

After the rehearsal, Susana picks me up in her new silver car. "Now, Virigina," she says, "keep my clothes and wear them to the rehearsals. And promise me you won't just change there. It would look bad, like you're ashamed. You have to wear them to the rehearsal. Promise me."

My stomach is starting to hurt. How can I leave the restaurant for rehearsals dressed like this? Maybe I can sneak out the back door.

Susana parks in front of the hotel. She's staring at me, trying to figure me out. "Virginia, you're *indígena*. You look beautiful in *indígena* clothes. Why don't you dress as an *indígena*?"

"I just—I—I don't know. When I was *indígena* I was poor and didn't go to school and my parents hit me all the time. And I don't want to be that person anymore. I left that behind me."

Her eyes soften; her face goes tender. "You can be *indígena* and be proud. You don't have to be like your parents. You can be educated and successful. You can speak Spanish *and* Quichua. You don't have to choose one or the other. You can take the best of both worlds, you know."

She kisses my cheek goodbye. Once she pulls away I sneak in the rear entrance and run straight to the basement and strip off her clothes and change back into a regular shirt and skirt. As I hang up the clothes, I feel a little sad and a little relieved and a little ashamed, all at the same time. And then, to top it off, I feel ashamed that I'm ashamed.

The next months are a whirlwind of rehearsals and events. I barely find time to do homework. My coworkers cover my shifts. We work out deals where they leave dirty dishes for me in the sink, and then, at nine or ten o'clock, after my rehearsals,

I sneak in the back door, change into my regular clothes, and wash the dishes in a sleepy daze. By midnight I'm finished, and try to keep my eyes open a few more hours to do my homework, and then, finally, I fall into bed, too tired to change into pajamas. It seems like only minutes later when my alarm clock goes off for school.

"What exactly are all these rehearsals for?" Don Lucho asks me.

"Queen stuff," I say vaguely.

"Sounds suspicious. Sure you're not training for the secret service?"

I force a laugh. "It's just this competition," I say. "Kind of a beauty pageant." And before he can ask for details, I say with a wink, "So, Lucho, I saw that cute *gringuita* making eyes at you earlier."

He blushes and smiles, and I'm off the hook for now.

Carmen is the only one besides Don Walter who knows what the rehearsals are really for, and, in an unspoken pact, she keeps quiet about the details. Sometimes she takes over my shifts if I'm too exhausted, or she lets me switch shifts with her. "Go, Virginia. I'll come early and do the prep for you and stay late and wash your dishes."

"Let me pay you, Carmen." Although as I say this, I have no idea how I would buy next semester's books if she accepted.

But she shrugs it off. "You're going to be queen, I know it. And I want to help you. You deserve it, *chica*."

I hug her and run off to the next rehearsal. I actually enjoy the rehearsals. We learn interesting things, things I can use in other parts of my life. We practice public speaking and how to converse with top government officials and important

302

businesspeople. Soon we'll all be representatives of our organizations, meeting high-profile public figures at dinners and luncheons. It worries me that the other girls have a head start on this since their families are already friends with the movers and shakers of Ecuador.

When Don Lucho finds out we're practicing refined manners, after a lot of teasing, he lends me *Modern Etiquette*, a well-worn paperback with water-stained, yellowed pages. I study it every spare second. I learn which fork to use with which course and how to sip soup quietly and what wine to drink with what kind of dish.

"This is like preparing to go to war!" I tell Don Lucho. And that's how I feel, that I'm arming myself for entering the world of the successful and wealthy, mastering skills that even the Doctorita and Niño Carlitos don't know.

When the other girls notice me dozing off during rehearsal break times and ask, "Why are you so tired?" I just say, "Oh, my classes are really hard this semester." I don't mention anything about being a dishwasher. And to my coworkers, I try not to complain about how worn out I am with only five hours of sleep a night.

I learn to leave out big parts of my past and present, depending on my audience. I learn to stretch the truth and give answers that let people draw conclusions that might not be exactly true.

It is exhausting being two different people.

As the competition draws near, newspaper reporters interview us. Each week they feature a different girl. The reporter who interviews me wears red plastic-rimmed glasses and scribbles my answers in a tiny notepad. I muster up all the skills I've learned and hold my head high, as if it's attached to a string, and look into his eyes and smile and enunciate my words and speak eloquently, with no *uhs* and *mmms*.

"I believe that preschool education is vital for indigenous children in poor communities. Many children don't even have access to books in their homes." I leave out that I used to be one of those poor indigenous children.

"What do you do when you're not in school or rehearsing?" he asks, tilting his head.

"I love talking to the tourists at my father's hotel." This lie slips off my tongue easily now, so easily I barely register it's a lie. "I tell them about everything that the Ecuadorian Andes have to offer. I enjoy spreading my pride in our country's rich cultural heritage." I leave out the dishwashing part.

He scribbles my answer, looking pleased. "Tell us about your family, your childhood."

My mind goes blank. I look at his glasses reflecting the lights above, a little smudge on the left lens. I have no idea what to say. He's waiting and looking at me expectantly.

Finally, I say, "That is a long story, a story that I would like to write a book about one day. A story of overcoming obstacles. A story that any girl could have, if only she has the courage to follow her dreams."

He nods, smiling, and records my answer in his little pad.

"How do you feel about participating in this competition?" he asks next, and I breathe out with relief that he's let the issue of my childhood drop.

Two days later, when Don Walter sees the article in the

paper, he clips it out and posts it above his desk. He doesn't object that I called him my father; in fact, he seems flattered, and keeps saying, "We're so proud of you, *m'hija!*"

My duties include going to dances and parties packed with all the richest, most important *indígenas* in town. Along with the other contestants, I wear a satin sash over my *indígena* clothes, which, like peacock feathers, attracts the attention of the young *indígena* men in the room. They flirt with us, looking handsome in their neat, long braids and pressed khaki pants and button-down shirts, all the best brand names.

"Señorita, do you care to dance?" one boy after another asks me with a little bow.

I remember what *Modern Etiquette* says about accepting a dance request. I smile graciously and nod like I'm already a queen and offer my hand delicately. They take it and lead me as I walk slowly with my head high. I dance with a smile on my face, even when my partners are ugly, or terrible dancers, so that they won't feel bad. Around ten or eleven, I sneak away, back to the hotel to change into my regular clothes and wash the dishes piled in the sink.

The competition organizers seem to like me, even though I doze off from time to time. Doña Amelia always uses me as an example during modeling practice. My only weakness—and it is a huge one—is public speaking in Quichua. Susana has helped me prepare a speech that I'll have to give during the competition. In rehearsals, I stumble over the words and talk in a high, nervous voice with terrible pronunciation.

One day, Doña Amelia takes me aside after a rehearsal. She

is tall and graceful, and reminds me of a waterbird. "Virginia, listen, I'll be straight with you. You have a good chance of being queen, but only if you improve your Quichua."

"Thank you, señora. I know my Quichua is awful. I practice every night in my room, but I don't live with my parents anymore and so I don't have the chance to talk Quichua."

"Why don't you go visit your parents, then? Go speak Quichua with them." She reaches out and tucks a loose strand of my hair behind my ear, then pats my cheek. At her touch, I remember the *mestiza* teacher and her cruel nails that pinched me and called me a stupid *longa* whenever I spoke Quichua.

Now, oddly enough, speaking Quichua is what I need most to have a chance at being queen. And, I realize, I do want to be queen, very badly. Being queen would be the opposite of crawling back to the Doctorita pregnant and begging for my job back. Being queen would show her that being *indígena* does not mean being a stupid, poor *longa*. It would show her that I am not only a star student with friends who love me but also a queen, a real, live queen.

chapter 35

Two DAYS LATER, in my parents' house in Yana Urku, I'm sitting awkwardly on the bed in a haze of pungent kerosene smoke. A chorus of crickets sings in the darkness just outside the walls. It's late; the children have already fallen asleep. Mamita is putting away the dishes, while Papito is talking to me in starts and stops. We sit close, leaning across the space between beds, keeping our voices soft so we won't wake the children.

"It's good to see you, *m'hija*," he says in Spanish, still a little bewildered at my sudden appearance earlier this evening. "What made you come visit us after so many months?"

"I just felt like it," I say in Spanish, shrugging. Then I take a deep breath and force my mouth to make the sounds of Quichua. "Talk Quichua, Papito," I say with such a terrible accent that he looks at me blankly until I whisper in Spanish, "Papito, please, can you speak in Quichua with me?"

"Why?" Lantern flames make spots of light and dark move over his face.

I hesitate. "I don't know." I can't bring myself to tell the truth. I want to keep my lives separate—Virginia the poor *indígena* in Yana Urku, Virginia the rich *indígena* at queen rehearsals; Virginia the dishwasher at the hotel, Virginia the star student at school. And my father wouldn't understand anyway. Even in Spanish, he wouldn't know the words for *newspaper interview* or *modern etiquette* or *public speaking*. These words are like stars in another galaxy, light-years from his reality. "I just— I just want to speak better Quichua is all."

"All right," he says in Quichua, but then neither of us can think of anything to say, so finally he says, "Good night, Daughter," and lies down in his bed. Soon he is snoring lightly.

By now Mamita has finished with the dishes, and she sits next to me on the other bed and hands me a cup of steaming lemon balm tea.

"*Pagui*, Mamita," I say in Quichua, thanking her.

She smiles at my effort.

I look at her, trying to form a question. I realize, all of a sudden, that this is the first time since I was a little girl that I've felt she has something to teach me. It's the first time I've made an effort to understand her.

And I think she's been waiting for this moment. She looks at me patiently.

"Tell me"—I'm still unsure what to say—"tell me about me, when little girl," I finally finish in choppy Quichua, pointing to myself, then gesturing with my hand to the height of a young child.

For a moment, she watches me, her eyes shiny in the lantern light. Then, from beneath the bed, she pulls out a water-stained, warped cardboard box, sets it between us, and opens it slowly.

Inside are a small *anaco* and blouse, and a pile of fabric scraps of all colors, faded and frayed. She holds up each piece, one by one. They are ancient, full of tears and holes and ground-in dirt stains. After holding each one up, she presses it to her face. She speaks slowly, resting her hand on my knee. "Your old things, my daughter."

I pick them up and yes, I recognize my blouse, the coarse cotton mottled with berry and blood stains. When I left with the Doctorita and Niño Carlitos, I must have kept this set of clothes at home, thinking I'd wear it on the monthly visits that never happened. My fingers brush over the soft fabric scraps— my pretend clothes for sale, which I used to sell to my cousins for leaves. Holding up the bits of material, I remember how I envisioned a good life for myself, in the same way *Secrets to a Happy Life* says you should. *The first step is imagining.*

"*Pusaq wata,*" Mamita says, holding up eight fingers. *Eight years.* She is crying now and wiping the tears with the clothes and fabric scraps. "Eight years I cried for you, my daughter. Every night I held your clothes and cried for you."

I speak slowly in Quichua, each word an effort. "Mamita." I point to her tears, then to my own face. "I cry, too. So many years. I miss you, too. I cry so many years."

She nods, tears streaming down her face. "*Ñuka guagua.*" My daughter.

"Many years I think about you," I whisper. I look at my brother and sister sleeping, their toes poking out from the blanket that barely covers them. "But, Mamita, you have other children." I motion to Hermelinda and Manuelito. I don't know how to express what I feel. I'm not even sure I know what I feel. Finally, I put my hand on my chest, right over my heart. "To you, I don't matter." I can't hold my tears in anymore.

She shakes her head and holds up one finger. "Each child is unique. Each one is special."

I sniff and wipe my eyes. "Many years ago, Mamita, you say, 'Leave, Daughter,'" and here I point to myself, and gesture toward the door. "You say, 'I happy you leave.'" And now my voice is trembling and I am sobbing.

She shakes her head vehemently and a frantic string of Quichua words pours from her mouth.

"Slow, Mamita, slow." I look at this woman here beside me, half stranger, half mother. I look at her weathered face that is old and worn and aching with regrets.

"*Ñuka guagua.*" She takes my hands in hers. "I love you, my daughter." These words I understand perfectly; these are the words I've wanted to hear my whole life.

"I love you too, Mamita."

The next morning, we're all sitting together around the fire pit, waiting for the potato soup to reheat—my parents, Manuelito and Hermelinda, and some little cousins who have wandered over for breakfast. Mamita is stirring the soup with a long wooden spoon, and I'm thinking what *Modern Etiquette* would say about this meal. No napkins to spread neatly on your lap, no silverware to use from outside to inside from first to last course, not even a single spoon to avoid slurping noisily from, no chair to sit straight in, no butter to ask to be passed rather than reached for, no table to keep your elbows off of . . . The

Modern Etiquette author would either faint or run screaming from the house. I smile at this thought, and then see that my toddler cousin Ivan has noticed my smile and is smiling back at me.

"How are you this morning?" I ask him in broken Quichua.

"Fine," he says, giggling.

From the corner of my eye, I catch Papito staring at me, with something close to a smile on his face. "You should speak Quichua more often, Daughter," he says.

"*Ari*," I agree in Quichua, letting myself smile back.

The dogs start barking outside, in a friendly way, and soon Matilde and Santiago are standing in the doorway, backlit by morning sunshine.

"Virginia!" Matilde cries, throwing her arms around me. "Little sister, what are you doing here?"

"Just visiting."

"But you never visit! Santiago and I come almost every weekend and we never see you here!"

"I've been busy, with school and work and stuff. But this weekend, I don't know, I just felt like it."

Mamita offers her stool to Santiago and moves to the floor, where she kneels with the children. I offer my stool to Matilde, but she insists, "No, stay there."

While the soup is heating, we sip lemon balm tea and Matilde chats about married life and her new neighbors and projects that she and Santiago are doing in their house in Quito, to get ready for their baby. It turns out she's three months pregnant.

Mamita begins serving the soup, ladles the biggest potato into a bowl, and hands it to me. "*Mana*, Mamita," I say in Quichua, shaking my head. "Give Matilde big potato."

311

Matilde laughs. "Since when do you speak Quichua, little sister?"

"I'm trying to learn it," I say, guilty I haven't told anyone the truth about why. My coming here, my attempting to learn Quichua—these alone are big steps for me. But I still don't feel comfortable taking the next one—merging my two lives. If I tell my family about the queen competition, they might want to come, and then the other contestants will see my real father and mother and realize we belong to the class of poor *indígenas*. No, I can't tell my family about the competition.

I can't invite my classmates and coworkers to the competition either, not even Carmen and Esperanza and Sonia. If they see me wearing an *anaco* and lacy blouse and gold beads, they might start to treat me as an *indígena*—maybe a well-off one, but an *indígena* all the same. Even imagining them looking at me that way quickens my heartbeat, makes me break out in a terrified sweat. So to be safe, I've invited no one.

Mamita passes Matilde the bowl with the biggest potato, and Matilde says, "No, Mamita, give it to Virginia. We have to treat her well so she'll come back to visit more often!"

Mamita hands the bowl to me, and I accept it, but stealthily pass it over to Ivan. The youngest child never gets the biggest potato, never gets served first. I remember feeling rage over this injustice as a little girl. "Here, Ivan," I say in Quichua. "Eat big potato!"

After breakfast, Matilde and I help Mamita with the dishes, and then it's time for me to go. "I have to get back to Otavalo for the lunch shift," I say, and find that instead of desperately wanting to leave, I'm actually enjoying myself.

They protest for a bit, "Stay, Virginia!" and "Stay, Daughter!" and "Stay, Sister!" and finally Matilde says, "Fine, but let me walk you to the bus stop."

We walk down the dusty street, lined with fields of knee-high corn. The sky is cloudless except for the far-off mists over the mountains Imbabura and Cotacachi. I'm wearing my track shoes, which I bought for gym class—they come in handy here. It's hard to believe I walked down this road barefoot, so many times, years ago.

I remember once when Matilde and I were out looking for berries. I spotted some bright red ones and pointed them out, but she got to them first and started eating them. I lost my temper, tackled her to the ground, and sat on her chest, pummeling her, screaming, "They're my berries! You stole them! I saw them first! I hate you!" She ran away, crying, "I'm telling on you!" I followed her up this very same road, calling her a tattletale. Once Mamita heard, she beat me with a eucalyptus stick and said, "You're a terrible sister!"

I'm embarrassed at the memory. "Matilde?" I ask. "Why are you so nice to me now, after I hit you and yelled at you and was so mean to you when I was little?"

She laughs. "You weren't mean. You were just an annoying little sister who I loved but who drove me crazy."

"Remember that time you took the berries I wanted and I pushed you down and beat you up?"

"What are you talking about?" she says with a grin. "The only time I remember you hitting someone was Papito. Whenever he was drunk and hit Mamita, you tried to defend her. You ran up to him and hit him with a stick and yelled, 'You're a bad man!' I admired your gumption. I was too scared to stand up to

313

Papito myself. But at the same time, I felt protective, because you were my little sister, and I didn't want him to hurt you. I felt so guilty for working in Quito, leaving you alone with Papito and his temper."

"Really? That's what you remember? That's how you felt?"

"And you know, I think in a way, Mamita and Papito respected you for your spunk. Sure you drove them crazy, but you didn't let anyone walk all over you. You stood up and fought. No matter how much they beat you, you stuck out your chin and told them you'd be a rich, famous business lady one day. That's who I remember you being, little sister." She laughs. "And look at you now, going to your fancy *colegio*, living in your fancy hotel. Nothing stops you! You have as much spunk as ever, little sister."

chapter 36

I PEER OUT FROM THE DARKNESS behind the curtain. Doña
Amelia is onstage, in the spotlight, talking into the microphone. Every one of the five hundred seats before her is full.
She's talking about how hard we all worked and how we all be-
came friends and how really, every one of us is a queen in her
eyes. She introduces the judges, in the front row, who stand up
and wave at the audience.

In the wings, the other girls are nervously whispering. Our
hair is shiny, every strand in place, our lips pink, our teeth
smeared with Vaseline to make them glow. Susana did my
makeup—sparkly silver eye shadow on the lids, a dark pencil
to make my eyebrows dramatic, blush to accentuate my cheek-
bones.

The smell of hair spray and gel and perfume clouds the air
backstage, and the girls ask each other, "Do I have lipstick on
my teeth? Is my blouse tucked in evenly?" I run my tongue over
my own teeth and check my *faja*. I've tied it super tight to make

315

sure it stays up; the worst thing in the world would be if it came unwound and fell down in front of hundreds of people.

"And now," Doña Amelia says, "I present to you . . . our lovely contestants!"

At that, the audience applauds, an ocean of clapping and whistling. As we've rehearsed dozens of times before, we stream onstage from both wings, shortest to tallest, dancing an indigenous harvest dance. We dance down the stairs and along the side aisles and then meet in the back to dance down the center. The spotlights follow us and people crane their heads and murmur, "Look, how beautiful."

We divide into two lines again, one on either side of the stage, graceful and smiling, and then disappear behind the curtains. A huge wave of applause sounds. Our next three dances go smoothly, each one met with loud cheers and whistles.

After the dancing segment, each girl walks like a model across the stage when her name is called, silently praying she won't trip and fall. She stops in the center, turns around, and pauses with a smile pasted on her face as Doña Amelia reads a little about her. Most every girl is a star student, loves her friends and family, hopes for world peace.

When my name is called, I glide across the stage, imagining I'm a bird or a deer as Doña Amelia suggested in our lessons. I pause at the center and smile big and let my eyes dance. *Stand tall, little radish flower.* Doña Amelia says nice things about how I'm on the honor roll and especially excel in science class.

Next comes the part that has kept me up worrying at night. The speech in Quichua. Every night I've gone over it, again and again in bed, struggling to get the intonations right and strike the perfect nasal tone. It's a flowery speech, more or less written by Susana, about how important preschool is for indigenous kids.

The girl in front of me, Luz, is talking about her organization, which helps bring health education to the indigenous communities, and although she rocks back and forth nervously, her words flow effortlessly from her mouth, her accent perfect, her sounds flawless. I can't understand most of what she says, but it sounds noble, about how we all have rights to good health care.

At the end of her speech, the audience applauds. Their applause is getting a little weaker, because it's been two hours and they've already heard about forty girls give one-minute speeches, and they're ready for the queens to be chosen already. Luz curtsies, and a few people call out, "Way to go, Sis! You're great, Cousin!" Everyone but me seems to have their whole extended family here to cheer them on.

"María Virginia Farinango," Doña Amelia calls.

I glide onstage, imagining a golden string holding up my head. *Querer es poder*, I say silently. *Yo puedo, yo puedo. I can do it, I can do it.* I stand behind the microphone. The spotlight is so bright in my eyes, I can't make out any faces. I hear people moving and shifting, and some babies babbling and their mothers shushing them.

My mind is as blank as a cloudless sky. I can't remember a single word in Quichua. I can't remember the first line of the speech that I've repeated hundreds of times.

Think, Virginia, think. Just remember the first line and then the rest will come to you.

But the moment has stretched out as long as it can and I have to do something.

I open my mouth, praying the Quichua words will tumble out. Instead, Spanish emerges. *"Buenas noches,"* I begin. Good evening.

Talk about education, Virginia. Preschool education for indigenous kids. Talk!

"I grew up in Yana Urku," I hear myself saying in Spanish. This is not my planned speech. This is something entirely different, and I don't know where it's headed, but I keep going. "In the poorest of the poor indigenous communities around Otavalo. There was not a single book in my house. My parents couldn't read. They thought school was a waste of time. They thought I would grow up to be a farmer like them, renting out land from *mestizos*. They thought I'd have no need for an education.

"I went to school for six weeks, but then I stopped. I stopped because when the teacher heard me speak Quichua she pinched my ear and called me a stupid *longa*."

Murmurs ripple through the audience. The room is humming with a new energy. I can feel the audience listening, hanging on my words.

"I thought that speaking Quichua was a bad thing. When I was seven, my parents gave me to a *mestizo* family, and I worked for them for free. For eight years. My boss called me a stupid *longa*. She said that *longas* are not meant to read. That they're meant to serve. And during that time I forgot how to speak my language. I learned to feel ashamed of my culture."

Again, the audience murmurs; although I can't see their faces, I feel their presence. I feel them with me in my story.

"My boss refused to let me go to school, so I studied in secret. I taught myself to read. I taught myself about the wonders of nature, like photosynthesis. The wonders of the world and

318

the wonders of the universe. After I escaped from this family, I knew that the most important thing for me was to go to school. I knew that education was the way I would succeed, the way I would have a career and a voice in the world."

More murmurs. "*Sí, sí, sí,*" people whisper. *Yes, yes, yes.*

"I represent an organization that believes education is a right everyone should have, indigenous or not. This education should begin early, at preschool. And it should be an education that values our language and our traditions as *indígenas*. No child should feel that her mother tongue is bad. No child should grow up in a house with no books. No child should be told she is only fit for serving. I ask you—"

I pause, because tears are slipping from my eyes and my voice is quavering, not from nervousness, but from the sheer force of speaking from my heart. I wipe my eyes and take a deep breath and go on. "I ask you to support our organization so that no child has to go through what I did. So that every child can learn about the richness of her world, the richness of her culture, the richness of her self."

I give a small curtsy. "*Pagui,*" I say in Quichua. Thank you.

A burst of applause sounds, so loud it fills me. As I walk off-stage into the wings, it's as though I'm swimming through a sea of sounds—clapping and whistling and foot-stamping and whooping.

Backstage, the other girls hug me and whisper, "That was incredible, Virginia!" and I whisper, "Thanks," but I can't say anything else because my knees are weak and my heart is pounding. As the last ten girls give their speeches, I feel my pulse race and think how good it feels to say what I believe with every molecule in my body, while hundreds of people listen. It doesn't matter that my speech wasn't in Quichua, that there's no way I can be voted queen now. Something inside me feels full.

After the last girl gives her speech, a band comes onstage, an *indígena* band, playing the panpipe music MacGyver played on his cassette years ago. It fills the room, creating landscapes of mountains and valleys and lakes with its wind notes. The musicians blow into their flutes with passion, their cheeks puffed out, their braids swinging. The music swirls around me and sweeps me up and makes my heart swell with pride.

During this time, the judges are conferring in another room, deciding on the winning queens. Five songs pass, and the band moves off the stage as the judges file onto it. All of us girls are onstage, too, in three rows—the tallest in back, shortest in front. I'm wedged in the middle row, hoping that Luz will be one of the winners, since she's always helped the other girls with the dance steps. Who will the other winners be—maybe Elsa or Cristina? Elsa has always made an effort to be friendly to everyone, especially to the shy girls. I'd be happy if she won.

Doña Amelia stands behind the microphone, excited. "It wasn't easy, but the judges have chosen the winners. First, we'll announce the Queen of Sky, then the Queen of Water, and finally, the star, the Queen of Corn."

The news reporters are crouched in front of the stage, cameras ready to snap photos. In the audience people are whispering about who they think will win. I'm holding hands with the girls next to me, and we squeeze each other's sweaty hands.

"For the Queen of Sky . . . Elsa Quimbo!"

Screams and squeals of joy erupt from one row of seats, which must be her family. "Elsa!" they shout, and rush to the stage with flowers. "Sister! Cousin! Niece!" There are at least a dozen of them—parents and brothers and sisters and aunts and uncles. They reach up their hands, whistling and clapping and glowing with pride. Doña Amelia puts a blue sash around Elsa that reads, in Quichua, *The Queen of Sky*. TV cameramen push through to get a better angle, and the reporters are snapping photos like crazy.

Once the applause calms, Doña Amelia says, "And now for the Queen of Water . . . María Virginia Farinango!"

The audience explodes in applause and whistles and whoops. I look around, thinking there must be some mistake. I couldn't have won. My speech wasn't in Quichua. Maybe I'm dreaming. Maybe I've gone overboard with one of my fantasies.

But Doña Amelia is looking at me and the girls are hugging me and pushing me forward to receive the sash. Doña Amelia hugs me and whispers, "Beautiful speech," into my ear. As she puts the sash around me, the journalists are clicking their cameras frantically and Susana is running up to the stage with a bouquet of lilies. No one else runs up to me, no family or friends, but plenty of people I don't even know are cheering and calling "María Virginia!" The applause goes on and on, and I stand, dazed and smiling, holding the flowers and sweating in the spotlight. Finally, Doña Amelia has to hold up her hands to make the audience settle down.

The Queen of Corn is next. It's Luz, and as she steps forward, we hug, and whisper "Congratulations" in each other's ears. In the midst of more applause and photo snapping, her family rushes up, showering her with flowers and cheers.

Maybe I should have invited my parents and brother and sister and cousins and friends and coworkers. It might have been nice for them to be here. It would feel good if all the pieces of my life could find a way to somehow fit together.

We three queens hold hands as Doña Amelia talks about our prizes—all-expenses-paid trips to the Galápagos Islands. I think of myself as a little girl perched in the tree, pretending to be an elegant, beautiful *indígena* riding in my truck to exciting places. I think of how wishes can come true, but not always in the way you expect. I think of what Matilde said about who I really am. Someone with spunk, someone who lets nothing stop her from reaching her dreams.

chapter 37

ON MONDAY MORNING, I walk from the bus stop to school full of jumpy energy, wondering how people at school will react. My picture along with those of the other queens is on the front page of this morning's newspaper. The article is long, describing the ceremony and quoting parts from my speech. Anyone in town who missed reading about it in the newspapers will have seen it on the morning news, which showed close-up footage of us queens in our sashes.

Earlier this morning, I was sipping my *jugo de tomate* in the hotel café when Don Lucho cried, "Look! It's our Virginia!" My coworkers stopped what they were doing and crowded around the TV in the corner. Even the *gringuitos* took their noses out of their guidebooks to watch Doña Amelia putting the sash over me.

Now I turn the block and walk toward the school, my insides leaping around. My coworkers are one thing, but the students and teachers are another. What will they say? Will they act differently toward me from now on? Will I no longer be one of them? I barely reach the gate when a crowd of students rushes over to me, not just seventh graders but upperclassmen, too.

"Congratulations, Queen Virginia!"

"Why didn't you tell us, Virginia? You're so modest!"

"Wow! You look beautiful in the pictures!"

All morning long, students I hardly know are asking me to run for class president, begging me to join their clubs, their sports teams, to sit with them at lunch. My teachers keep me after every class to congratulate me.

My science teacher is especially excited. "Virginia!" she says. "We're so proud of you! Now I understand why your grades haven't been as high as usual lately. All these rehearsals, all this work!"

I nod. "Yes, it's been busy."

"You should have told us what was going on!"

"Yes, I should have." And it's true, I should have.

After school, I have an hour before work starts, so Carmen and Sonia and Esperanza and I decide go to the ice cream stall at the food market to celebrate. A few people stop and stare as I pass, and some ask, "Aren't you one of the queens?"

My friends giggle, loving this. "It's like being with a celebrity!" Sonia says.

I blush and lick my ice cream cone, a little embarrassed, but mostly happy.

"Hey, Virginia," Esperanza says, "why don't you wear your *indígena* clothes more? Like at work and hanging out. I bet they'd even let you wear them to school instead of a uniform."

"Why would I do that?" I ask, shifting on my stool.

"Because you look gorgeous in them!" Carmen says, throwing her arm around my shoulder. "*Chica*, those pictures in the paper were amazing!"

"Maybe," I say.

"But now you have a responsibility to dress that way," she insists. "You're the Queen of Water! You're representing this organization! It's your queenly duty, *chica!*"

A week later, on Sunday afternoon, before the dinner shift, I put on Susana's *anacos* and blouse and jewelry—which she insisted I keep as a gift. As I leave the hotel, all my coworkers ooh and ahh and whistle. "*¡Qué guapa, esta reina!*" How beautiful, this queen!

Outside, I walk down the street slowly, relishing how strangely comfortable I am. I don't feel the need to scurry along quickly, hiding my face, as I did during all the rehearsals. As I pass, a few people murmur to each other, "Is that one of the queens?" At the square, my girlfriends are waiting for me by the fountain, under an apple tree.

"Yay! You did it!" Carmen says. The girls touch the beads around my neck, the red beads at my wrist, the shiny blouse, the soft *anaco* fabric, the ribbon wrapped around my ponytail.

"You look so pretty!" Esperanza says.

And Sonia chimes in, "Can you let me try this on sometime?"

Not long after the election, an official invitation arrives at the hotel, addressed to me. The card is thick creamy linen paper with raised gold lettering, with so many swirls and flourishes it's hard to read.

Esteemed Señorita María Virginia Farinango,
We request the honor of your presence at a luncheon at
the Hotel Otavalo at one in the afternoon on Saturday the
first of June . . .

I already know about the luncheon from Don Walter talking about it. It's a big deal, with the daughter of the president of Ecuador coming. At the hotel we've hosted big, fancy luncheons and dinners before, but nothing quite this big.

The whole week before the event, Don Walter and the cooks and waiters are excitedly planning the menu and ordering fresh lilies and roses for the table in the formal dining room upstairs. "The president's daughter!" everyone is buzzing. "Here, in our hotel!"

I can't quite bring myself to tell them that I will be one of the guests, so I just help them with the preparations, giving a new coat of wax to the wood floors, polishing the banister to a high sheen. I've told them I won't be able to work that day because of a queen commitment, but when I try to tell them the truth, it stops in my throat. I want my worlds to come together, but I'm not sure how. How can I be a queen and a dishwasher at the same time?

Saturday arrives. At eleven, my coworker Quines and I are checking the table, making sure all the napkins are perfectly folded, all the silverware perpendicular to the table edge, the flowers arranged just right.

"Virginia," he says, placing the glasses of water from a tray onto the table, "if you have time before your royal duties, why don't you stay and help us? There are only three servers and we'll be super-busy."

"Well, Quines." I pluck off a few wilted rose petals, stalling. "Actually, this *is* my royal duty. I'm a guest at this luncheon."

He nearly drops the tray of water glasses. "What? You're eating with the president's daughter?"

"I should change now, actually," I say, and run downstairs, leaving him there, bewildered.

An hour later, I'm dressed in my *indígena* clothes, sitting with the other queens at a long table with the president's daughter. Panpipe music is playing lightly from the speakers, and reporters and photographers are snapping photos and talking to the more-famous guests—senators and city council members. The president's daughter looks about thirty years old, around Susana's age, and is an expert on mingling and posing graciously for pictures. She wears a tailored blue suit with a white ruffled blouse and low heels and a pretty pin at her neck.

Niçoise salad is the first course, which I spent all morning making, arranging the hard-boiled eggs and olives perfectly on each of the twenty-five plates. Daintily, I pick up the proper fork to use for the salad, and notice that two of the councilmen use their main-course forks by mistake.

I know the menu by heart. Next will come cream of asparagus soup topped with blue cheese crumbles, then sautéed chicken in a mushroom-raisin-wine sauce garnished with curlicues of carrot and sprigs of fresh cilantro. The cilantro and carrot curlicues were my idea, from a magazine I read, and Don Walter agreed it would be a nice touch. Finally, for dessert, dark chocolate mousse layered with fresh raspberry coulis and topped with a dollop of whipped cream.

As Quines collects our dirty dishes, I whisper, "Delicious salad."

He shakes his head, grinning. "Good thing Lucho lent you *Modern Etiquette*," he whispers back. Before rehearsals, he and Lucho would quiz me on which spoon to use for soup, which for iced tea, when to put the napkin in your seat to signal you'll be back or on the table to signal you're finished.

During the soup course, the president's daughter starts talking to me. "What a lovely blouse you have. Those flowers must have taken someone a long time to stitch!"

"Thank you," I say, a little tongue-tied. I remember *Modern Etiquette*. When someone compliments you, say something nice back. "Your outfit is beautiful too. I like your pin." It's a gold cameo with a creamy pink face in the center.

We sip our soup soundlessly. Everything looks different from this spot at the table, compared with when I'm clearing dishes. It's easy to revel in the elegance, trust that everything will flow smoothly, like silk. And I can sink into this, but at the same time, I can imagine the scene in the kitchen—Quines and my other friends whizzing around and sweating and frantically getting twenty-five plates of food ready, making them look perfect, timing all the courses so they're the right temperature when they come out: the salad cool and fresh, the soup hot but not too hot.

"Mmm," the president's daughter says. "This soup is delicious, isn't it? I'll have to ask for the recipe to give to the cook at our house."

I want to say, *Thank you! The blue cheese topping was Quines's idea.* I want to tell her I picked out the soup with Don Walter and went shopping at the market for the ingredients and helped blend up the asparagus. I want to tell her these things, but they might shatter my image as queen.

But I wonder, what if I tell her the truth about my life? Will she still think I belong at this table? Is she willing to know what's beneath the surface, behind the scenes? Or is she content to take me at face value, a cardboard cutout queen?

"The soup's easy," I say. "Steam the asparagus, sauté garlic and green onions, add some cream, blend it up, add salt and pepper."

"My, that does sound easy," she says. "So you enjoy cooking?"

"Actually, señora, I work here. I'm a dishwasher, but when we have big events I shop and cook, too. And I help with serving sometimes, but I can't today."

She stares, her spoon midair. "What an extraordinary girl you are! Tell me, how did you end up working here?"

Through the whole mushroom chicken course I tell her about going back to Yana Urku and needing money for school, and finding this job. As I talk, she nods and asks me questions, truly interested. It's as though the fabric scraps of my self are being sewn together, in tiny, almost invisible stitches, with the finest of threads.

While Quines is clearing the dishes and the others are setting out coffee, I notice the sweat beaded on their foreheads and I can see in their eyes that they're swamped. I know they need to serve the rest of the coffee and deal with the cream and sugar and then there's the chocolate mousse with fresh whipped cream that will droop if it's not brought out soon.

"Excuse me a moment," I tell the president's daughter, and put my napkin on my chair. I breeze into the kitchen and sure enough, there is a tray of chocolate mousse, the whipped cream dollops just on the verge of sagging.

"Thank goodness, Virginia," the cook says. "Please, take it

out now!" I emerge from the kitchen with my head high, as though it's attached to a golden string, the platter of mousse balanced on one upturned palm. Quines has just cleared the last of the main-course plates, and he gives me a surprised but grateful smile when he sees me with the platter.

Everyone turns to me as I put down their dessert, and says politely, "Thank you, Virginia," or "Thank you, señorita."

I am not at all invisible. I am the served and I am the server. I am queen and I am dishwasher. I am rich and poor, *indígena* and *mestiza*, and no one can put me in a box.

I save the last mousse for myself, sit down, choose the small dessert spoon. Then I notice the president's daughter. She has waited for me to take my seat before starting to eat. We raise our spoons in a kind of toast and dig in.

All week, more articles and pictures of me and the other queens have appeared in the newspaper. Don Walter cuts them out and puts them next to the others above his desk, and Don Lucho tapes some behind the café bar.

"Virginia!" Don Lucho calls to me on Saturday morning. "You have some visitors."

I'm sitting at a café table, covered with pink eraser dust, sipping orange juice and trying to solve a geometry problem. My head is full of isosceles triangles and hypotenuses and formulas. I'm trying to get all my homework done today, because tomorrow morning is the big procession, the culmination of all the queen events, when I'll be paraded through the city with Luz and Elsa.

I put down my pencil, glad of a break. "Who is it?"

"The president and his daughter," Don Lucho says, walking

330

over to me, peering at my homework. "She wants to hang out with you, since you're best friends now. She brought her dad along."

"Don Lucho!" I say, hitting him playfully.

He laughs and flashes his gold tooth.

"Do I really have visitors?"

"Yes, Your Highness. A woman and a man. But they didn't give their names."

Maybe it's Susana and José, here to tell me last-minute instructions for the big parade tomorrow. It could be anyone, really. For the past two weeks I've had all kinds of unexpected visitors. One young man who made dolls for tourists wanted to make *indígena* queen dolls, and he took my picture to use as a model. A photographer from France came, too, and we did a modeling shoot near Lake Mojanda for his magazine.

I take my hair out of its ponytail, smooth it back, and wrap the band around again. I brush the eraser dust from my skirt and breeze past Don Lucho, whispering, "And stop calling me Your Highness, King Lucho!"

With a smile still on my face, I walk to the foyer and look around, but no one's there. I go to the doors and glance outside.

The smile disappears.

It's them.

chapter 38

NIÑO CARLITOS AND THE DOCTORITA stand before me like pieces of an old dream I can't quite forget. For months I've dreamed of the satisfaction I'd get from them seeing me crowned queen. I've imagined their reaction to the newspaper articles, the TV clip. I've imagined how the Doctorita would have to eat her terrible words. I've imagined them coming and begging my forgiveness. But I've never imagined it happening so soon.

I thought it might happen in the distant future, once I'm a grown woman with an important job and my own house and a husband and children. I try to make my legs move to turn, to run back inside and hide somewhere.

The Doctorita spots me through the doorway. It's too late to run. I force my feet to walk out the door. I stand across from them on the sidewalk. They stare silently. Niño Carlitos's gaze is especially intense, full of feeling. Guilt? Happiness? Sadness? Hope? I can't tell. There's a toddler girl, holding on to his hand. The boys are shyly hanging back, behind the Doctorita. Her face is chubbier than I remember, her belly bigger, her hips wider. Her hair is dyed an orangey color, with gray-brown roots showing. She's wearing a dress I've never seen.

As I look at them, my legs feel about to collapse. So many feelings bombard me at once. There's the warmth of familiarity—memories of the Doctorita in her faded blue bathrobe in the mornings and Niño Carlitos building toys for us and telling me my food was *rrriquísimo*. The Doctorita making jokes and laughing at something and singing along with romantic songs on the radio and knitting her Baby Jesus dresses. Nights watching TV together, gasping when MacGyver was hanging on the edge of a cliff and sighing with relief when he rescued himself. Little Andrecito strapped to my back as I washed dishes, calling me Mamá and playing with my hair. Stealing fruit with Jaimito in the orchards, playing chase together.

At the same time, my neck grows tense and I feel myself shrink, hunching my shoulders protectively, ready to let my arms fly up and protect my face from the Doctorita's fists. Ready to cringe and duck away from Niño Carlitos's groping hands.

And I feel myself sweating, my heart beating in anger, as I remember their last words to me. *In three months you'll be crawling back to us on your knees, pregnant, begging for us to take you in. Just like all longas.*

I remind myself I am the Virginia with spunk, the Virginia who never rolls belly-up, the Virginia who stands tall like a radish flower. I am Virginia the Queen of Water. I straighten up and swing my ponytail over my shoulder, keeping my distance.

The Doctorita raises her arms and cries, "Oh! My daughter!" and comes toward me. I go rigid as she wraps her arms around me. Her perfume brings back a new rush of memories

333

that make me queasy. She holds her arms at my shoulders. "My, you've grown up!" Her chins jiggle.

I step back, leaving her with her hands dangling.

"Hello, señora," I say in what I hope is a cool, detached voice.

Meanwhile, Niño Carlitos is hanging back with the kids and forcing a smile. "Hello, Don Carlos," I say.

I walk over to the boys. "Hello, Andrecito. Hello, Jaimito." They smile shyly but don't throw their arms around me in bear hugs like they used to. Two years is a long time for kids. They probably barely remember me.

Glancing up at the Doctorita, I take a long breath. I keep my head high, as though it's hanging from a golden string. "How did you know I was here?"

The Doctorita looks at Niño Carlitos. "You've been all over the newspapers."

I recall that yes, in one interview, I said I lived at the Hotel Otavalo. With Walter, my father. I wish Don Walter were here now, but he's out at a meeting. I wish he were next to me with his hand on my shoulder.

"Why did you come?" I ask flatly. I am not going to engage in polite small talk with them. I am not going to pretend anymore.

"Is that any way to treat us? Your family? I've always been like a mother to you. And Carlos has been like your father."

Niño Carlitos looks at the sidewalk.

I want to keep cool and collected, but the blood is rising to my face. "Why did you come?" I ask again, my voice not as steady now.

"Virginia," the Doctorita says, "we came to bring you

home." She takes a step toward me. Suddenly I'm terrified she'll grab me and throw me into the truck and take me away.

You're stronger than her now, I remind myself. *All you have to do is scream and in seconds, Don Lucho and Quines and Carmen and everyone else will be out here to defend you.* I do not step backward. I stand my ground and say in her face, "This is my home now."

She lowers her voice. "Look at you, working at a hotel like some low-class person. I thought you wanted to be a professional."

Arguing with her is like *la lucha libre*—freestyle wrestling, with almost no rules—and she has just given me a jab to the gut. I recover relatively quickly. "This job is what pays for my education. And in a few years, after I finish college, I'll have a career."

She shakes her head, pursing her lips as though she's trying to hold in her scorn. *"Ve tonta."* Look, fool.

"Don't call me *tonta.*"

She rolls her eyes. "Look, Virginia, we've come to make a generous offer. Even though you treated us terribly. Even though you abandoned us after all we did for you. Even though you left a distraught woman who had just given birth after a dangerous pregnancy. Even though you left her with a premature baby with no help. Even though you've shown us nothing but ingratitude."

I feel nauseated, hot, prickly, on the verge of fainting or throwing up.

"Yet because you are like a daughter to us," she says, "we have decided to pay for your high school and your college. You will come back to live with us. Where you belong."

I stare. Does she really want me back? Is it possible she really considers me family? Does she really think of me as a daughter? Is there any kernel of truth to what she says?

"Look, Virginia. Don't throw this away. We're offering you your own house and an education. Only a fool would hesitate."

Niño Carlitos looks at the Doctorita, then back at me. "You don't have to answer now, *m'hija*," he says softly. "Just think about it. We—we miss you. The boys miss you. We need your help with the baby. We haven't found anyone to replace you. No one could ever replace you."

He seems to be speaking honestly. Do they really need me? Have they truly realized I'm special, irreplaceable? Would they treat me differently now? Would they really pay for college and give me a house?

I say nothing, and finally the Doctorita snaps, "Think about it." She turns to the boys. "Say goodbye to Virginia."

"Goodbye, Virginia," they mumble.

"Give her a hug," she commands.

They hug me, shyly at first, and then warmly. "I love you, boys," I whisper, my eyes tearing up.

"Tell Virginia how much you want her to come home," the Doctorita urges.

"We want you to come home," they say simultaneously.

"We'll be back soon," the Doctorita says.

"Goodbye," I say, and turn to leave. They start climbing into their truck.

And then it hits me. Maybe she loves me a little and misses me a little. But most of all, she wants control over me. She wants to win. She wants me under her thumb. She wants to be able to say that she is responsible for how I've turned out.

She wants me to be indebted to her for my education, for my career, for my house. She wants to hold that over me, so I'll never be able to tell people the truth of what she did to me.

I remember my first newspaper interview, when I said that one day I would write a book about my childhood. I said that mainly to avoid more questions about my background, but what if, maybe, I do write a book someday? What if the Doctorita fears I'll expose her?

If I accept her offer, I could never write the book. Suddenly, this feels bigger than me and my small life. If I say yes, it won't just be her winning, it will be another *mestiza* oppressing an *indígena*.

They are in the truck with the engine warming up when I walk to the passenger window. "You never treated me like a daughter," I tell her. "You never put photos of me on the coffee table. You didn't let me go to school. You beat me. You stole my childhood from me. And you, Don Carlos—"

His knuckles are white on the steering wheel. He must be terrified I'll tell his secrets. "You showed me more kindness than your wife, but you did not treat me the way a father should treat a daughter. You never treated me like a daughter, either of you."

The Doctorita's eyes fill with tears, and I can't tell if they're genuine or conjured up. "But it's not my fault! I was only trying to break you in. That's how Carlos's mother told me to treat *longas*, break them so they serve you well. You were like a little animal when you came. You don't know how hard it was to train you—"

"I'm not an animal and I never was. I have always been just as human as your own children."

Tears roll down her face. "But—it was the only way—"

"I will never go back with you. Never. I will pay my own way through school and live like a normal teenage girl and have friends and a boyfriend and go to dances and parties and all the things I couldn't do with you. And then I will have a career and a husband and family. And I will know I succeeded not *because* of you, but *in spite* of you. And maybe someday I will forgive you. I hope someday I can."

I turn away. From the doorway, I watch the truck roll down the street, the two boys peering sadly from the back. My hands are shaking, my whole body trembling. Soon the truck disappears from sight.

Inside, sitting in front of my geometry homework again, I feel a new kind of freedom.

chapter 39

THE NEXT MORNING, the day of the parade, I walk through town in my *indígena* clothes, which feel comfortable now. I no longer have to tie the *faja* so tightly it strangles my rib cage for fear of my *anacos* falling down. The streets are already packed, *indígenas* and *mestizos* and tourists all crowded together, trying to find good spots for watching the parade. I weave my way through the throngs to the meeting place, where Susana and the organizers and the other queens are waiting.

As Doña Amelia gives us last-minute instructions, Susana fusses over me, dabbing silver eye shadow on my lids, gliding her lipstick over my lips, giving my hair a final spritz of hair spray. The marching band sets out just ahead of us, complete with trumpets and trombones and drums and cymbals. Off they go in a torrent of earsplitting music.

"You're next, Virginia," Doña Amelia says, helping me climb onto my throne, a gold-painted chair sitting on a wide plank held by four men. They lift me up so that I'm above everyone's shoulders. I can't help giggling.

During a rehearsal for this, Doña Amelia told us that it used to be an old custom in June to carry an image of an indigenous Goddess-Virgin from house to house, collecting some corn or coins as an offering of thanks for the harvest. This parade is to be the first one in more than a decade, and instead of a statue of the Virgin Mary, I will represent her, along with Elsa and Luz, who are at the middle and end of the procession.

Susana reaches her hand up toward me. "I'm proud of you, Virginia!"

"Thank you for everything, Susana!" I call out as they start carrying me away, into the crowd. People wave at me and I wave back, smiling big. I can see over everyone's heads, a clear view of the mountains on all sides. As we come closer to the main town square, the crowds grow even more packed, a solid mass of people. They cheer as I pass, *indígenas* and *mestizos* and foreigners alike, clapping and waving and whistling. They shower me with confetti that sticks to my skin and hair, and makes me laugh as I brush it from my face.

"Look! It's the Queen of Water!" someone shouts.

And I feel like the Queen of Water. I feel like water that transforms from a flowing river to a tranquil lake to a powerful waterfall to a freshwater spring to a meandering creek to a salty sea to raindrops gentle on your face to hard, stinging hail to frost on a mountaintop, and back to a river again. There have been so many different Virginias in my lifetime, yet really, they are all the same one.

Beyond the crowd, in the shadows of a doorway, I notice a young *indígena* girl, a maid, pausing in her sweeping, broom in hand, watching the procession, swaying slightly in rhythm to the music. She's pretending to sweep, longing for a closer view, or maybe she's daring to wish to be in a parade herself one day.

Come out! I want to tell her. *Come out into the world!*

Swiftly, I am carried past her, and my gaze moves over the crowd, resting here and there on familiar faces—classmates and teachers and shopkeepers and coworkers.

And then, a shout, booming, louder than the others. "My daughter, look at my daughter! María Virginia! The Virgin Mary! My daughter!"

It's Papito. He is one of the men wearing a worn hat, woven and frayed. One of the short men, the rough men, the men with the torn, stained shirts, the pants trimmed with dried mud, the manure-coated work boots, the leathery, lined faces, the thick, calloused hands, the fingernails caked with weeks' worth of dirt. He's waving at me.

Embarrassed, I continue my small beauty-queen waves to the crowd, keeping my smile even. People have turned to stare at this small indigenous man jumping around. I could let them think he's just a crazy man. Or I could wave and shout, *¡Hola, Papito! Yes, it's me! Your daughter.*

Which, after a long, stretched-out moment, is what I do, my tears blurring the sea of faces. "Papito, yes, it's me!"

He lights up at my voice. There's joy on his face, joy that makes it glow. And there's more. There's love. A love that enters my chest and expands until I feel I could burst. A rough, awkward, muddled love, but love all the same.

"My daughter!" he calls out again, beaming as I wave to him.

And then, slightly behind him, I notice my mother, bent

beneath the weight of a bundle strapped to her back, a bag of corn slung across her front, her arms heavy with fat sacks of beans. A bewildered smile spreads over her face, an expression of disbelief and pride. To her I call more softly in Quichua. "Hello, Mamita. It's me. Your daughter. Virginia."

As I pass, I look back over my shoulder at my parents. Maybe Matilde and Santiago are nearby too, and maybe the Doctorita and Niño Carlitos are somewhere in the crowd, and maybe the teacher who used to call me *longa,* and maybe Alfonso and Mariana. My girlhood trails behind me like fading notes of music. Melodies emerge, patterns that I couldn't quite make sense of at the time. Now I see that sometimes the person you thought was your enemy was really your teacher, or even, in an odd way, your savior. I see that wishes come true, in roundabout ways. I see that if you try to fit someone in a box, she might slip through the seams like water and become her own river.

I move onward, through the colors and cheers and music, floating into my future, and it is a clear, open space that stretches wider than the sky and higher than the Andes.

author's note

ONE SNOWY AFTERNOON IN COLORADO, I stopped by a small shop where María Virginia Farinango sold alpaca sweaters and scarves. I'd met her briefly before at the local community college where she was a student and I taught English to immigrants.

She was stunning. Thick strands of golden beads formed an upside-down halo around her neck. She looked about my age, thirty, but her eyes were old and young at once, a feature I've noticed in people who've lived extraordinary lives. From the moment I first saw her, I was certain: this was someone I wanted to know.

Because of the weather, her store was deserted except for the two of us and her toddler son. It felt cozy there, wrapped in musty wool smells. I ended up staying for hours, sitting cross-legged on the floor with her. She told me the story of her life, which began in a small Quichua community in the Ecuadorian Andes.

When María Virginia was a child, it was fairly common for impoverished indigenous families to send their young daughters—as young as six or seven—to live with wealthier families. The arrangements were often vague. There was a blurry line between giving daughters away, having them work as nannies or maids, and selling them. It was sometimes unclear to the girl how often she would return home for visits, how much—if anything—she would be paid, and even whether the arrangement was temporary or permanent. In some cases, when the wealthier families did not uphold their end of the vague bargain, the girls were essentially stolen. And in Ecuadorian society in the 1980s, poor indigenous families were so marginalized that they felt powerless to demand their daughters back.

María Virginia was one of these stolen daughters.

Yet as her story unfolded, I discovered that her past was surprisingly full of laughter, spunk, and, best of all, heart-swelling triumph. Throughout her story, the cultural anthropologist in me was riveted, and the writer in me was jumping up and down. I desperately wanted to write this story.

María Virginia concluded, "One of my dreams is to write a book about my life." She smiled. "But I want to do it with an experienced author."

I burst out, "I'd love to do it!"

For the next year, María Virginia and I met a few times a week. We spent dozens of hours tape-recording her memories, which I then translated from Spanish to English and transcribed onto my computer. Next, focusing on the major themes, I selected the most riveting and pivotal scenes; provided sociocultural context; added more dialogue and setting details; further developed characters; wove more imagery and metaphor into the narrative; and distilled series of similar events and realizations that took place over time into single scenes in order to create a cohesive and engaging story. Throughout the six-year process, María Virginia gave input, and we discussed her memories in more depth and detail—sometimes even acting them out—in a process that brought tears of sadness and laughter to us both.

I took two research trips to Ecuador, where I talked with several of her family members and friends and people who appear in the book. I experienced the landscapes and colors and sounds and tastes of her story. I was excited to come across a newspaper interview with her as a teenager, in which she was asked about her family. "That is a long story," she replied, "a story that I would like to write a book about one day."

I feel deeply grateful that María Virginia chose me to write her story. This book has changed my life. During our sessions, I began to know her memories so intimately, they sometimes haunted me. I almost felt as though they had happened to me. Interestingly, María Virginia said that as she told me her memories, little by little, a weight was lifted from her. After hundreds of hours together, sharing her stories, we've come to consider each other close friends; in some ways, even sisters.

It was hard to decide at what point to end this book, since María Virginia continued to lead an extraordinary life after becoming the Queen of Water. Throughout *colegio*, she excelled at track, public speaking, and other activities, and she graduated with academic honors. Since then, she has acted in a TV movie, had her own radio show, performed traditional dance, run an Andean crafts business, and traveled to Asia, Europe, and North America. She is now studying psychology at the

Universidad Técnica Particular de Loja and has recently started a small holistic day spa in Otavalo, where she lives with her son and her husband, Tino, a musician and composer. I'm thrilled that María Virginia has realized so many of her dreams, and especially thrilled that this book is one of them.

María Virginia's story is part of a larger story in Ecuadorian society. Over the past several decades, despite lingering racism in their country, many Otavaleño *indígenas* like María Virginia and her husband have embraced their culture and become world-traveling musicians or craft vendors. As a result of these people's successes, as well as indigenous rights movements, *indígenas* of the Ecuadorian Andes have gained a great deal of social, economic, and political power in recent years.

The bones and blood of the story you have read are true. My imagination has fleshed out the details and shaped it into its final form.* As much as possible, I've tried to let María Virginia's voice shine through. I hope that her story will stay with you, and even become part of you, as it has for me.

—Laura Resau, February 2010

*Some names have been changed for privacy protection. For a discussion of the specifics, please visit my website at lauraresau.com.

glossary and pronunciation guide

QUICHUA (also spelled Kichwa) is the native language of indigenous people of the Ecuadorian Andes. You may have heard the similar term *Quechua*, which refers to a related indigenous language and culture in Peru and Bolivia. Both languages have roots in the Incan empire, which ruled the region until the Spaniards came to South America. Over the past five hundred years, the Spanish language has influenced Quichua, and vice versa. For example, some modern Quichua words are actually combinations of Spanish and Quichua words, like *pobregulla*. Quichua words that have become integrated into Spanish include terms for native Andean foods, like *papa* (potato), *cuy* (guinea pig), and quinoa. As with many indigenous languages, pronunciation, vocabulary, and spelling of Quichua words may vary from village to village.

As you peruse the glossary, please note that:

- an *o/a* ending indicates that *o* is used for masculine and *a* for feminine forms.
- an *rr* indicates a rolled *r*.
- in Ecuadorian Spanish, it is very common to add an *ito* ending to names; this is meant to show affection, and sometimes respect.
- an asterisk indicates that the term is either Quichua or specifically Andean/Ecuadorian Spanish.

adiós   ah-dee-OHS   goodbye
ala de pollo   AH-lah day POH-yo   chicken wing
amo*   AH-moh   a title of respect
anaco*   ah-NAH-koh   traditional long, wraparound skirt made with thick fabric. A dark *anaco* is usually worn as an outer layer and a cream-colored *anaco* as an inner layer.
api*   AH-pee   soup
ari*   AH-ree   yes
bruta   BROO-tah   fool
buenas noches   BWAY-nahs NOH-chays   good evening
buenas tardes   BWAY-nahs TARR-days   good afternoon
buenos días   BWAY-nohs DEE-ahs   good morning
capulí   cah-poo-LEE   a tiny red fruit
chica   CHEE-cah   girl
chilca   CHEEL-cah   tree whose leaves may be used medicinally
choclo   CHOH-cloh   ear of corn
chushac*   CHOO-shahc   empty
colegio   coh-LAY-hee-oh   combined junior high and high school
compañera   cohm-pahn-YAYR-ah   companion, classmate, or coworker
cortido*   corr-TEE-doh   an Ecuadorian salad made with lime juice, tomatoes, cucumber, onion, and other raw vegetables
Dios   dee-OHS   God

Doctorita dohc-toh-REE-tah literally, "Little Doctor." A term of respect and affection that Virginia was forced to use with Romelia.

Doña DOHN-yah Mrs.

espanto ays-PAHN-toh "fright"—a condition that may cause illness and misfortune, according to cultural beliefs

"Estrellita de la tarde" ays-tray-YEE-tah day lah TAHRR-day "Little Evening Star"—a romantic song

estera* ays-TAY-rah woven mat

estúpida ays-TOO-pee-dah stupid

fachalina* fah-chah-LEE-nah traditional wool cape, usually cream or black, used by Quichua women as either a shawl or a head covering

faja* FAH-hah piece of traditional clothing—a long strip of embroidered fabric that is wrapped around the waist, over the *anaco*, holding it up

gelatina hay-lah-TEE-nah gelatin (popular dessert)

gente de clase HAYN-tay day CLAH-say upper-class people

gracias GRAH-see-ahs thank you

gringuito/a green-GUEE-toh/green-GUEE-tah little gringo/a (affectionate term for a North American)

grosera groh-SAY-rah rude woman

guagua* WAH-wah child

guaguita* wah-WEE-tah little child (affectionate term)

guapa GWAH-pah beautiful (girl or woman)

hermanita ayr-mah-NEE-tah little sister

hija EE-hah daughter, term of affection for a girl

hola OH-lah hi

Imbabura* eem-bah-BOO-rah the northern Ecuadorian province where this story takes place. It's named after a huge mountain, which is sacred to the indigenous people of the area.

india/o EEN-dee-ah/EEN-dee-oh "Indian"—often used as an insult

indígenas een-DEE-hay-nahs indigenous (people)

jugo de tomate HOO-goh day toh-MAH-tay juice of an orange fruit called *tomate*

klya' kee-TAH moon

Kunu Yaku KOO-noo YAH-koo fictitious name for the small, rural town where Virginia lived with the *mestizos*

la gente que puede lah HAYN-tay kay PWAY-day people of means

la lucha libre la LOO-chah LEEB-ray freestyle wrestling

limpieza leem-pee-AY-sah spiritual cleansing

longo/a* LOHN-goh/LOHN-gah offensive word for an indigenous person

longuito/a* lohn-GUEE-toh/lohn-GUEE-tah literally, "little *longo*." Offensive word for an indigenous person.

MacGyver mah-GEE-vayrr American TV show popular in the 1980s (Virginia was stunned when I told her how we pronounce the name in English!)

machacar mah-chah-CAHRR to pound, bruise, or crush (things)

machucar mah-choo-CARR to pound, bruise, or crush (people)

maestra mah-AYS-trah teacher

mal viento MAHL vee-AYN-toh evil air, negative energy, according to cultural beliefs

mana* MAH-nah no

mestizo/a mays-TEE-soh/mays-TEE-sah ethnic category used in parts of Latin America, generally referring to a person of mixed race. In Ecuador, it often refers to people who are not indigenous.

m'hija MEE-hah literally, "my daughter." Also, a term of affection for a girl or young woman.

m'hijita mee-HEE-tah my little daughter (term of affection for a girl)

mi amor mee ah-MORR my love

misha copetona* MEE-sha coh-pay-TOH-nah mestiza with the ridiculous bun

mishu* MEE-shu offensive Quichua word for *mestizo*

nina* NEE-nah fire

Niño* NEEN-yoh literally, "child." Virginia was forced to use this term of respect and affection as Carlitos's title.

ñuku guagua* NYOO-koo WAH-wah my daughter

pagui* PAH-guee thank you

patroncito pah-trohn-SEE-toh literally, "little boss." A title of respect.

plastona plahs-TOH-nah lazy woman (an insult)

pobrecito/a poh-bray-SEE-toh/poh-bray-SEE-tah poor thing

pobregulla* poh-bray-GOO-yah poor thing (affectionate Quichua term)

por favorcito pohr fah-vohr-SEE-toh pretty please

puro POO-roh alcohol made from sugarcane

pusaq wata* POO-sahk WAH-tah eight years

querer es poder kay-RAYRR ays poh-DAYRR To want is to be able. To want is power.

"Rabanito" rrah-bah-NEE-toh "Little Radish (Flower)"—a folk song

reina RRAY-nah queen

rezador(es) rray-sah-DOHR-(ays) people who pray

rial(es)* rree-AHL-(ays) unit of money used before Ecuador switched to the dollar in the year 2000

rrriquísimo rrree-KEE-see-moh very delicious (three r's here indicate that the r is rolled emphatically)

sambo SAHM-boh a kind of squash

señor sayn-YOHR sir, Mr.

señora sayn-YOH-rah ma'am, lady, Mrs.

señorita sayn-yoh-REE-tah miss

soga SOH-gah whip

sucre* SOO-cray small unit of money used before Ecuador switched to dollars in 2000

taita* tah-EE-tah mister or father

tía TEE-ah aunt

tonta/o TOHN-tah/TOHN-toh fool(ish)

uchafa* oo-CHAH-fah ash

urku* OOR-koo mountain

venipe* vay-NEE-pay come here

viejita vee-ay-HEE-tah old lady

¡Viva la libertad! VEE-vah la lee-bayrr-TAHD Long live freedom!

vivísima vee-VEE-see-mah very clever

Yana Urku* YAH-nah OOR-koo fictitious name for Virginia's native village

yo la machuco yoh lah mah-CHOO-coh I pound her.

yo puedo yoh PWAY-doh I can [do it].

yumbo* YOOM-boh refers to babies who died before baptism and are believed to be stuck in limbo

zapalla* sah-PY-ah pumpkin